¡¡MANU!!

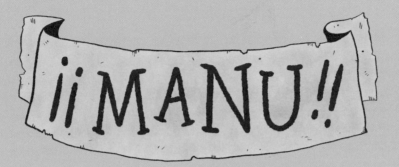

Kelly Fernández

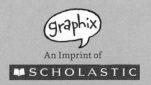

An Imprint of

SCHOLASTIC

Library of Congress Control Number: 2020946443

ISBN 978-1-338-26419-7 (hardcover)
ISBN 978-1-338-26418-0 (paperback)

10 9 8 7 6 5 4 3 2 1   21 22 23 24 25

Printed in China   62
First edition, October 2021

Edited by Cassandra Pelham Fulton
Book design by Kelly Fernández and Steve Ponzo
Creative Director: Phil Falco
Publisher: David Saylor

TO ANYONE LOST
IN A DEEP, DARK CAVE

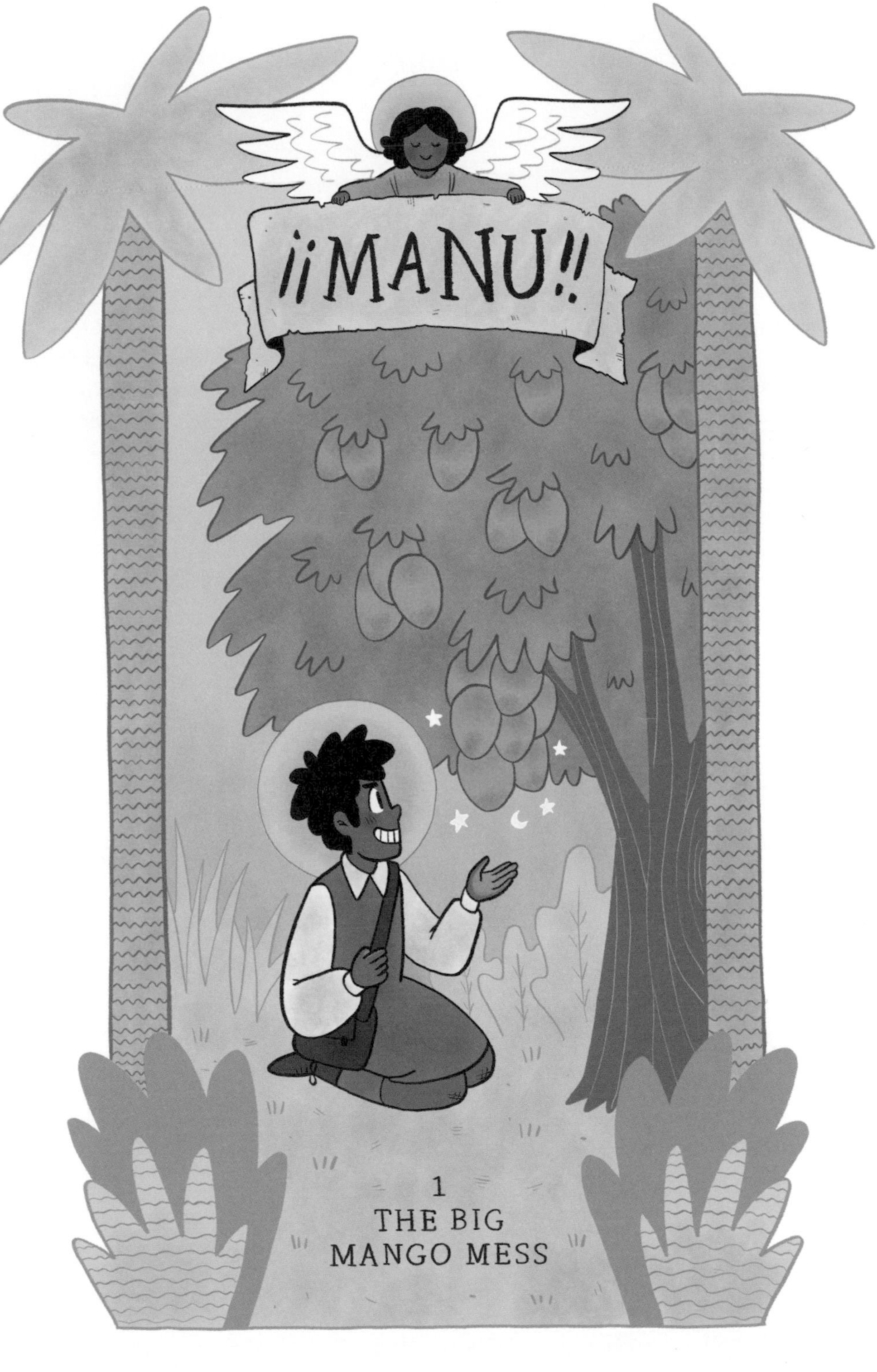
¡¡MANU!!

1
THE BIG MANGO MESS

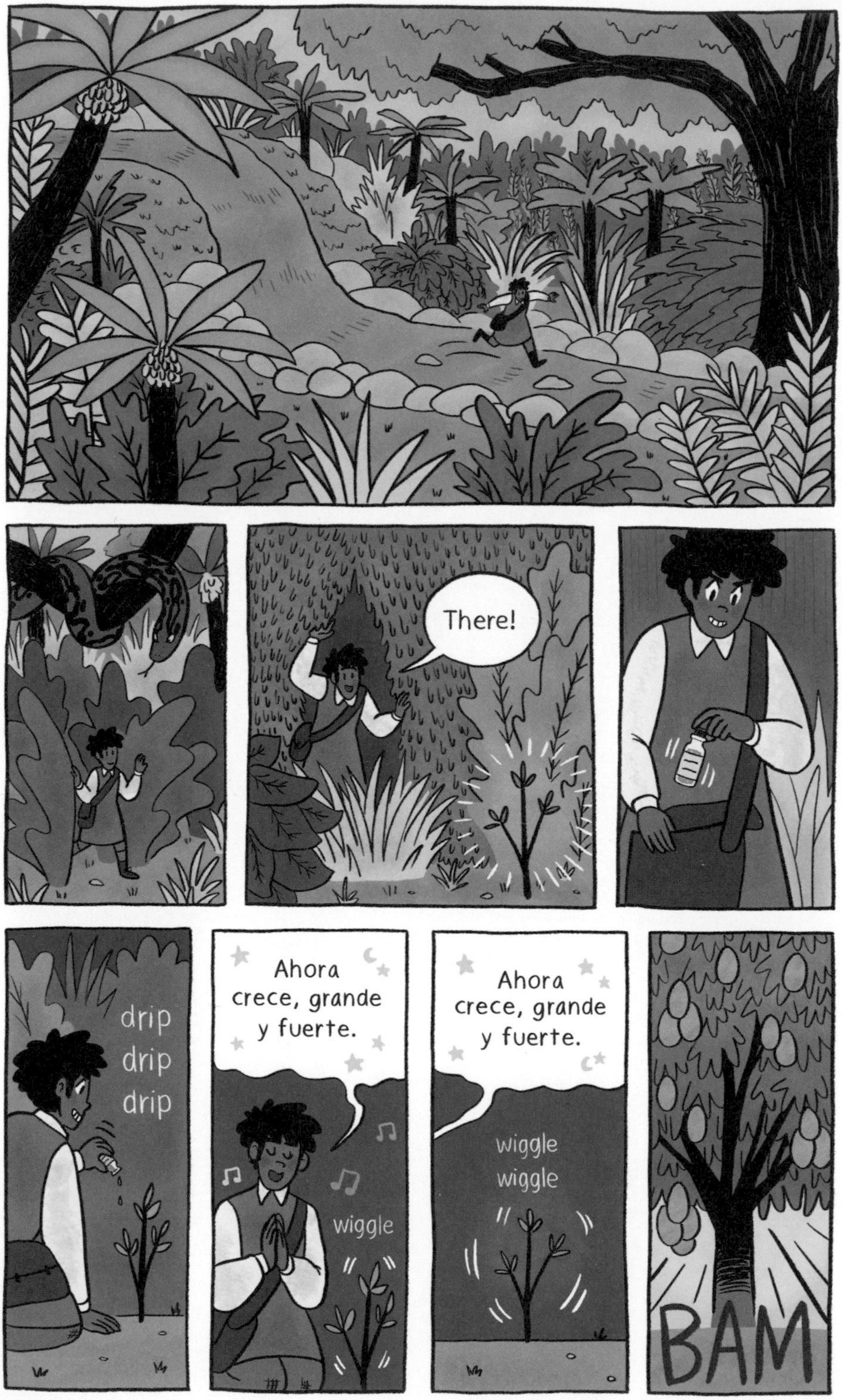
There!
drip
drip
drip
Ahora crece, grande y fuerte.
wiggle
Ahora crece, grande y fuerte.
wiggle
wiggle
BAM

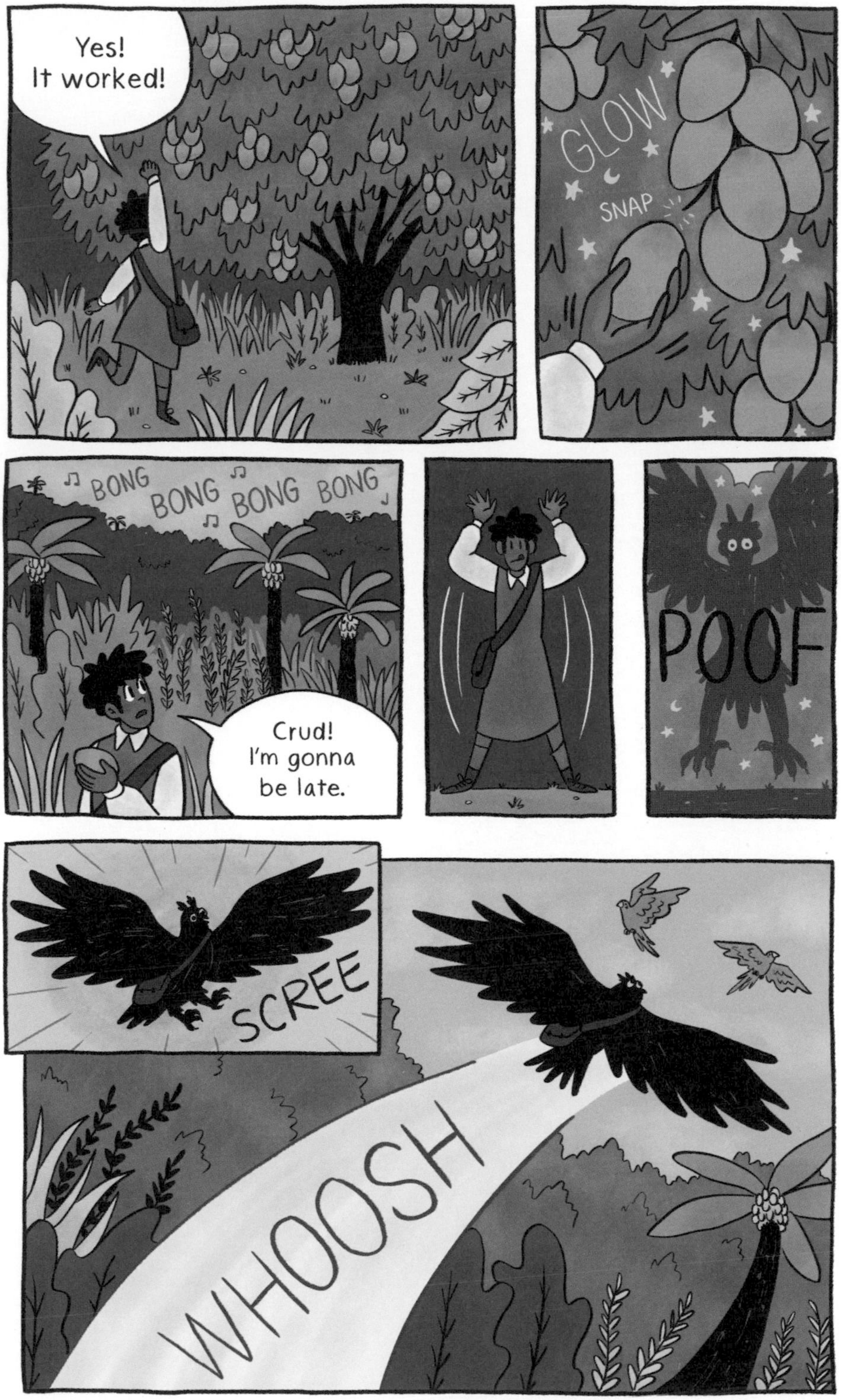
Yes! It worked!
GLOW
SNAP
BONG BONG BONG BONG
Crud! I'm gonna be late.
POOF
SCREE
WHOOSH

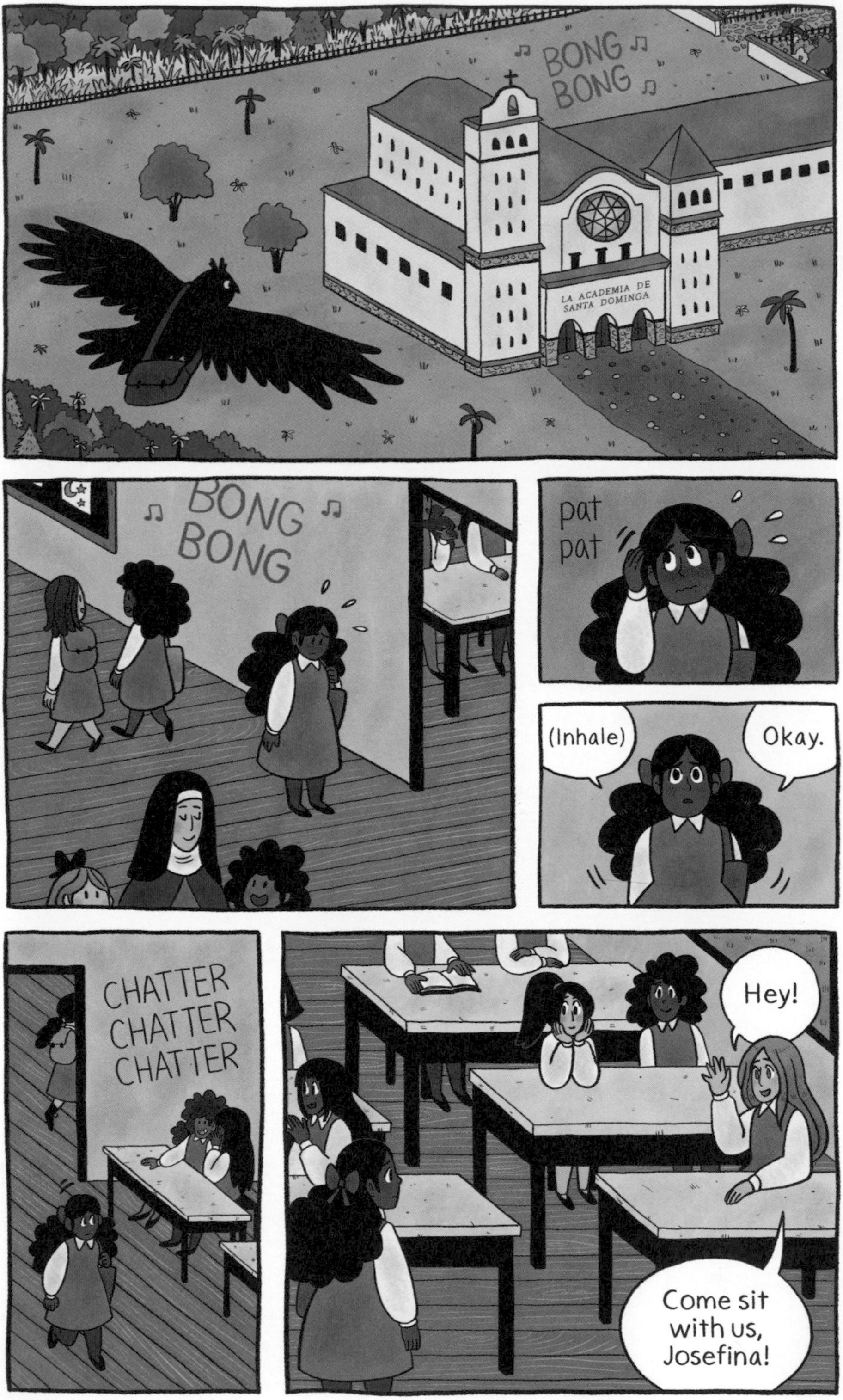
BONG
BONG
LA ACADEMIA DE
SANTA DOMINGA
BONG
BONG
pat
pat
(Inhale)
Okay.
CHATTER
CHATTER
CHATTER
Hey!
Come sit with us, Josefina!

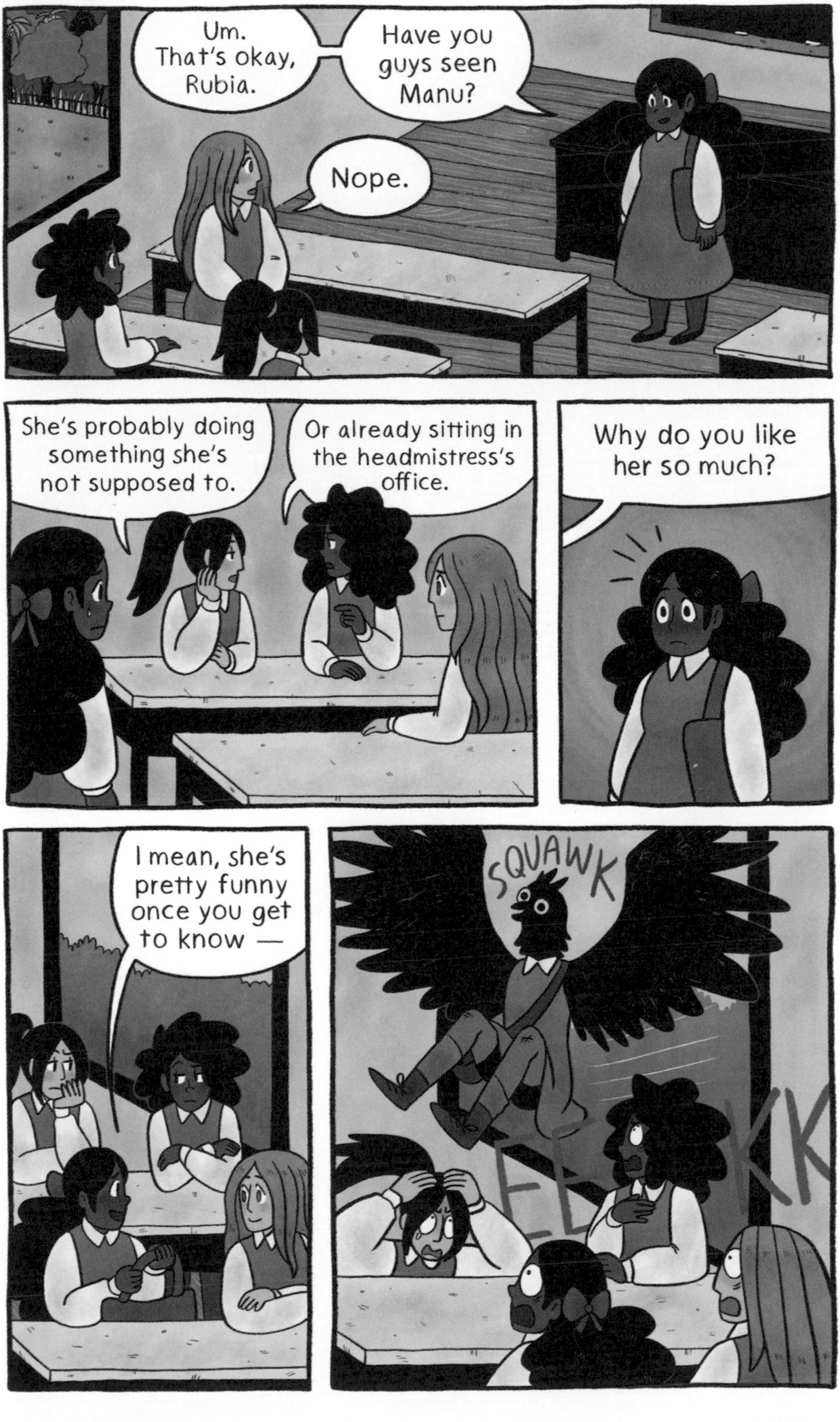
Um. That's okay, Rubia.
Have you guys seen Manu?
Nope.
She's probably doing something she's not supposed to.
Or already sitting in the headmistress's office.
Why do you like her so much?
I mean, she's pretty funny once you get to know —
SQUAWK
EEKK

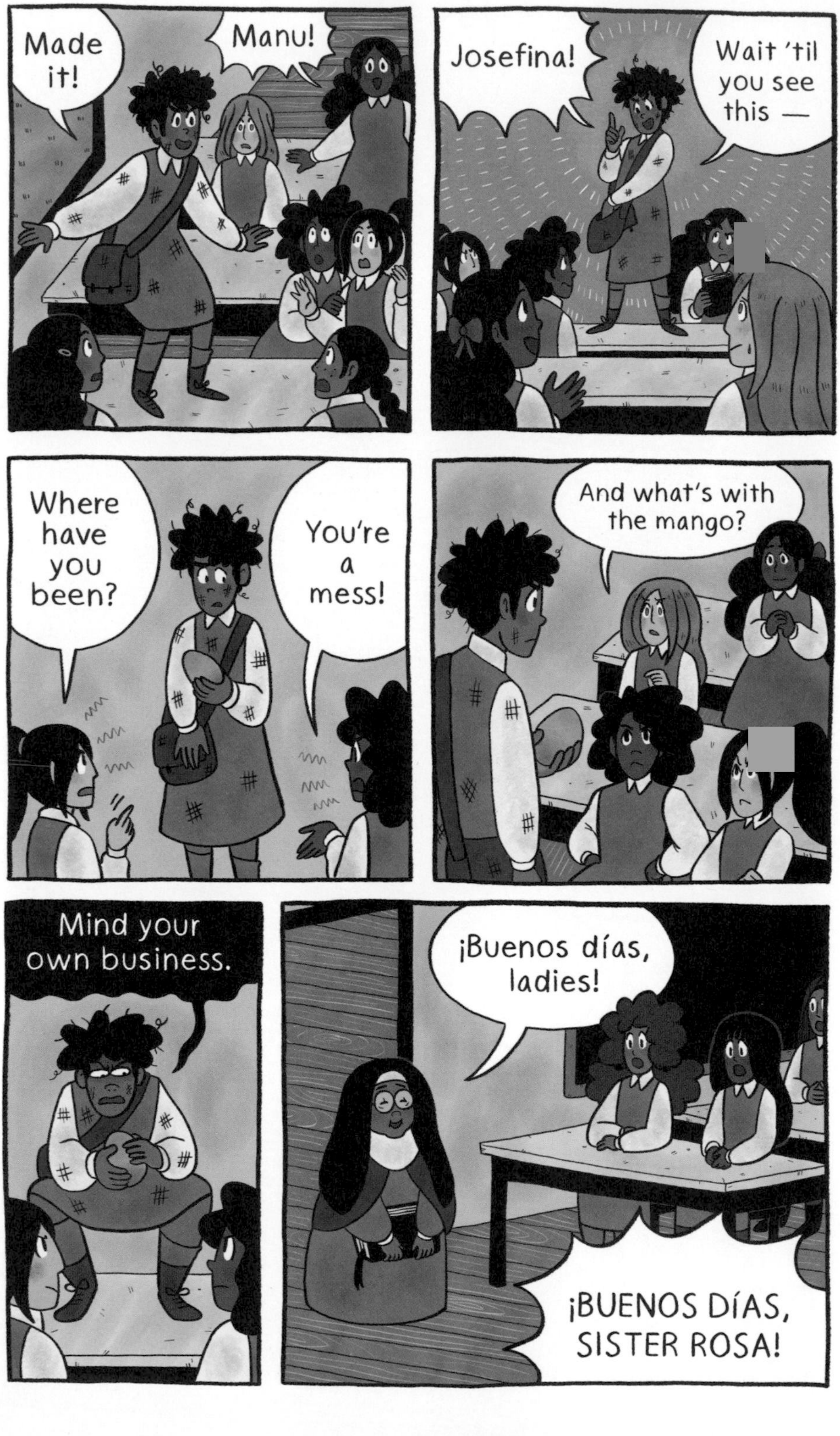
Made it!
Manu!
Josefina!
Wait 'til you see this —
Where have you been?
You're a mess!
And what's with the mango?
Mind your own business.
¡Buenos días, ladies!
¡BUENOS DÍAS, SISTER ROSA!

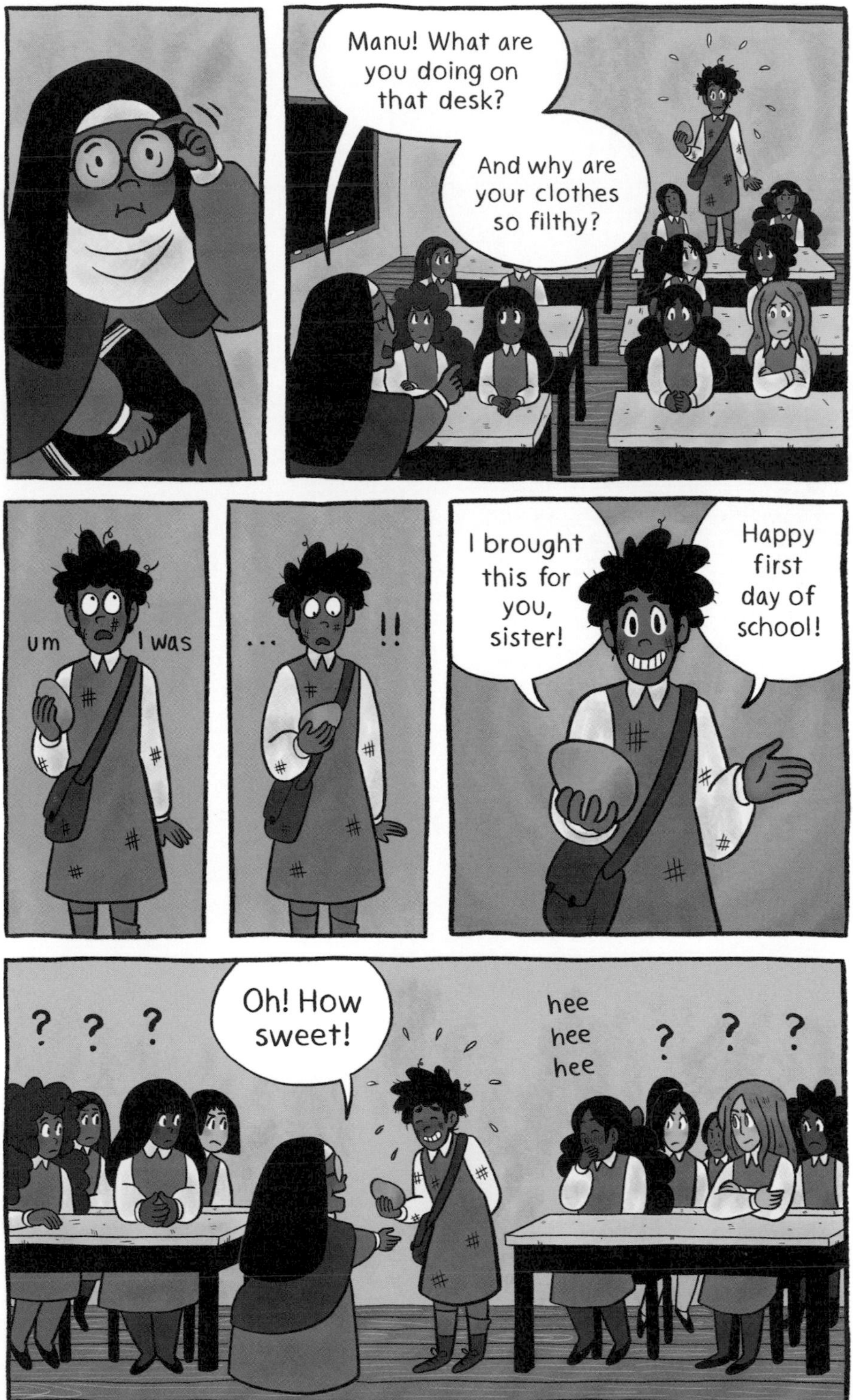
Manu! What are you doing on that desk?
And why are your clothes so filthy?
um
I was
...
!!
I brought this for you, sister!
Happy first day of school!
? ? ?
Oh! How sweet!
hee hee hee
? ? ?

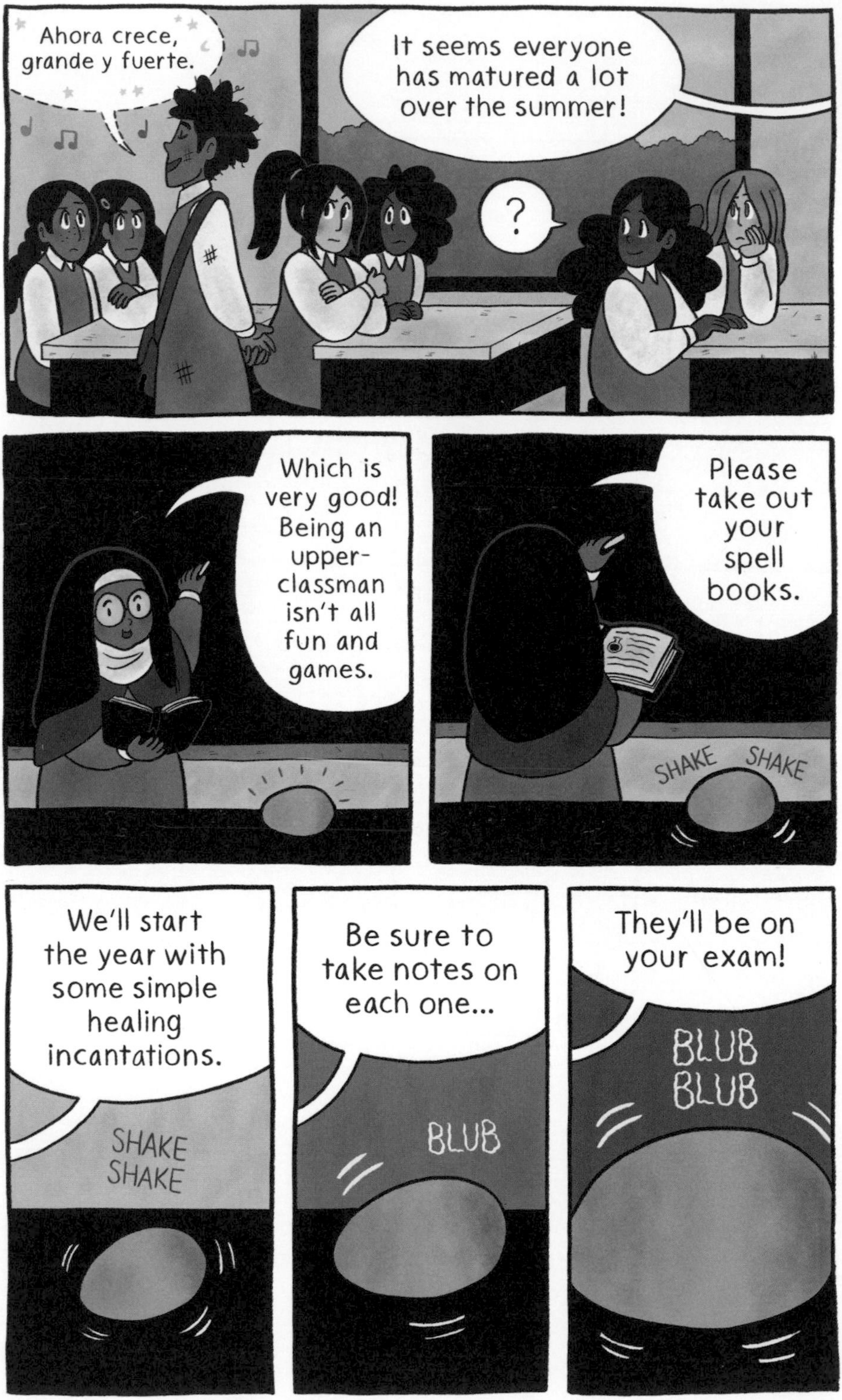
Ahora crece, grande y fuerte.
It seems everyone has matured a lot over the summer!
?
Which is very good! Being an upper-classman isn't all fun and games.
Please take out your spell books.
SHAKE SHAKE
We'll start the year with some simple healing incantations.
SHAKE SHAKE
Be sure to take notes on each one...
BLUB
They'll be on your exam!
BLUB BLUB

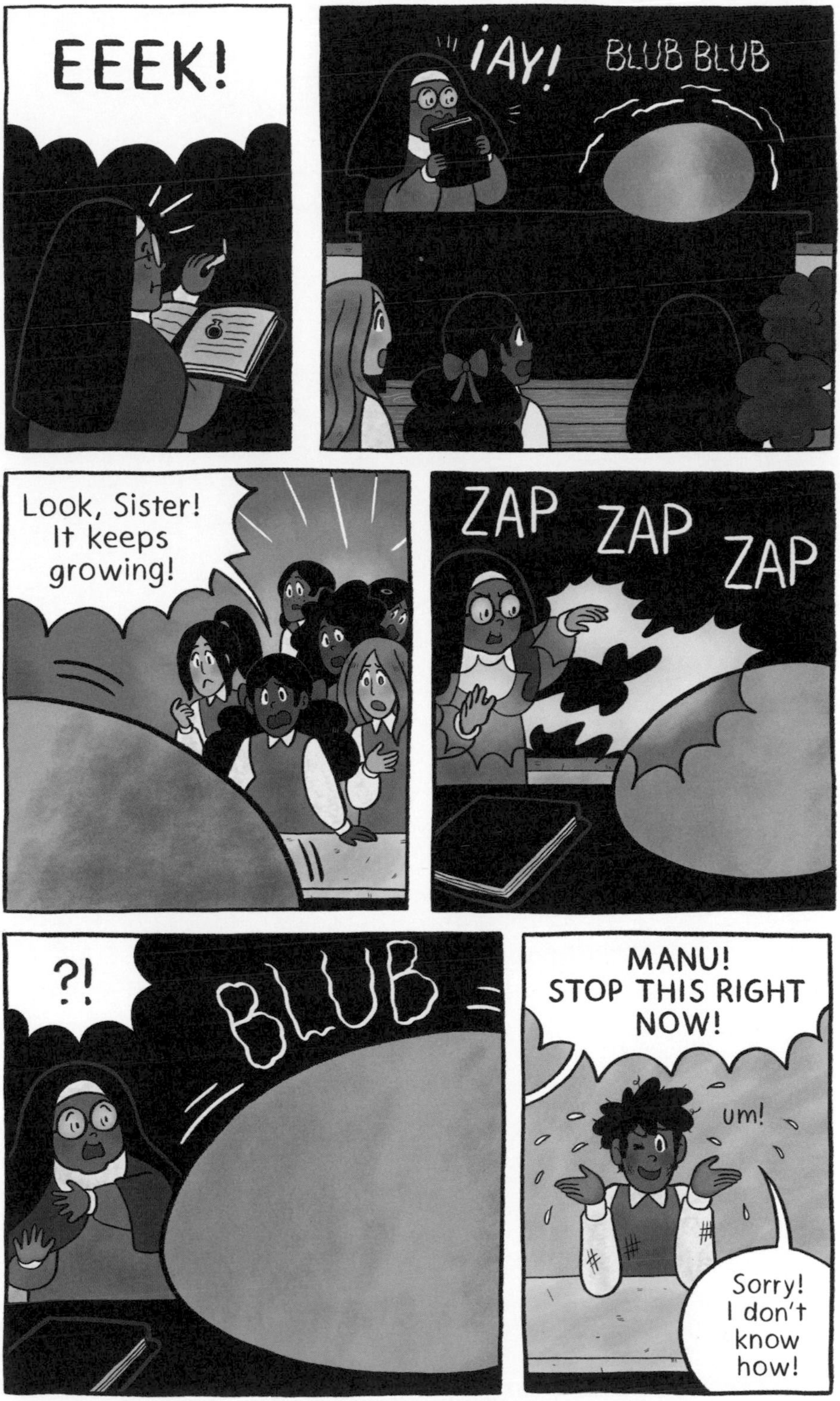
EEEK!
¡AY!
BLUB BLUB
Look, Sister! It keeps growing!
ZAP
ZAP
ZAP
?!
BLUB
MANU! STOP THIS RIGHT NOW!
um!
Sorry! I don't know how!

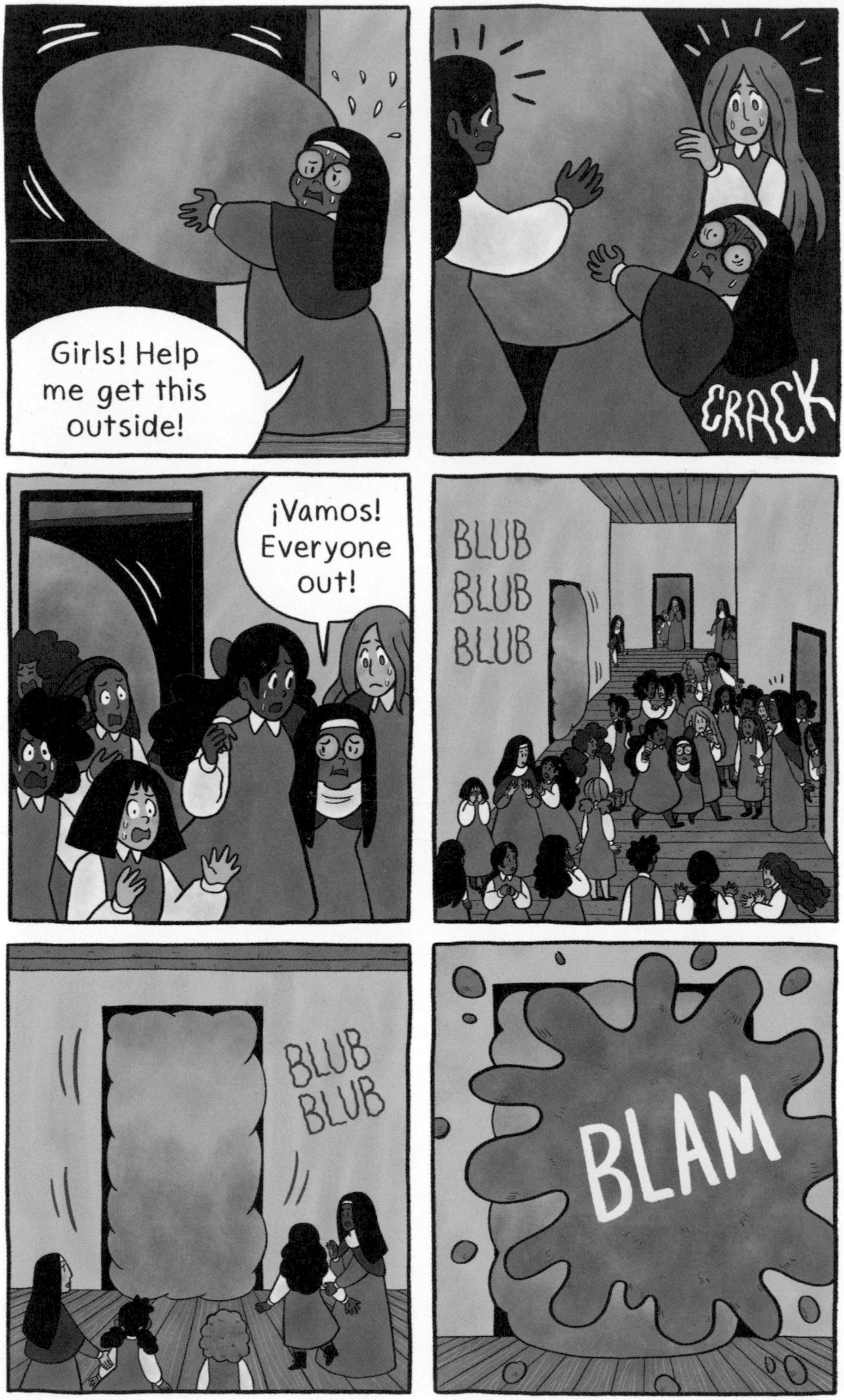
Girls! Help me get this outside!
CRACK
¡Vamos! Everyone out!
BLUB BLUB BLUB
BLUB BLUB
BLAM

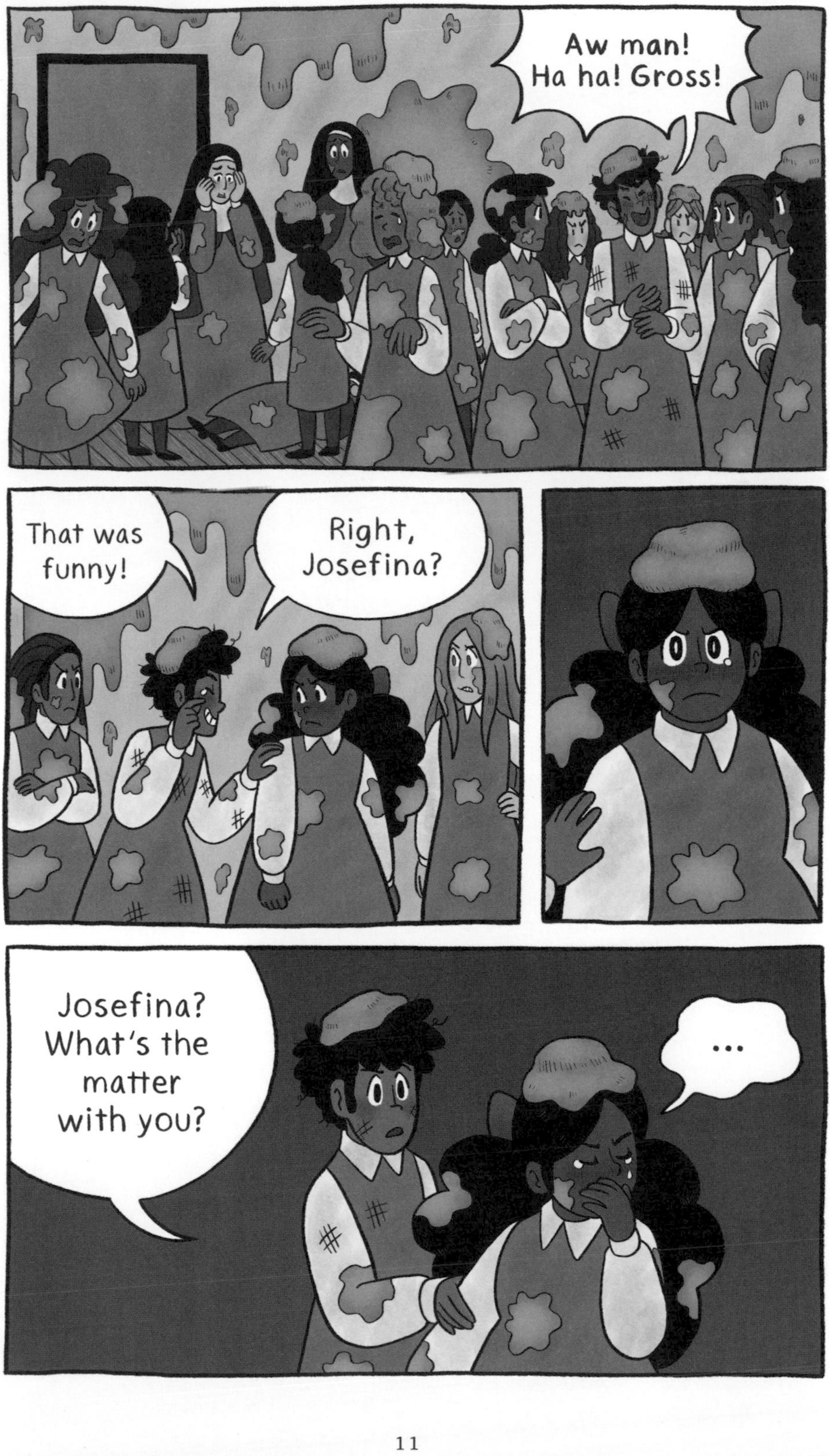
Aw man!
Ha ha! Gross!
That was funny!
Right, Josefina?
Josefina? What's the matter with you?
...

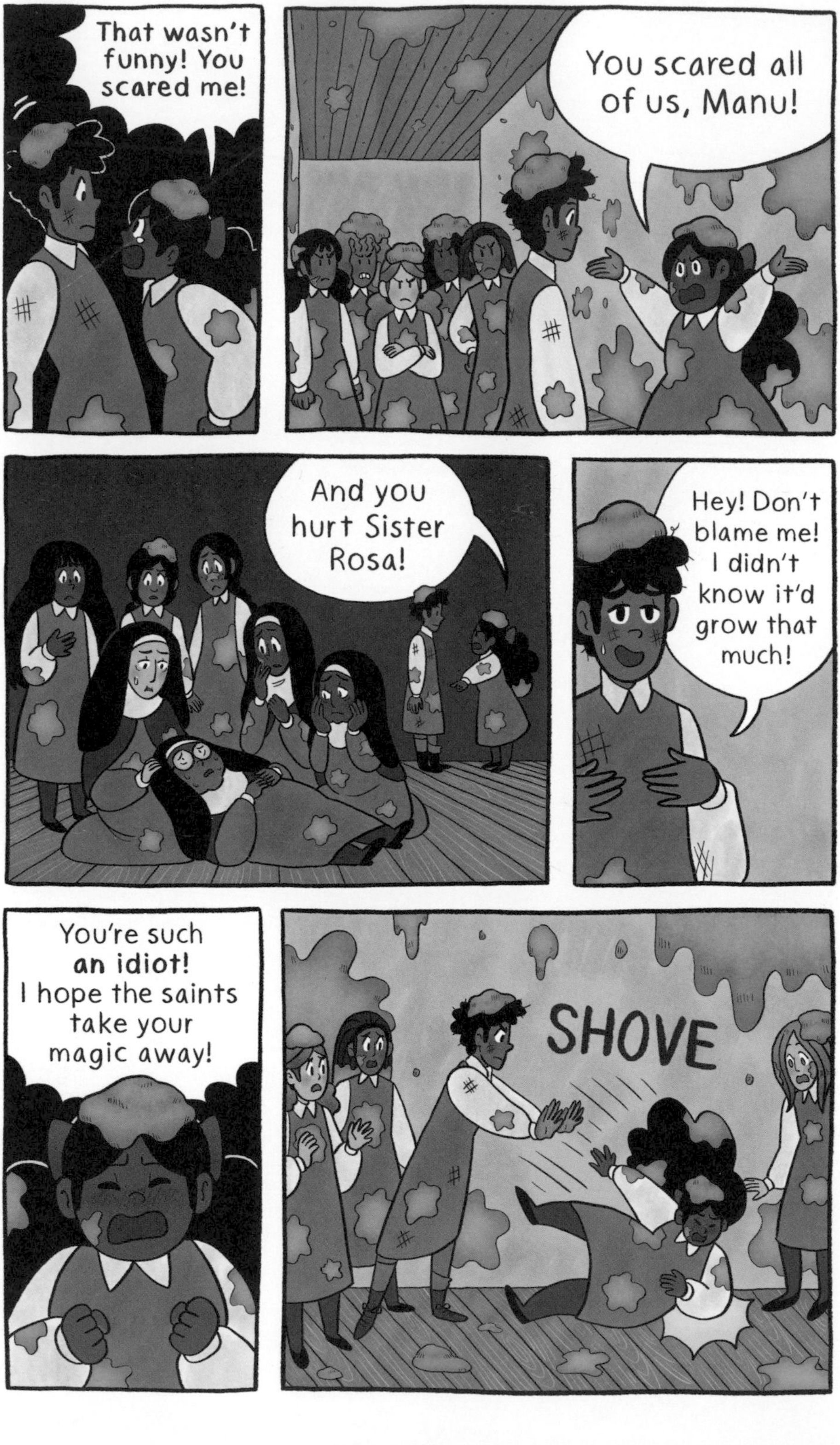
That wasn't funny! You scared me!
You scared all of us, Manu!
And you hurt Sister Rosa!
Hey! Don't blame me! I didn't know it'd grow that much!
You're such **an idiot!** I hope the saints take your magic away!
SHOVE

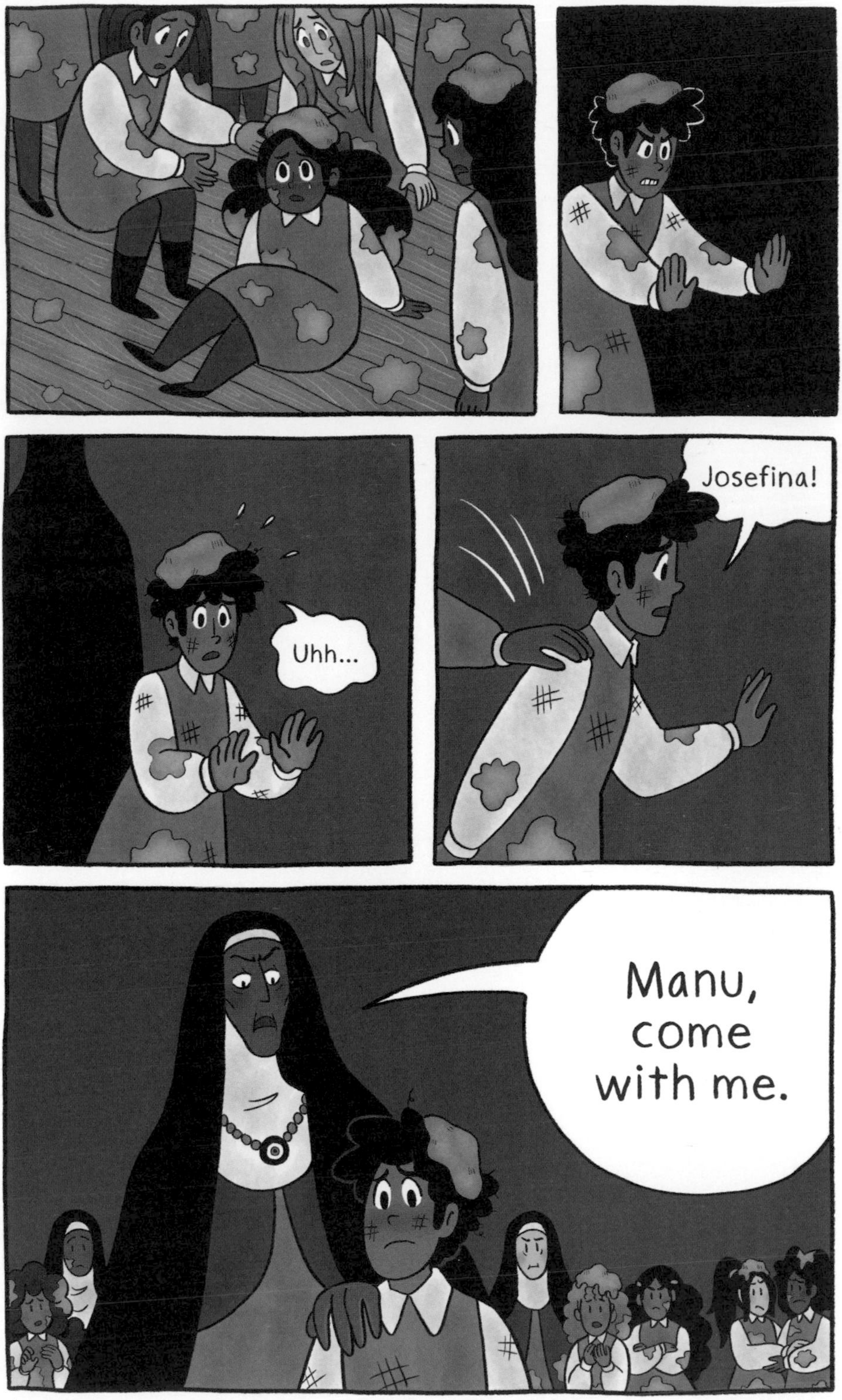
Uhh...
Josefina!
Manu, come with me.

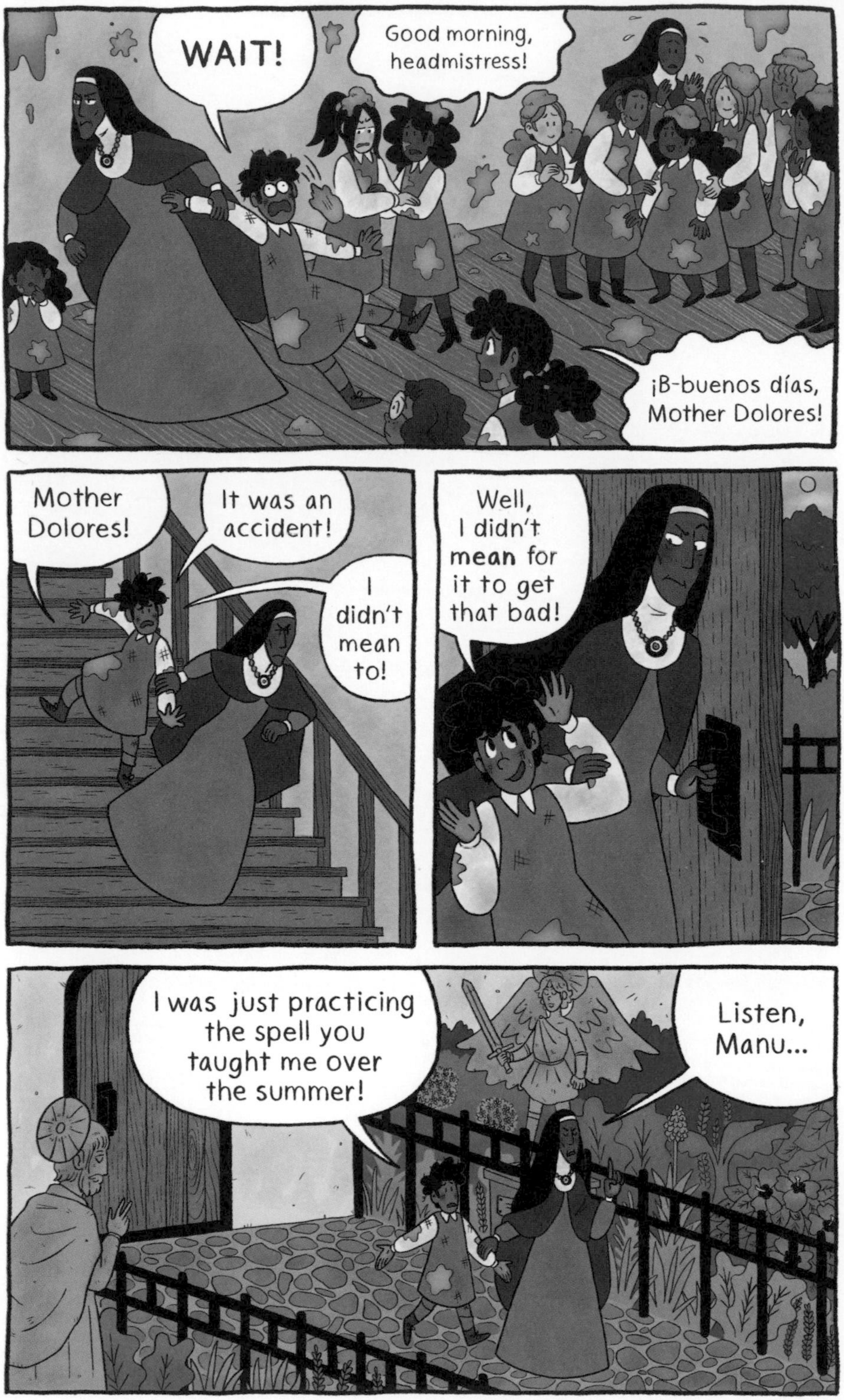
WAIT!
Good morning, headmistress!
¡B-buenos días, Mother Dolores!
Mother Dolores!
It was an accident!
I didn't mean to!
Well, I didn't **mean** for it to get that bad!
I was just practicing the spell you taught me over the summer!
Listen, Manu...

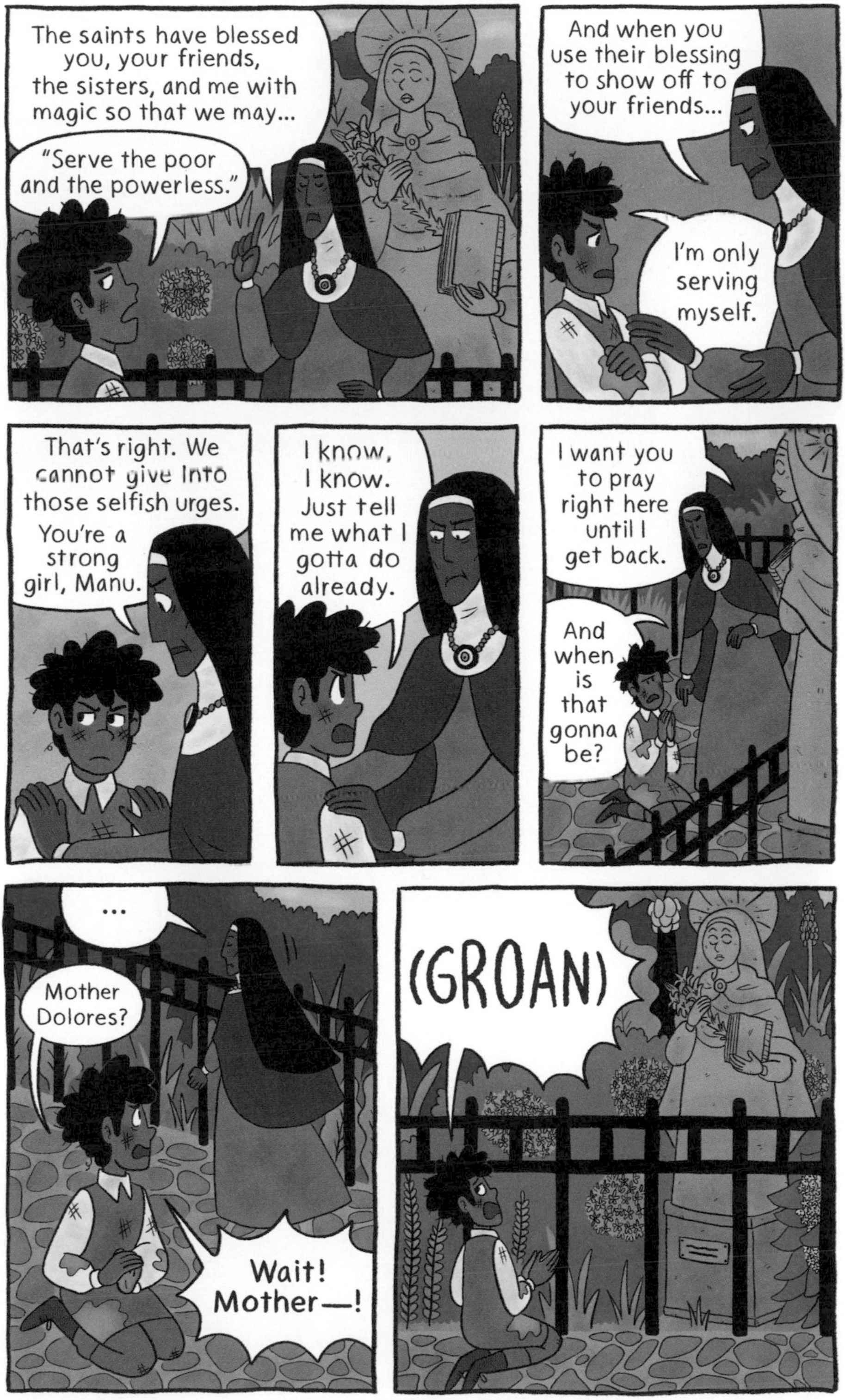
The saints have blessed you, your friends, the sisters, and me with magic so that we may...
"Serve the poor and the powerless."
And when you use their blessing to show off to your friends...
I'm only serving myself.
That's right. We cannot give into those selfish urges.
You're a strong girl, Manu.
I know, I know. Just tell me what I gotta do already.
I want you to pray right here until I get back.
And when is that gonna be?
...
Mother Dolores?
Wait! Mother—!
(GROAN)

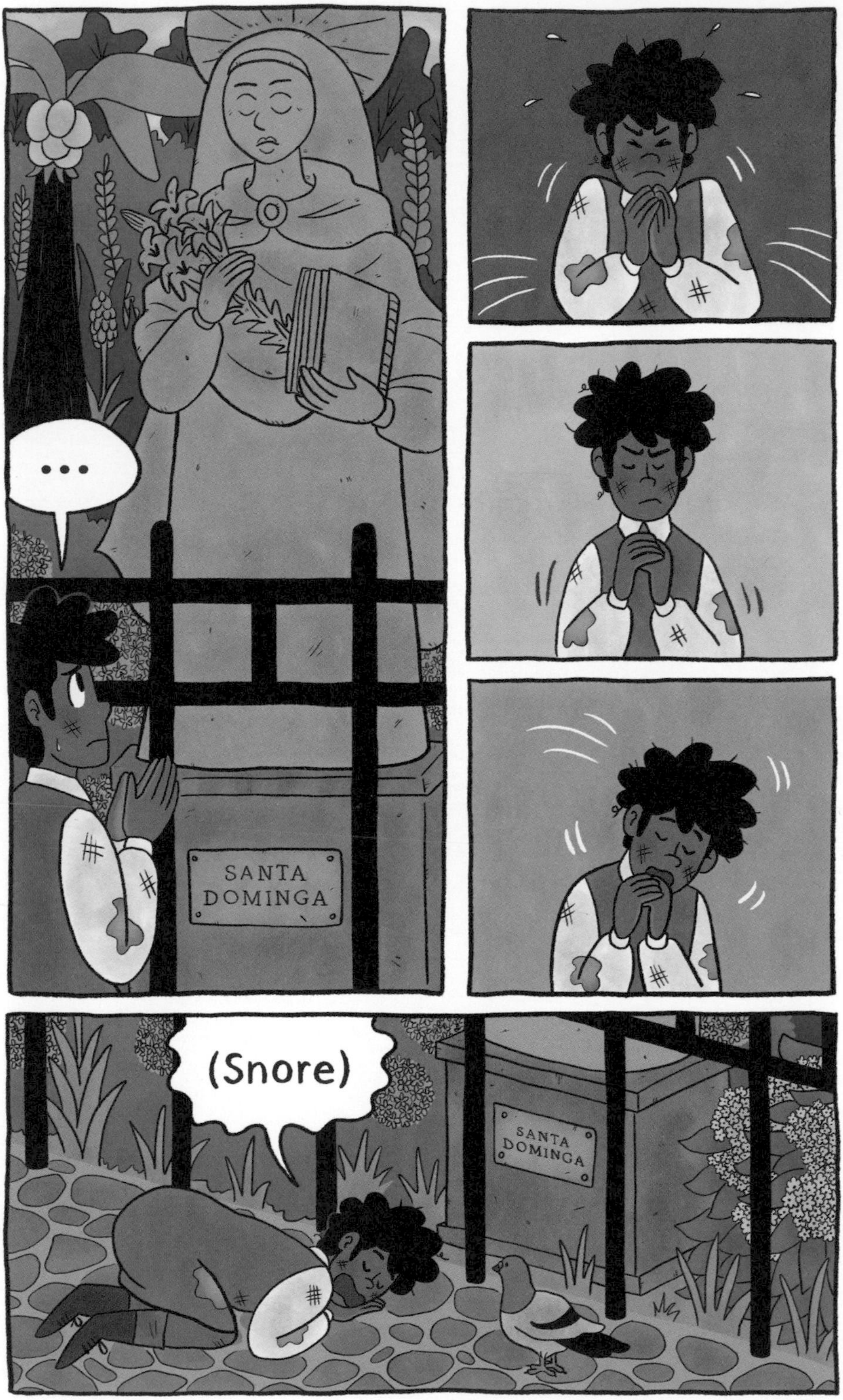
...
SANTA DOMINGA
(Snore)
SANTA DOMINGA

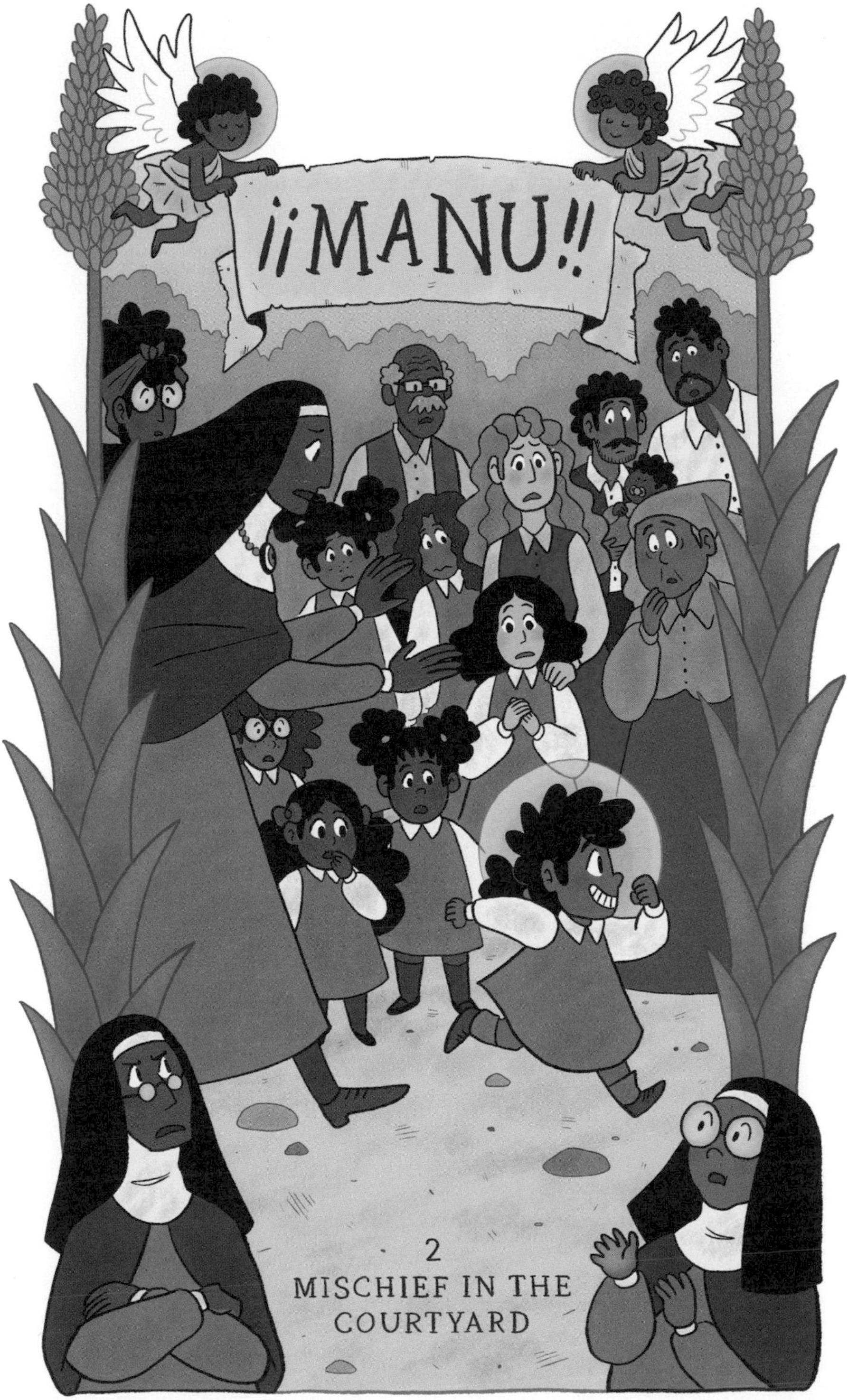
¡¡MANU!!

2
MISCHIEF IN THE COURTYARD

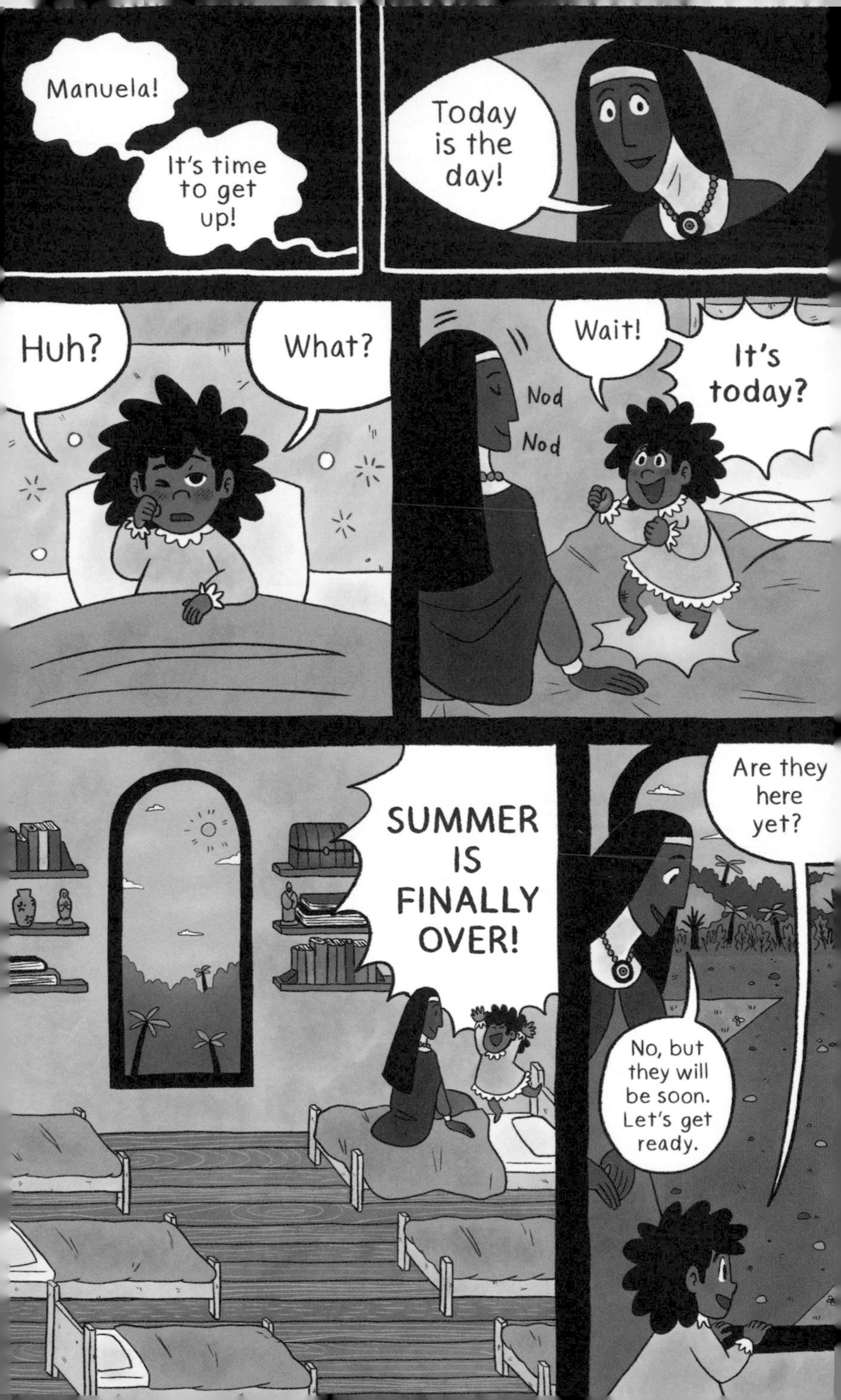
Manuela!
It's time to get up!
Today is the day!
Huh?
What?
Nod
Nod
Wait!
It's today?
SUMMER IS FINALLY OVER!
Are they here yet?
No, but they will be soon. Let's get ready.

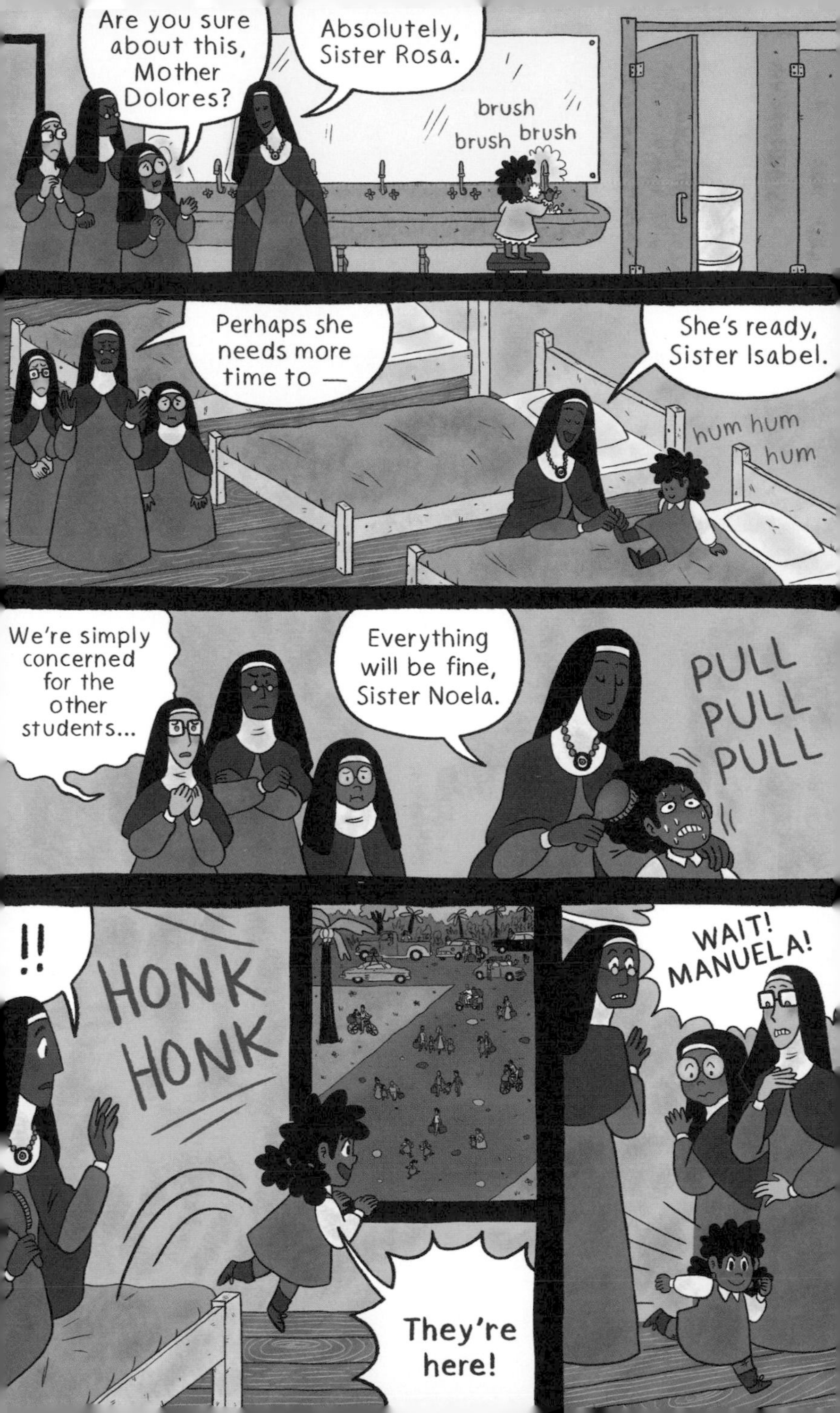
Are you sure about this, Mother Dolores?
Absolutely, Sister Rosa.
brush brush brush
Perhaps she needs more time to —
She's ready, Sister Isabel.
hum hum hum
We're simply concerned for the other students...
Everything will be fine, Sister Noela.
PULL PULL PULL
!!
HONK HONK
They're here!
WAIT! MANUELA!

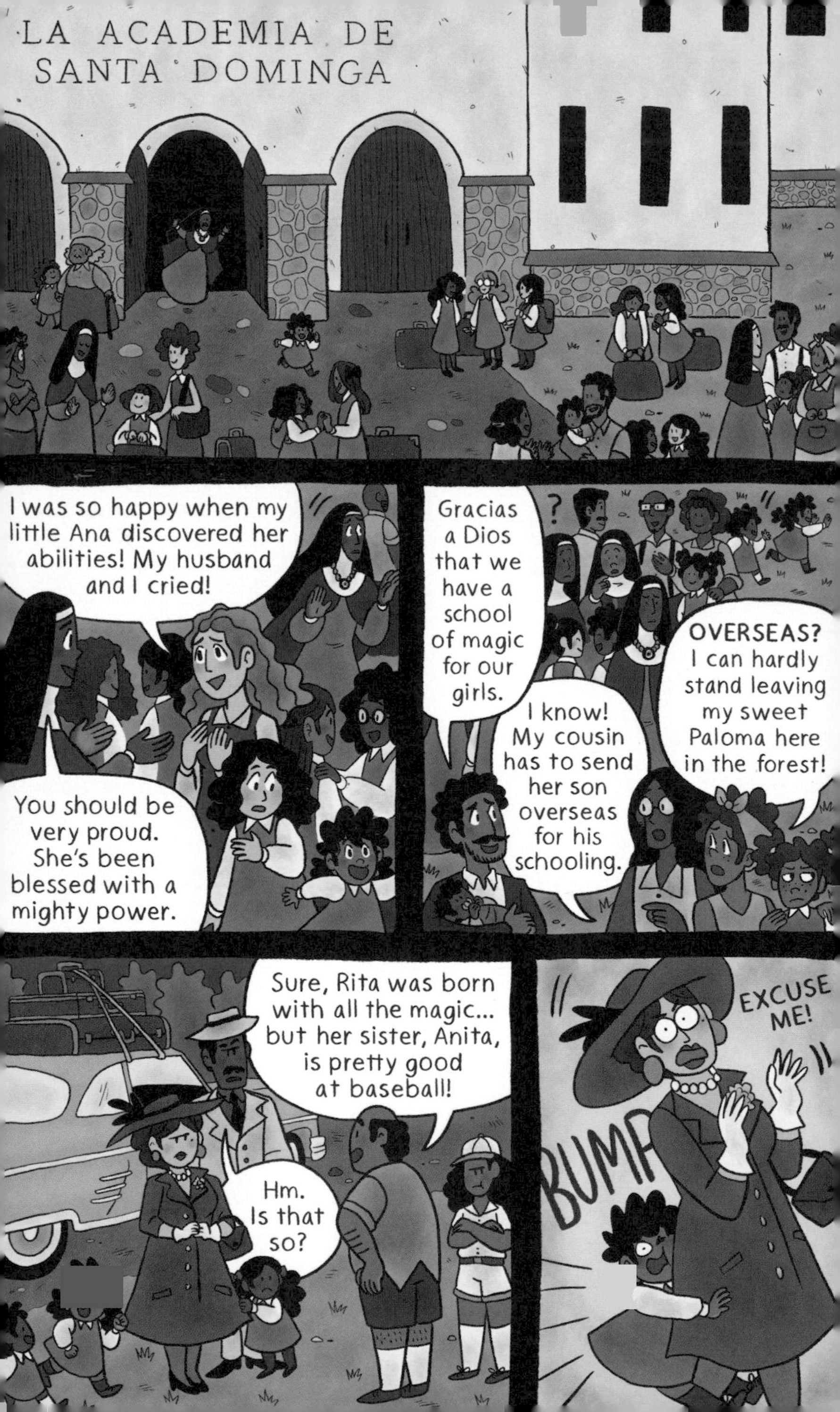
LA ACADEMIA DE SANTA DOMINGA
I was so happy when my little Ana discovered her abilities! My husband and I cried!
You should be very proud. She's been blessed with a mighty power.
Gracias a Dios that we have a school of magic for our girls.
I know! My cousin has to send her son overseas for his schooling.
OVERSEAS? I can hardly stand leaving my sweet Paloma here in the forest!
?
Sure, Rita was born with all the magic... but her sister, Anita, is pretty good at baseball!
Hm. Is that so?
EXCUSE ME!
BUMP

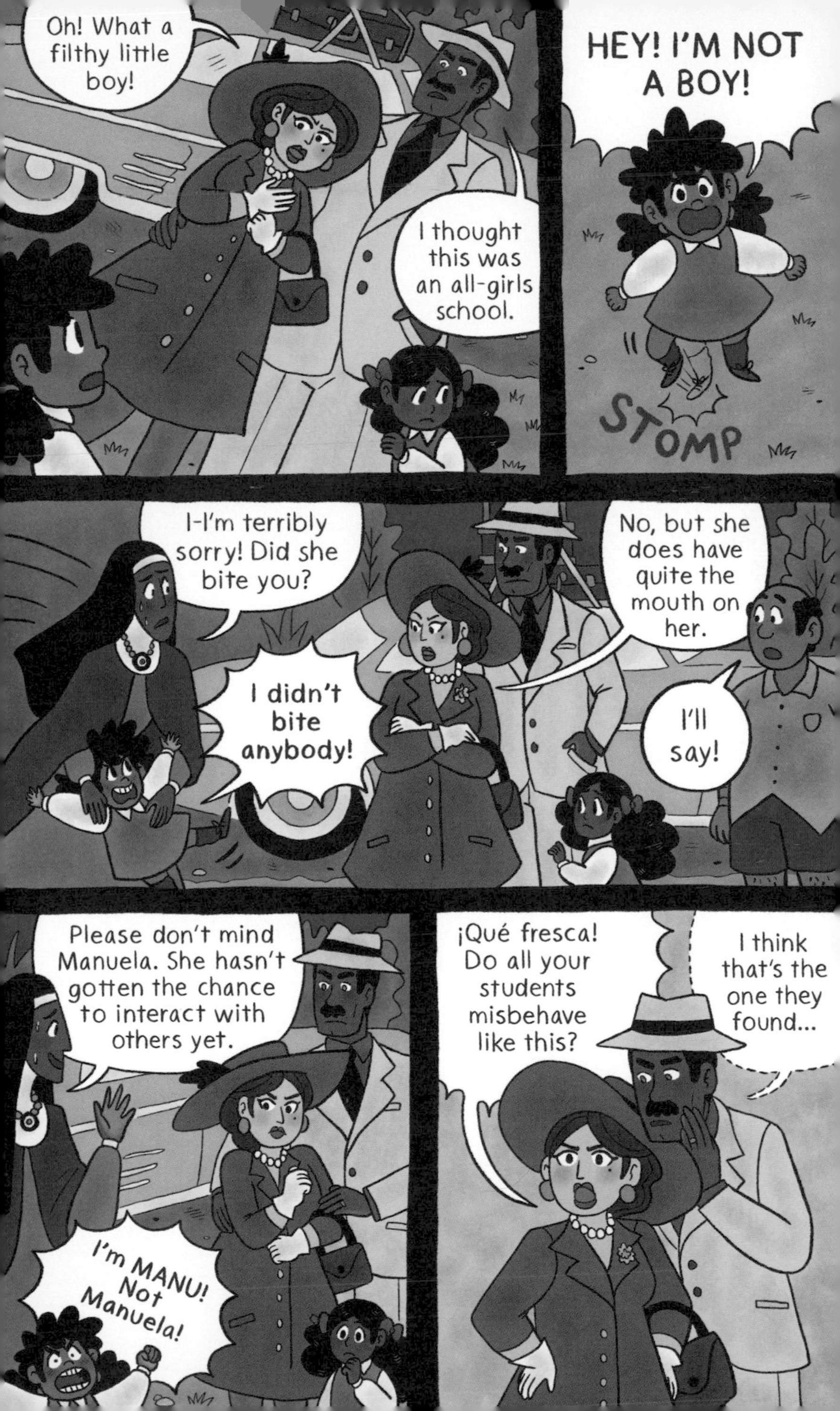

Oh! What a filthy little boy!
I thought this was an all-girls school.
HEY! I'M NOT A BOY!
STOMP
I-I'm terribly sorry! Did she bite you?
I didn't bite anybody!
No, but she does have quite the mouth on her.
I'll say!
Please don't mind Manuela. She hasn't gotten the chance to interact with others yet.
I'm MANU! Not Manuela!
¡Qué fresca! Do all your students misbehave like this?
I think that's the one they found...

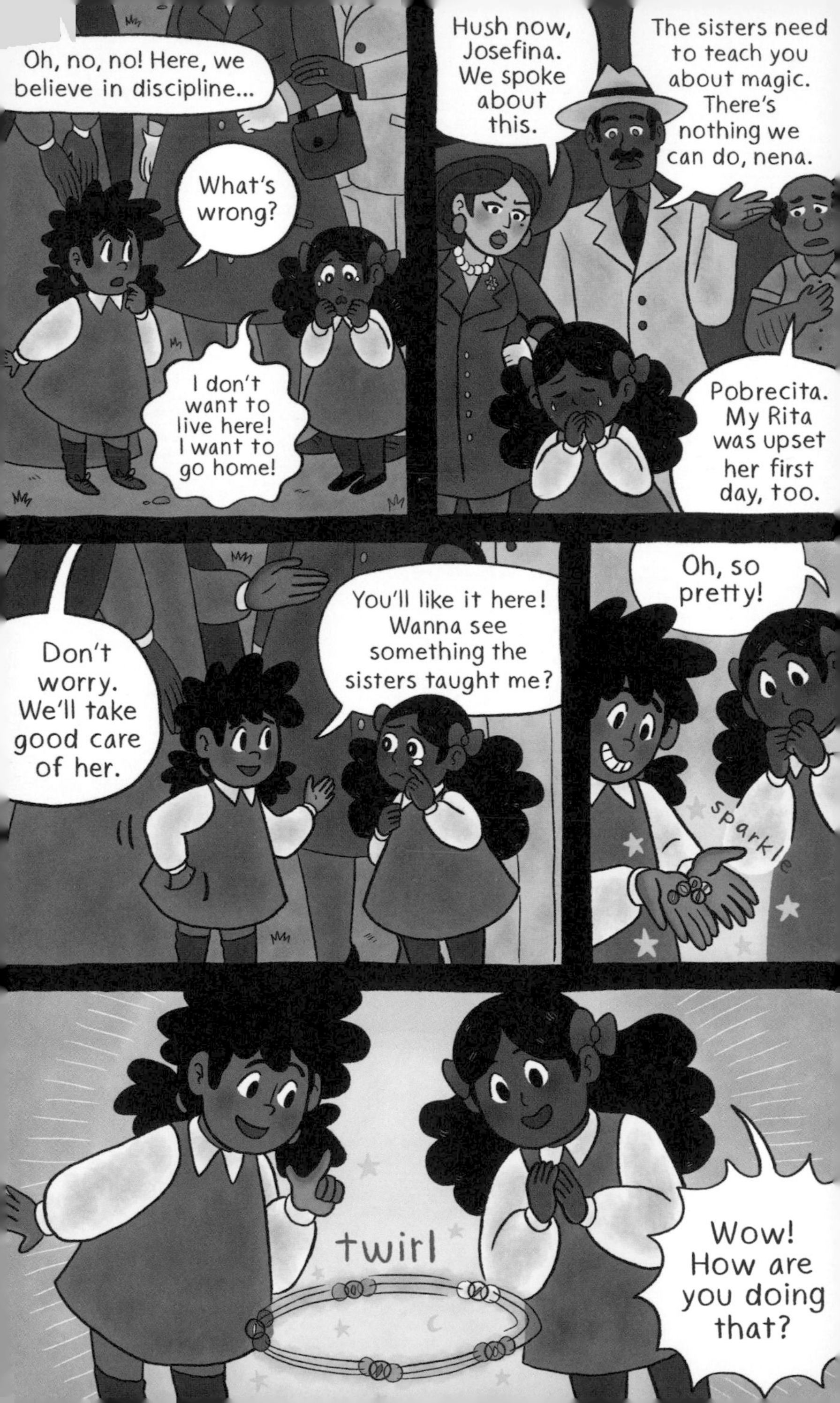
Oh, no, no! Here, we believe in discipline...
What's wrong?
I don't want to live here! I want to go home!
Hush now, Josefina. We spoke about this.
The sisters need to teach you about magic. There's nothing we can do, nena.
Pobrecita. My Rita was upset her first day, too.
Don't worry. We'll take good care of her.
You'll like it here! Wanna see something the sisters taught me?
Oh, so pretty!
sparkle
twirl
Wow! How are you doing that?

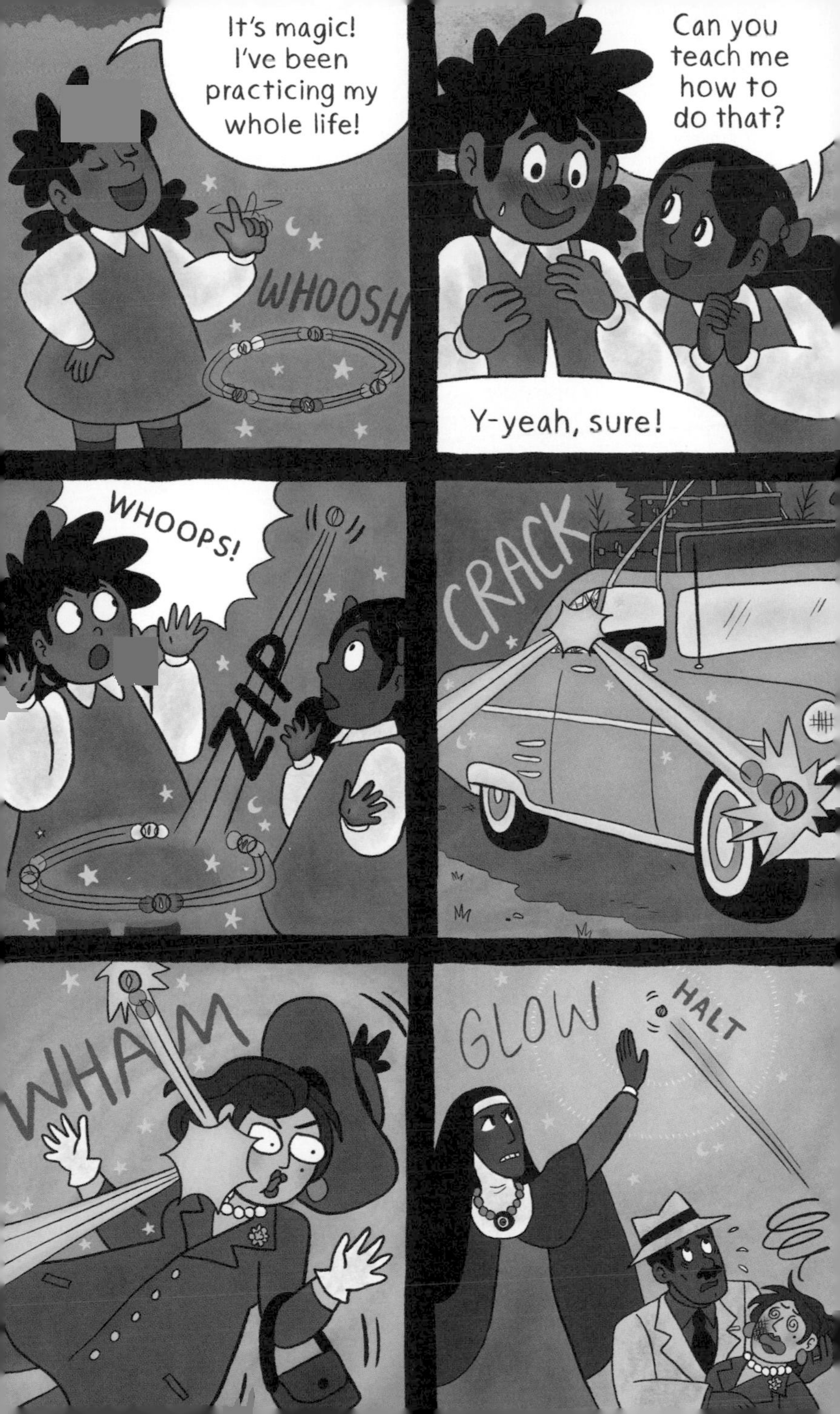
It's magic! I've been practicing my whole life!
WHOOSH
Can you teach me how to do that?
Y-yeah, sure!
WHOOPS!
ZIP
CRACK
WHAM
GLOW
HALT

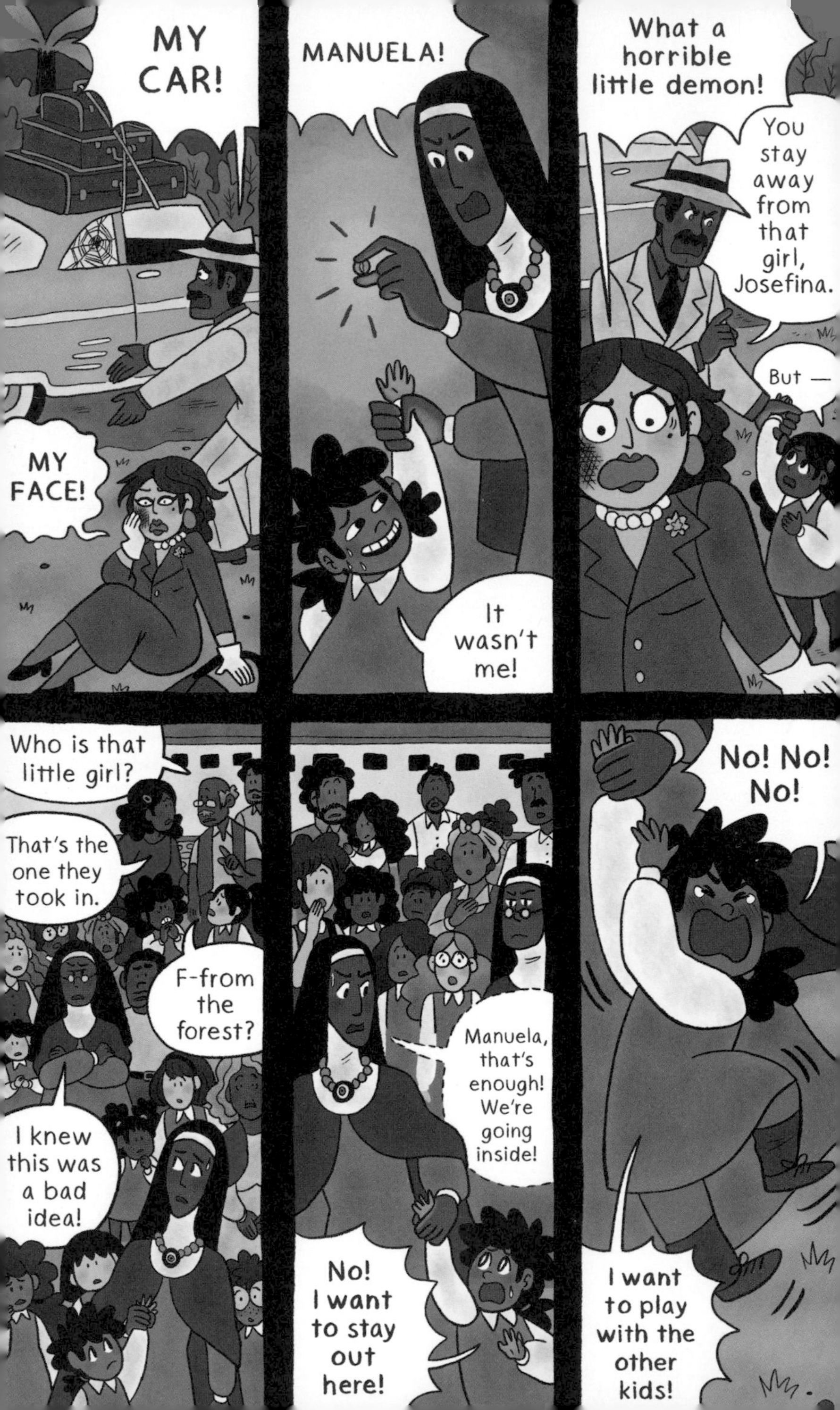
MY CAR!
MY FACE!
MANUELA!
It wasn't me!
What a horrible little demon!
You stay away from that girl, Josefina.
But —
Who is that little girl?
That's the one they took in.
F-from the forest?
I knew this was a bad idea!
Manuela, that's enough! We're going inside!
No! I want to stay out here!
No! No! No!
I want to play with the other kids!

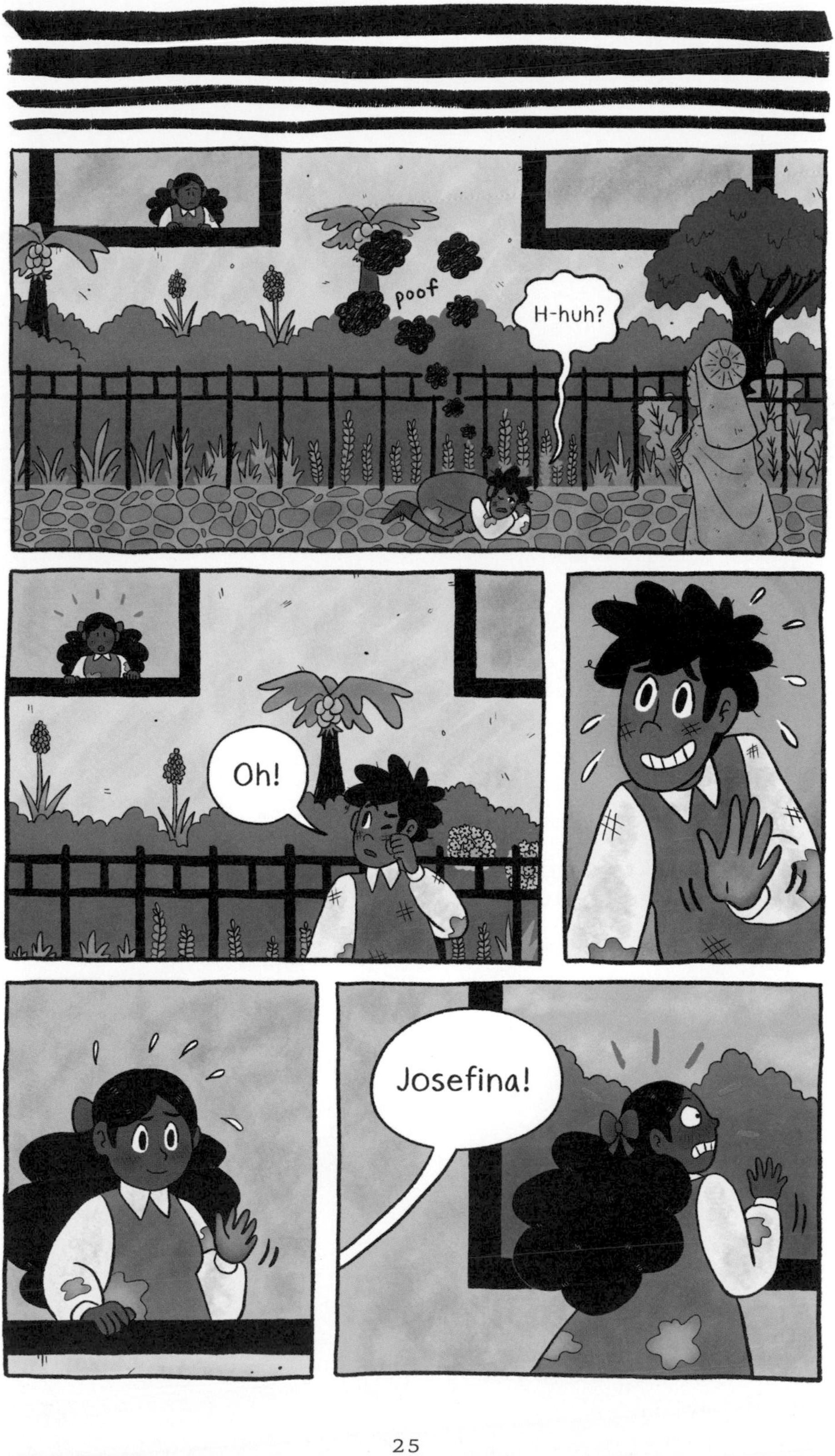
poof
H-huh?
Oh!
Josefina!

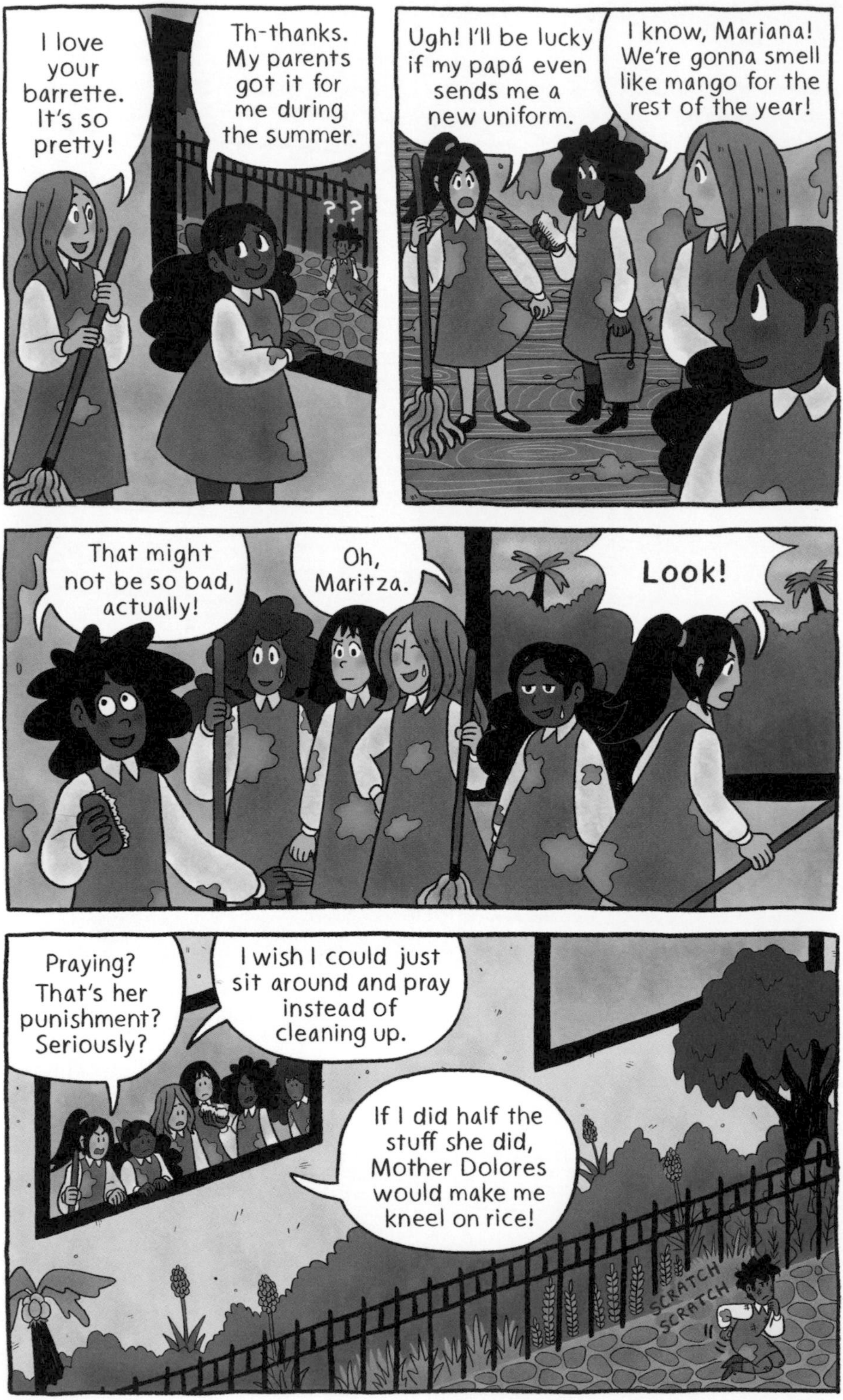
I love your barrette. It's so pretty!
Th-thanks. My parents got it for me during the summer.
? ?
Ugh! I'll be lucky if my papá even sends me a new uniform.
I know, Mariana! We're gonna smell like mango for the rest of the year!
That might not be so bad, actually!
Oh, Maritza.
Look!
Praying? That's her punishment? Seriously?
I wish I could just sit around and pray instead of cleaning up.
If I did half the stuff she did, Mother Dolores would make me kneel on rice!
SCRATCH
SCRATCH

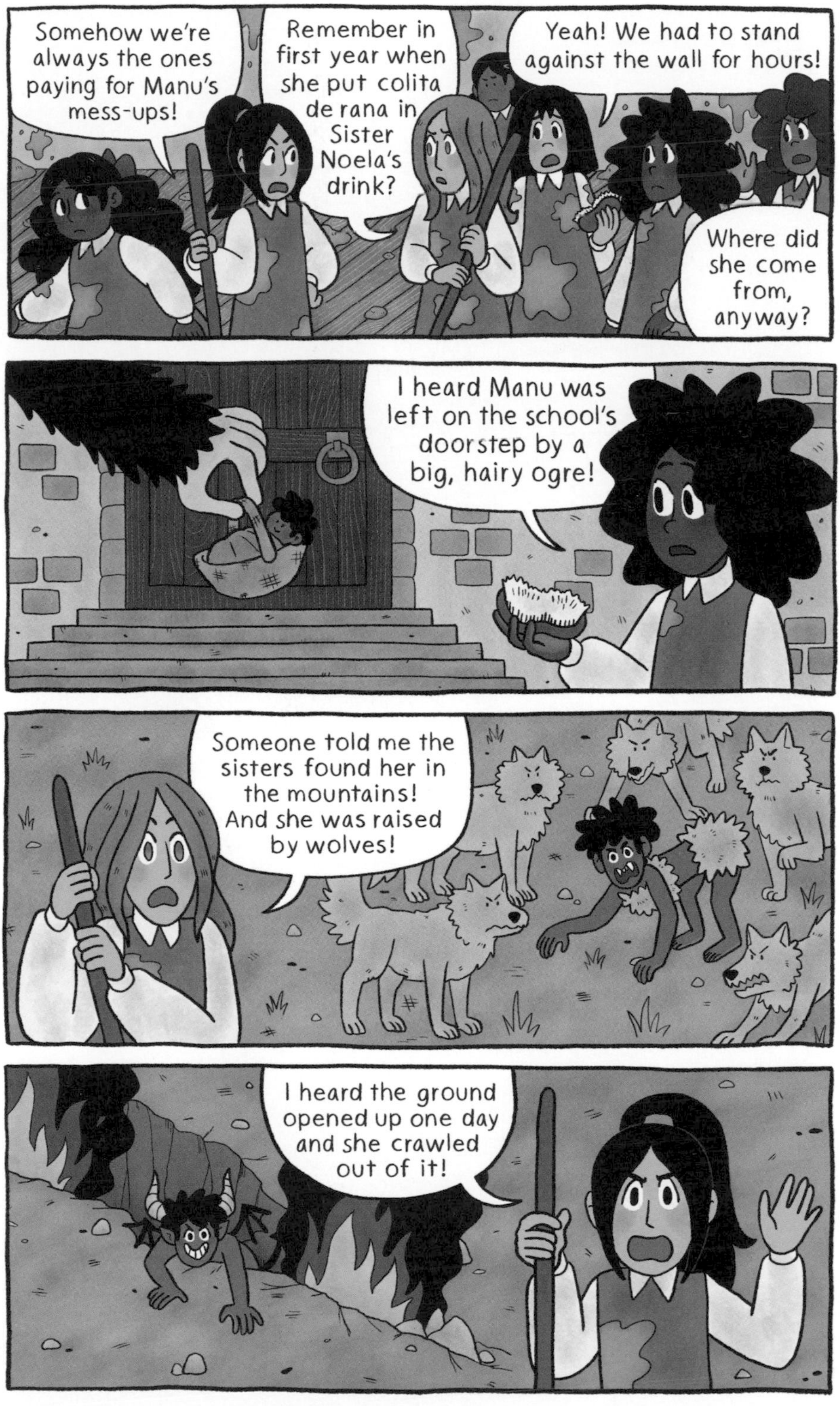
Somehow we're always the ones paying for Manu's mess-ups!
Remember in first year when she put colita de rana in Sister Noela's drink?
Yeah! We had to stand against the wall for hours!
Where did she come from, anyway?
I heard Manu was left on the school's doorstep by a big, hairy ogre!
Someone told me the sisters found her in the mountains! And she was raised by wolves!
I heard the ground opened up one day and she crawled out of it!

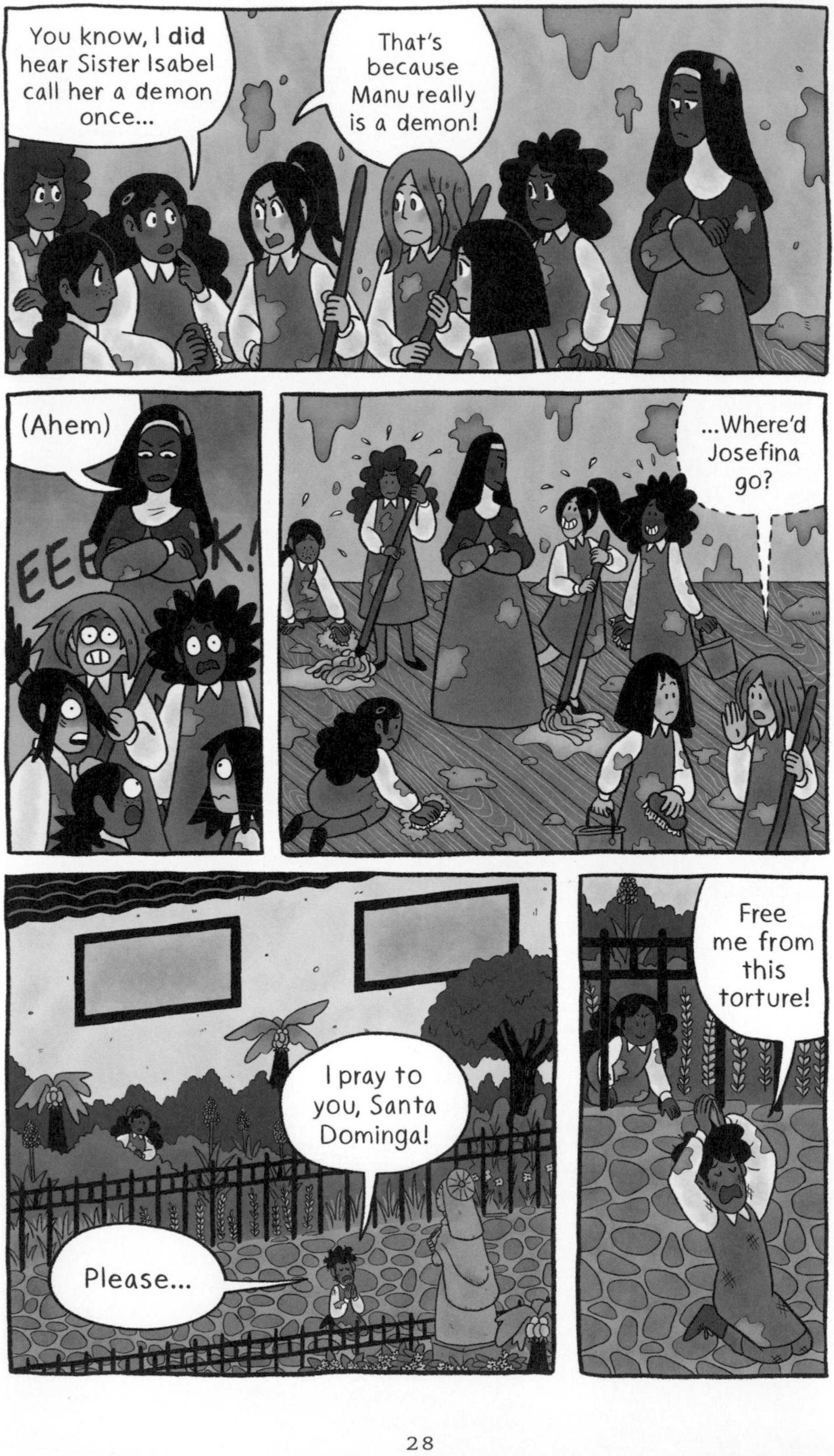
You know, I did hear Sister Isabel call her a demon once...
That's because Manu really is a demon!
(Ahem)
...Where'd Josefina go?
I pray to you, Santa Dominga!
Please...
Free me from this torture!

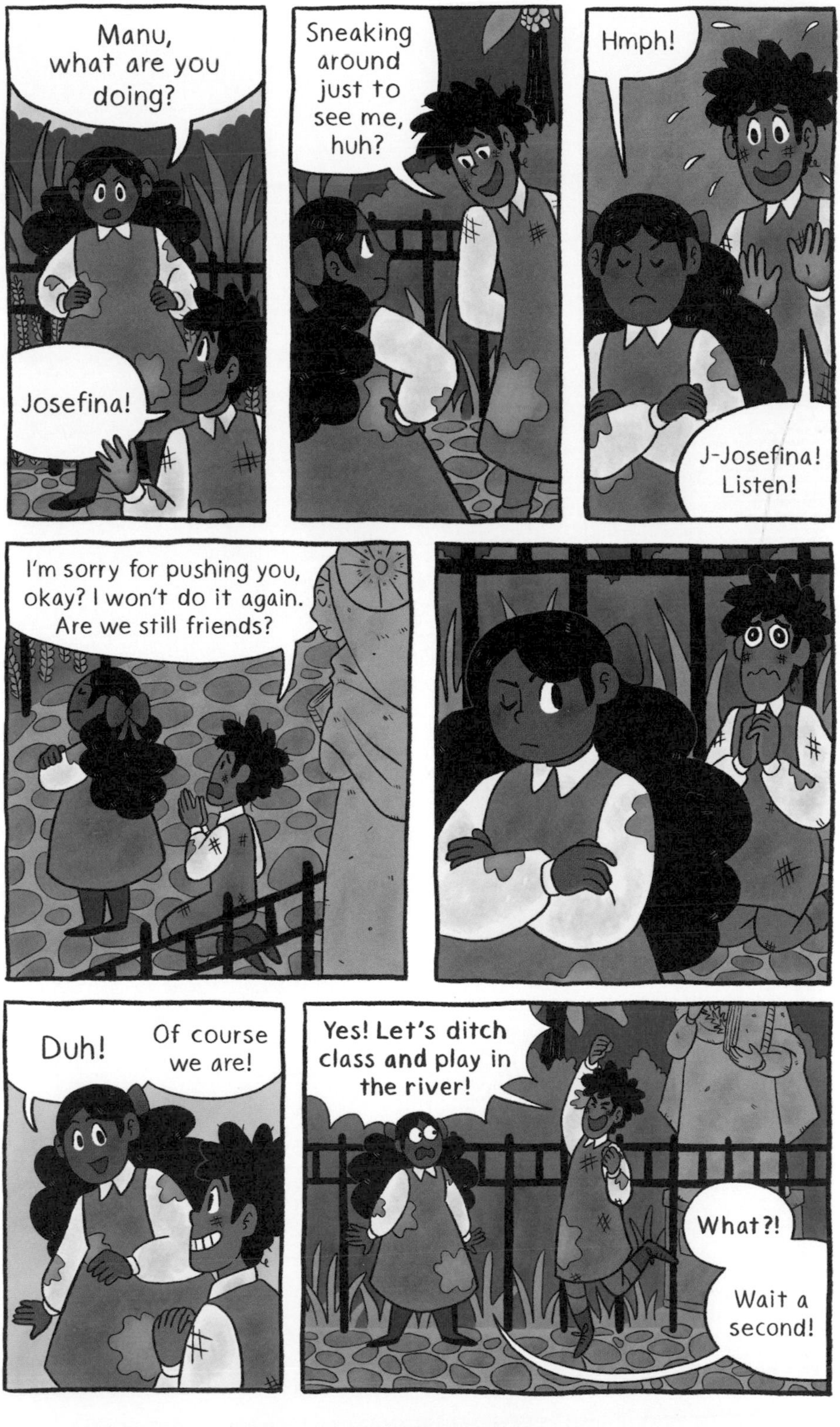
Manu,
what are you
doing?
Josefina!
Sneaking
around
just to
see me,
huh?
Hmph!
J-Josefina!
Listen!
I'm sorry for pushing you,
okay? I won't do it again.
Are we still friends?
Duh!
Of course
we are!
Yes! Let's ditch
class and play in
the river!
What?!
Wait a
second!

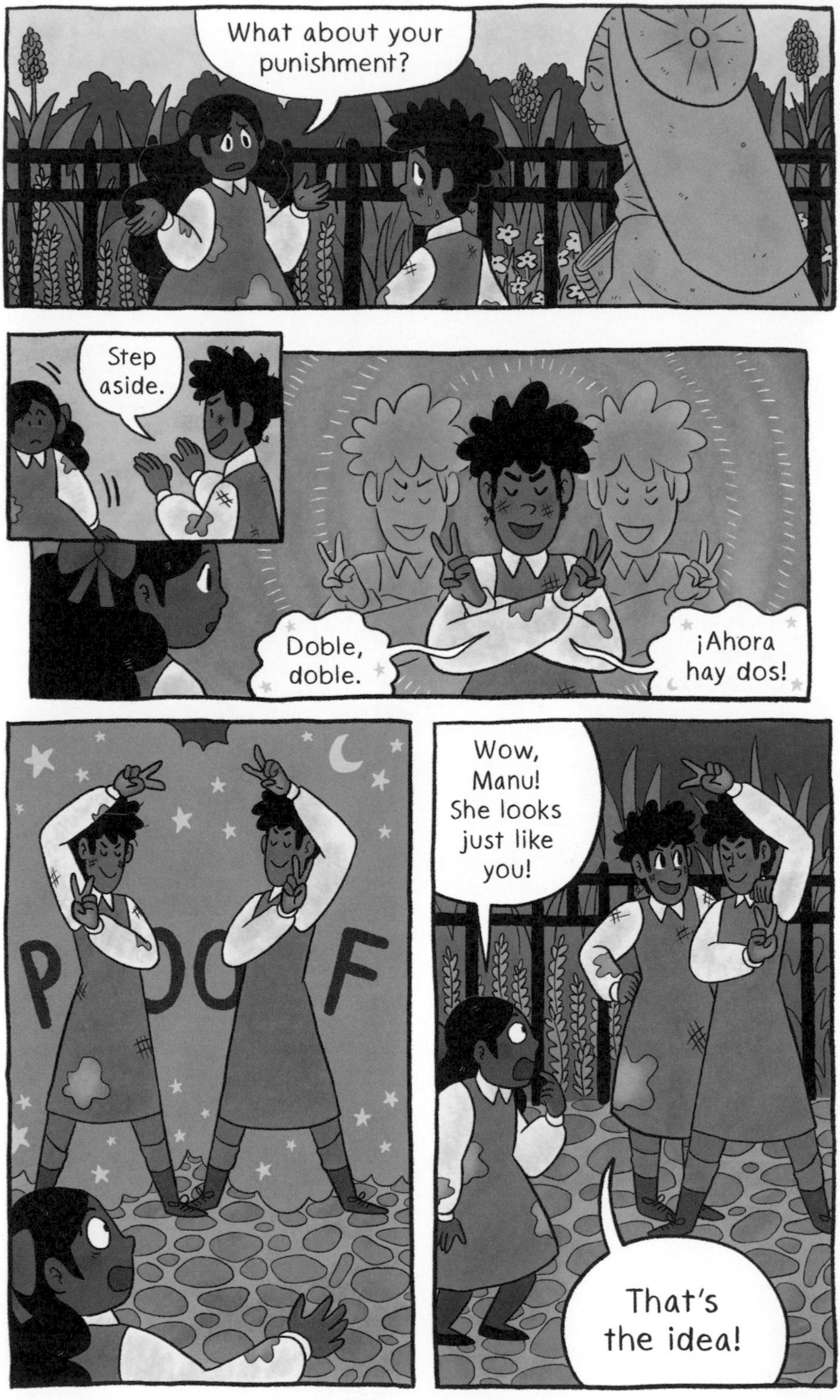
What about your punishment?
Step aside.
Doble, doble.
¡Ahora hay dos!
POOF
Wow, Manu! She looks just like you!
That's the idea!

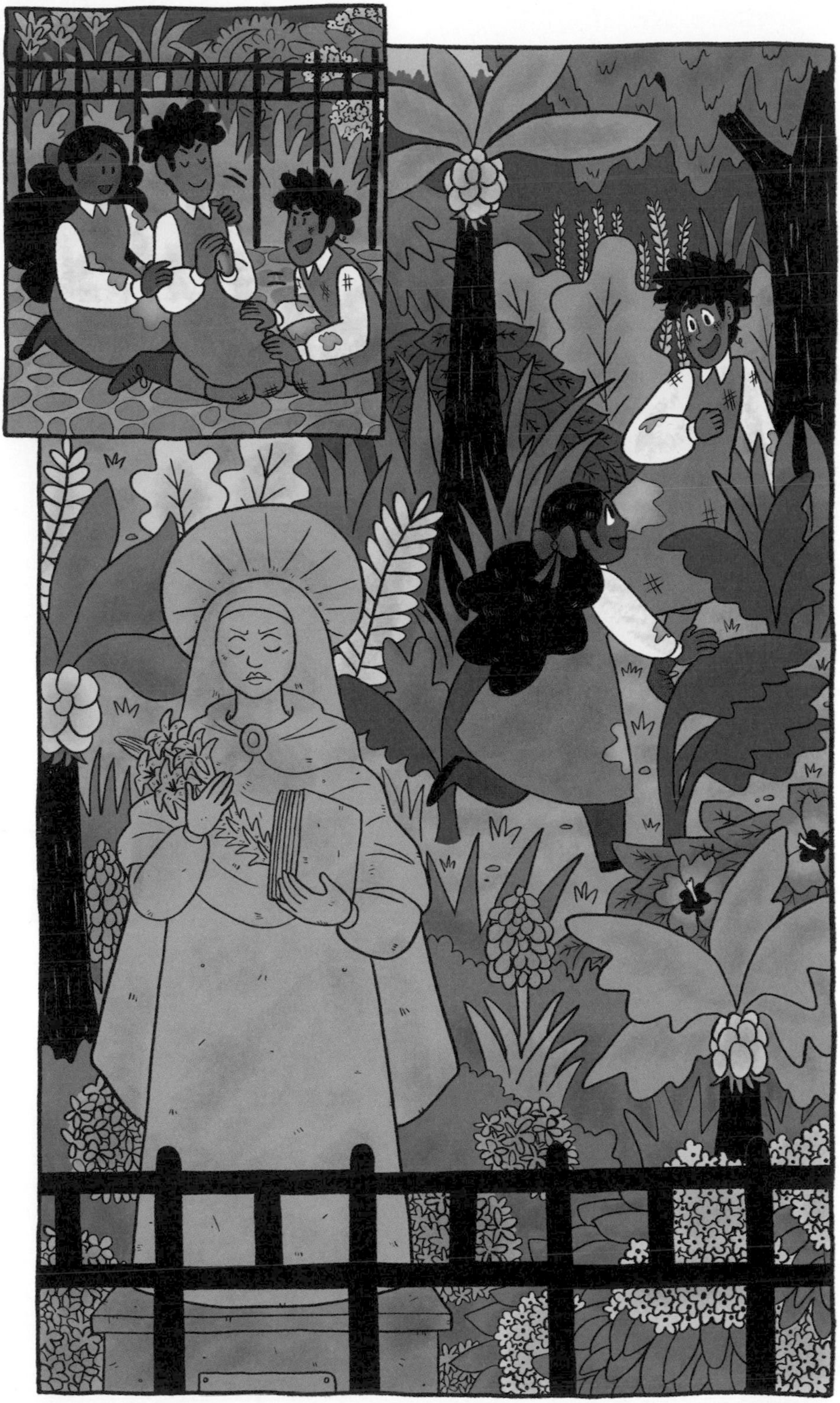

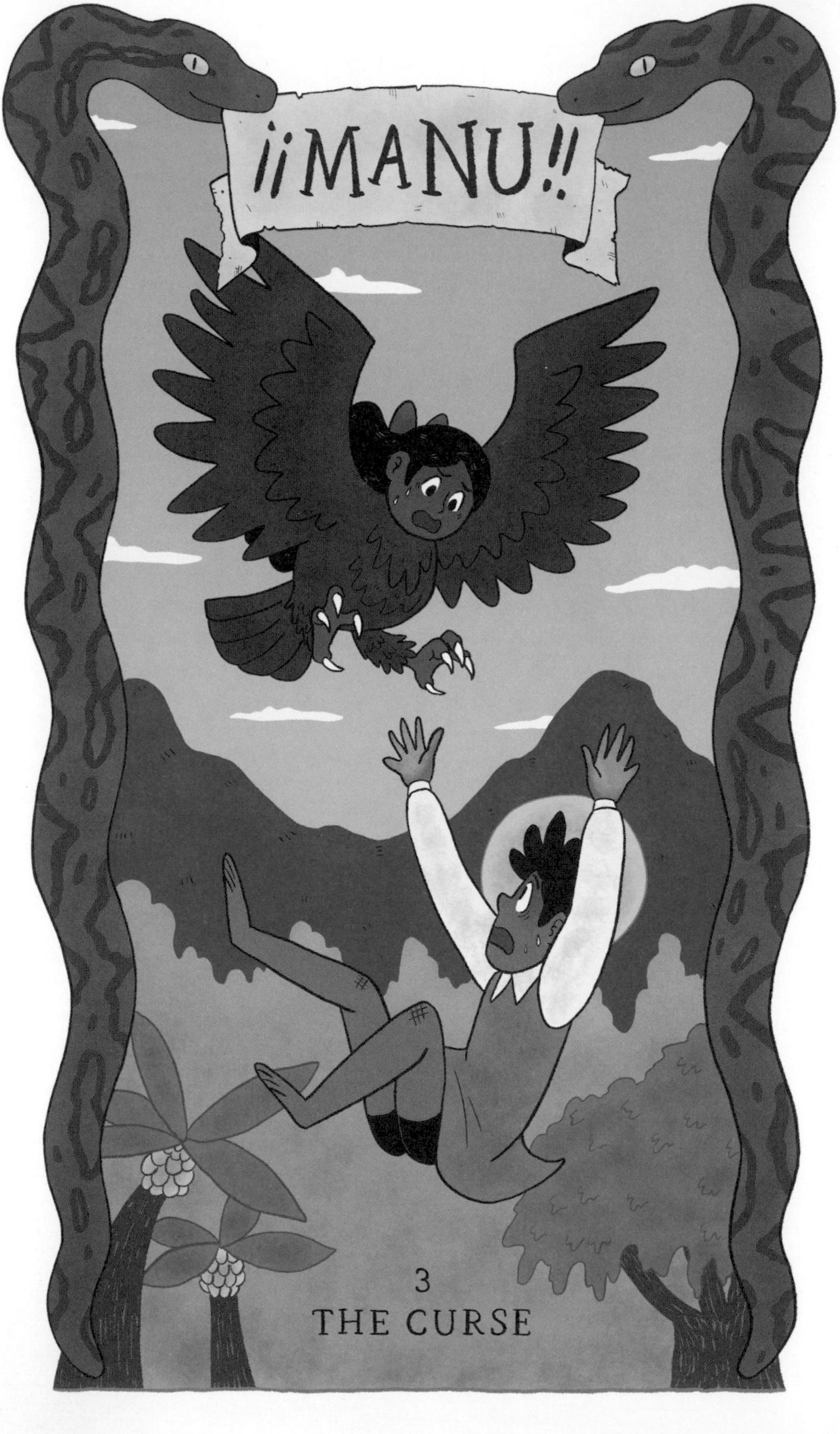
¡¡MANU!!

3
THE CURSE

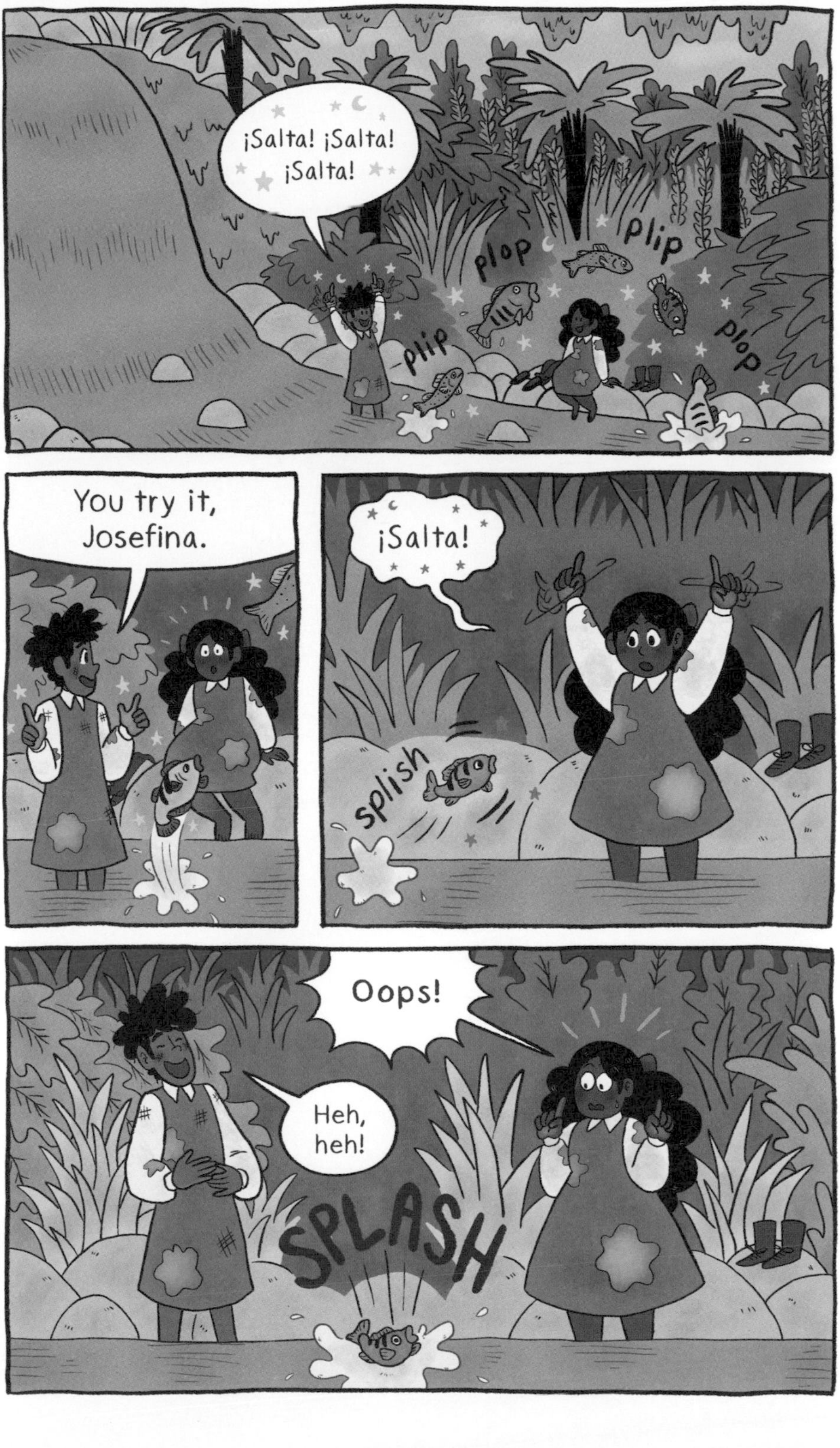
¡Salta! ¡Salta! ¡Salta!
plop
plip
plip
plop
You try it, Josefina.
¡Salta!
splish
Oops!
Heh, heh!
SPLASH

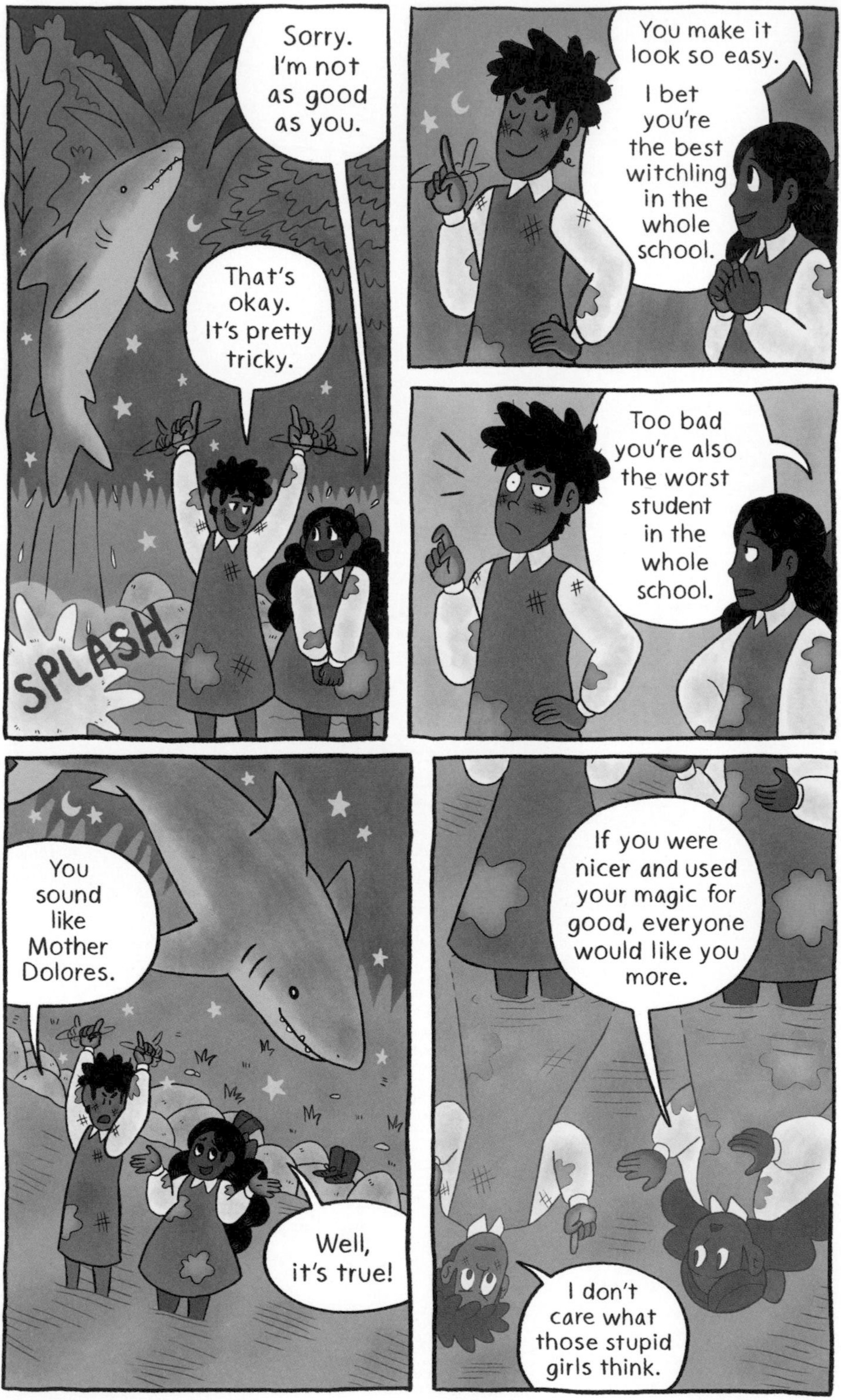
Sorry. I'm not as good as you.
That's okay. It's pretty tricky.
SPLASH
You make it look so easy.
I bet you're the best witchling in the whole school.
Too bad you're also the worst student in the whole school.
You sound like Mother Dolores.
Well, it's true!
If you were nicer and used your magic for good, everyone would like you more.
I don't care what those stupid girls think.

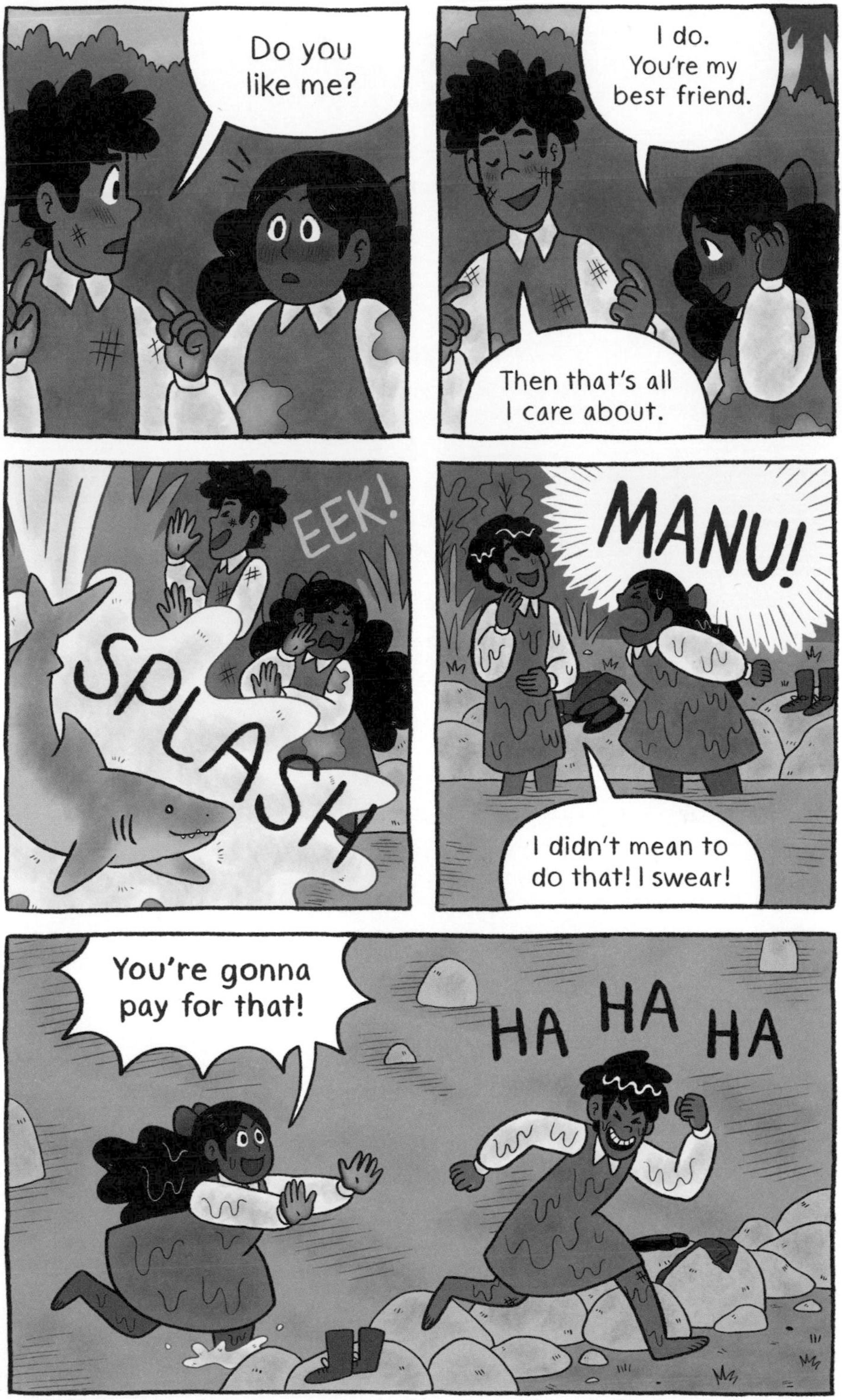

Do you like me?
I do. You're my best friend.
Then that's all I care about.
EEK!
SPLASH
MANU!
I didn't mean to do that! I swear!
You're gonna pay for that!
HA HA HA

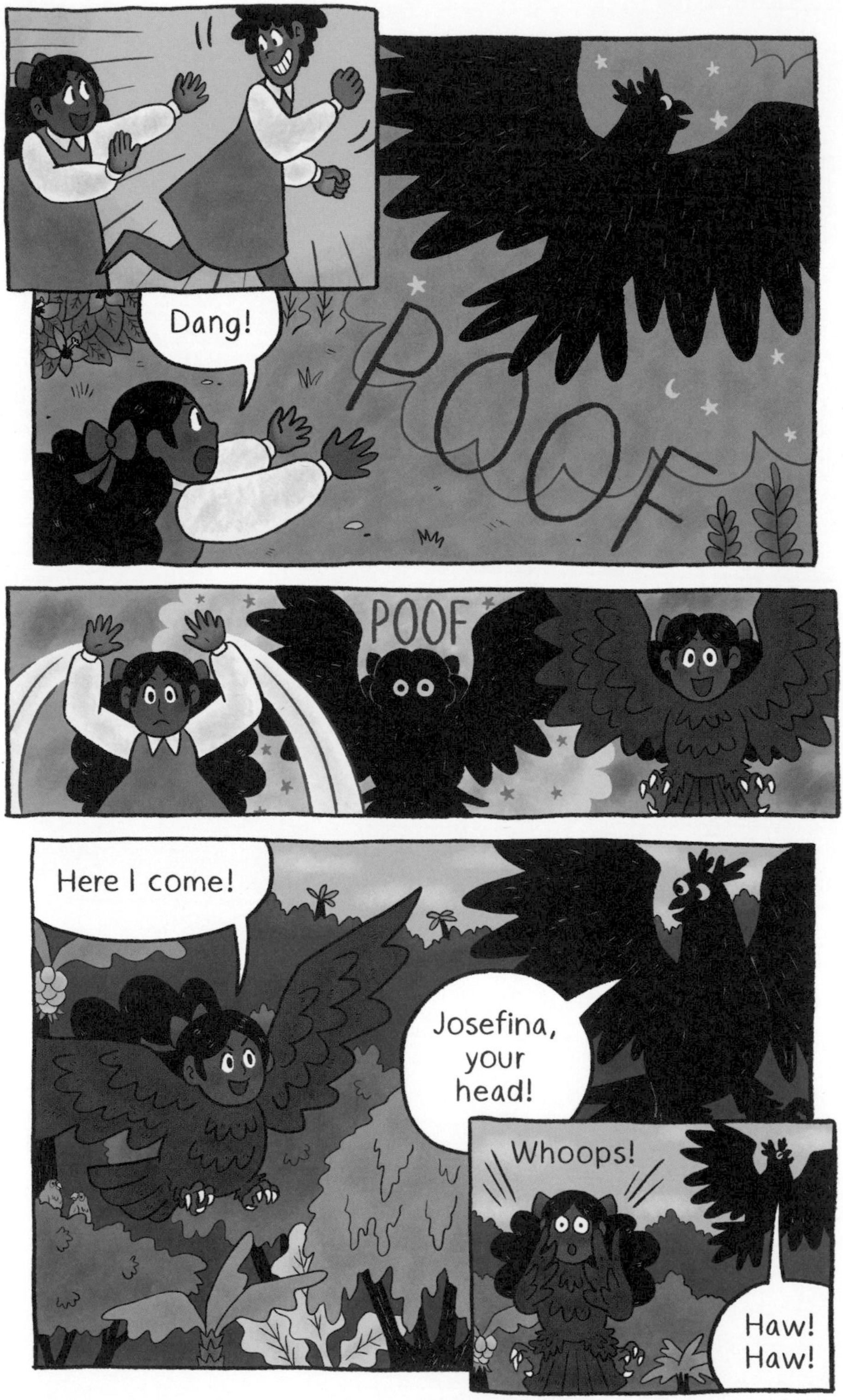
Dang!
POOF
POOF
Here I come!
Josefina, your head!
Whoops!
Haw! Haw!

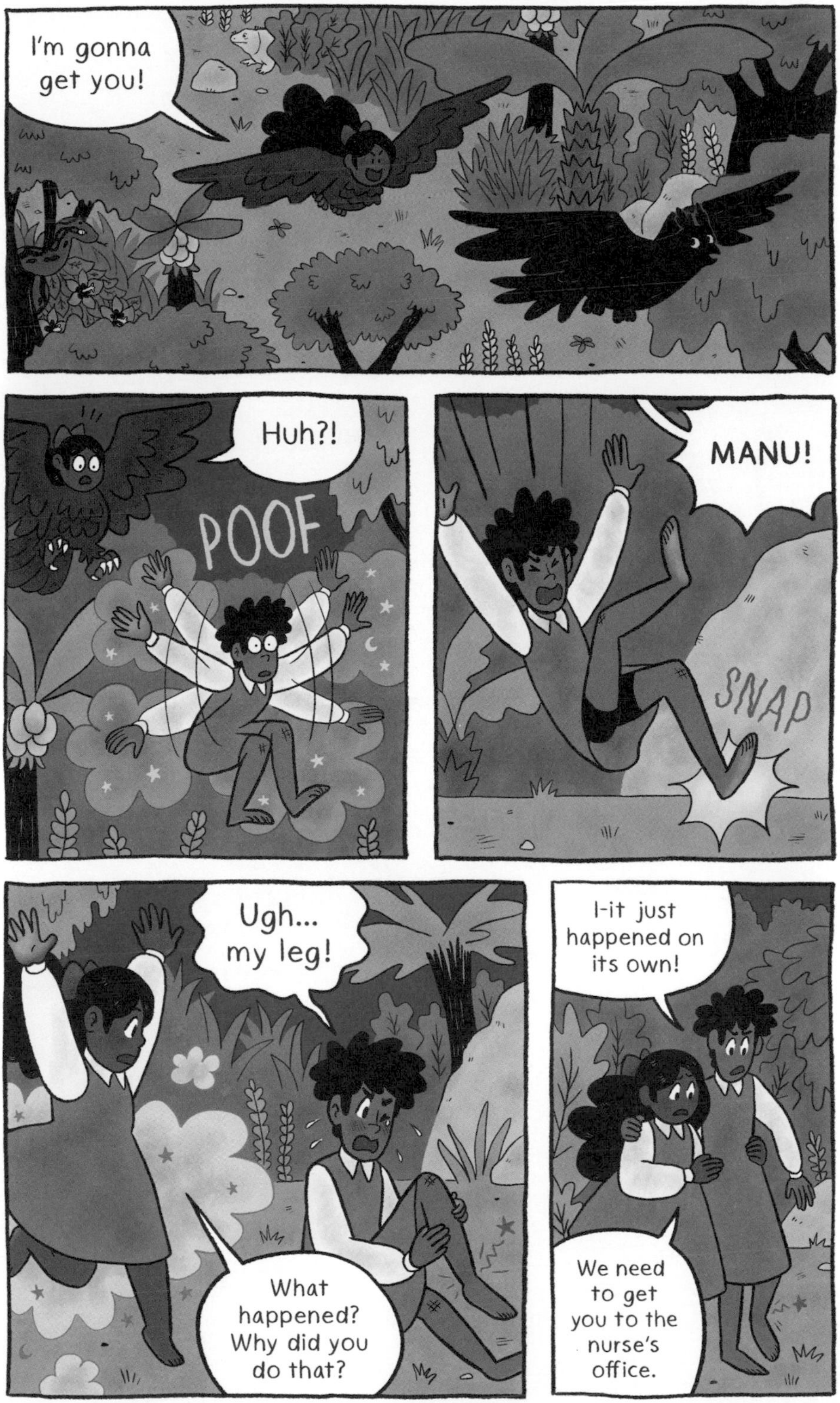
I'm gonna get you!
Huh?!
POOF
MANU!
SNAP
Ugh... my leg!
What happened? Why did you do that?
I-it just happened on its own!
We need to get you to the nurse's office.

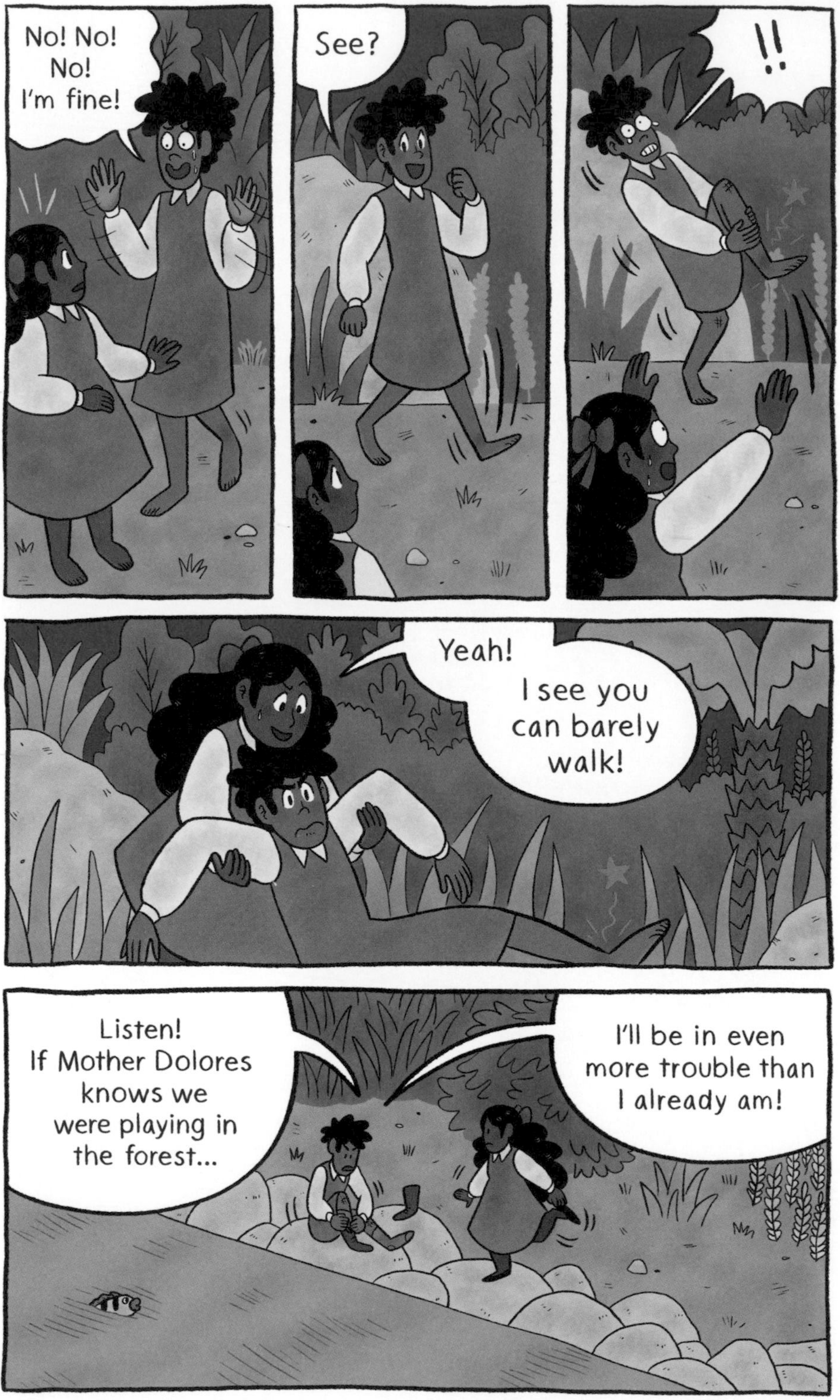
No! No! No! I'm fine!
See?
!!
Yeah!
I see you can barely walk!
Listen! If Mother Dolores knows we were playing in the forest...
I'll be in even more trouble than I already am!

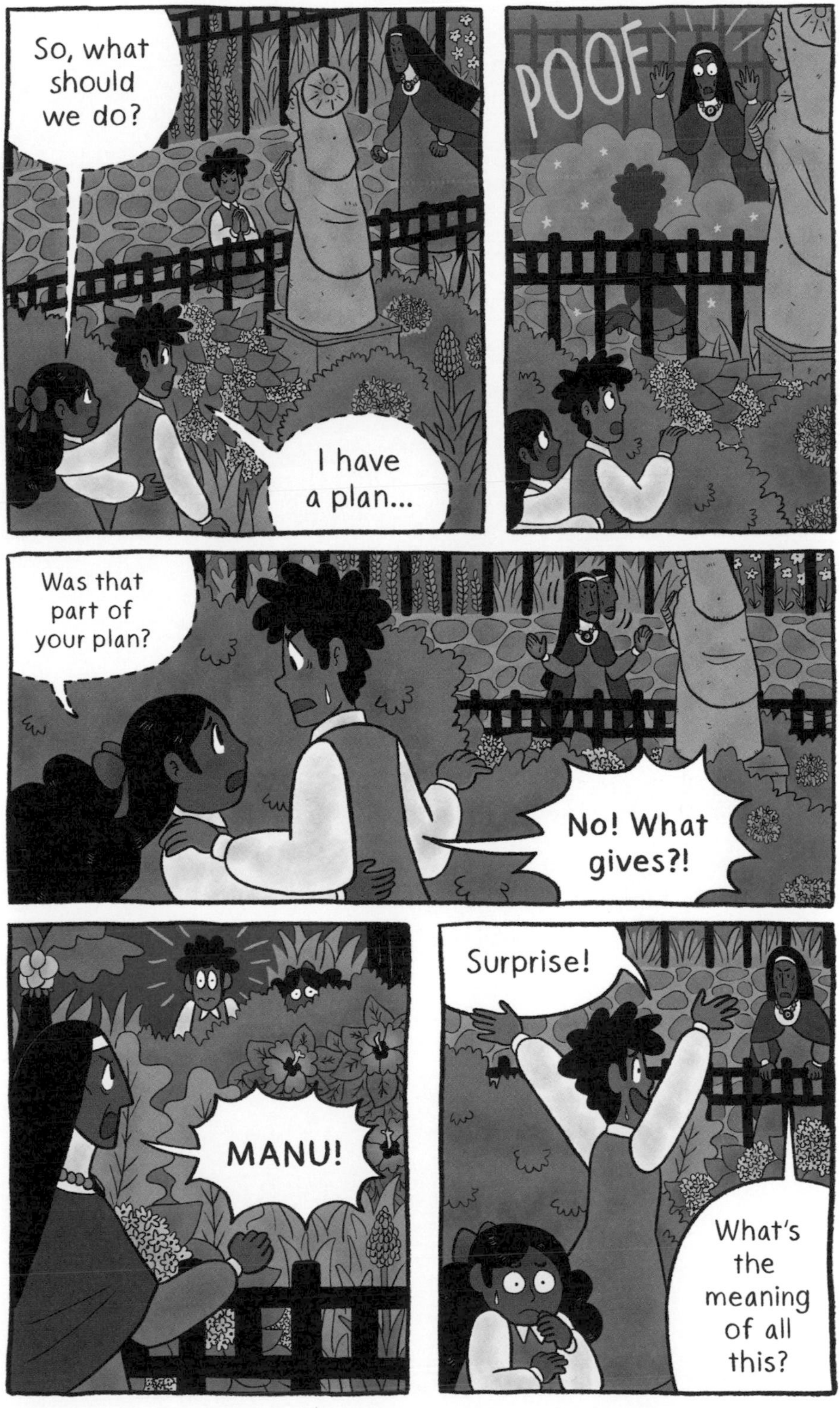
So, what should we do?
I have a plan...
POOF
Was that part of your plan?
No! What gives?!
MANU!
Surprise!
What's the meaning of all this?

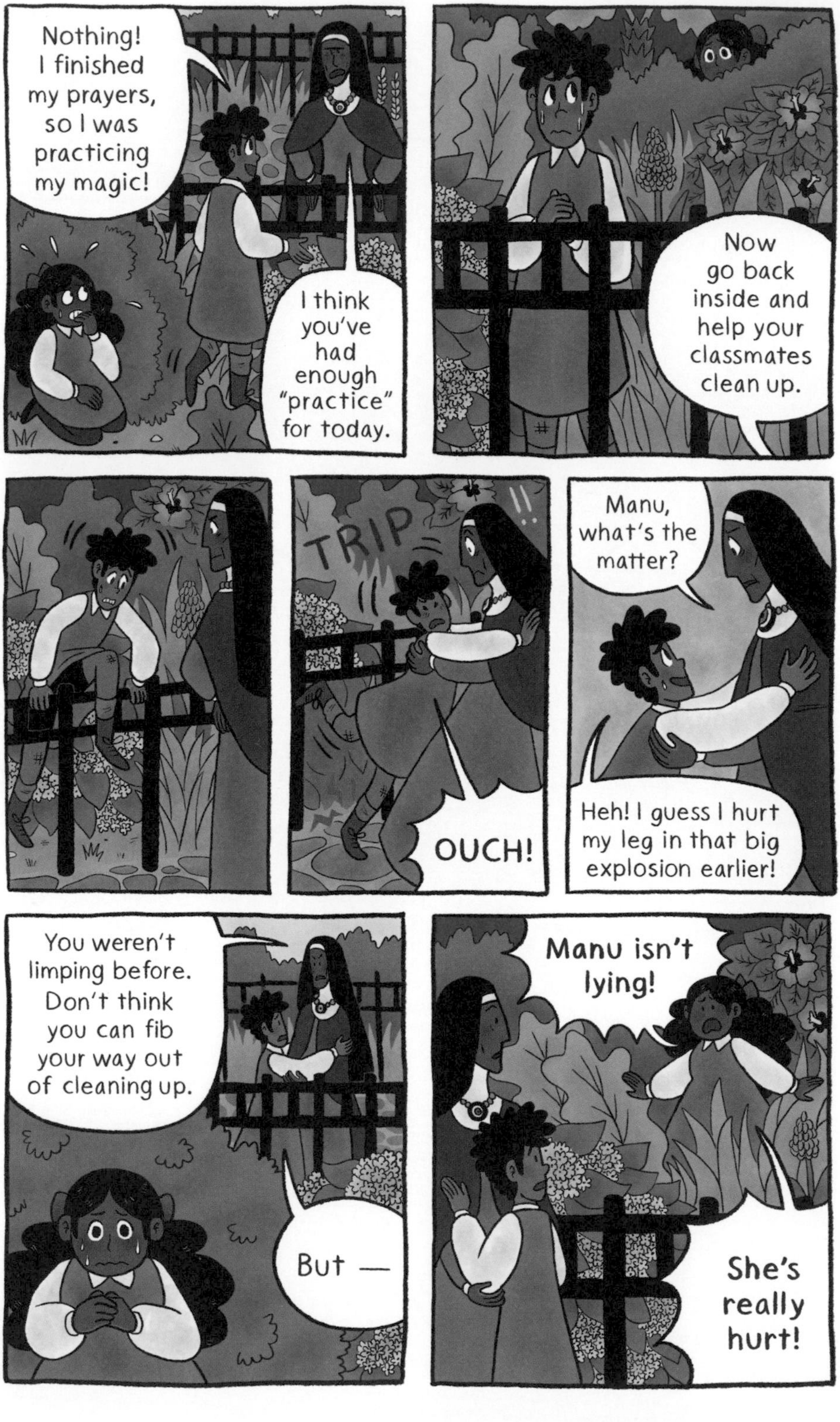

Nothing! I finished my prayers, so I was practicing my magic!
I think you've had enough "practice" for today.
Now go back inside and help your classmates clean up.
TRIP
!!
OUCH!
Manu, what's the matter?
Heh! I guess I hurt my leg in that big explosion earlier!
You weren't limping before. Don't think you can fib your way out of cleaning up.
But —
Manu isn't lying!
She's really hurt!

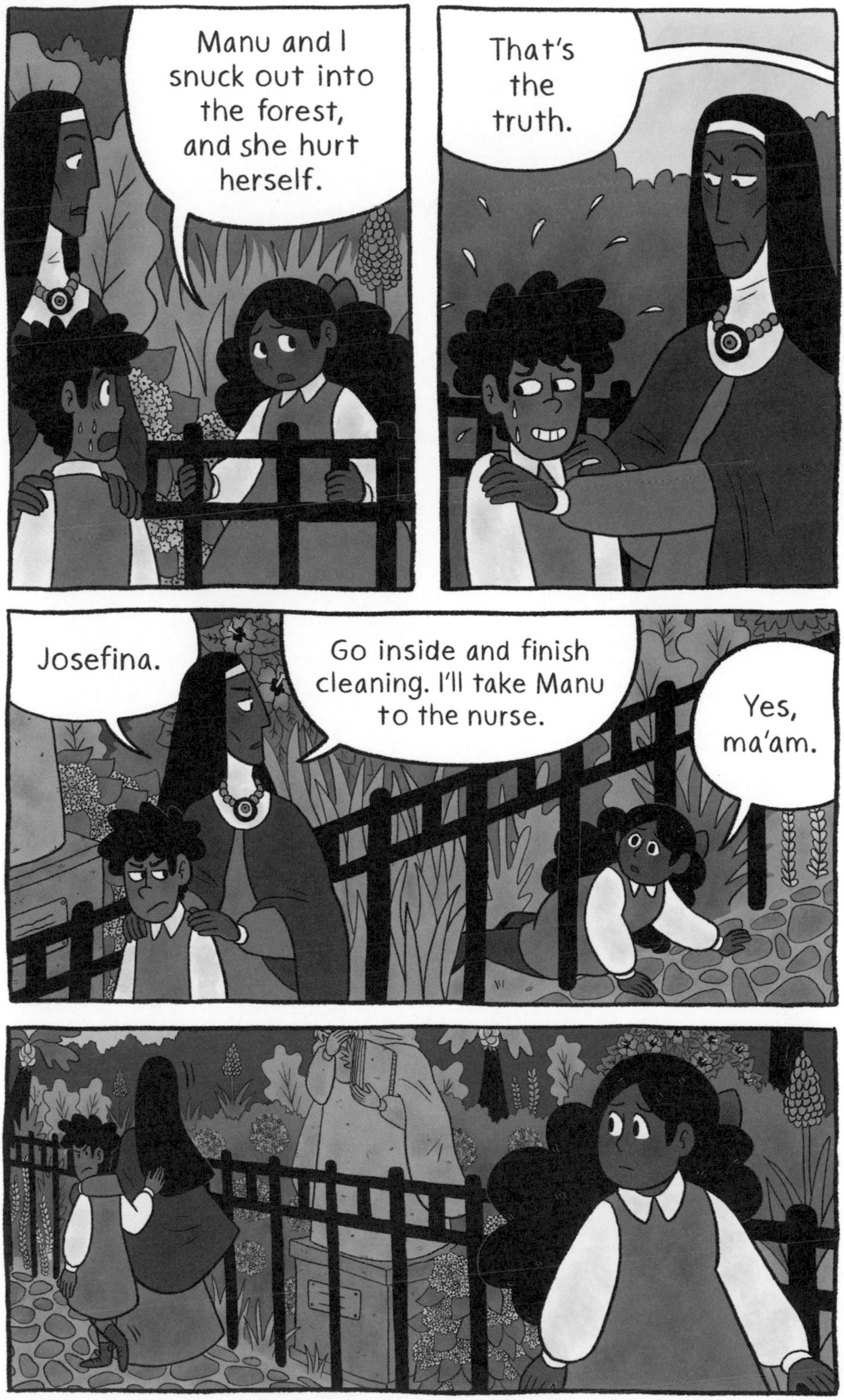
Manu and I snuck out into the forest, and she hurt herself.
That's the truth.
Josefina.
Go inside and finish cleaning. I'll take Manu to the nurse.
Yes, ma'am.

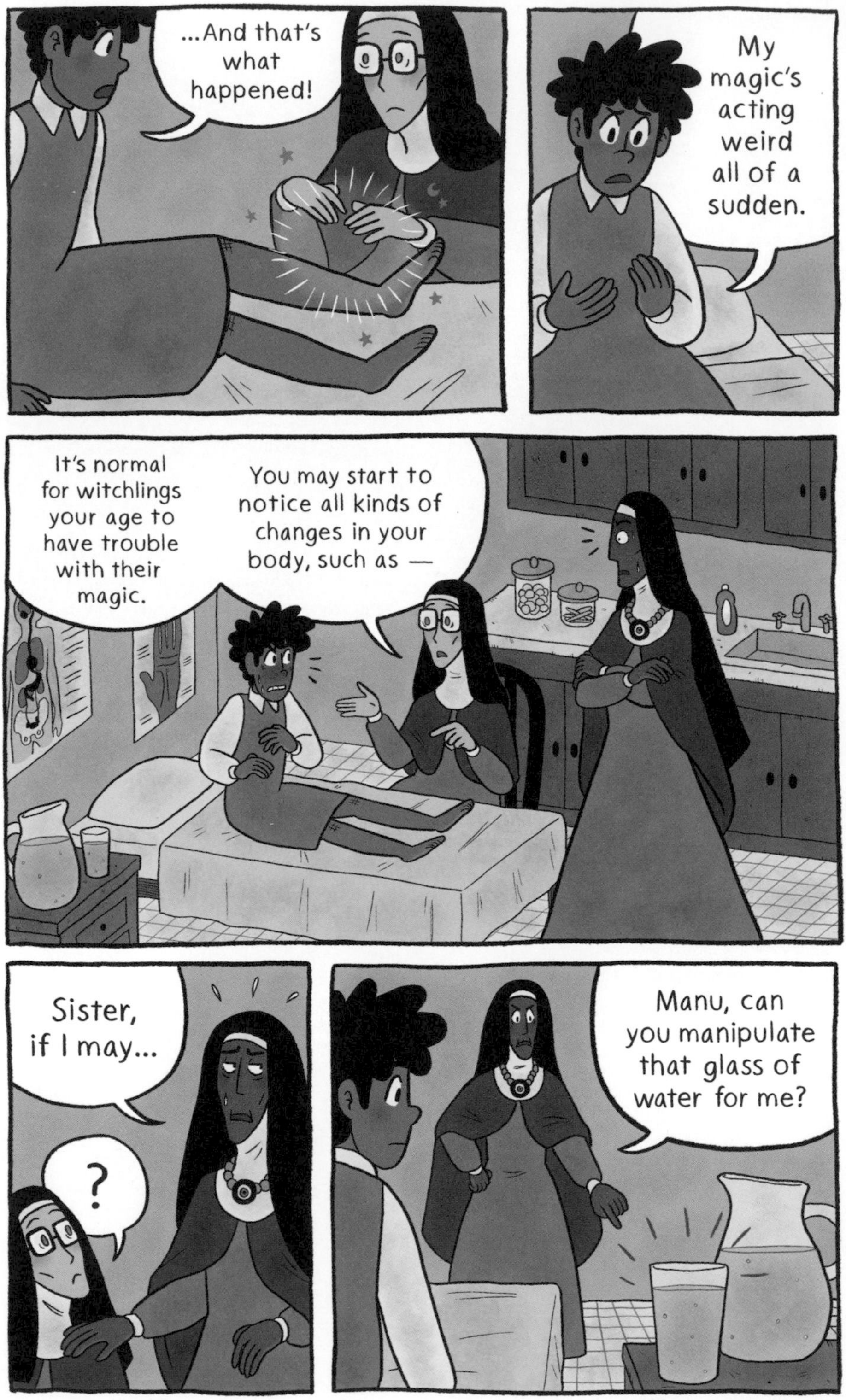
...And that's what happened!
My magic's acting weird all of a sudden.
It's normal for witchlings your age to have trouble with their magic.
You may start to notice all kinds of changes in your body, such as —
Sister, if I may...
?
Manu, can you manipulate that glass of water for me?

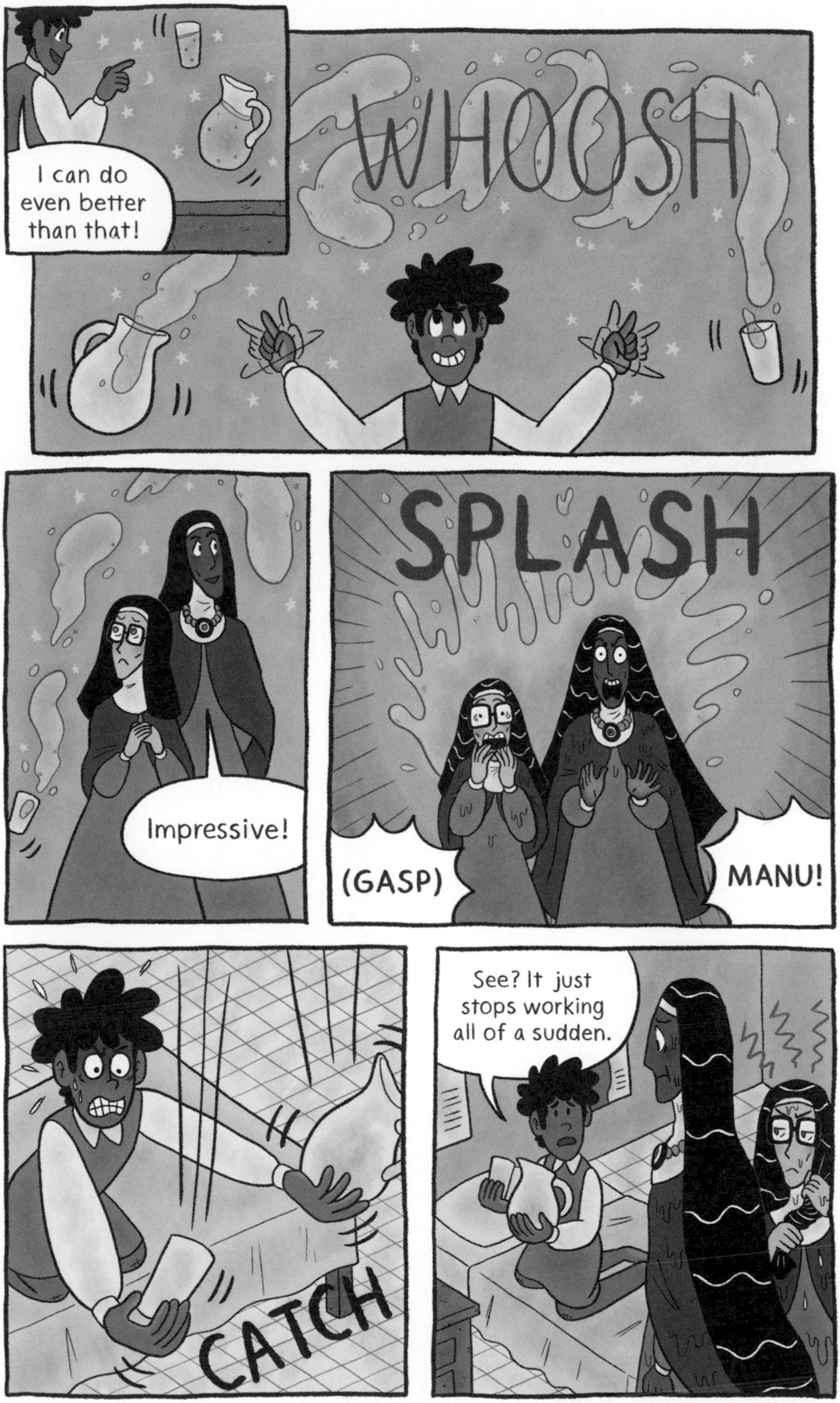

I can do even better than that!
WHOOSH
Impressive!
SPLASH
(GASP)
MANU!
CATCH
See? It just stops working all of a sudden.

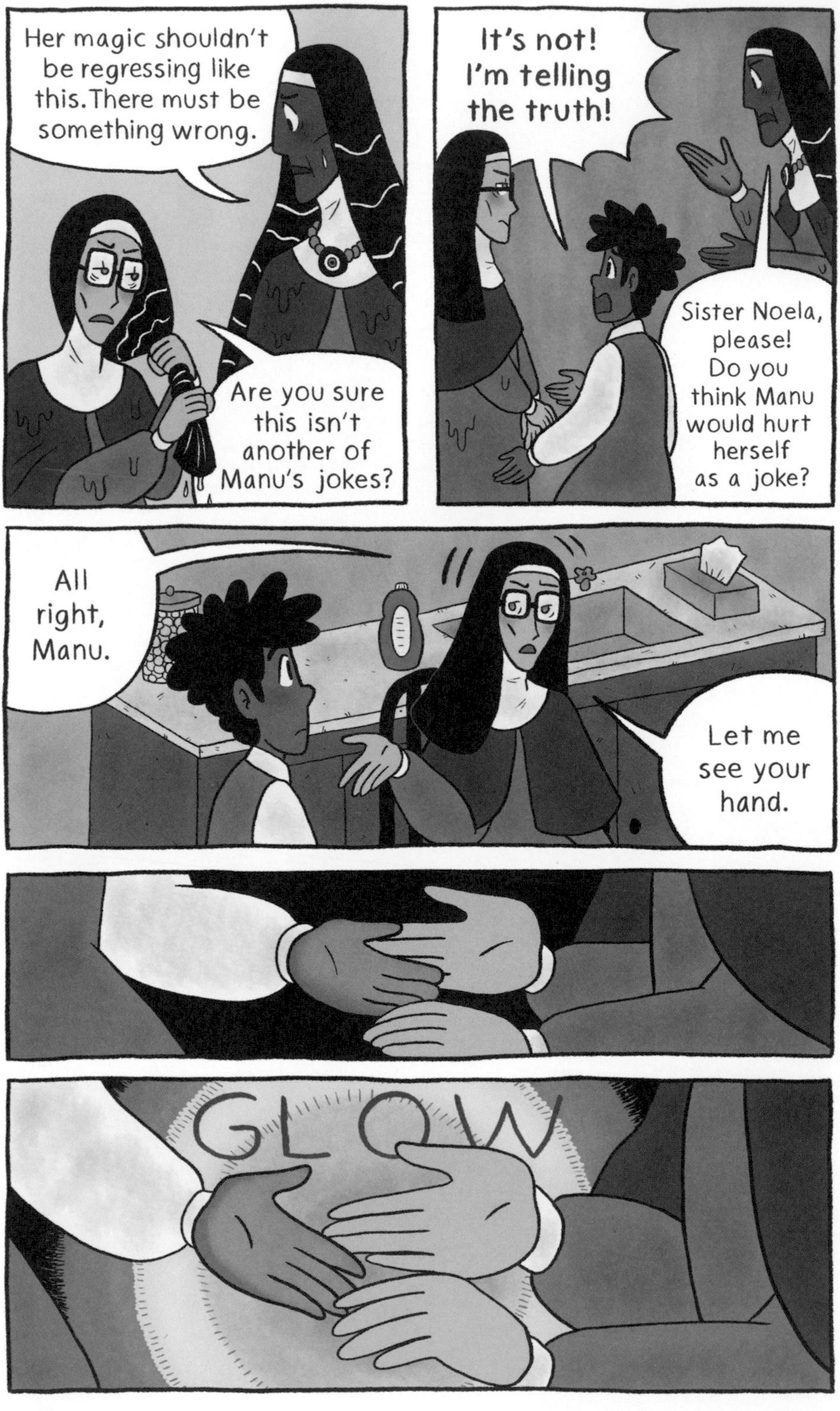
Her magic shouldn't be regressing like this. There must be something wrong.
Are you sure this isn't another of Manu's jokes?
It's not! I'm telling the truth!
Sister Noela, please! Do you think Manu would hurt herself as a joke?
All right, Manu.
Let me see your hand.
GLOW

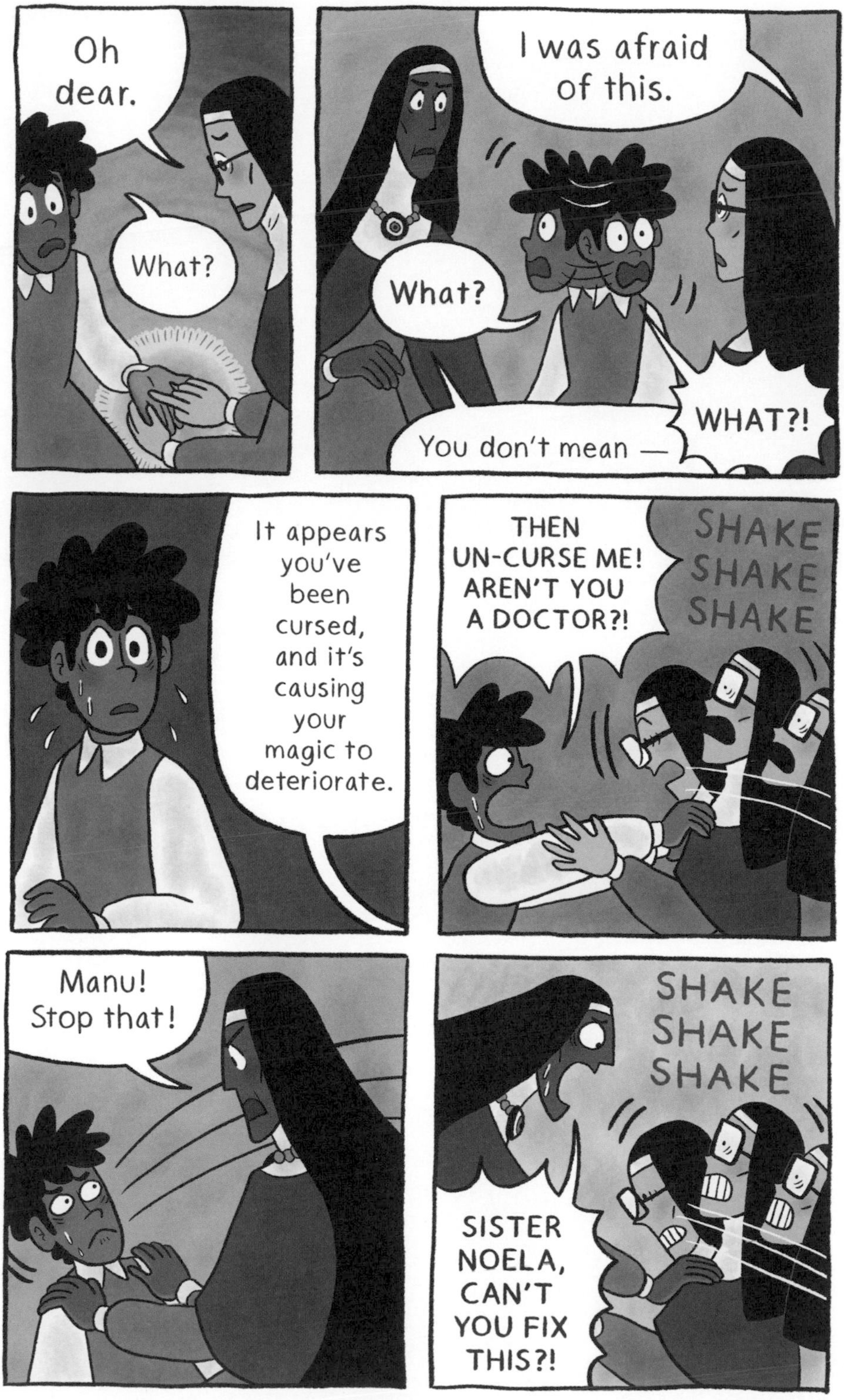
Oh dear.
What?
I was afraid of this.
What?
You don't mean —
WHAT?!
It appears you've been cursed, and it's causing your magic to deteriorate.
THEN UN-CURSE ME! AREN'T YOU A DOCTOR?!
SHAKE SHAKE SHAKE
Manu! Stop that!
SHAKE SHAKE SHAKE
SISTER NOELA, CAN'T YOU FIX THIS?!

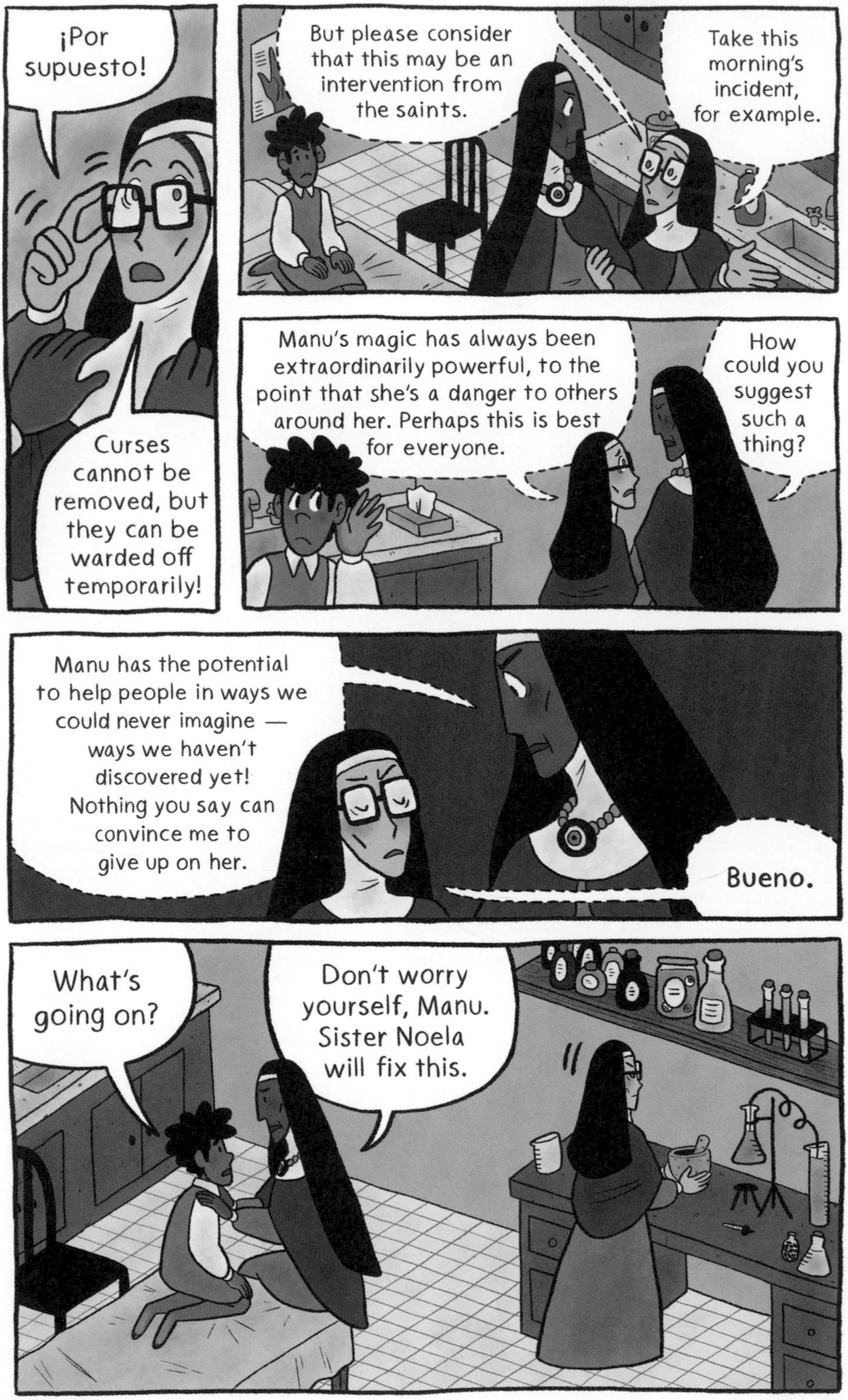
¡Por supuesto!
Curses cannot be removed, but they can be warded off temporarily!
But please consider that this may be an intervention from the saints.
Take this morning's incident, for example.
Manu's magic has always been extraordinarily powerful, to the point that she's a danger to others around her. Perhaps this is best for everyone.
How could you suggest such a thing?
Manu has the potential to help people in ways we could never imagine — ways we haven't discovered yet! Nothing you say can convince me to give up on her.
Bueno.
What's going on?
Don't worry yourself, Manu. Sister Noela will fix this.

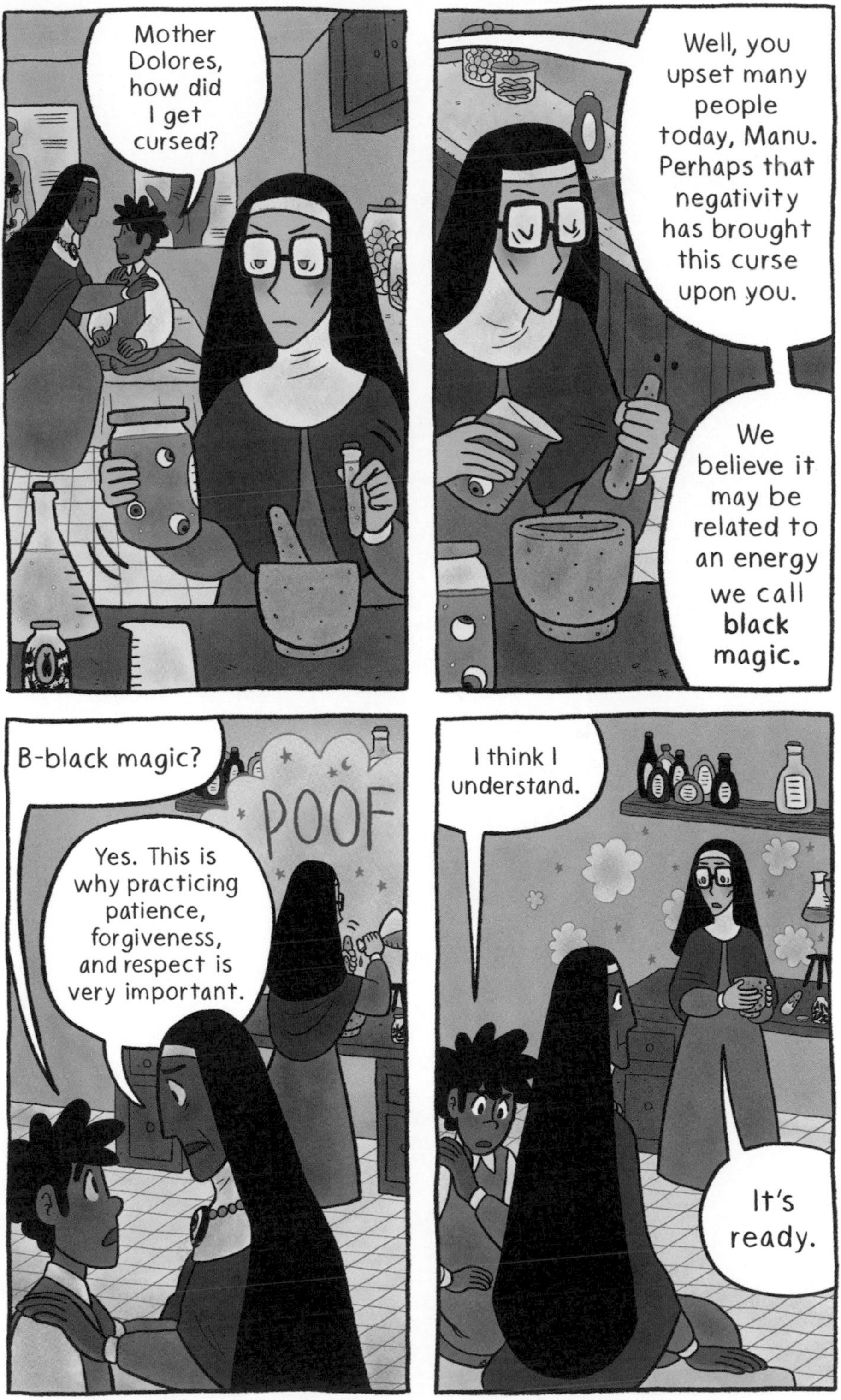
Mother Dolores, how did I get cursed?
Well, you upset many people today, Manu. Perhaps that negativity has brought this curse upon you.
We believe it may be related to an energy we call **black magic.**
B-black magic?
POOF
Yes. This is why practicing patience, forgiveness, and respect is very important.
I think I understand.
It's ready.

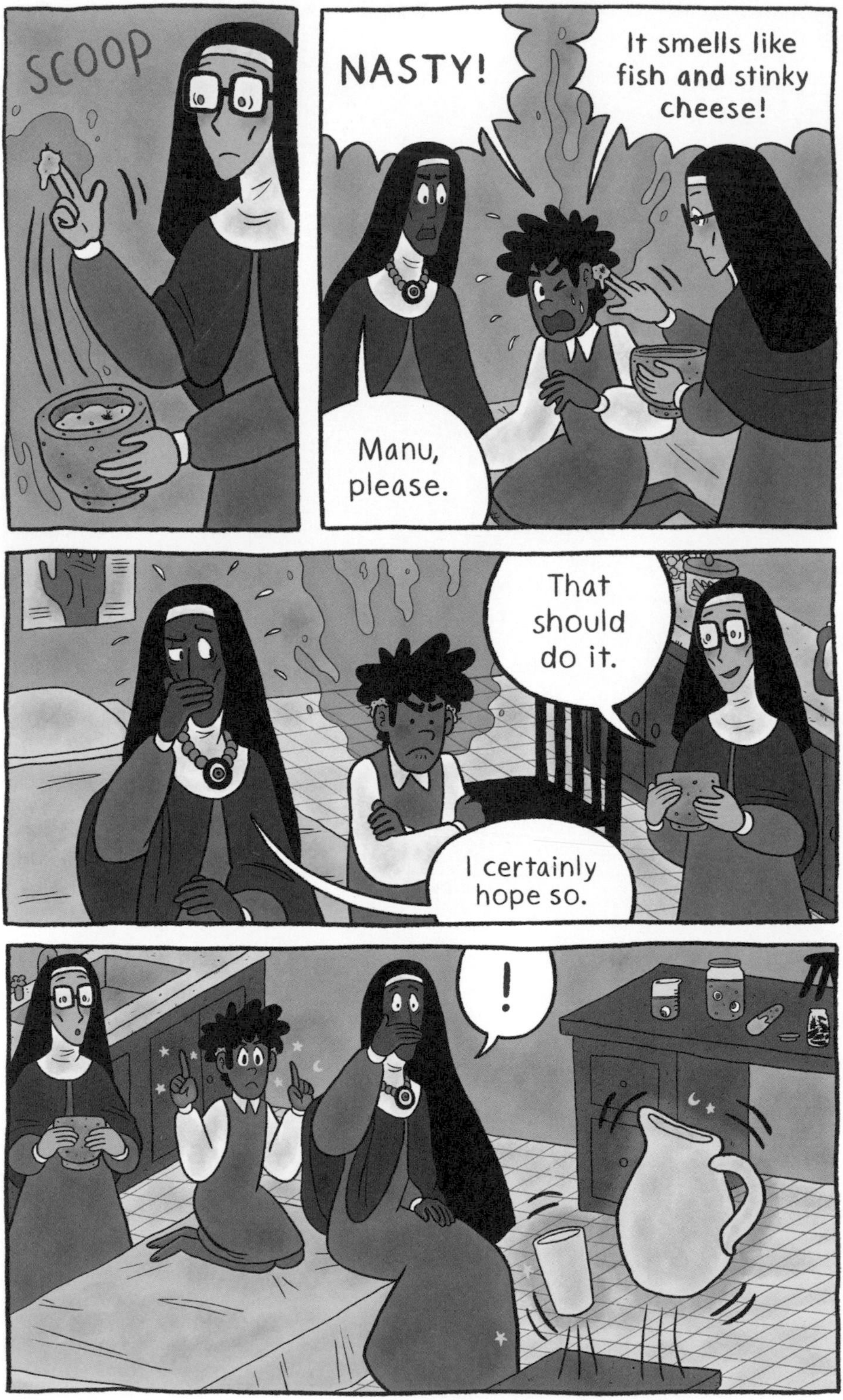
SCOOP
NASTY!
It smells like fish and stinky cheese!
Manu, please.
That should do it.
I certainly hope so.
!

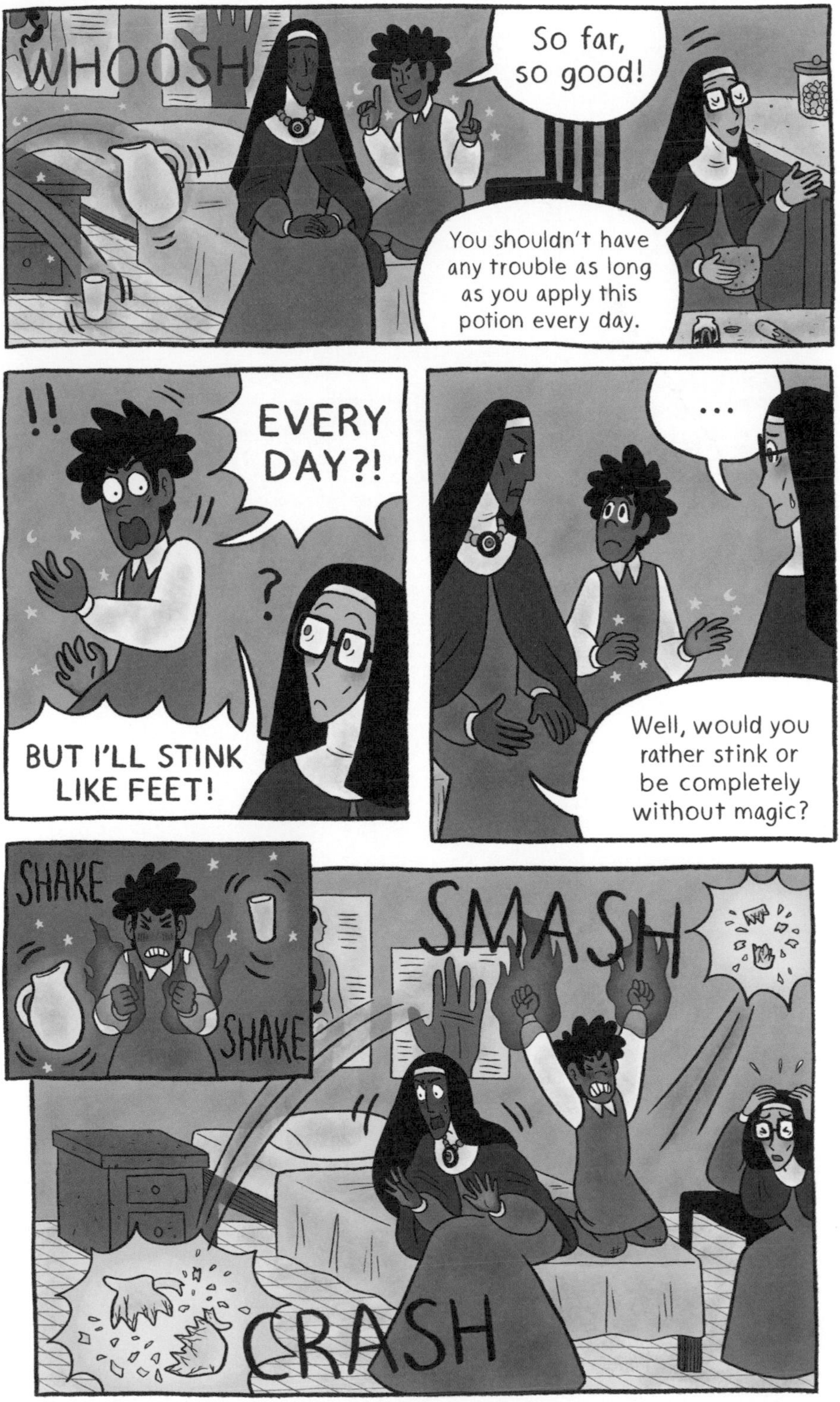
WHOOSH
So far, so good!
You shouldn't have any trouble as long as you apply this potion every day.
!!
EVERY DAY?!
BUT I'LL STINK LIKE FEET!
?
...
Well, would you rather stink or be completely without magic?
SHAKE
SHAKE
SMASH
CRASH

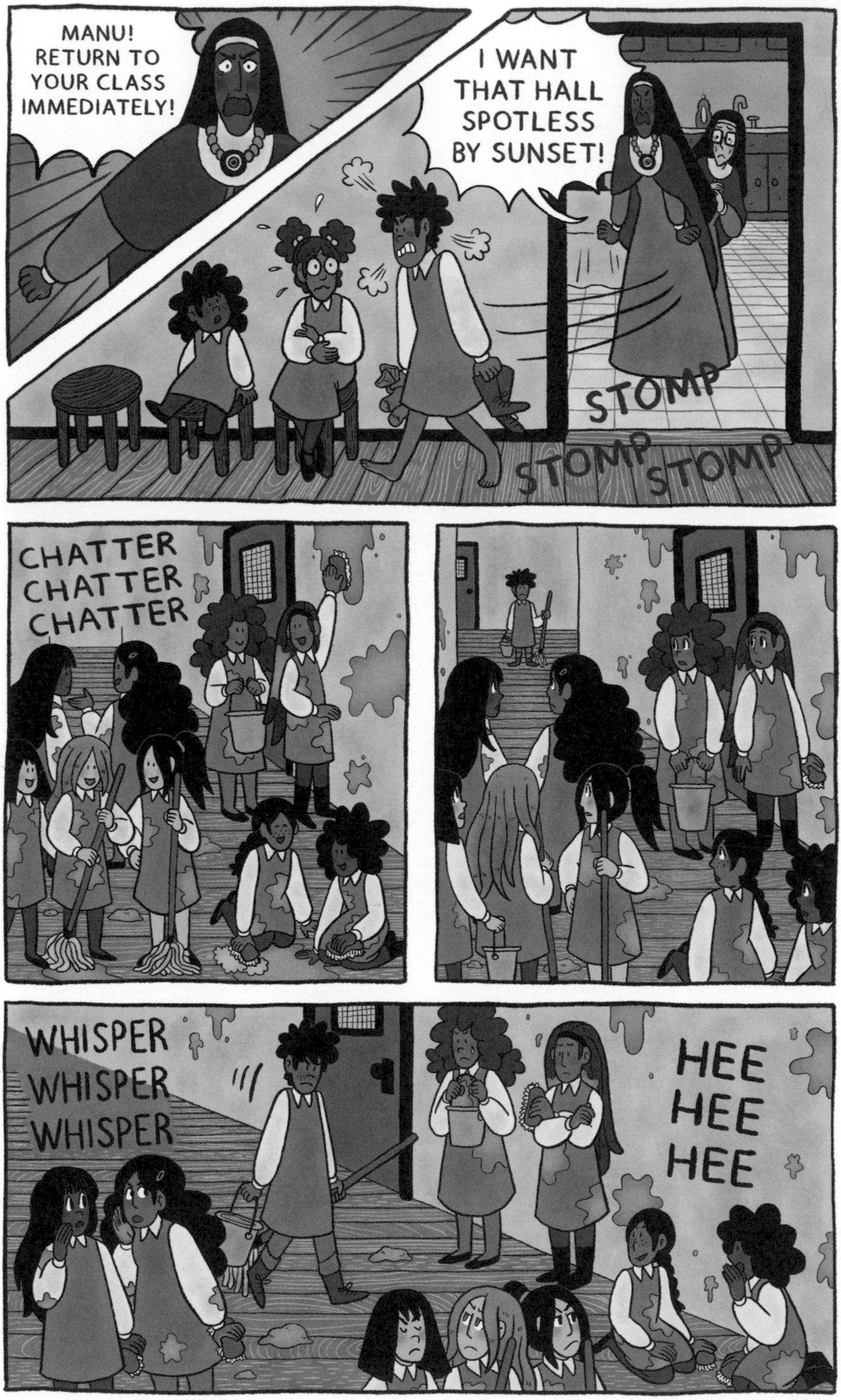
MANU! RETURN TO YOUR CLASS IMMEDIATELY!
I WANT THAT HALL SPOTLESS BY SUNSET!
STOMP
STOMP STOMP
CHATTER CHATTER CHATTER
WHISPER WHISPER WHISPER
HEE HEE HEE

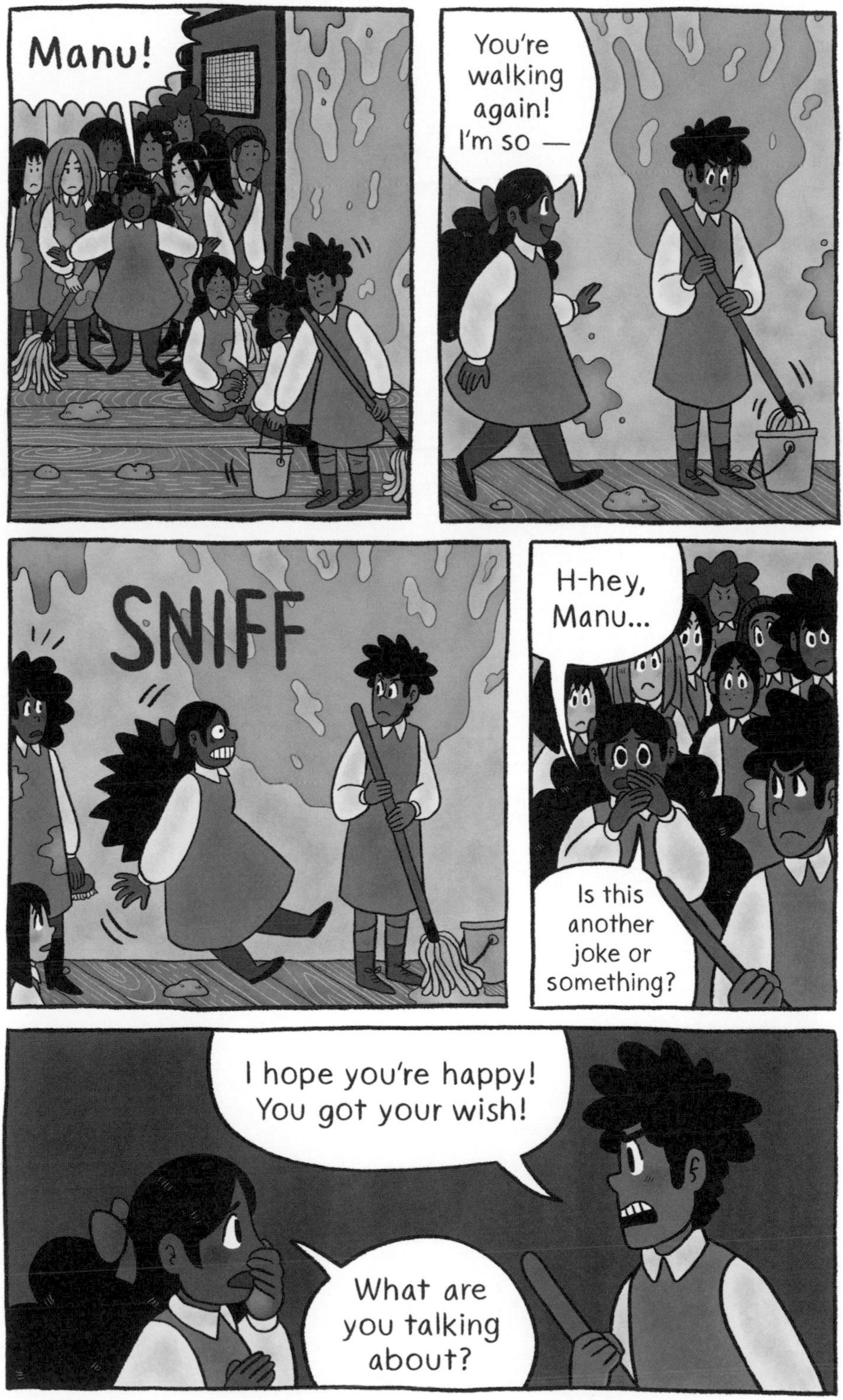
Manu!
You're walking again! I'm so —
SNIFF
H-hey, Manu...
Is this another joke or something?
I hope you're happy! You got your wish!
What are you talking about?

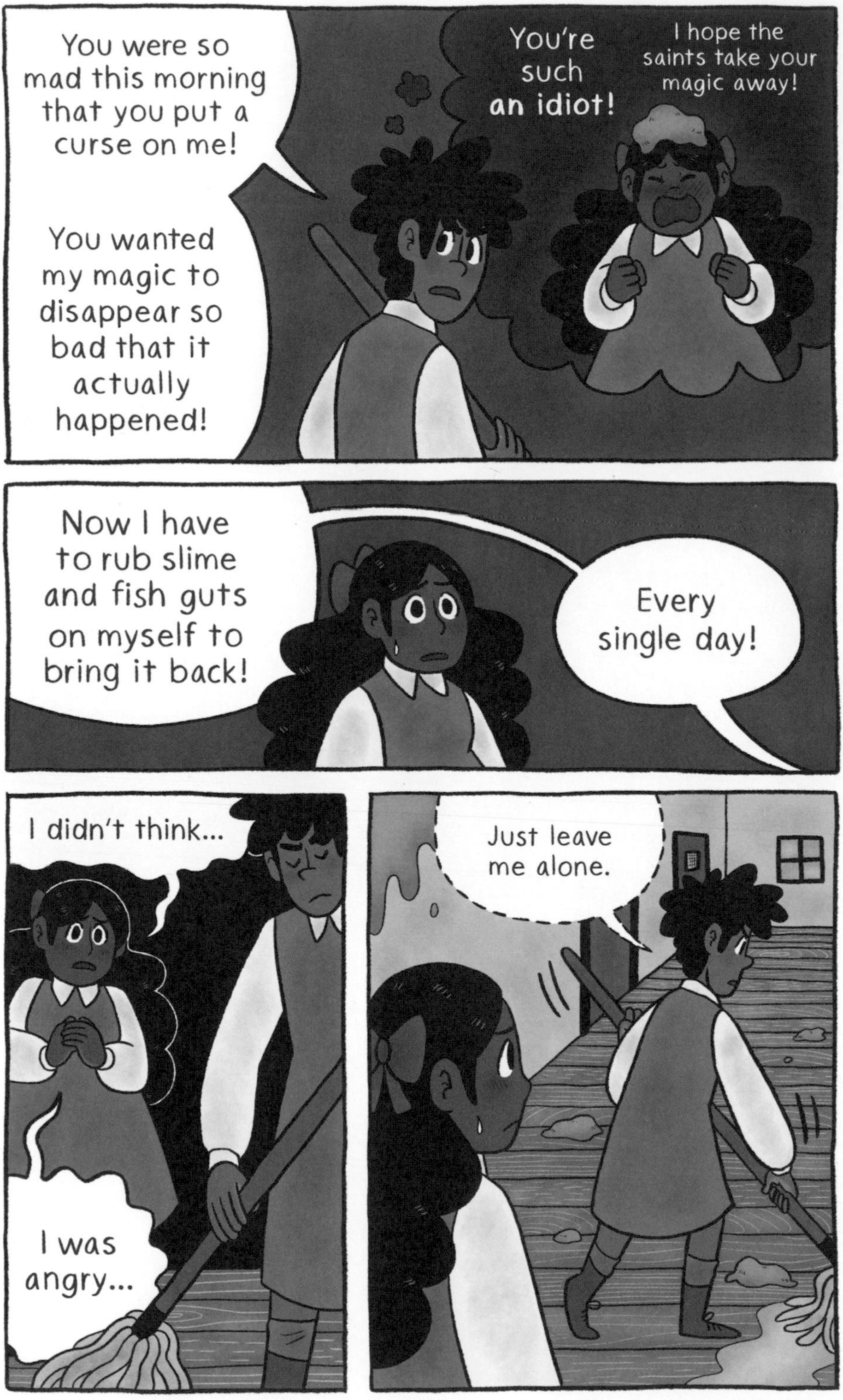
You were so mad this morning that you put a curse on me!
You wanted my magic to disappear so bad that it actually happened!
You're such an idiot!
I hope the saints take your magic away!
Now I have to rub slime and fish guts on myself to bring it back!
Every single day!
I didn't think...
I was angry...
Just leave me alone.

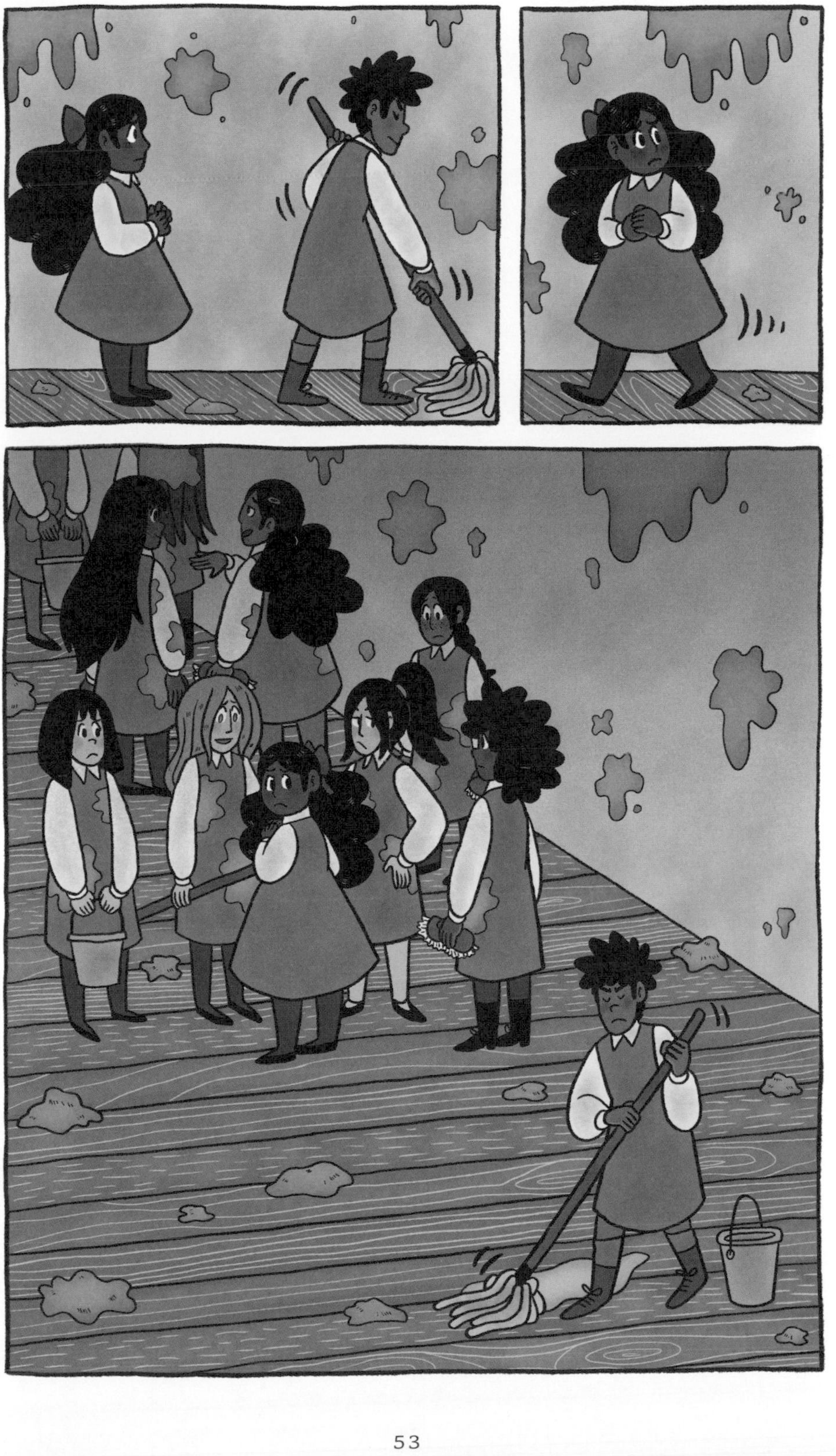

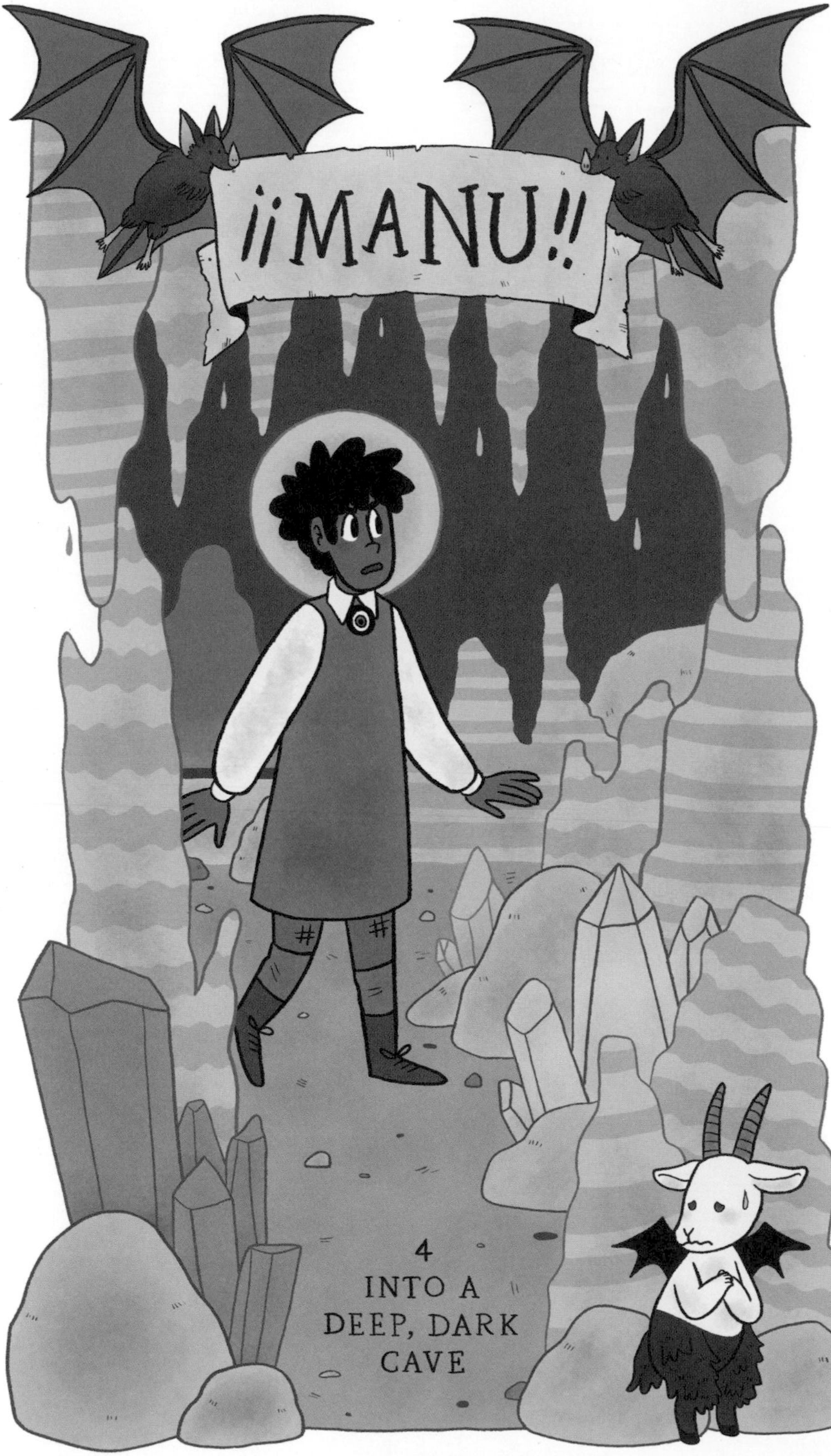
¡¡MANU!!
4
INTO A
DEEP, DARK
CAVE

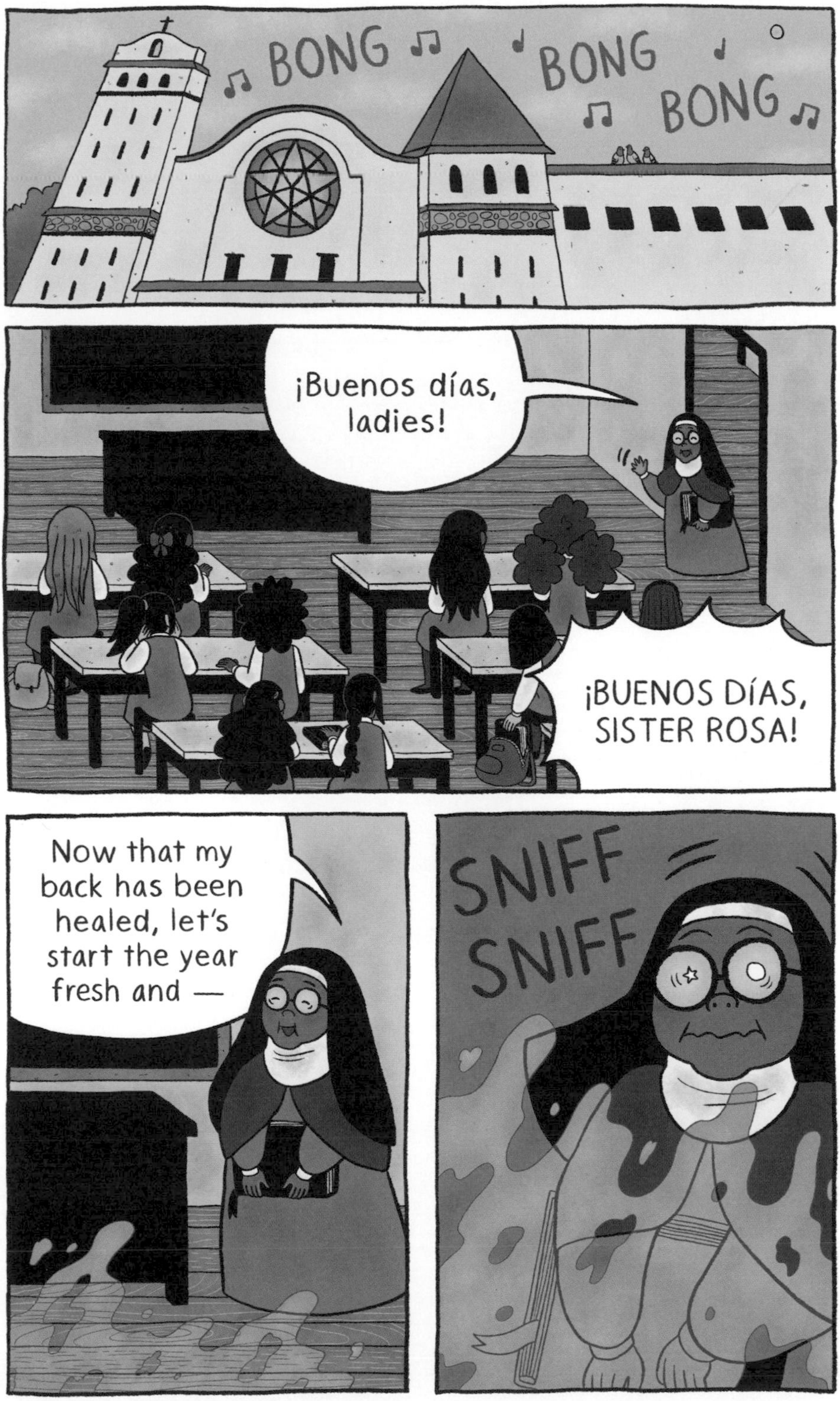
BONG
BONG
BONG
¡Buenos días, ladies!
¡BUENOS DÍAS, SISTER ROSA!
Now that my back has been healed, let's start the year fresh and —
SNIFF SNIFF

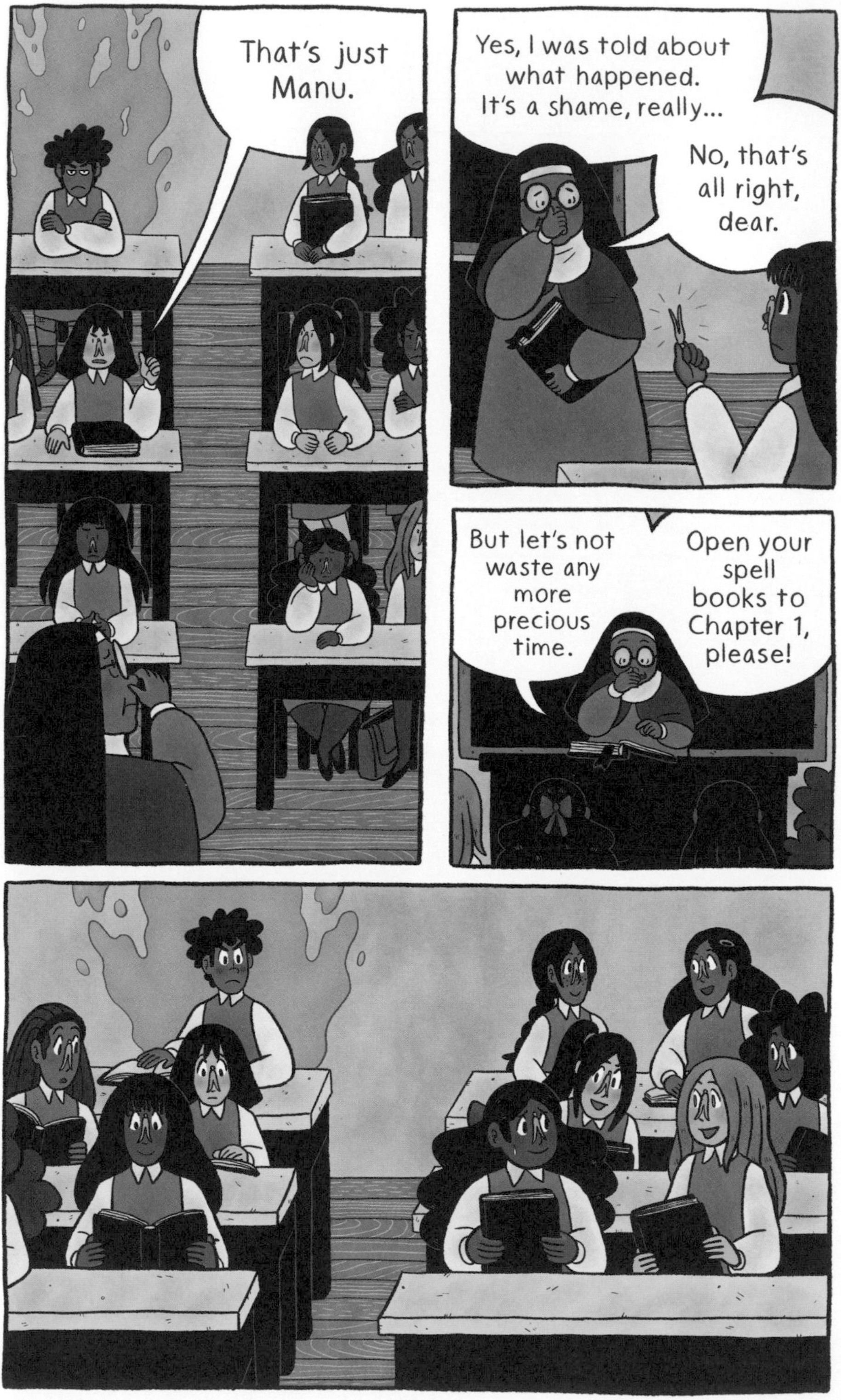
That's just Manu.
Yes, I was told about what happened. It's a shame, really...
No, that's all right, dear.
But let's not waste any more precious time.
Open your spell books to Chapter 1, please!

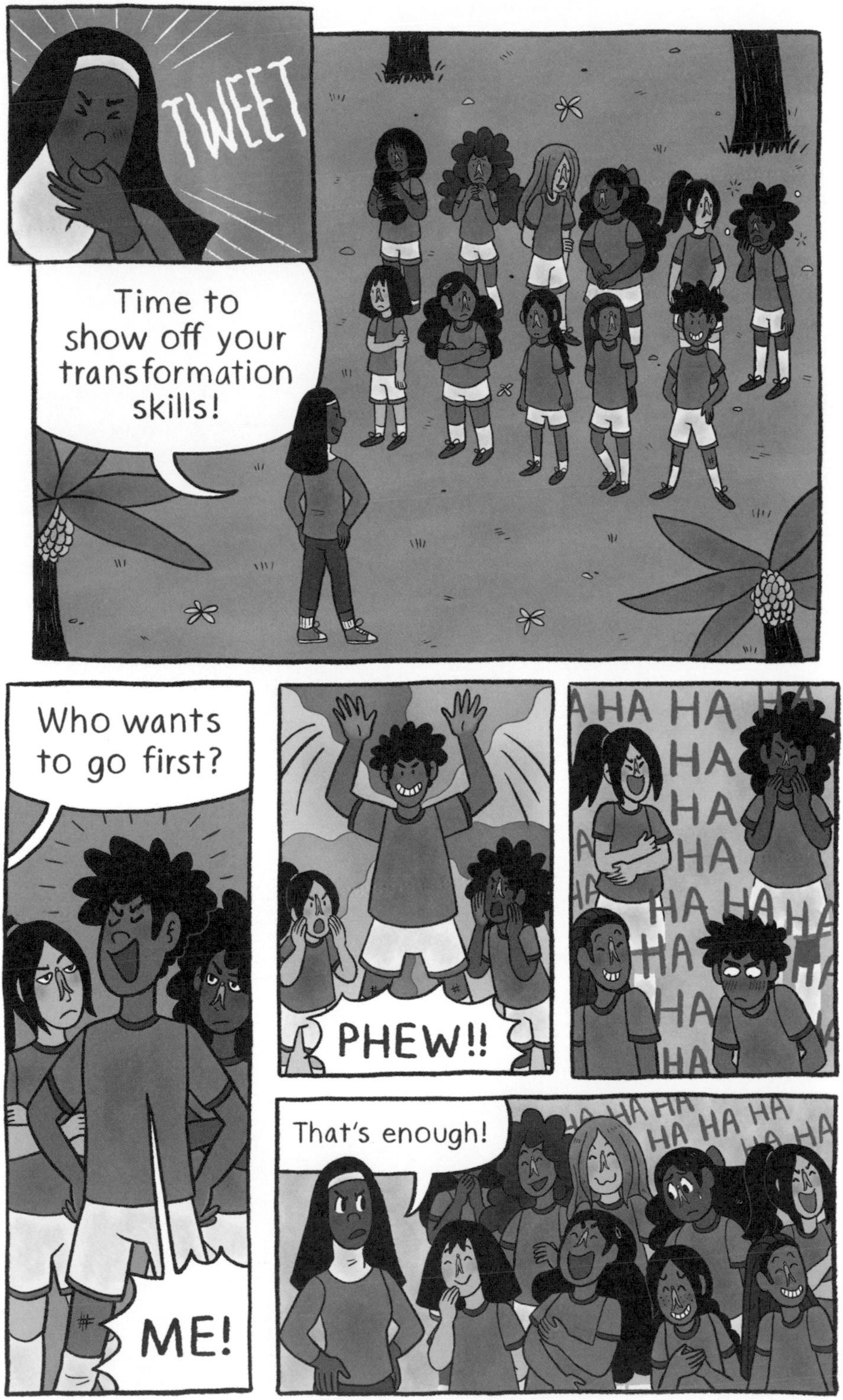
TWEET
Time to show off your transformation skills!
Who wants to go first?
ME!
PHEW!!
HA HA HA HA HA HA HA HA HA HA HA HA HA
That's enough!
HA HA HA HA HA HA HA HA

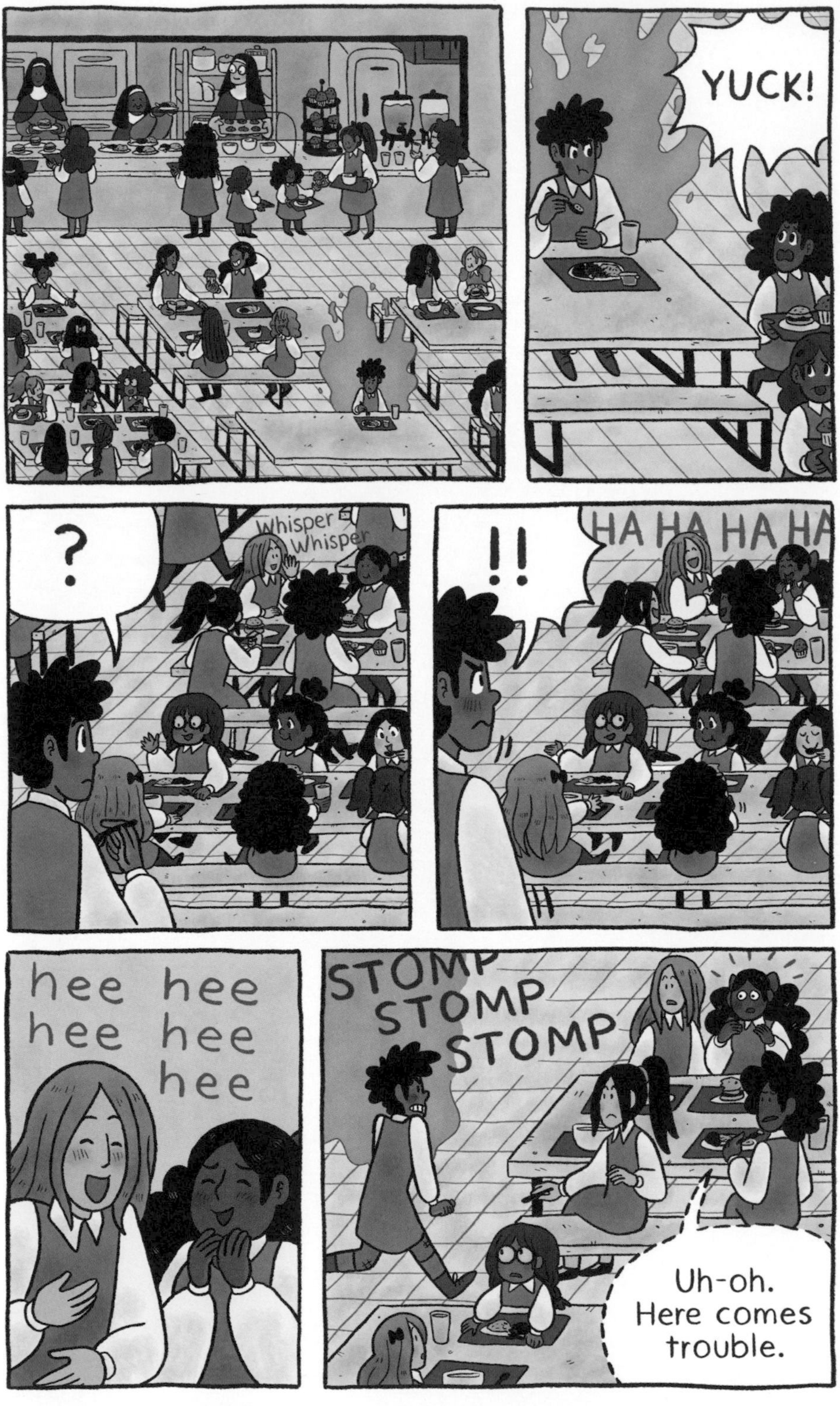
YUCK!
?
Whisper Whisper
!!
HA HA HA HA
hee hee hee hee hee
STOMP STOMP STOMP
Uh-oh. Here comes trouble.

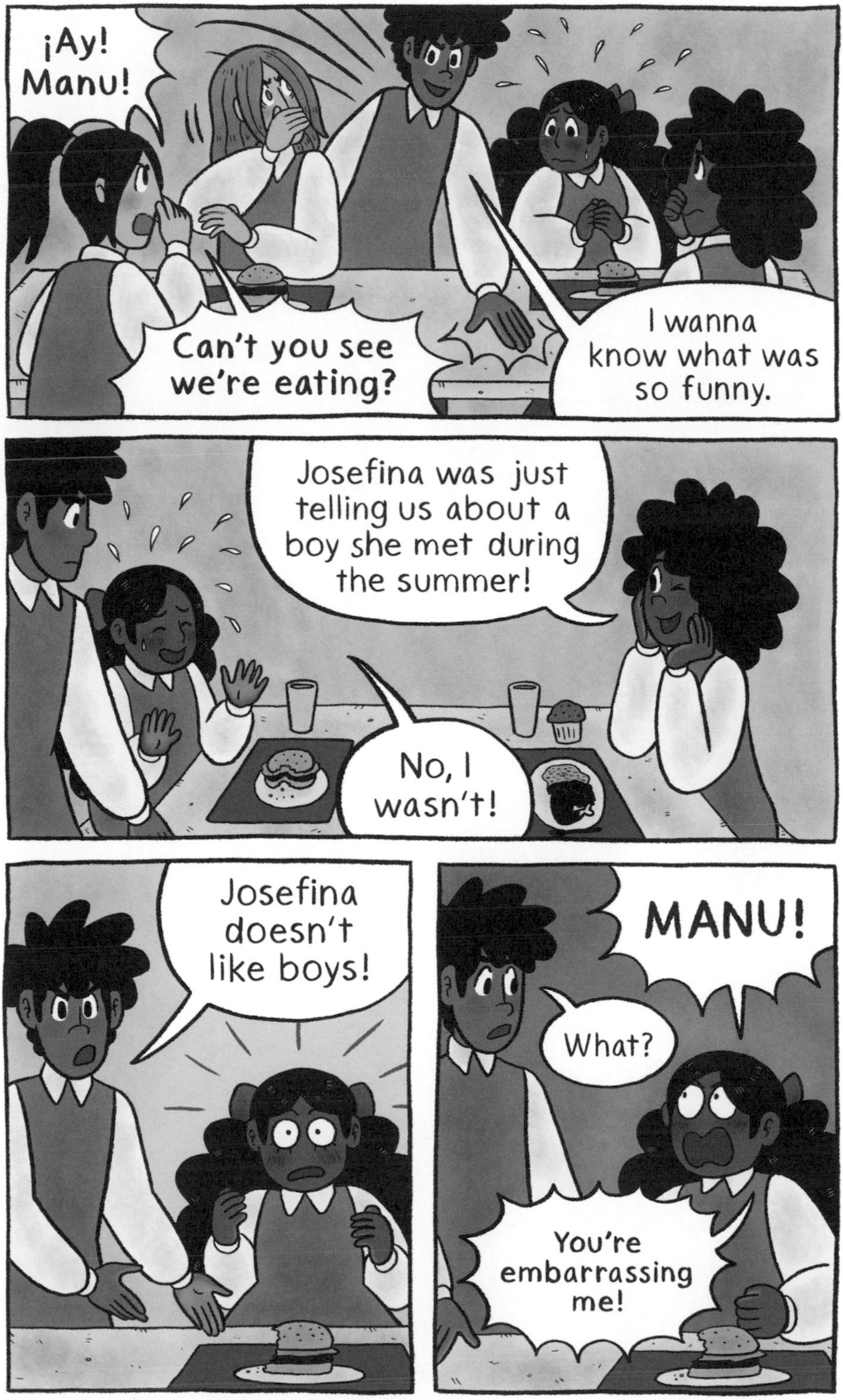
¡Ay! Manu!
Can't you see we're eating?
I wanna know what was so funny.
Josefina was just telling us about a boy she met during the summer!
No, I wasn't!
Josefina doesn't like boys!
MANU!
What?
You're embarrassing me!

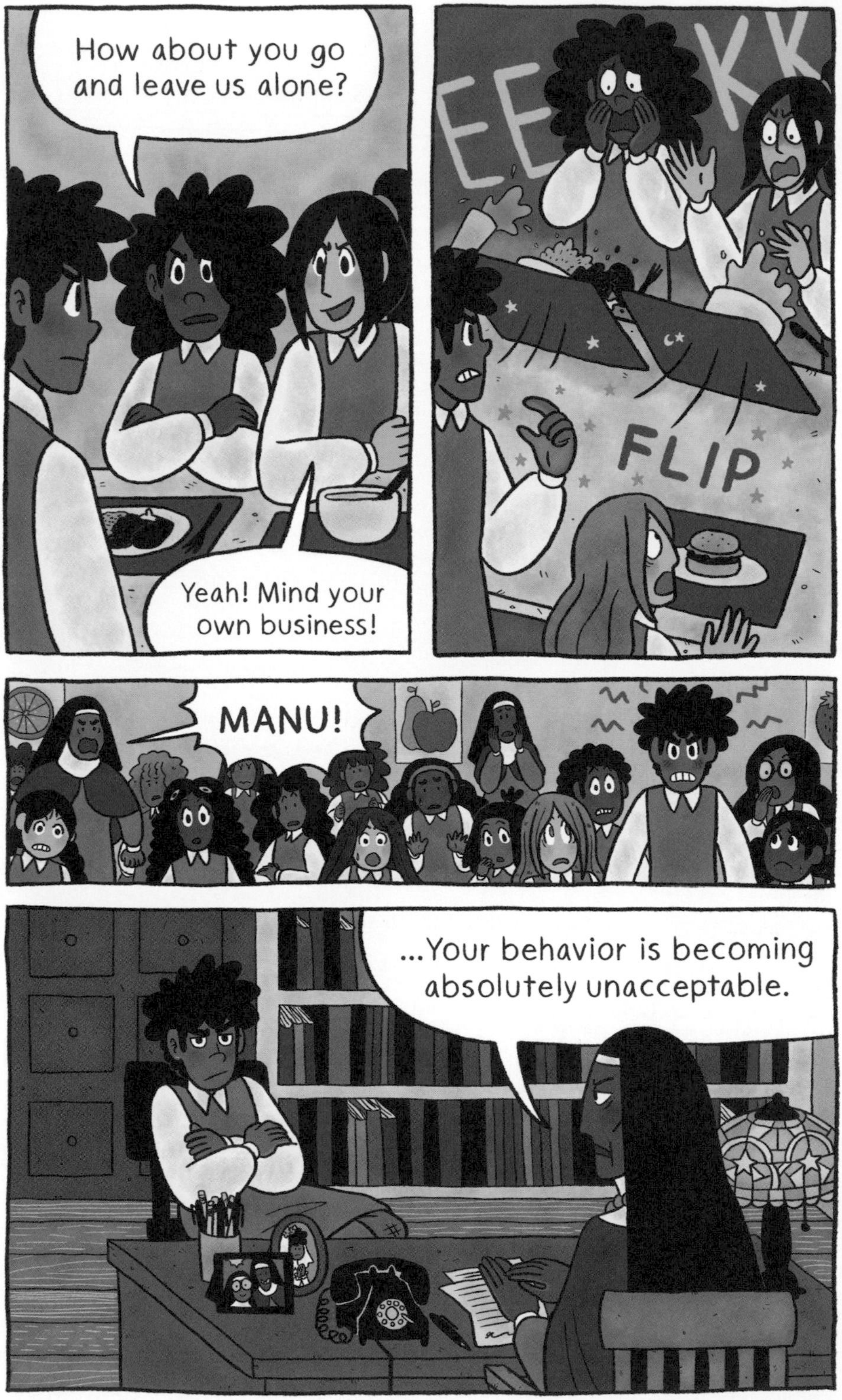
How about you go and leave us alone?
Yeah! Mind your own business!
EEKK
FLIP
MANU!
...Your behavior is becoming absolutely unacceptable.

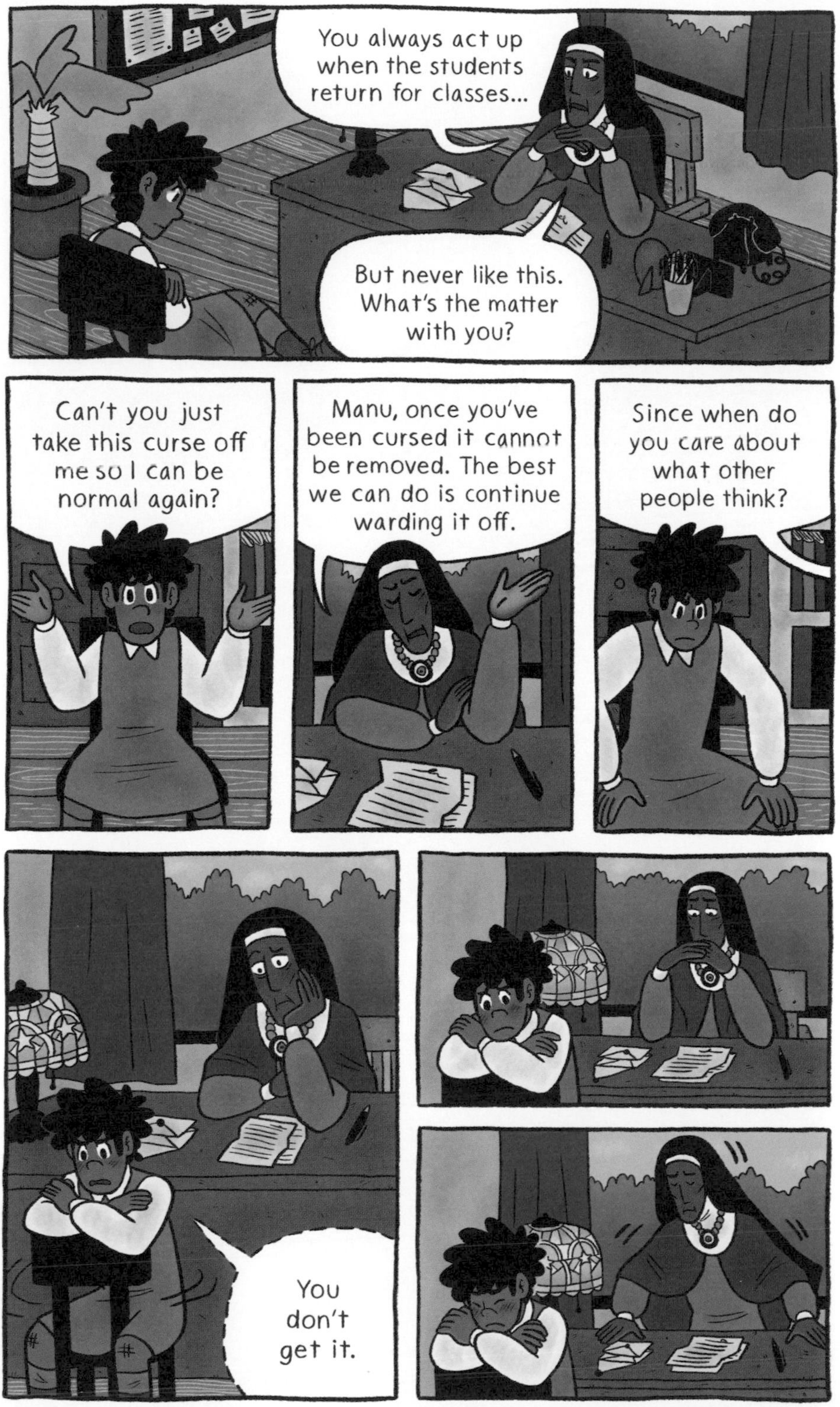
You always act up when the students return for classes...
But never like this. What's the matter with you?
Can't you just take this curse off me so I can be normal again?
Manu, once you've been cursed it cannot be removed. The best we can do is continue warding it off.
Since when do you care about what other people think?
You don't get it.

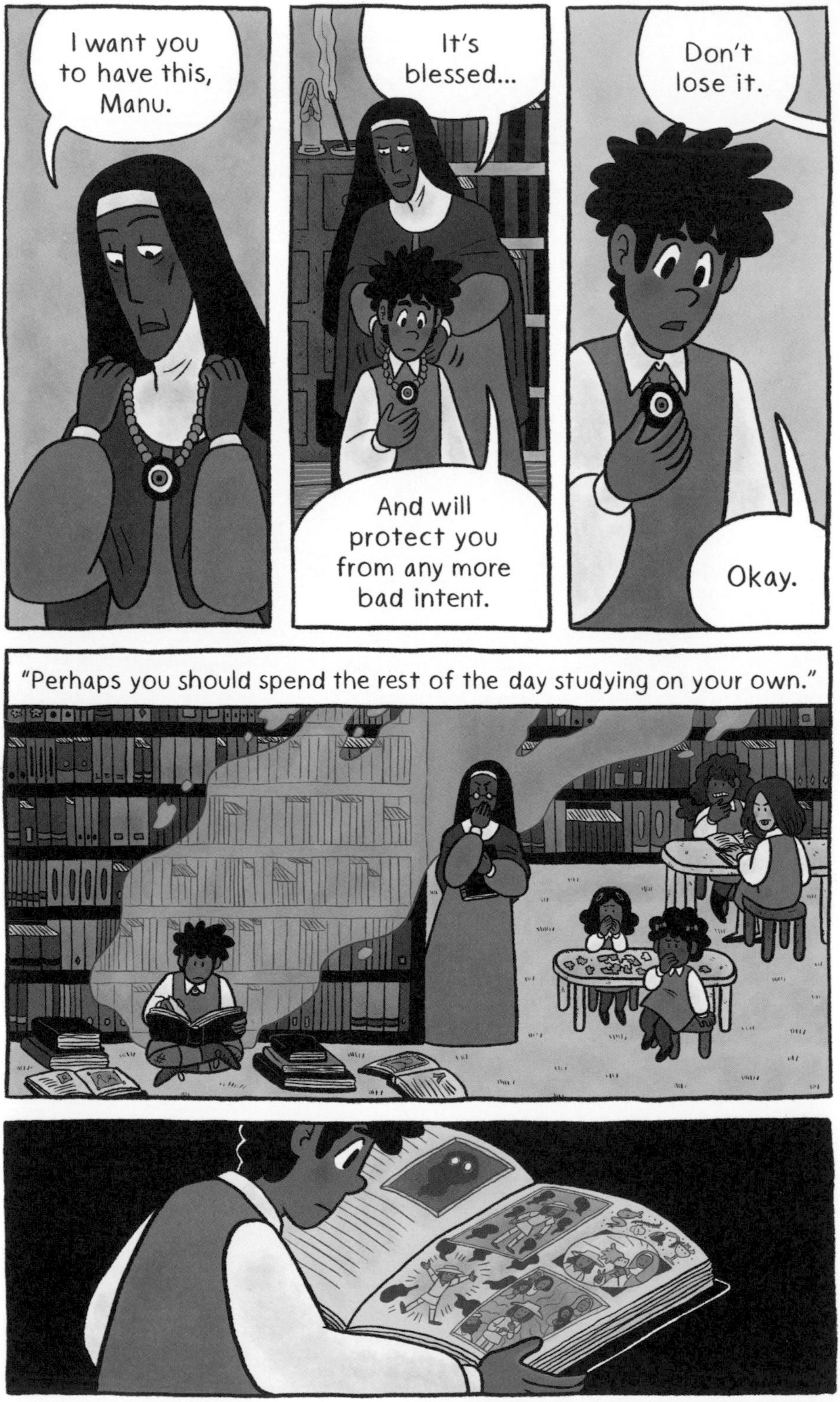

I want you to have this, Manu.
It's blessed...
And will protect you from any more bad intent.
Don't lose it.
Okay.
"Perhaps you should spend the rest of the day studying on your own."

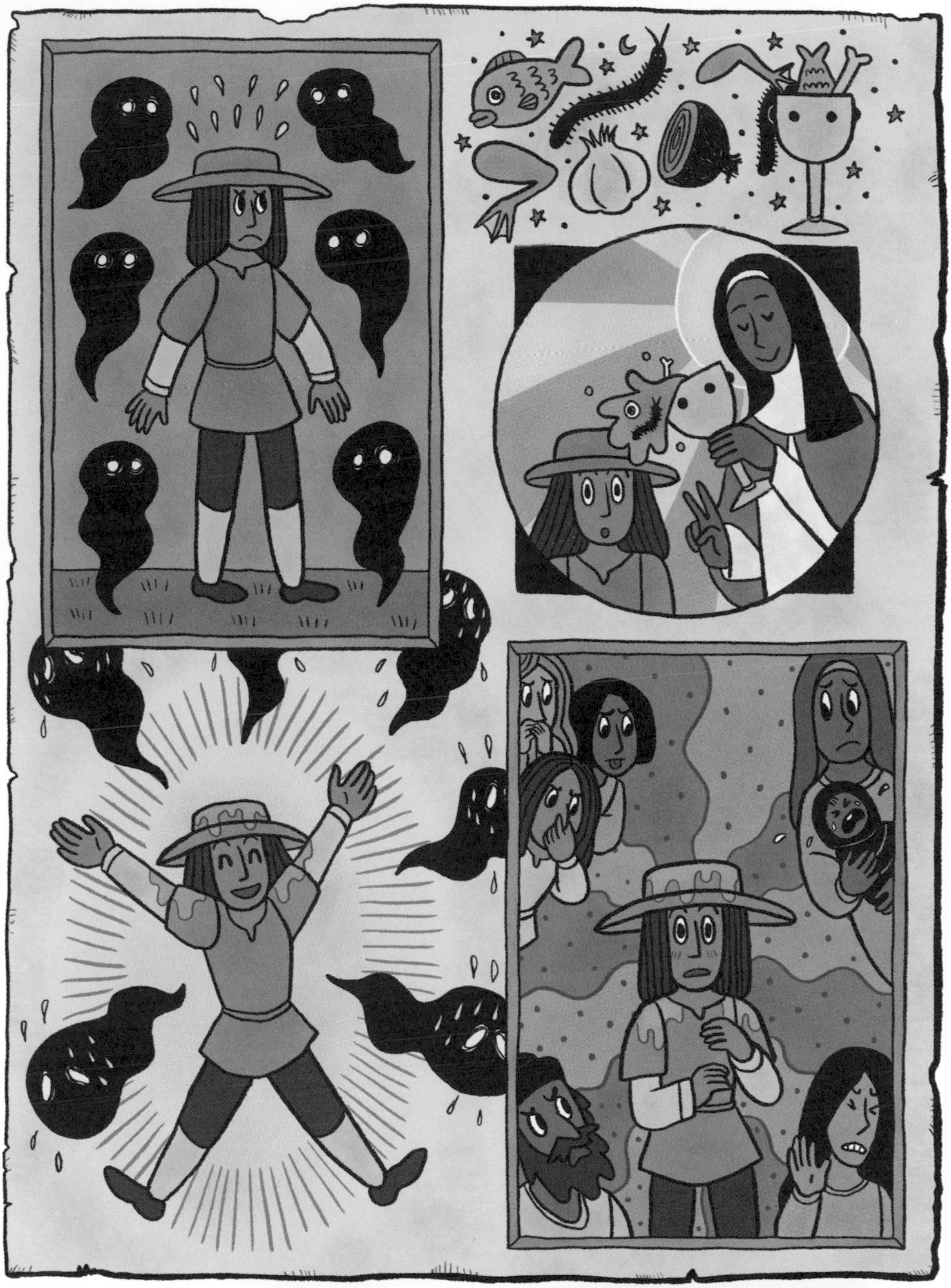

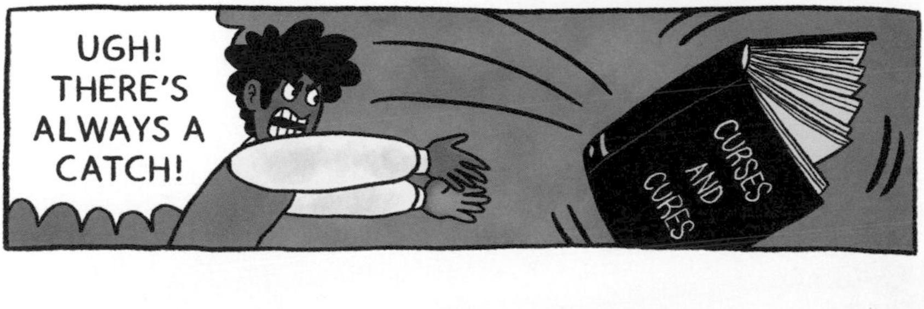
UGH! THERE'S ALWAYS A CATCH!
CURSES AND CURES

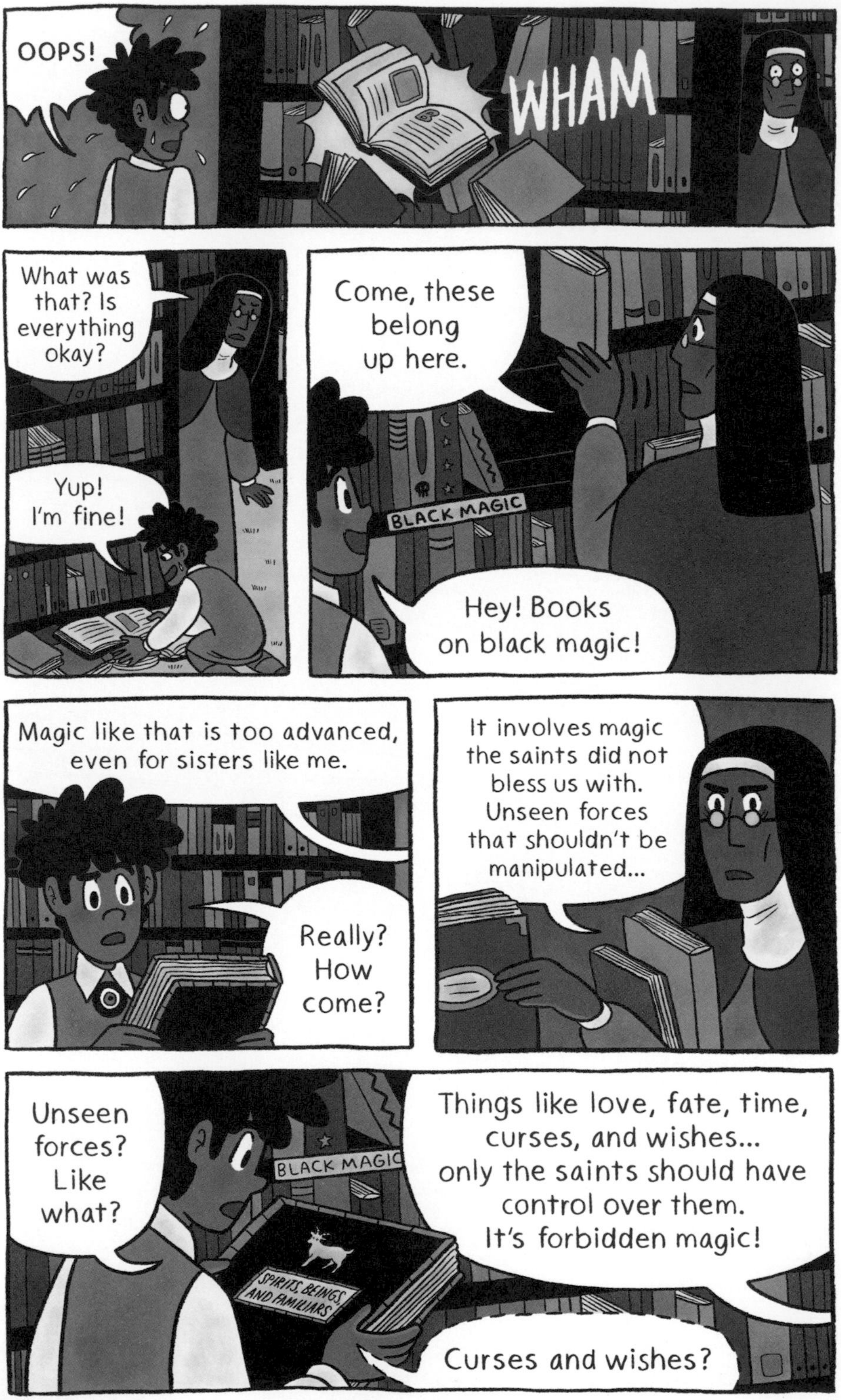
OOPS!
WHAM
What was that? Is everything okay?
Yup! I'm fine!
Come, these belong up here.
BLACK MAGIC
Hey! Books on black magic!
Magic like that is too advanced, even for sisters like me.
Really? How come?
It involves magic the saints did not bless us with. Unseen forces that shouldn't be manipulated...
Unseen forces? Like what?
BLACK MAGIC
Things like love, fate, time, curses, and wishes... only the saints should have control over them. It's forbidden magic!
SPIRITS, BEINGS, AND FAMILIARS
Curses and wishes?

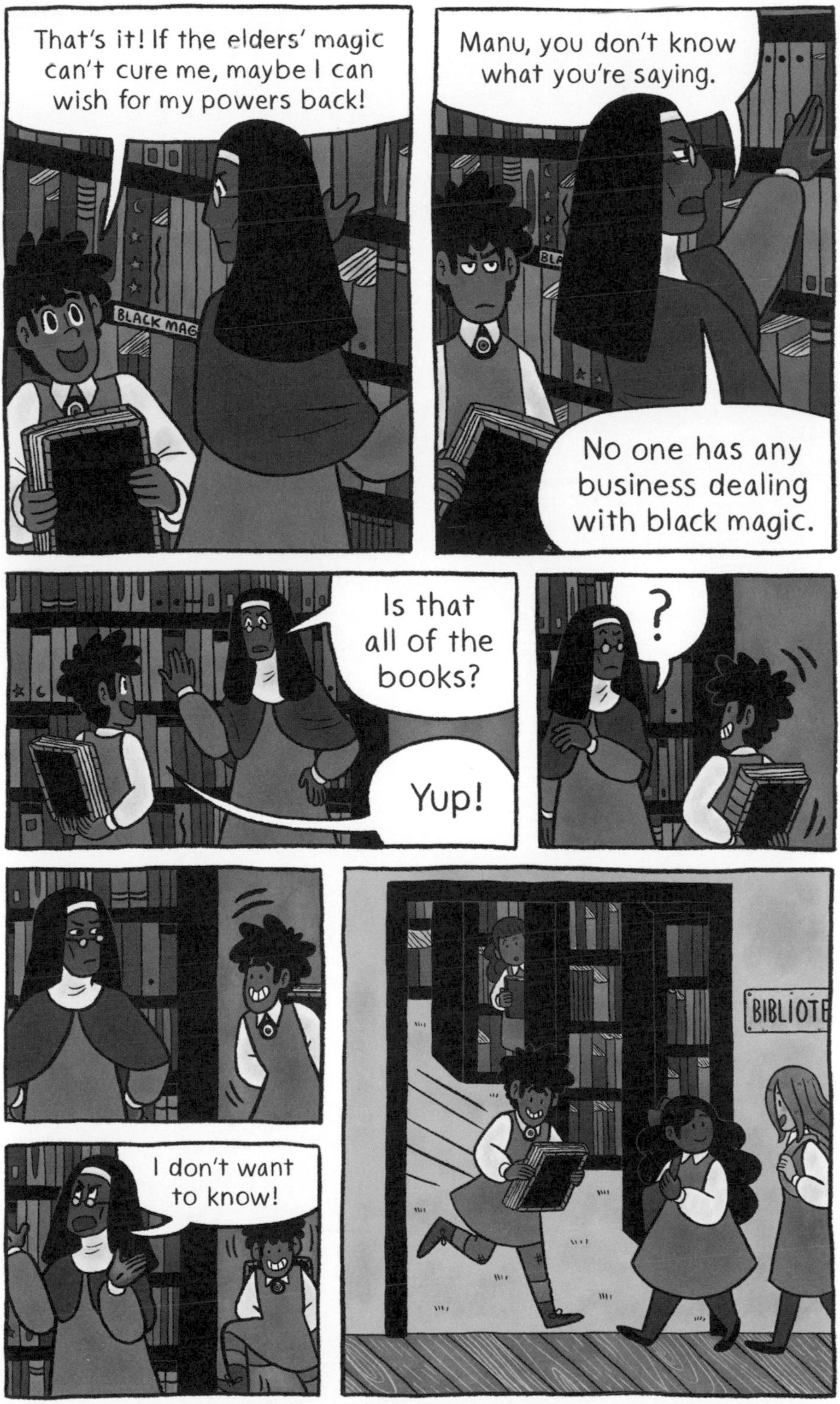
That's it! If the elders' magic can't cure me, maybe I can wish for my powers back!
BLACK MAG
Manu, you don't know what you're saying.
BLA
No one has any business dealing with black magic.
Is that all of the books?
Yup!
?
I don't want to know!
BIBLIOTE

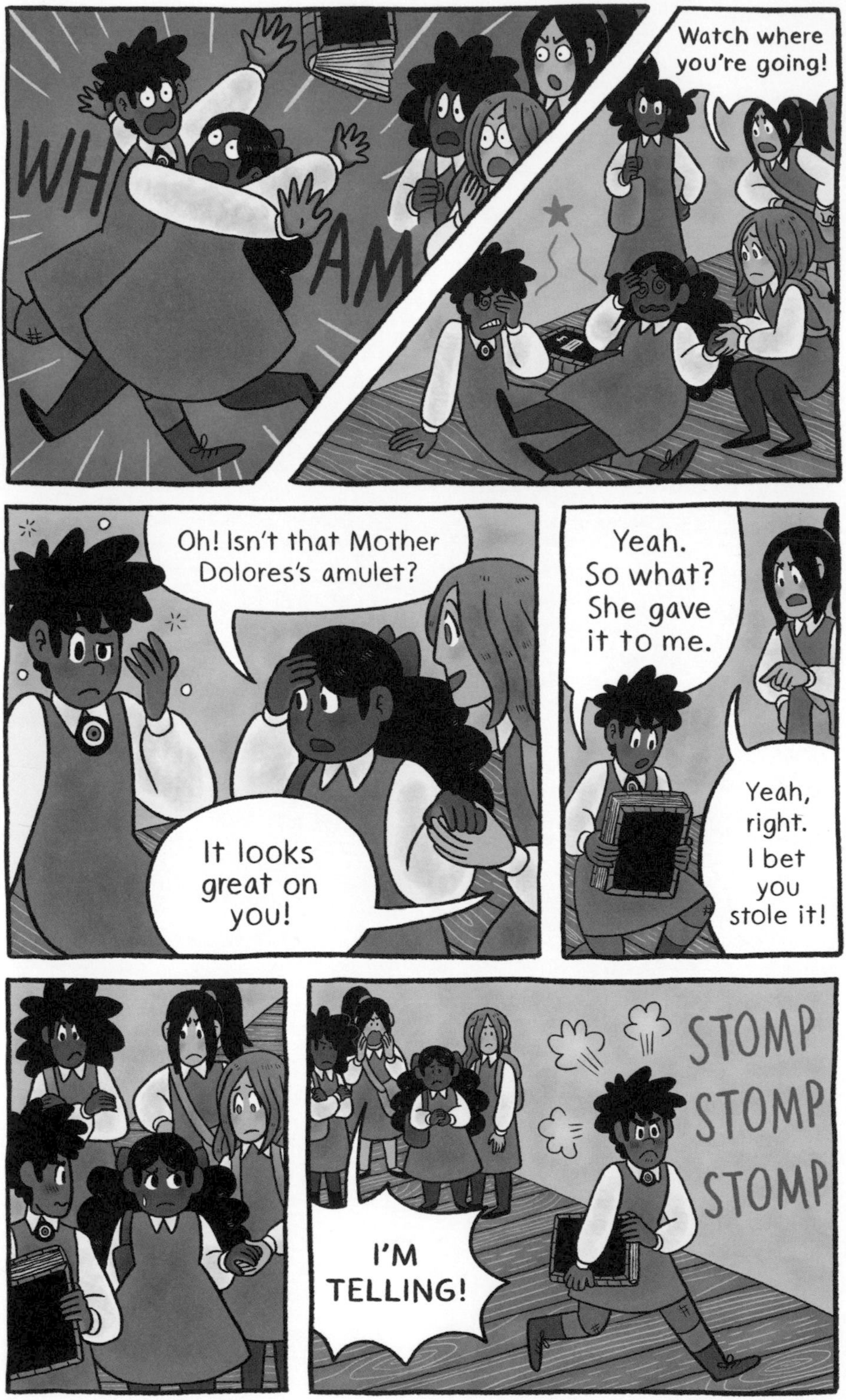
WH
AM
Watch where you're going!
Oh! Isn't that Mother Dolores's amulet?
It looks great on you!
Yeah. So what? She gave it to me.
Yeah, right. I bet you stole it!
I'M TELLING!
STOMP
STOMP
STOMP

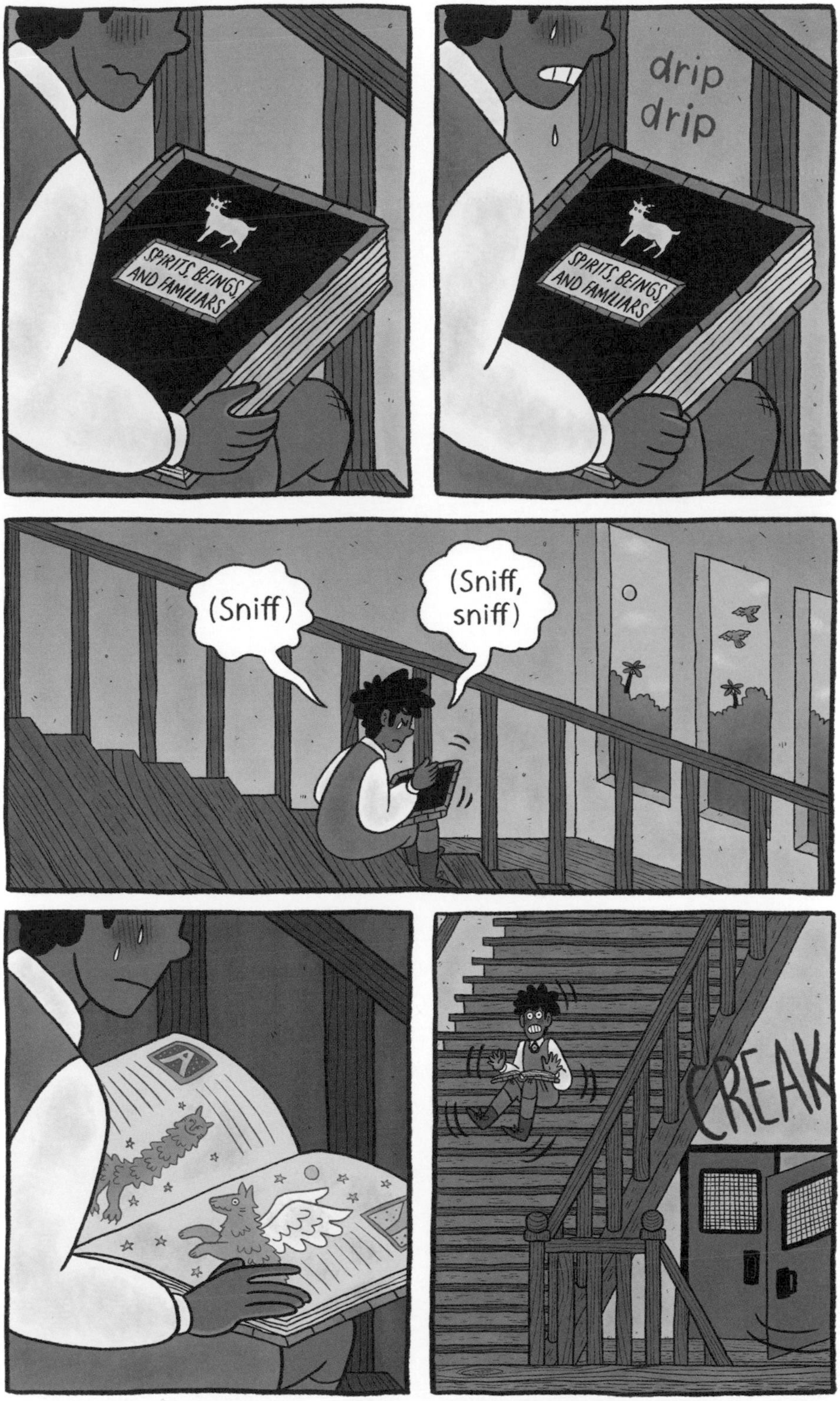
SPIRITS, BEINGS, AND FAMILIARS
drip drip
SPIRITS, BEINGS, AND FAMILIARS
(Sniff)
(Sniff, sniff)
A
CREAK

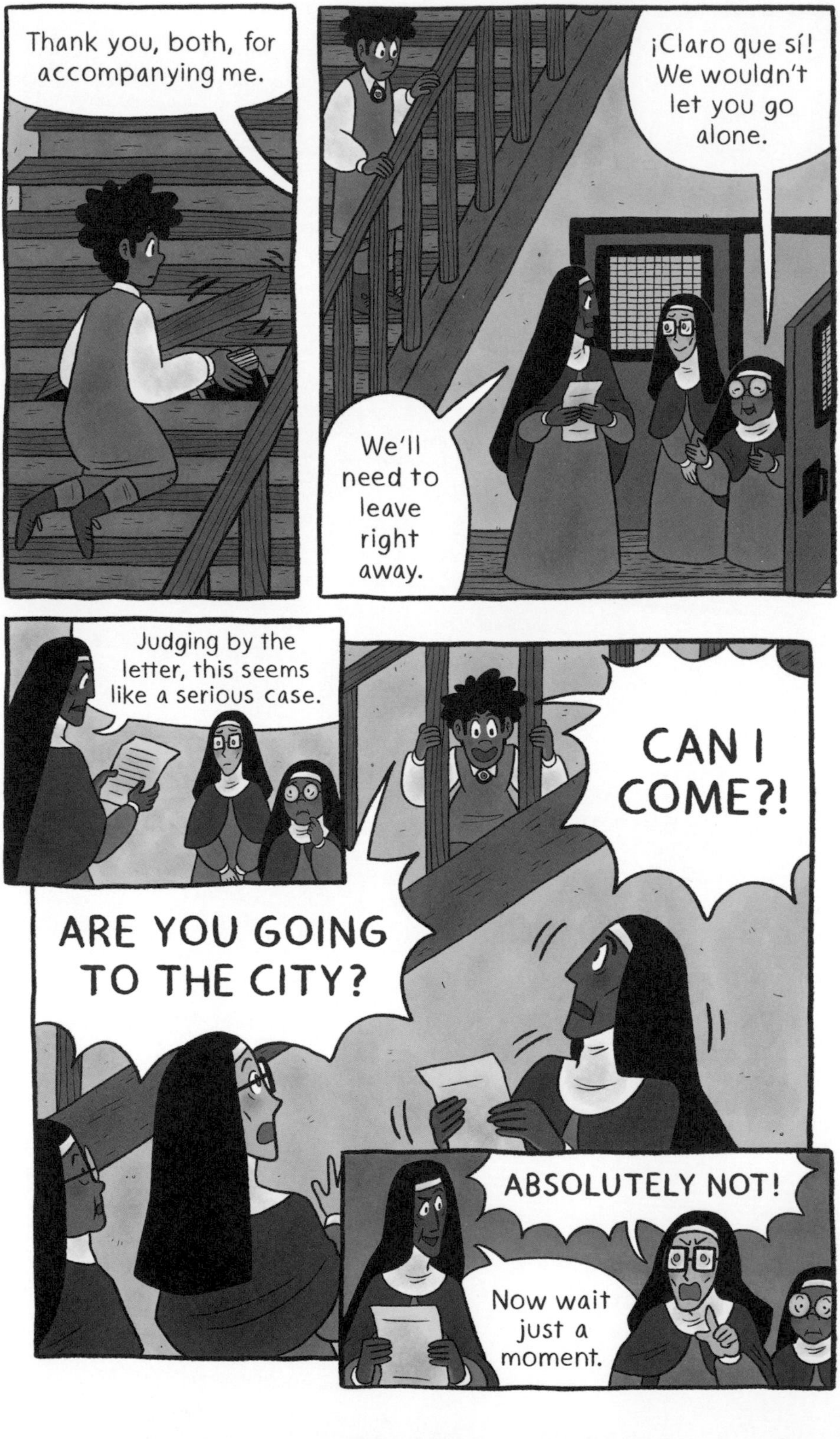
Thank you, both, for accompanying me.
¡Claro que sí! We wouldn't let you go alone.
We'll need to leave right away.
Judging by the letter, this seems like a serious case.
CAN I COME?!
ARE YOU GOING TO THE CITY?
ABSOLUTELY NOT!
Now wait just a moment.

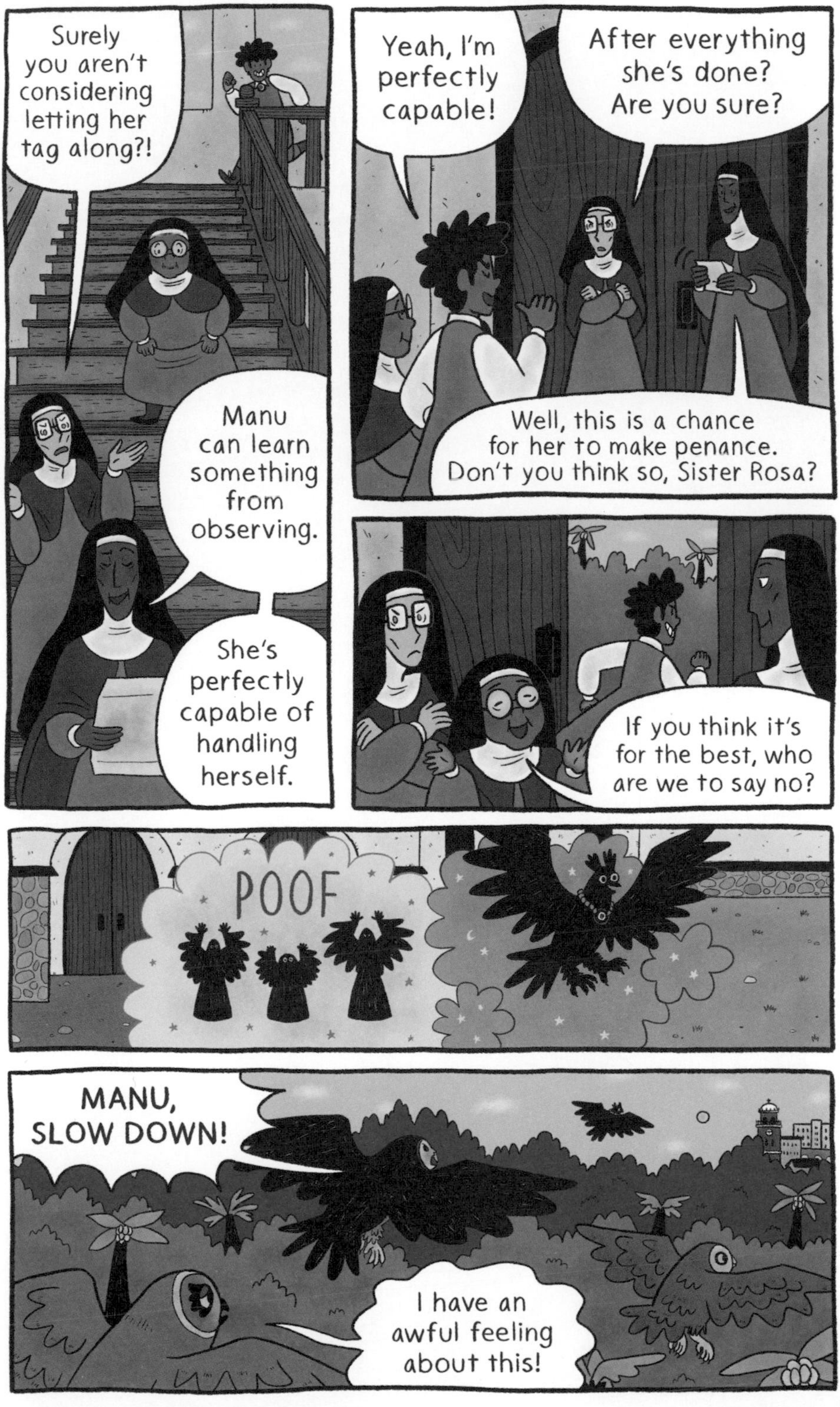
Surely you aren't considering letting her tag along?!
Manu can learn something from observing.
She's perfectly capable of handling herself.
Yeah, I'm perfectly capable!
After everything she's done? Are you sure?
Well, this is a chance for her to make penance. Don't you think so, Sister Rosa?
If you think it's for the best, who are we to say no?
POOF
MANU, SLOW DOWN!
I have an awful feeling about this!

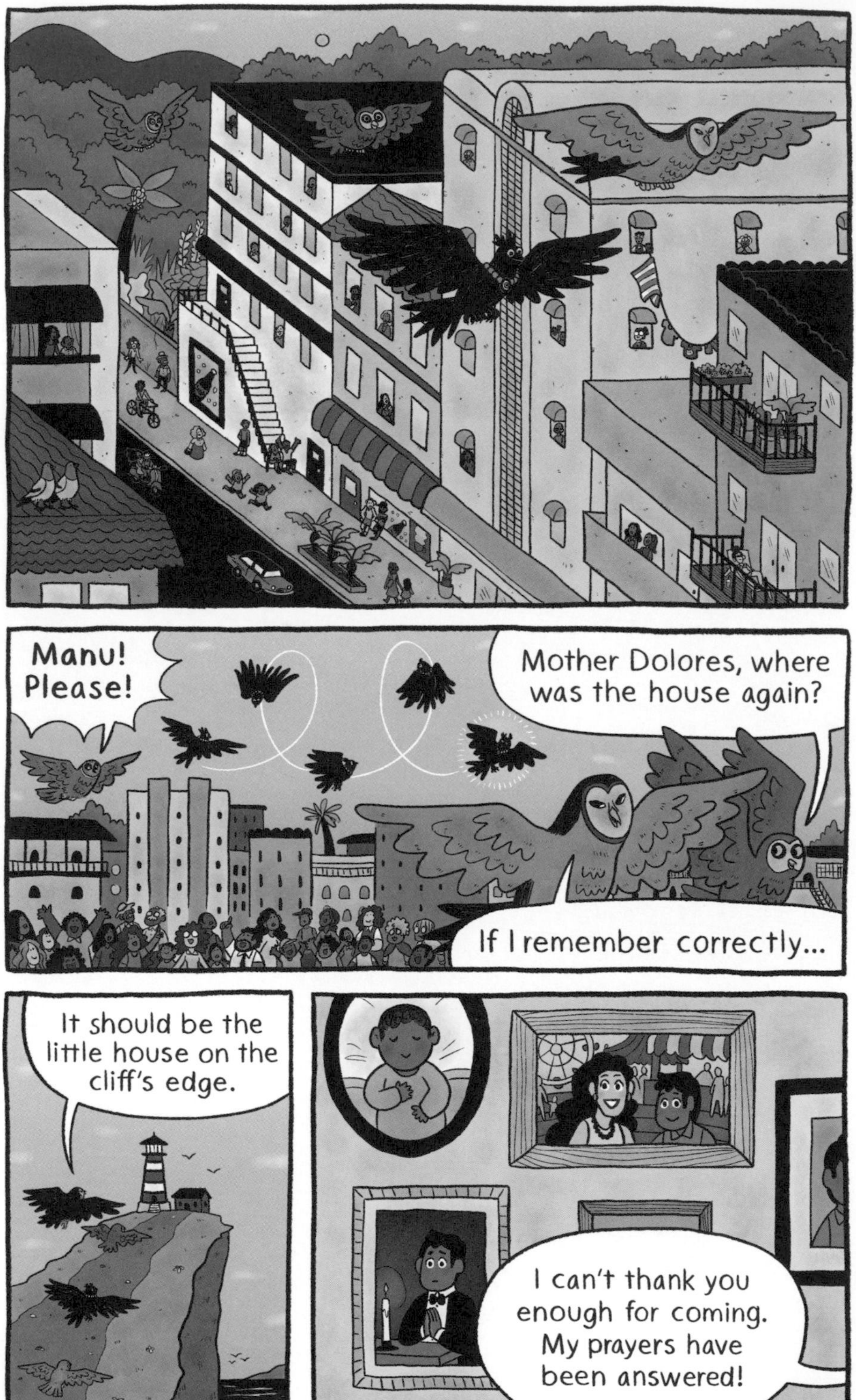
Manu!
Please!
Mother Dolores, where was the house again?
If I remember correctly...
It should be the little house on the cliff's edge.
I can't thank you enough for coming. My prayers have been answered!

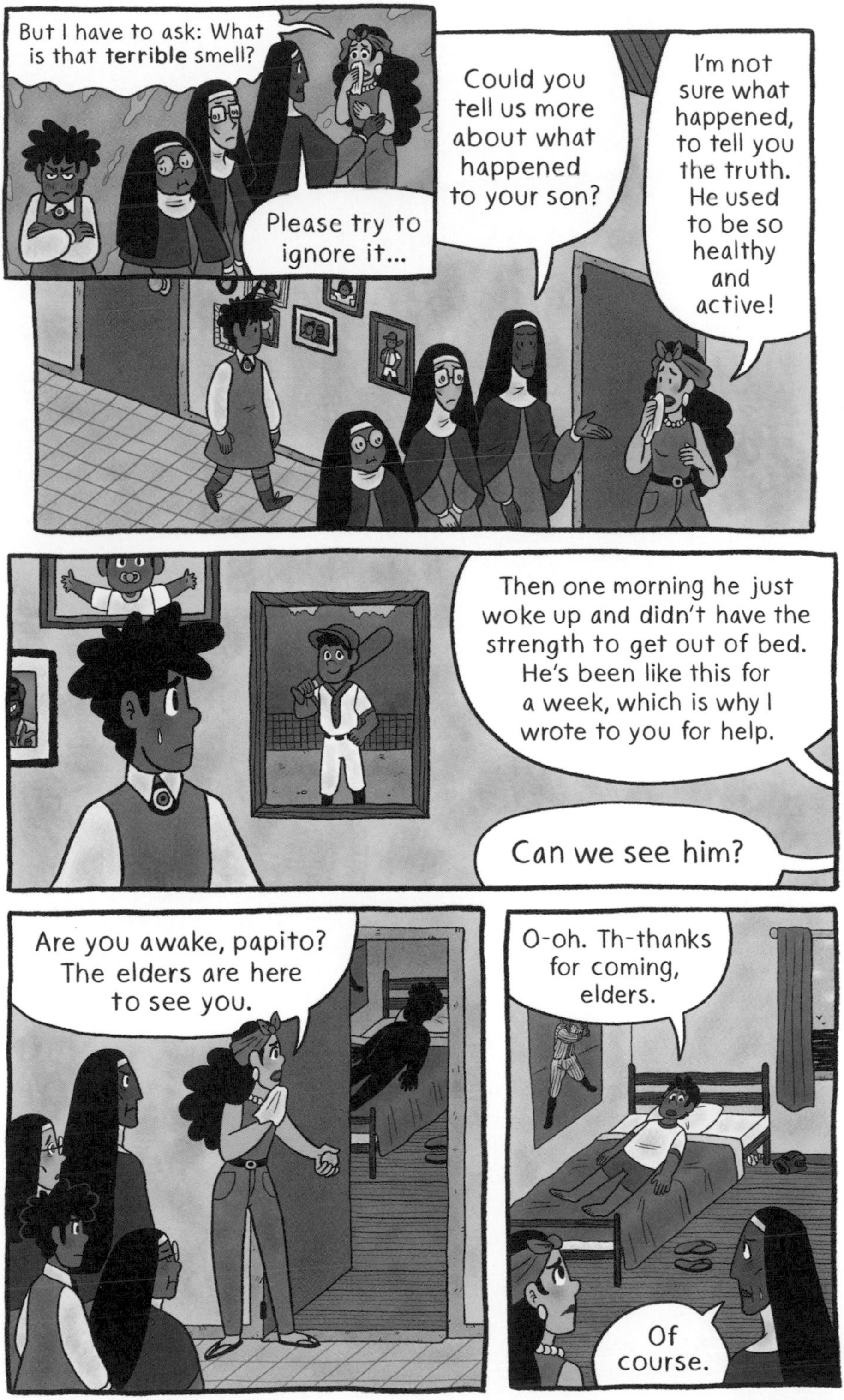
But I have to ask: What is that **terrible** smell?
Please try to ignore it...
Could you tell us more about what happened to your son?
I'm not sure what happened, to tell you the truth. He used to be so healthy and active!
Then one morning he just woke up and didn't have the strength to get out of bed. He's been like this for a week, which is why I wrote to you for help.
Can we see him?
Are you awake, papito? The elders are here to see you.
O-oh. Th-thanks for coming, elders.
Of course.

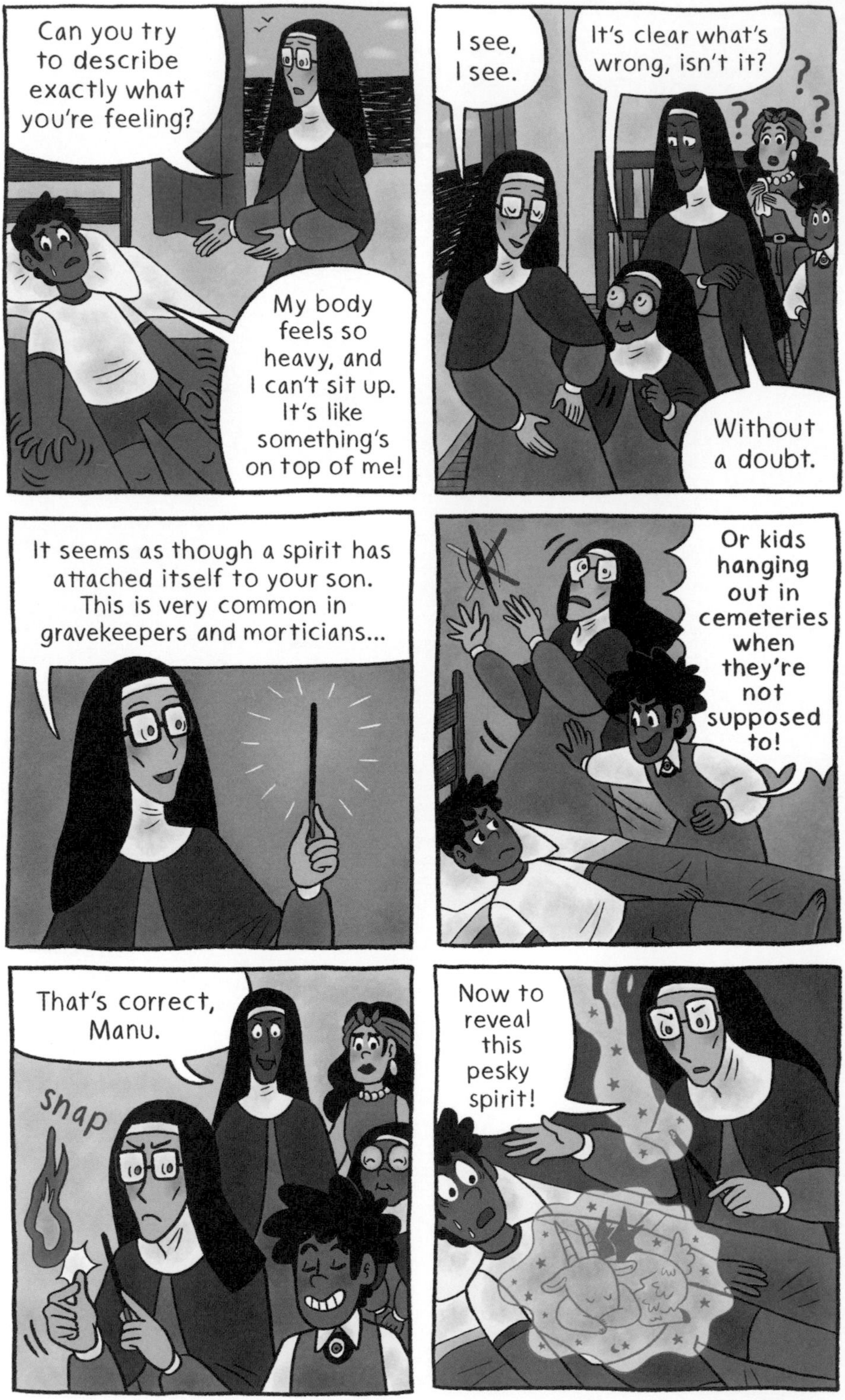
Can you try to describe exactly what you're feeling?
My body feels so heavy, and I can't sit up. It's like something's on top of me!
I see, I see.
It's clear what's wrong, isn't it?
? ? ?
Without a doubt.
It seems as though a spirit has attached itself to your son. This is very common in gravekeepers and morticians...
Or kids hanging out in cemeteries when they're not supposed to!
That's correct, Manu.
Snap
Now to reveal this pesky spirit!

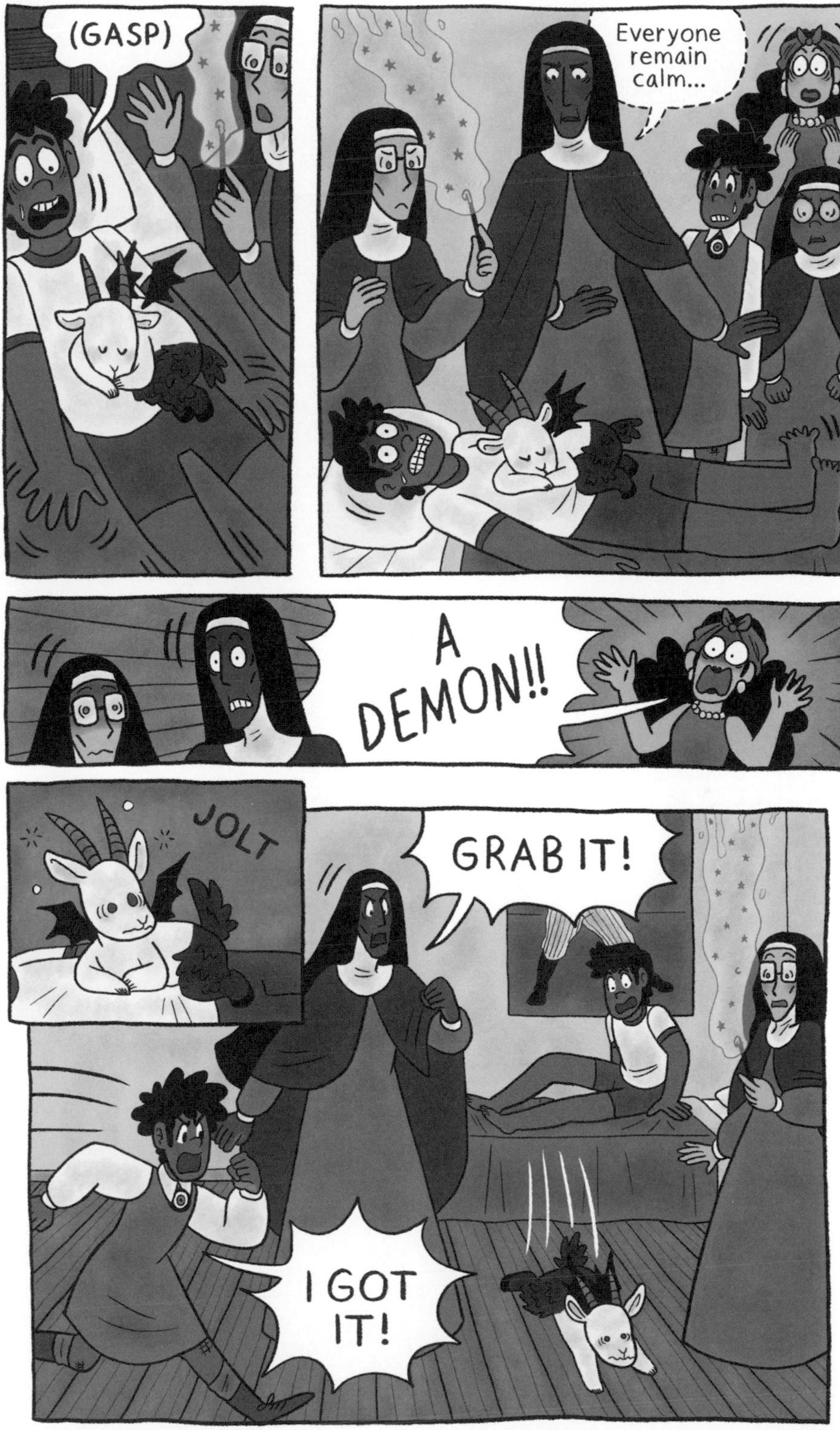
(GASP)
Everyone remain calm...
A DEMON!!
JOLT
GRAB IT!
I GOT IT!

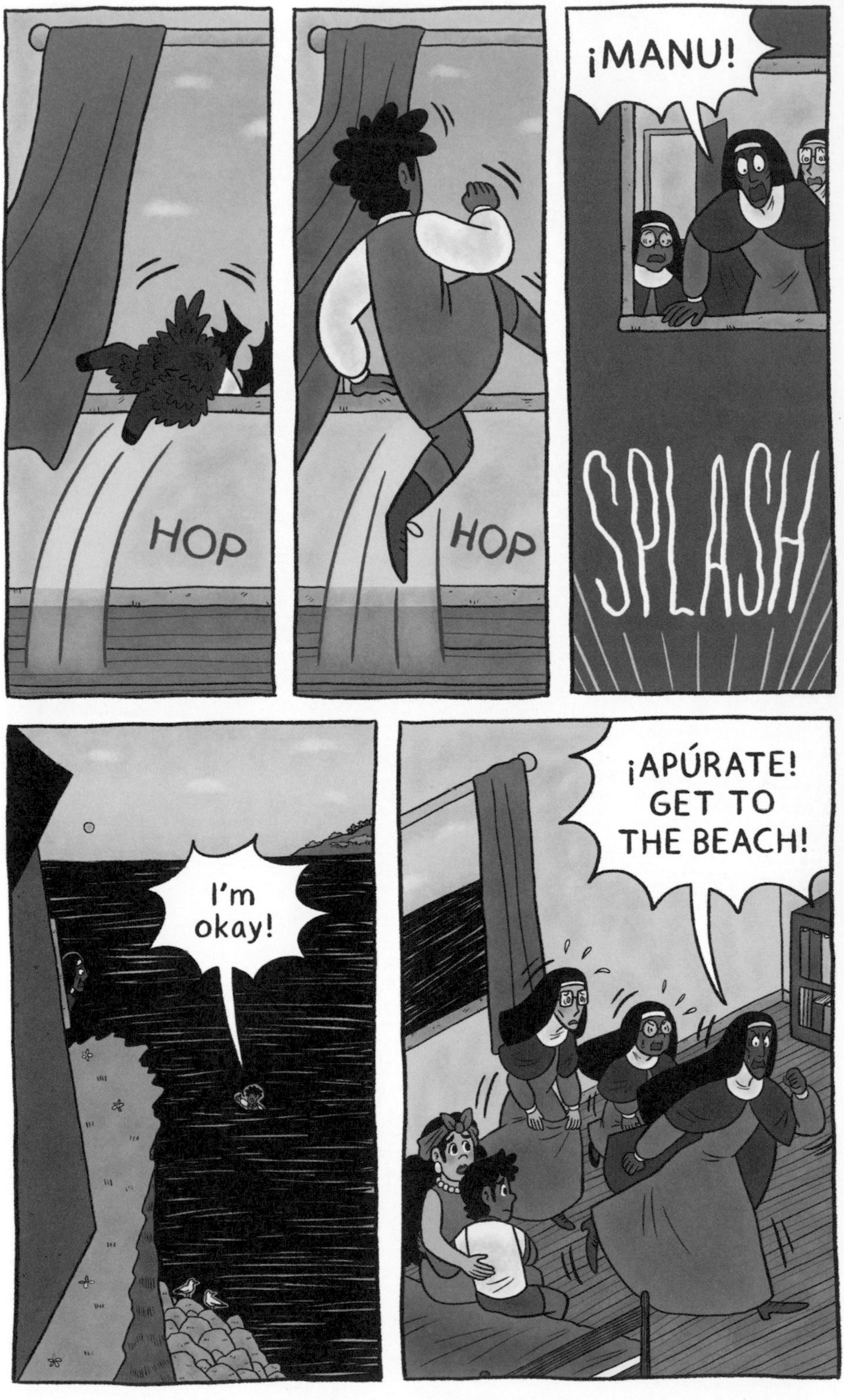
HOP
HOP
¡MANU!
SPLASH
I'm okay!
¡APÚRATE! GET TO THE BEACH!

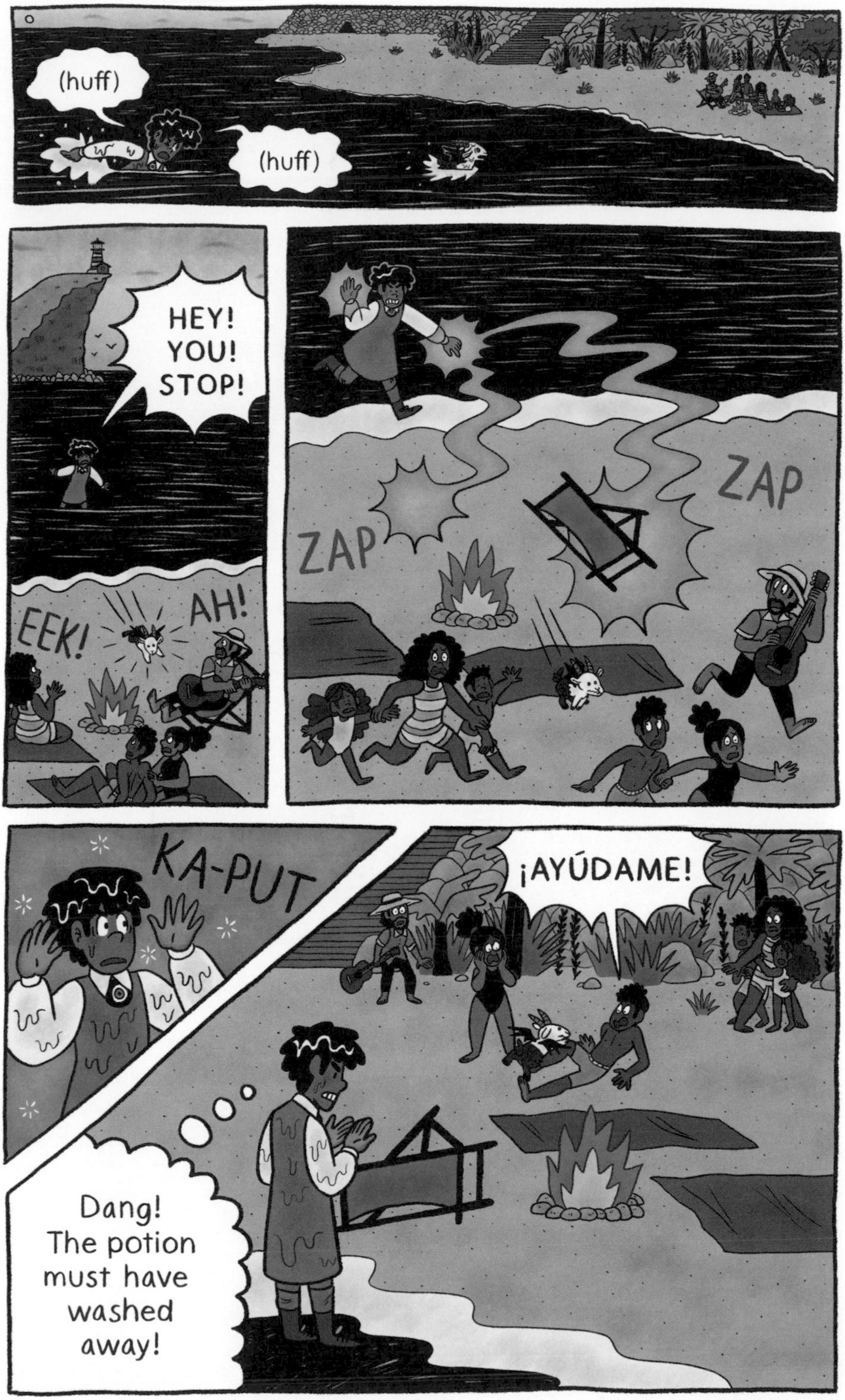
(huff)
(huff)
HEY! YOU! STOP!
EEK!
AH!
ZAP
ZAP
KA-PUT
¡AYÚDAME!
Dang! The potion must have washed away!

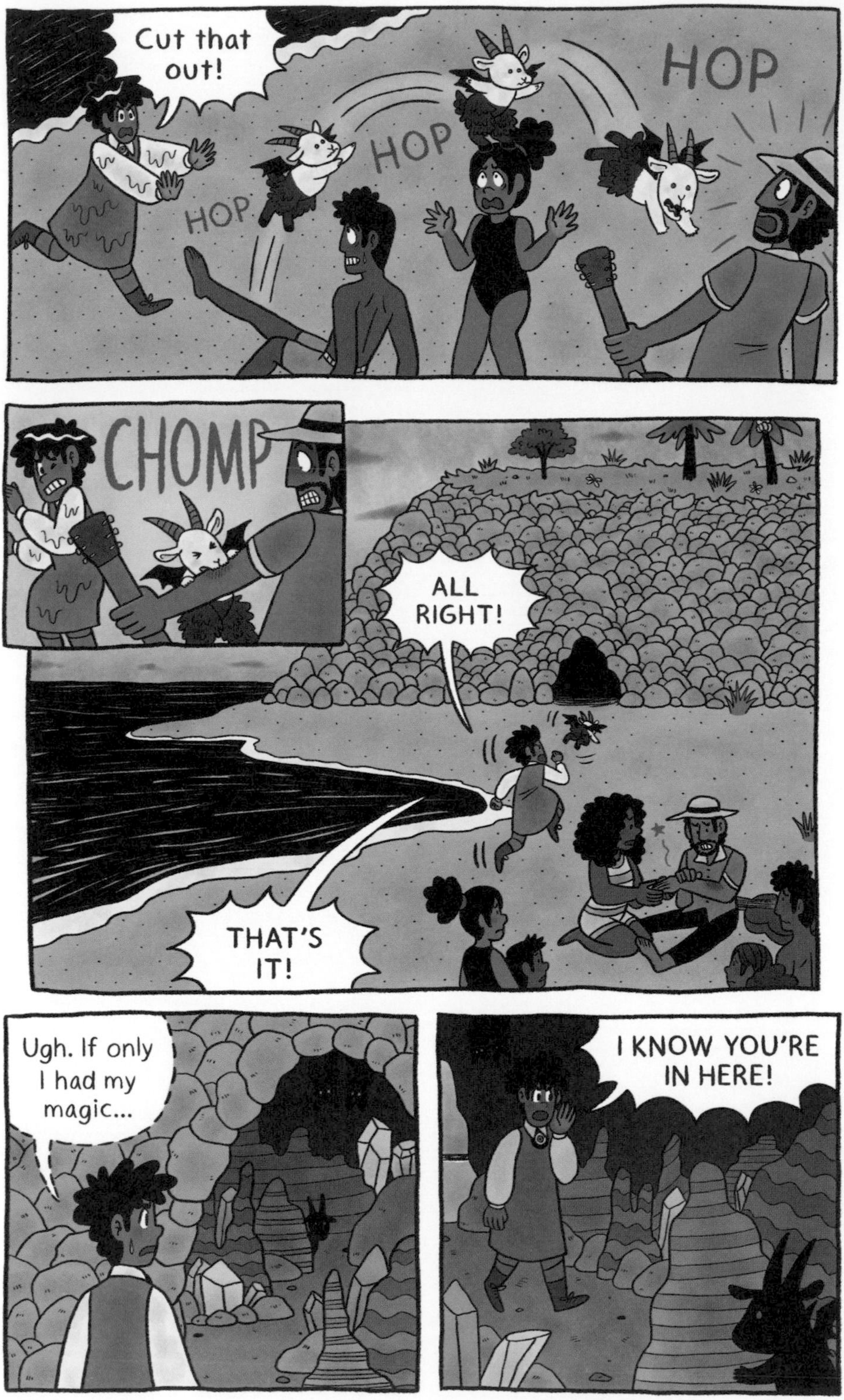
Cut that out!
HOP
HOP
HOP
HOP
CHOMP
ALL RIGHT!
THAT'S IT!
Ugh. If only I had my magic...
I KNOW YOU'RE IN HERE!

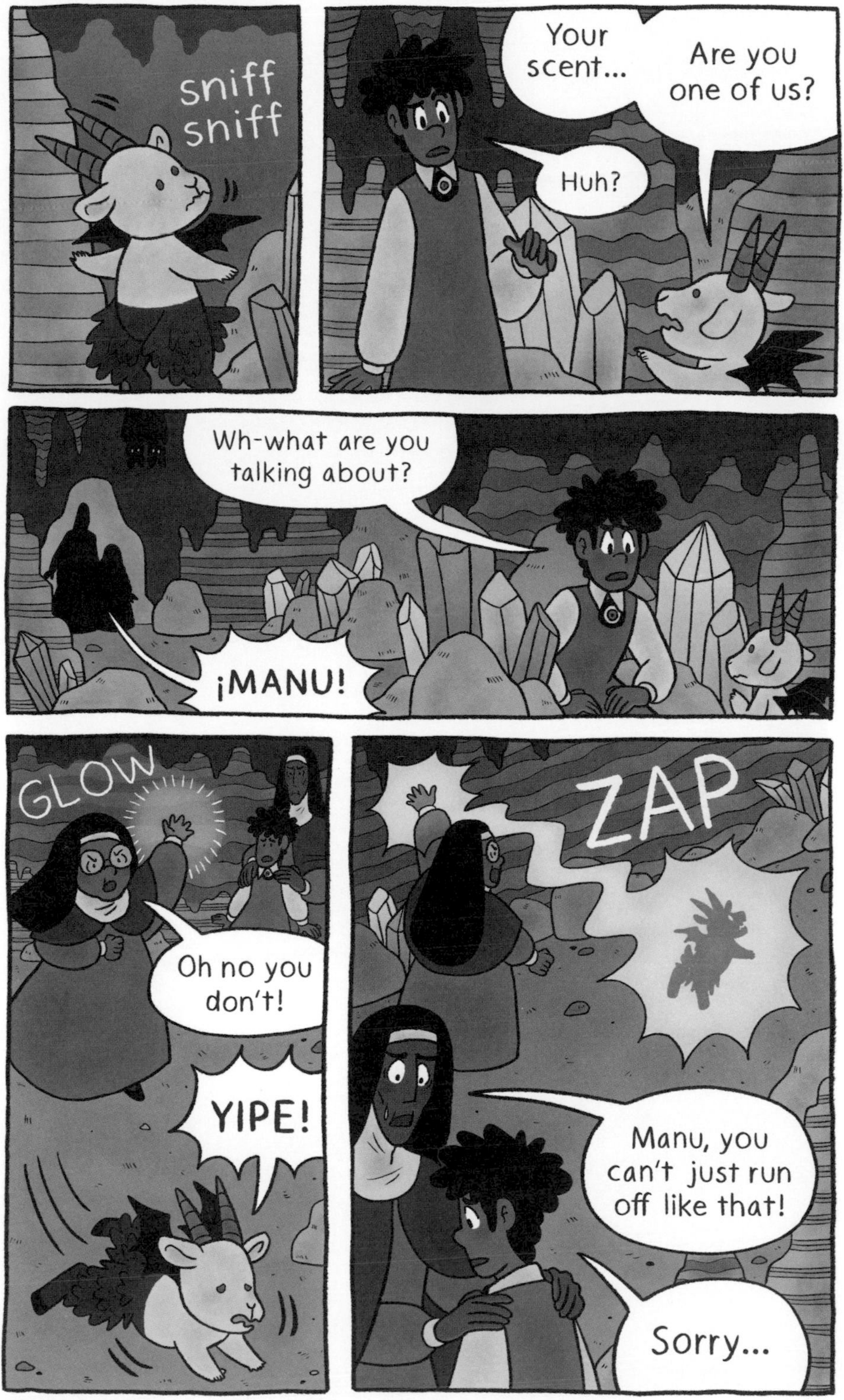
sniff sniff
Your scent...
Are you one of us?
Huh?
Wh-what are you talking about?
¡MANU!
GLOW
Oh no you don't!
YIPE!
ZAP
Manu, you can't just run off like that!
Sorry...

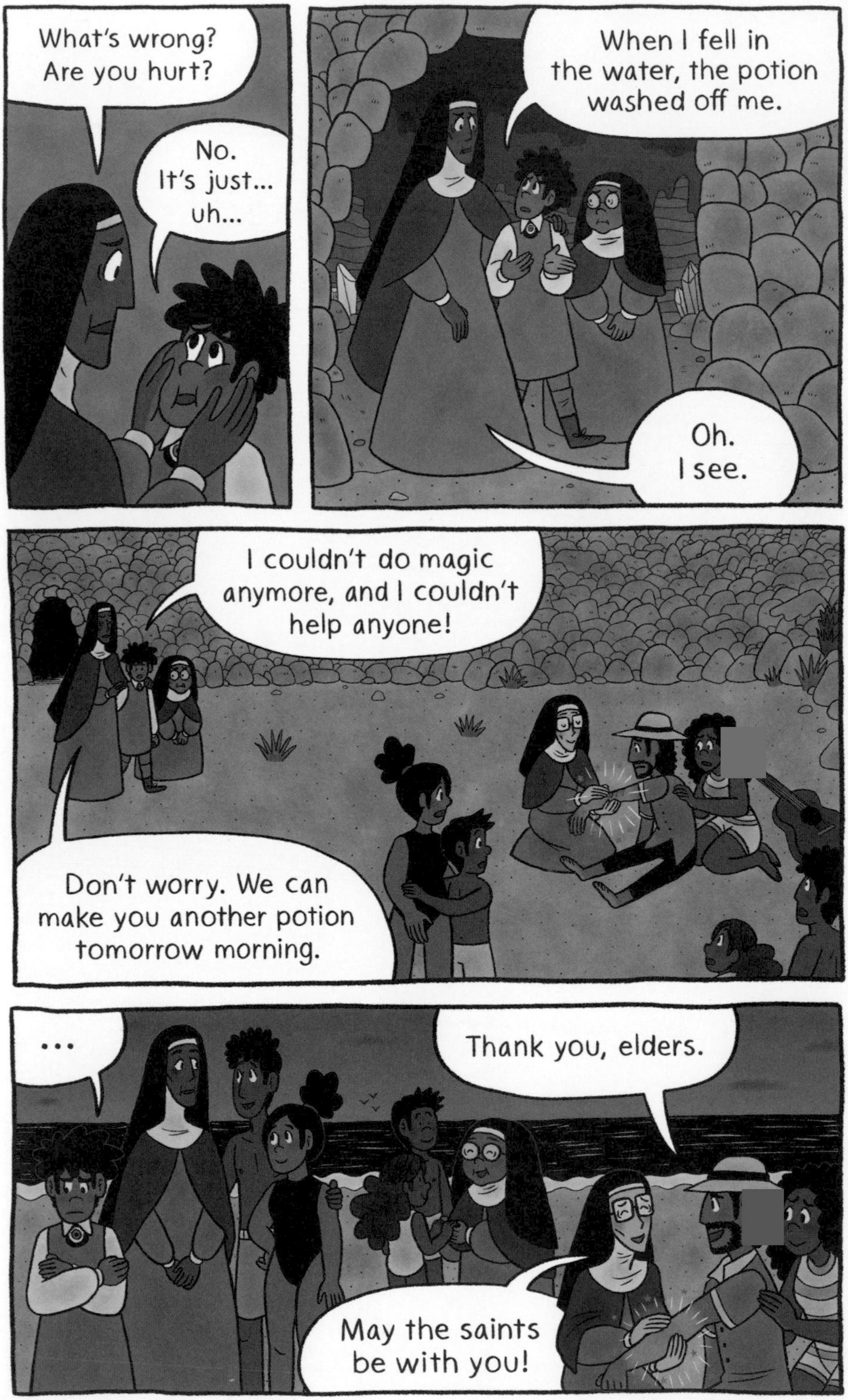
What's wrong? Are you hurt?
No. It's just... uh...
When I fell in the water, the potion washed off me.
Oh. I see.
I couldn't do magic anymore, and I couldn't help anyone!
Don't worry. We can make you another potion tomorrow morning.
...
Thank you, elders.
May the saints be with you!

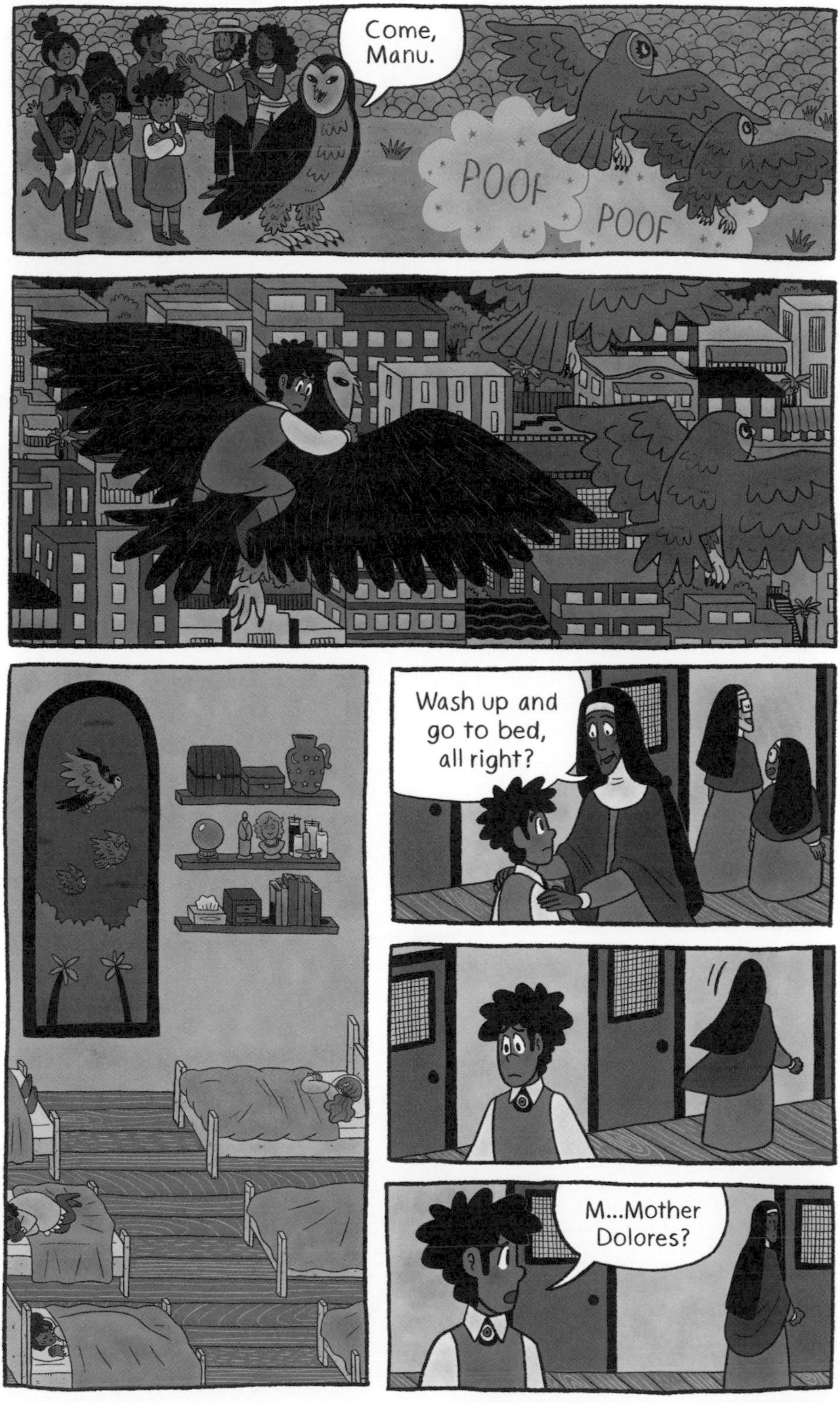
Come, Manu.
POOF
POOF
Wash up and go to bed, all right?
M...Mother Dolores?

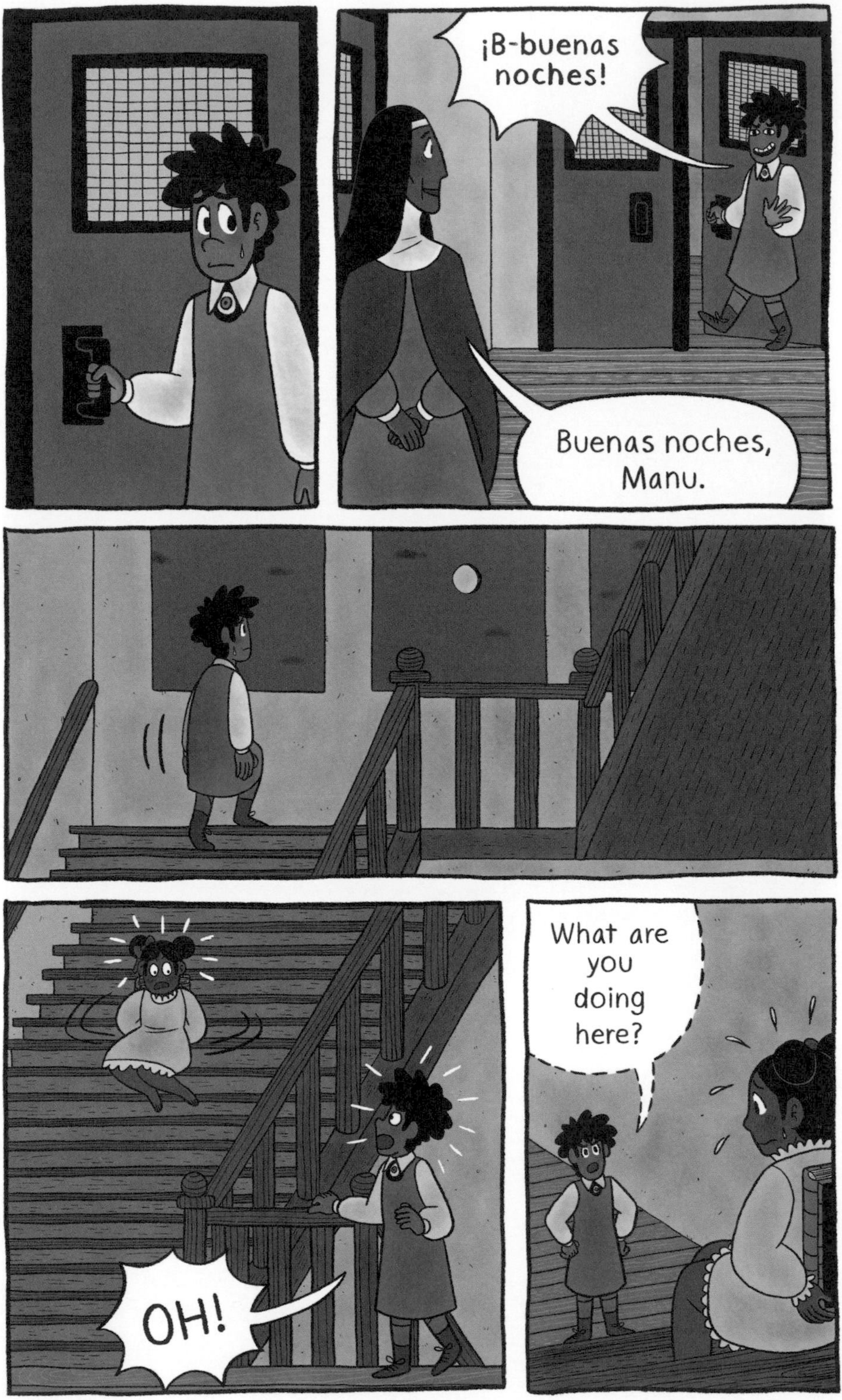

¡B-buenas noches!
Buenas noches, Manu.
OH!
What are you doing here?

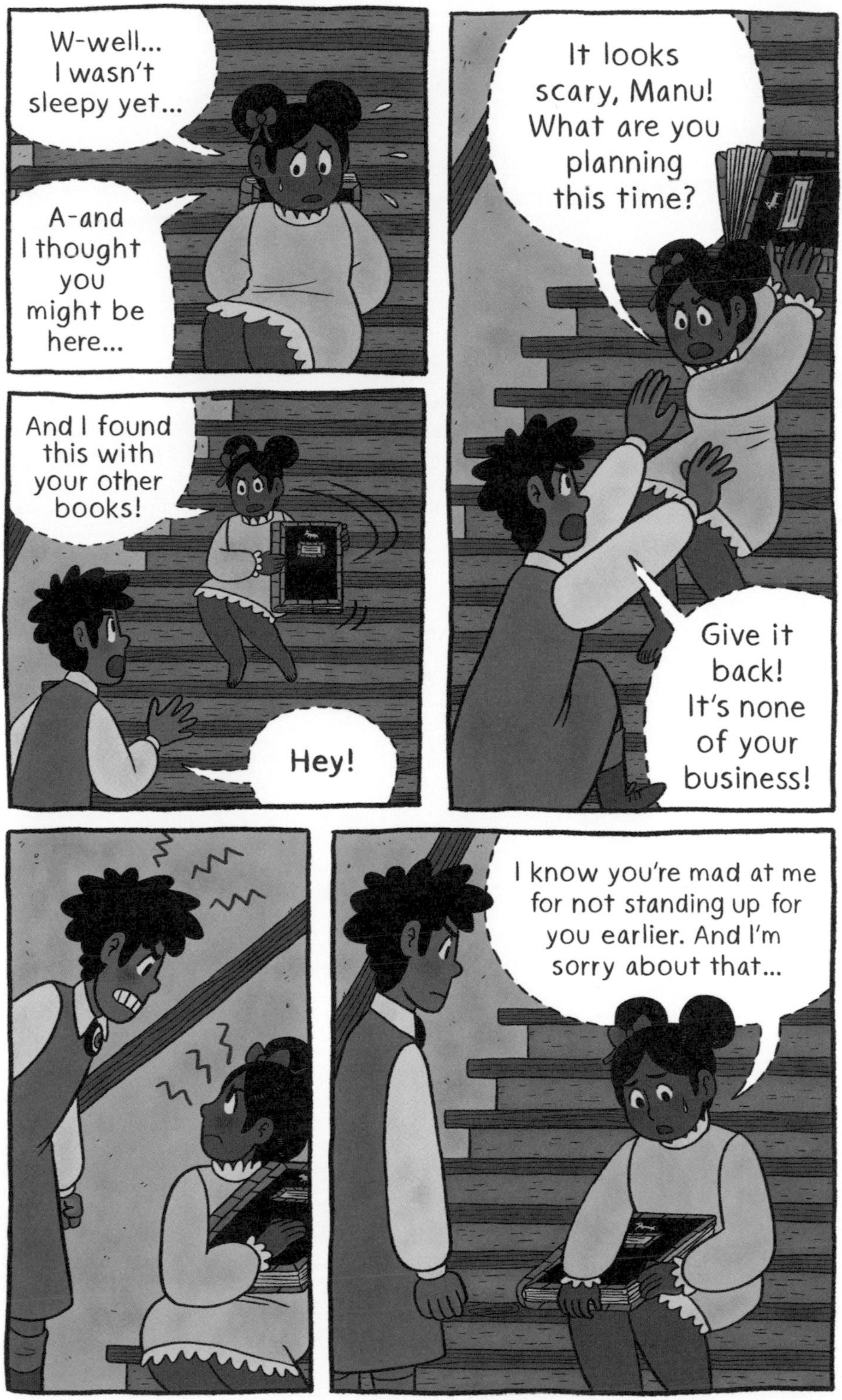

W-well... I wasn't sleepy yet...
A-and I thought you might be here...
And I found this with your other books!
Hey!
It looks scary, Manu! What are you planning this time?
Give it back! It's none of your business!
I know you're mad at me for not standing up for you earlier. And I'm sorry about that...

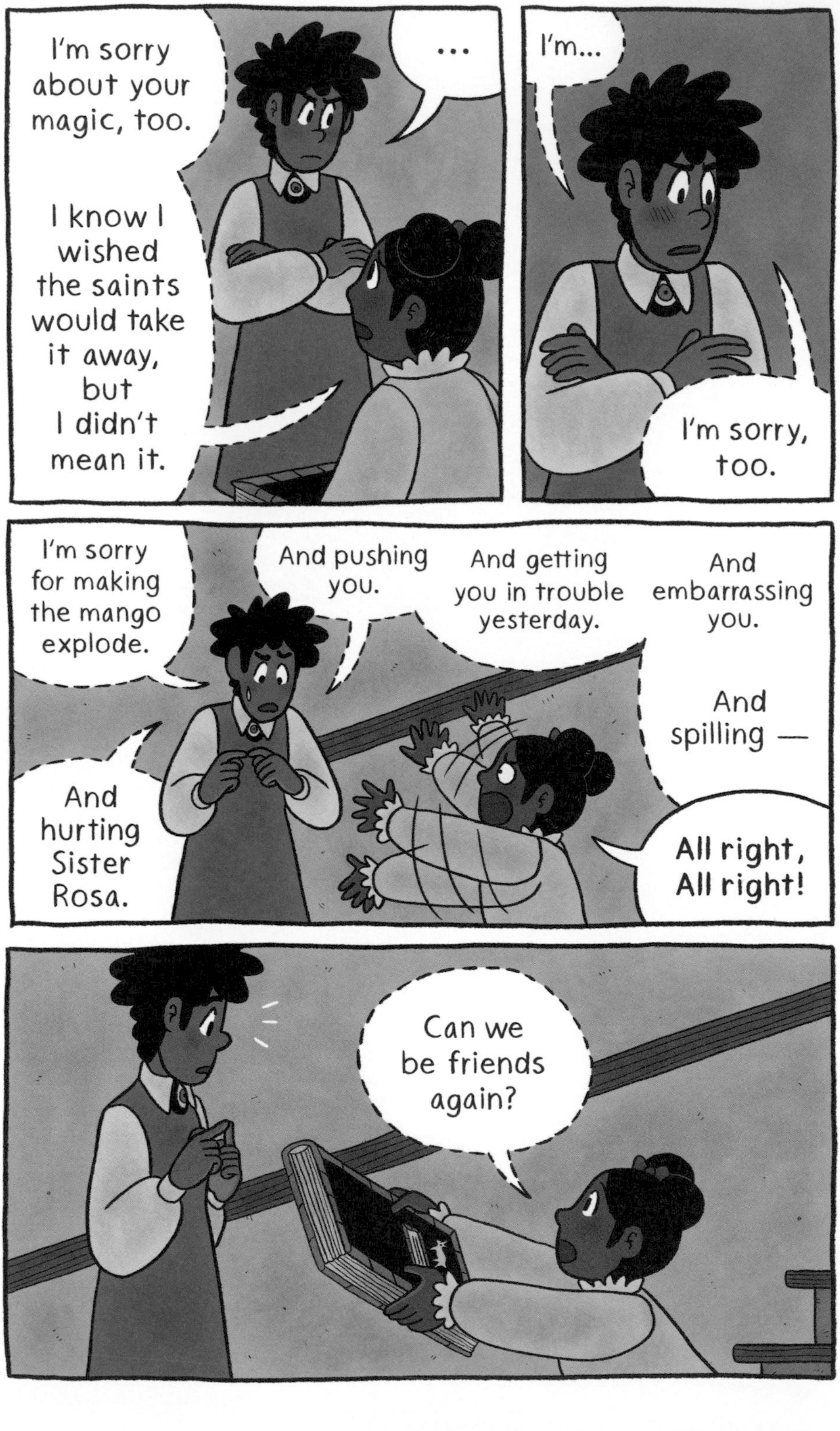
I'm sorry about your magic, too.
I know I wished the saints would take it away, but I didn't mean it.
...
I'm...
I'm sorry, too.
I'm sorry for making the mango explode.
And pushing you.
And getting you in trouble yesterday.
And embarrassing you.
And hurting Sister Rosa.
And spilling —
All right, All right!
Can we be friends again?

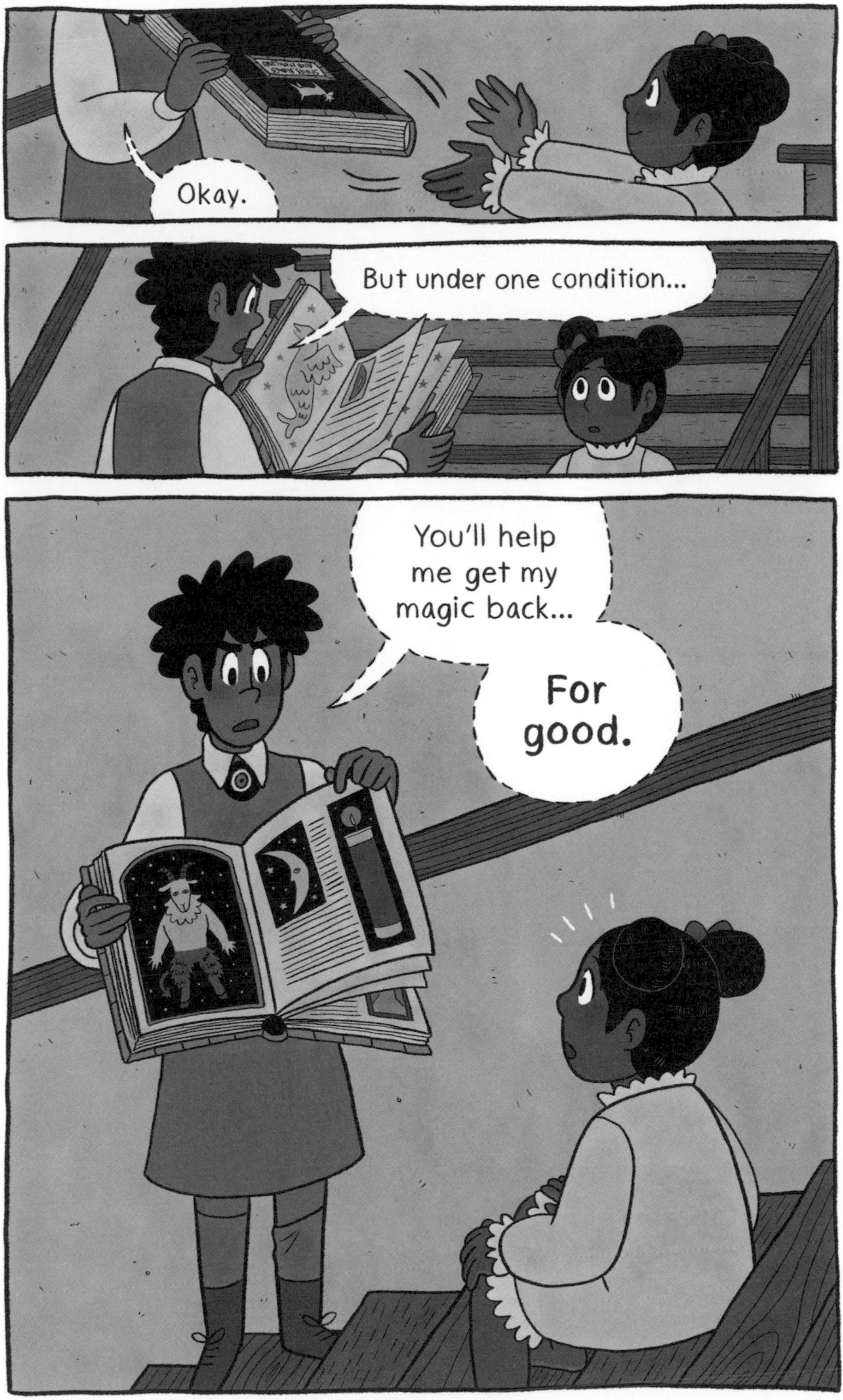
Okay.
But under one condition...
You'll help me get my magic back...
For good.

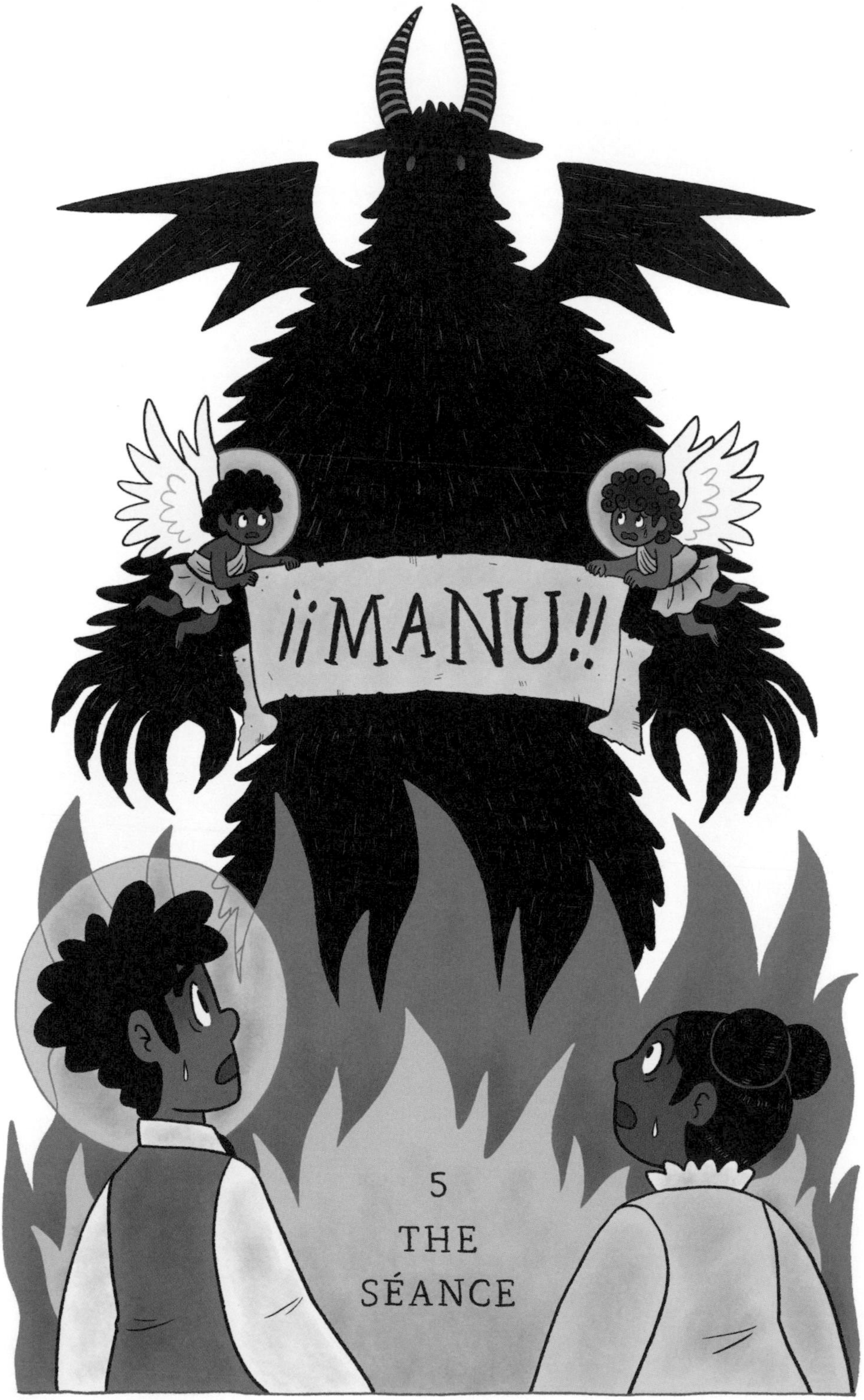
¡¡MANU!!

5
THE SÉANCE

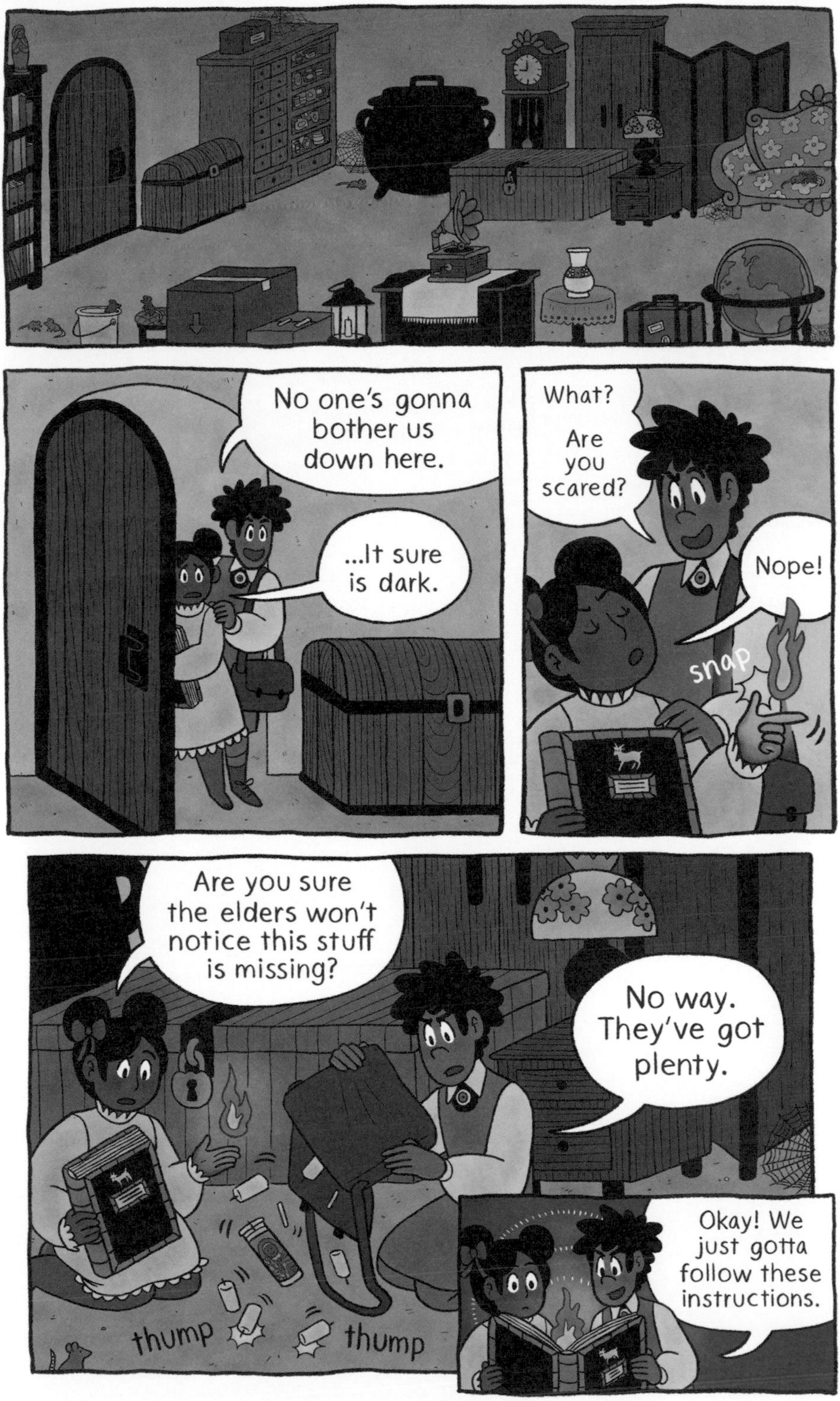
No one's gonna bother us down here.
...It sure is dark.
What?
Are you scared?
Nope!
snap
Are you sure the elders won't notice this stuff is missing?
No way. They've got plenty.
thump
thump
Okay! We just gotta follow these instructions.

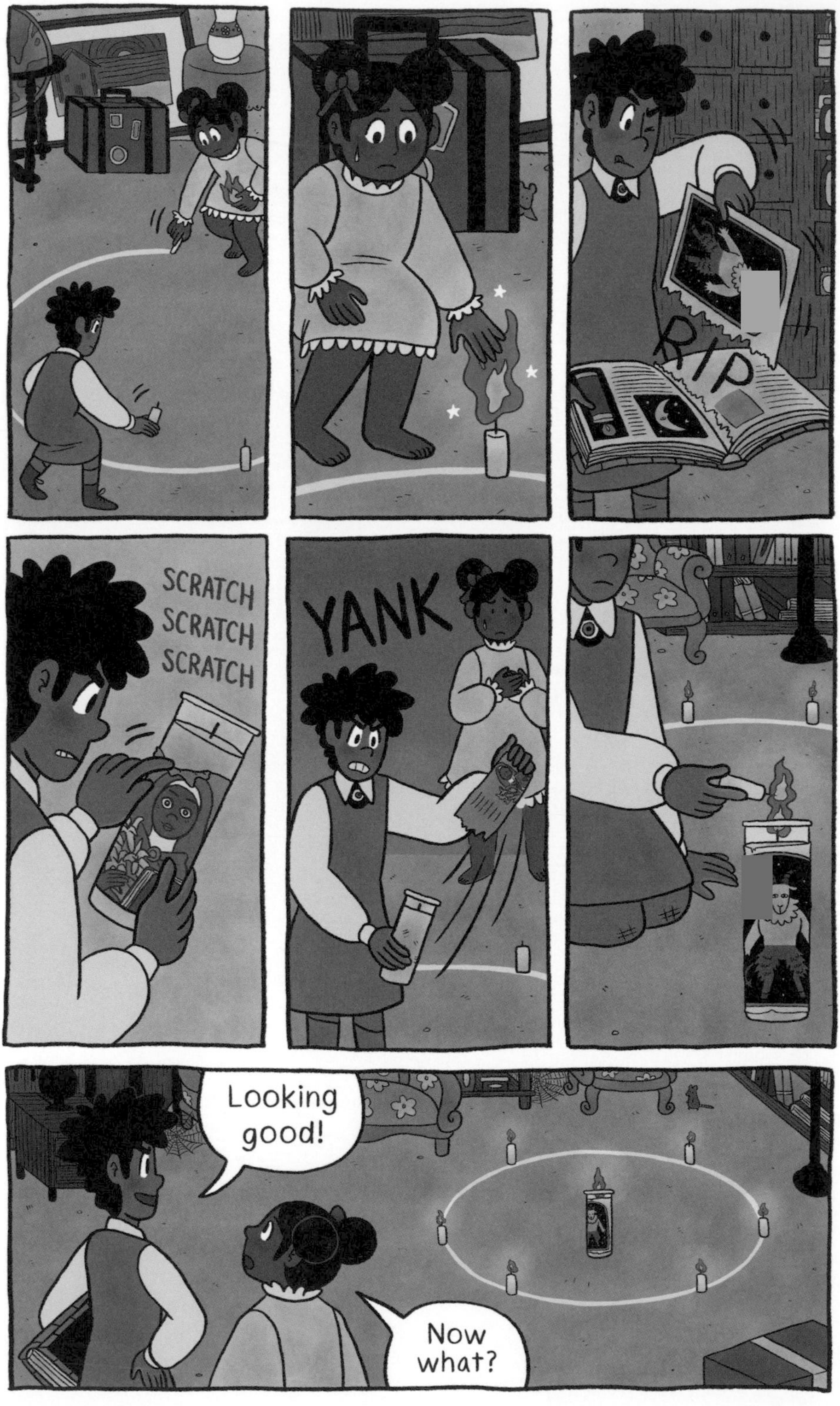
RIP
SCRATCH
SCRATCH
SCRATCH
YANK
Looking good!
Now what?

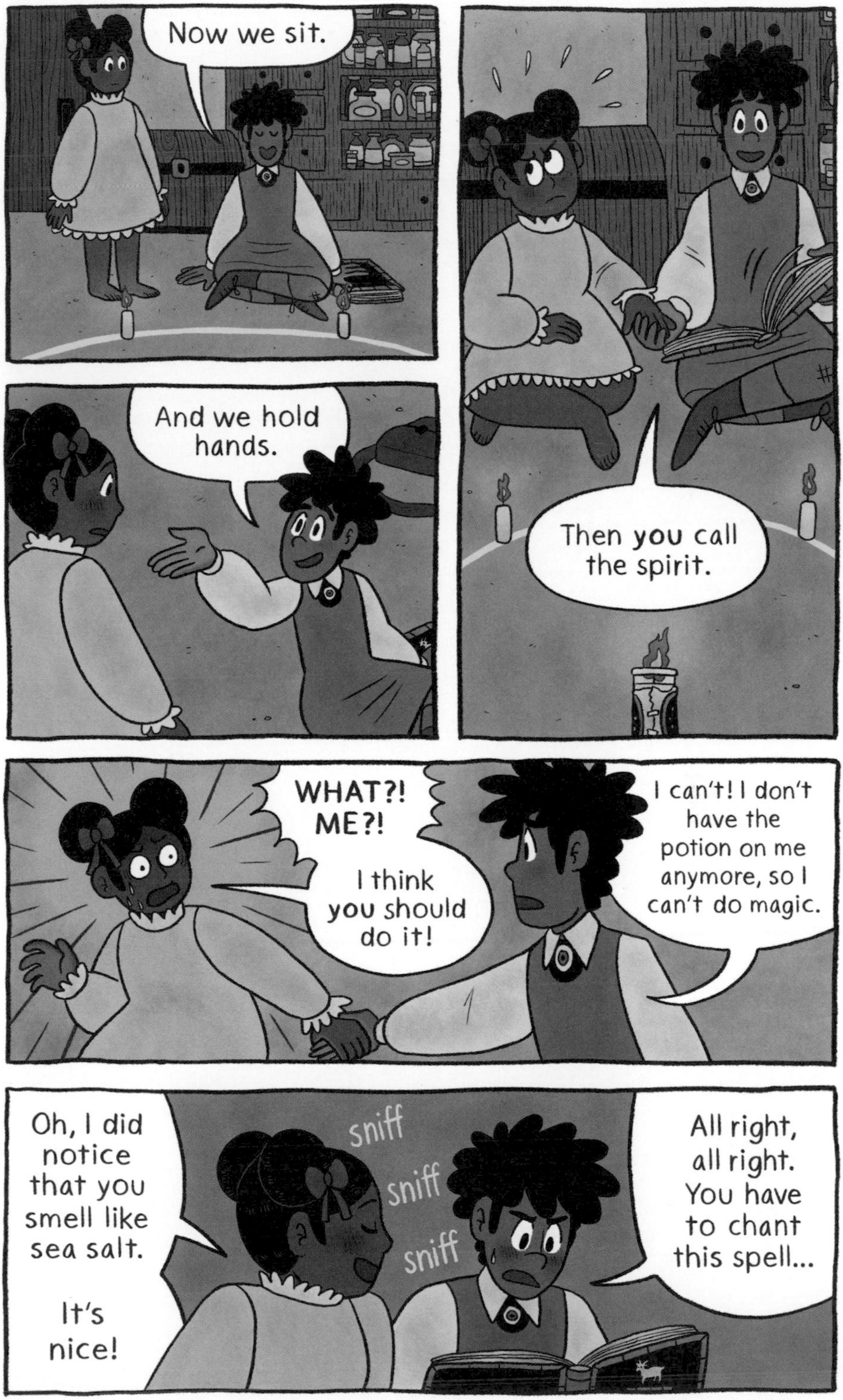
Now we sit.
And we hold hands.
Then you call the spirit.
WHAT?! ME?!
I think you should do it!
I can't! I don't have the potion on me anymore, so I can't do magic.
Oh, I did notice that you smell like sea salt.
It's nice!
sniff
sniff
sniff
All right, all right. You have to chant this spell...

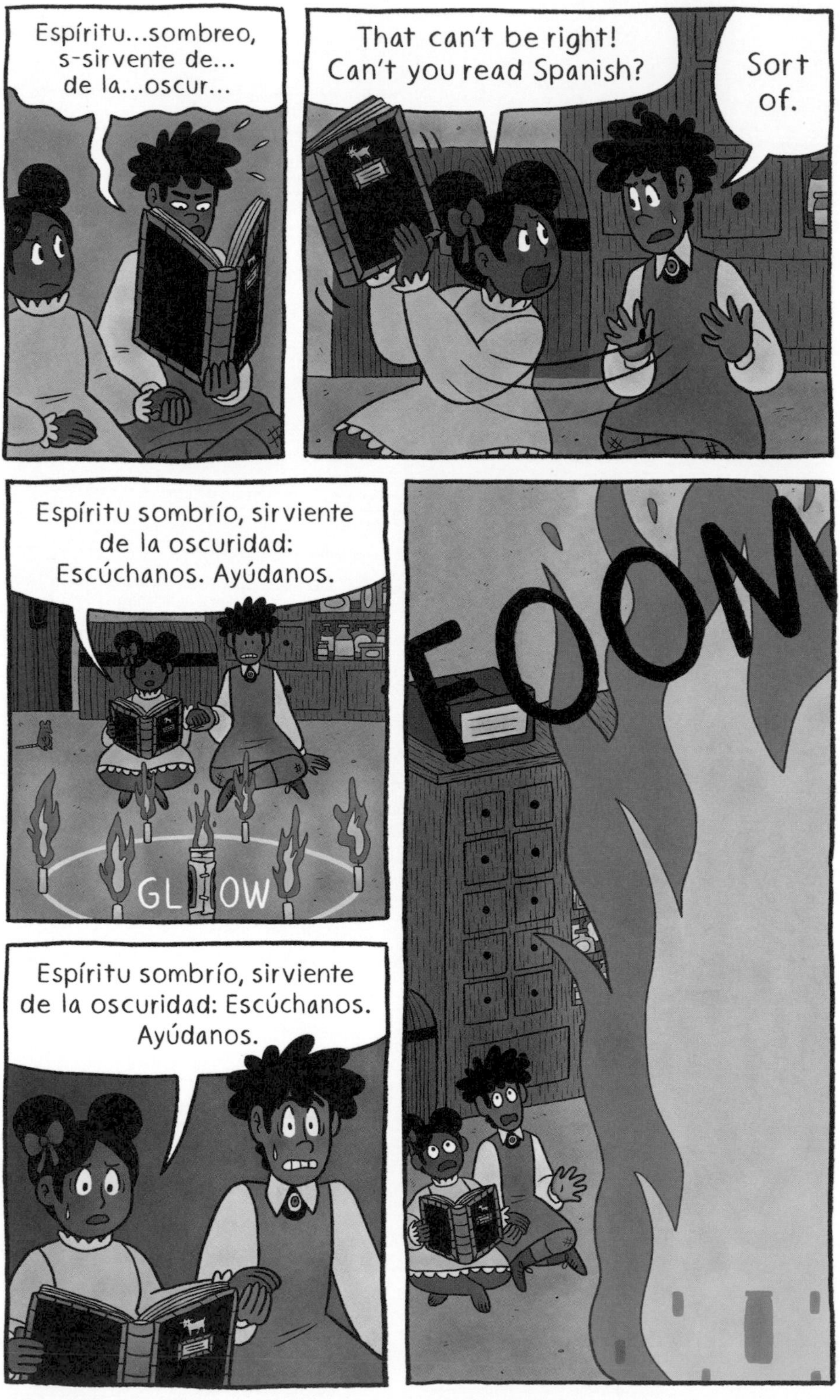
Espíritu...sombreo, s-sirvente de... de la...oscur...
That can't be right! Can't you read Spanish?
Sort of.
Espíritu sombrío, sirviente de la oscuridad: Escúchanos. Ayúdanos.
GLOW
Espíritu sombrío, sirviente de la oscuridad: Escúchanos. Ayúdanos.
FOOM

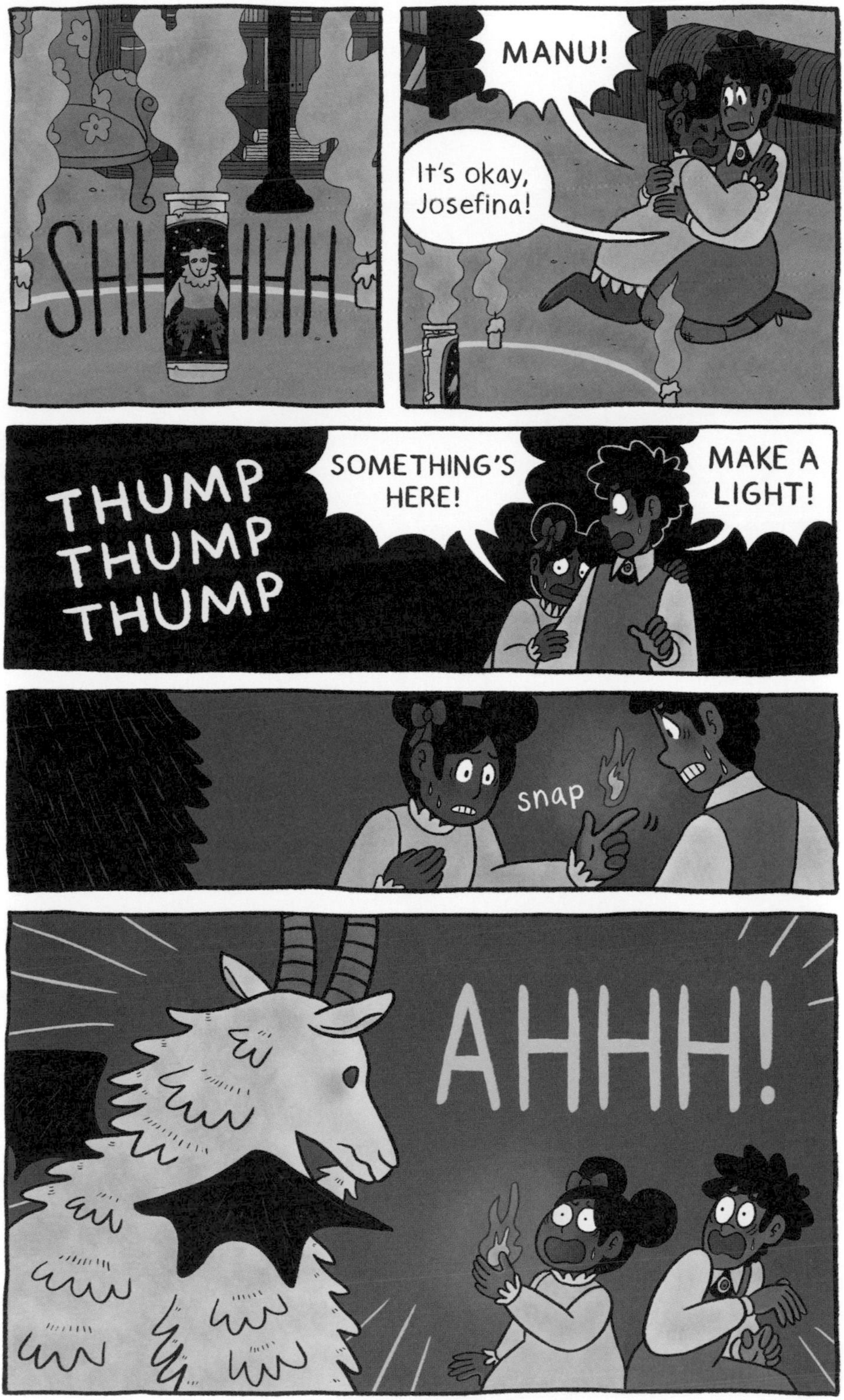
SHHHHHH
MANU!
It's okay, Josefina!
THUMP THUMP THUMP
SOMETHING'S HERE!
MAKE A LIGHT!
snap
AHHH!

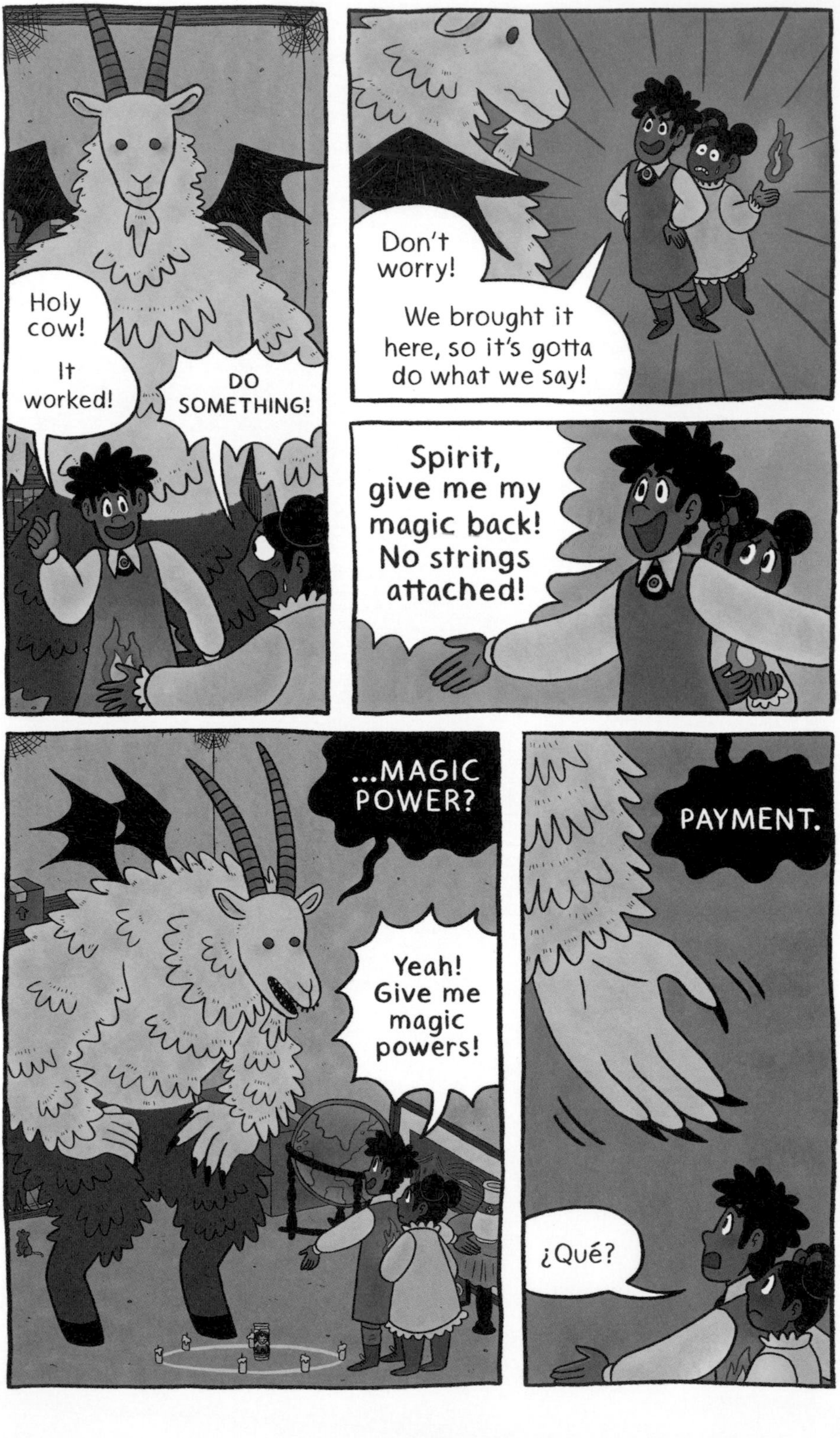
Holy cow!
It worked!
DO SOMETHING!
Don't worry!
We brought it here, so it's gotta do what we say!
Spirit, give me my magic back! No strings attached!
...MAGIC POWER?
Yeah! Give me magic powers!
PAYMENT.
¿Qué?

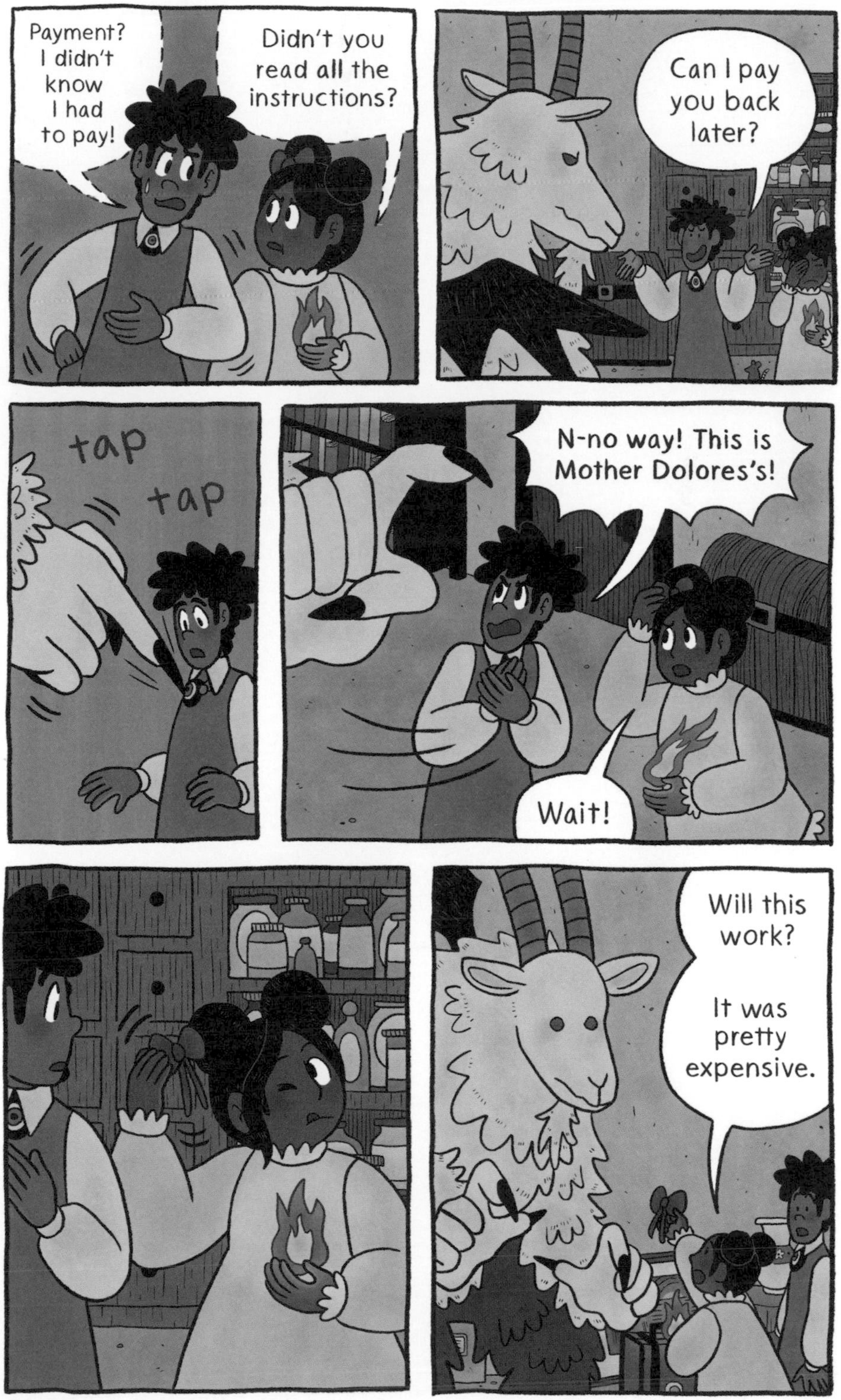
Payment? I didn't know I had to pay!
Didn't you read all the instructions?
Can I pay you back later?
tap
tap
N-no way! This is Mother Dolores's!
Wait!
Will this work?
It was pretty expensive.

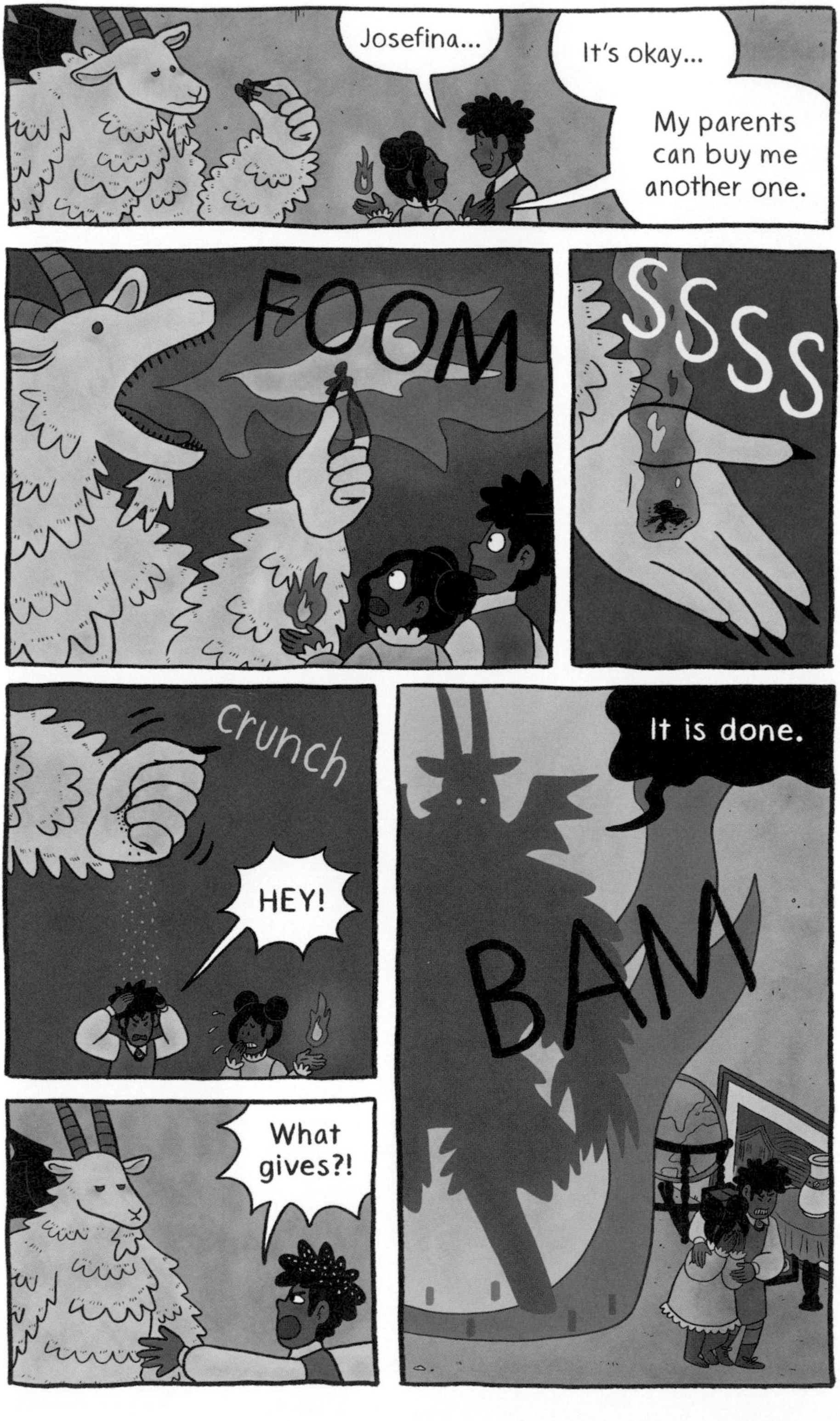
Josefina...
It's okay...
My parents can buy me another one.
FOOM
SSSS
crunch
HEY!
What gives?!
It is done.
BAM

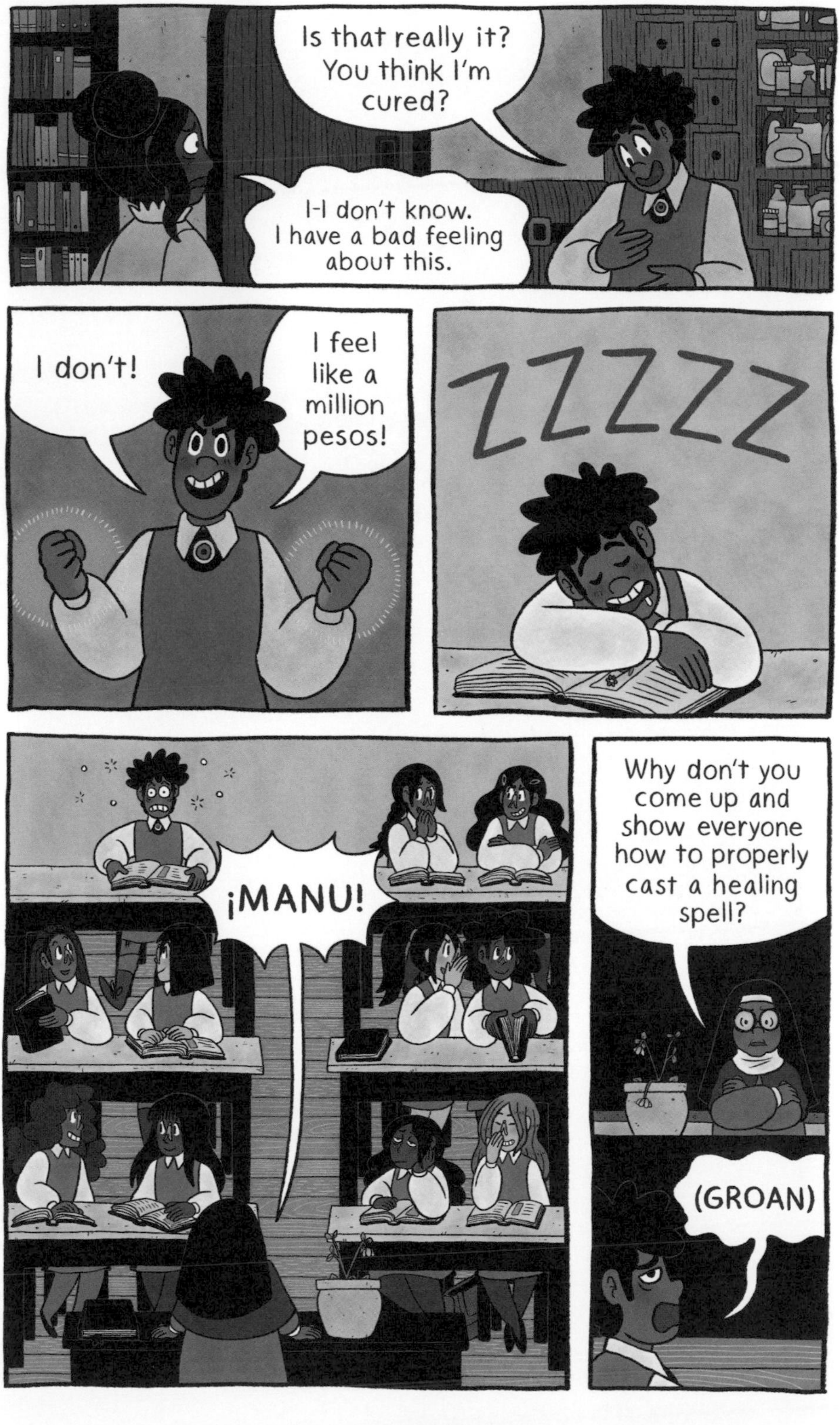
Is that really it? You think I'm cured?
I-I don't know. I have a bad feeling about this.
I don't!
I feel like a million pesos!
ZZZZZ
¡MANU!
Why don't you come up and show everyone how to properly cast a healing spell?
(GROAN)

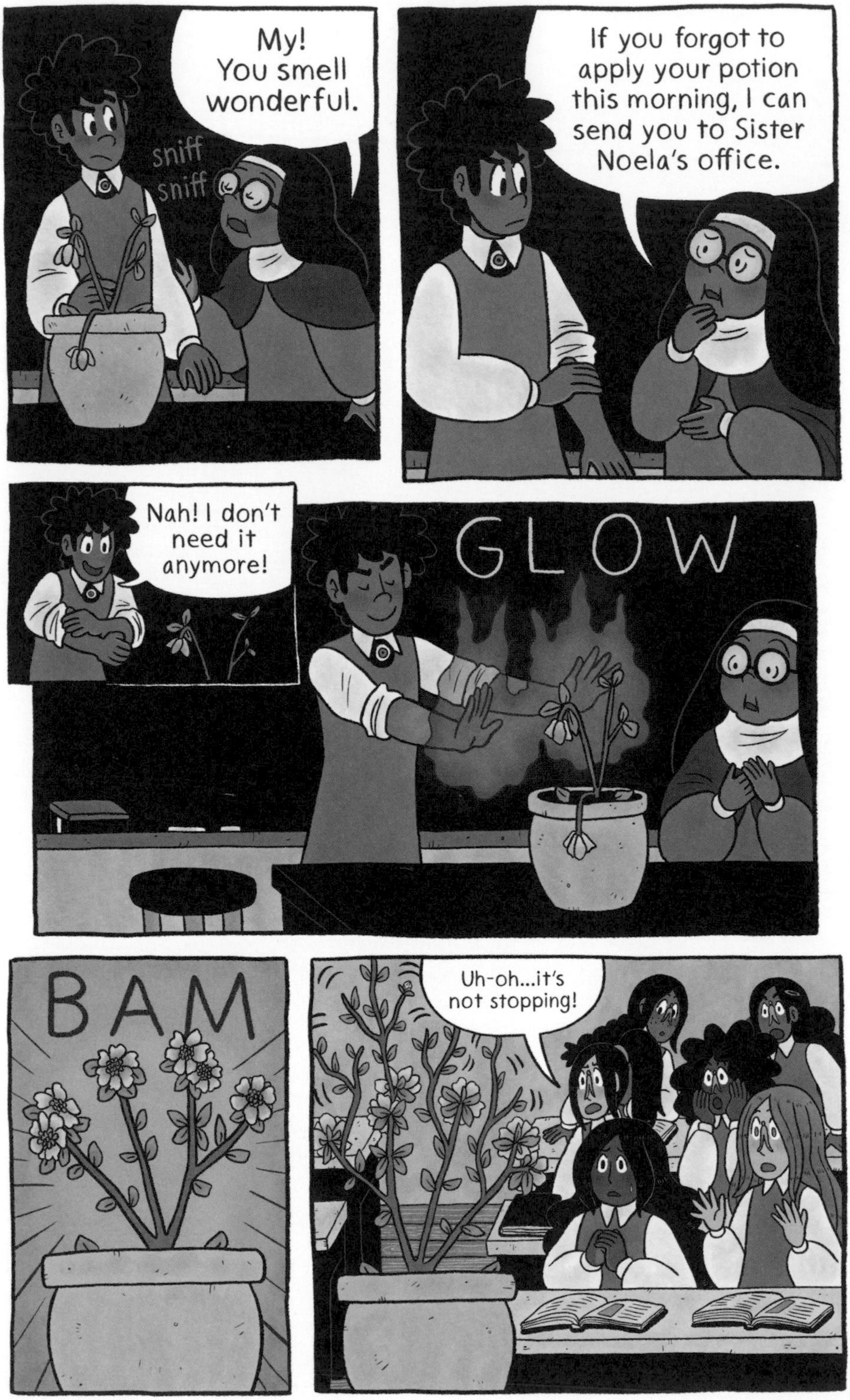
My! You smell wonderful.
sniff sniff
If you forgot to apply your potion this morning, I can send you to Sister Noela's office.
Nah! I don't need it anymore!
GLOW
BAM
Uh-oh...it's not stopping!

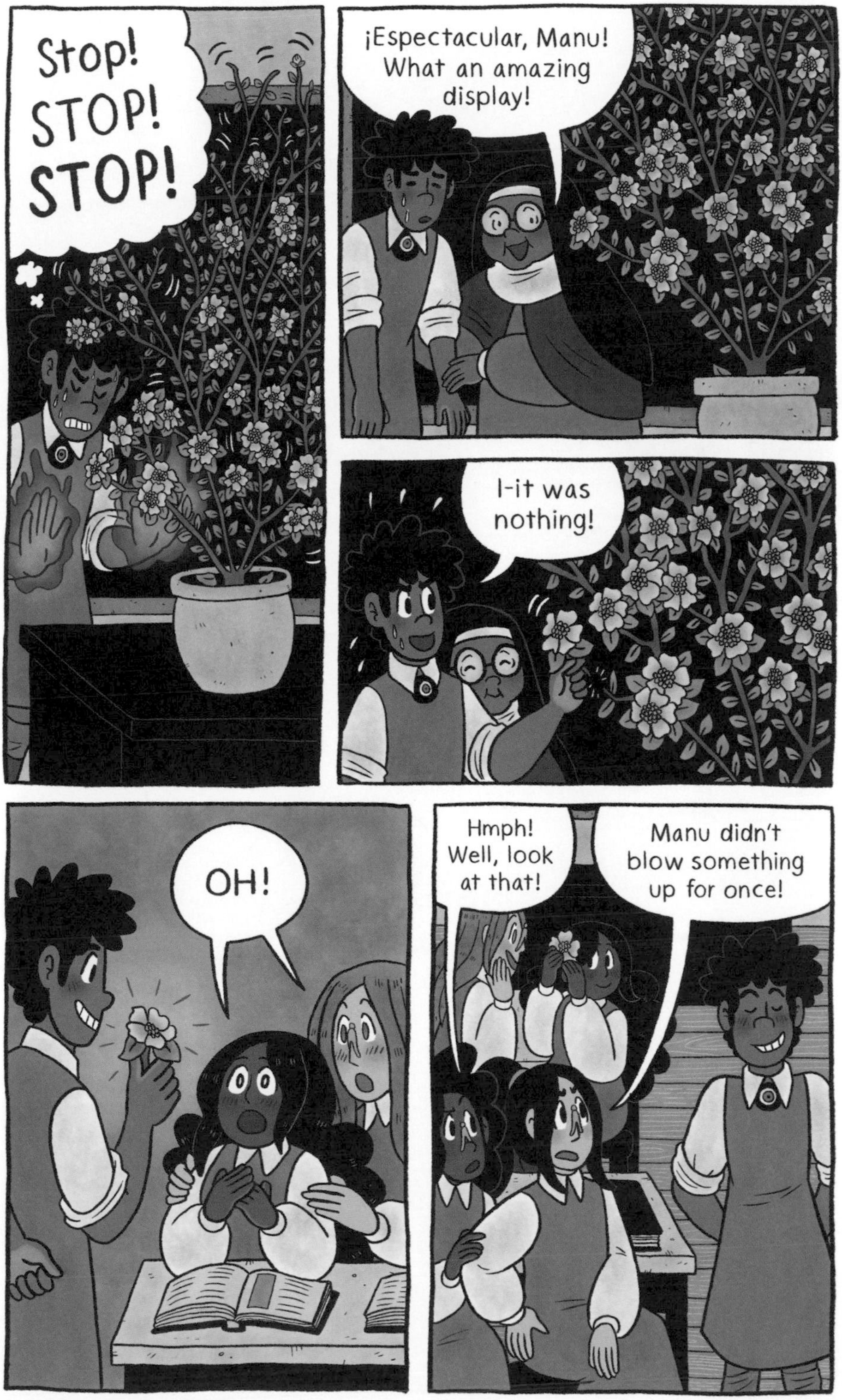
Stop!
STOP!
STOP!
¡Espectacular, Manu! What an amazing display!
I-it was nothing!
OH!
Hmph! Well, look at that!
Manu didn't blow something up for once!

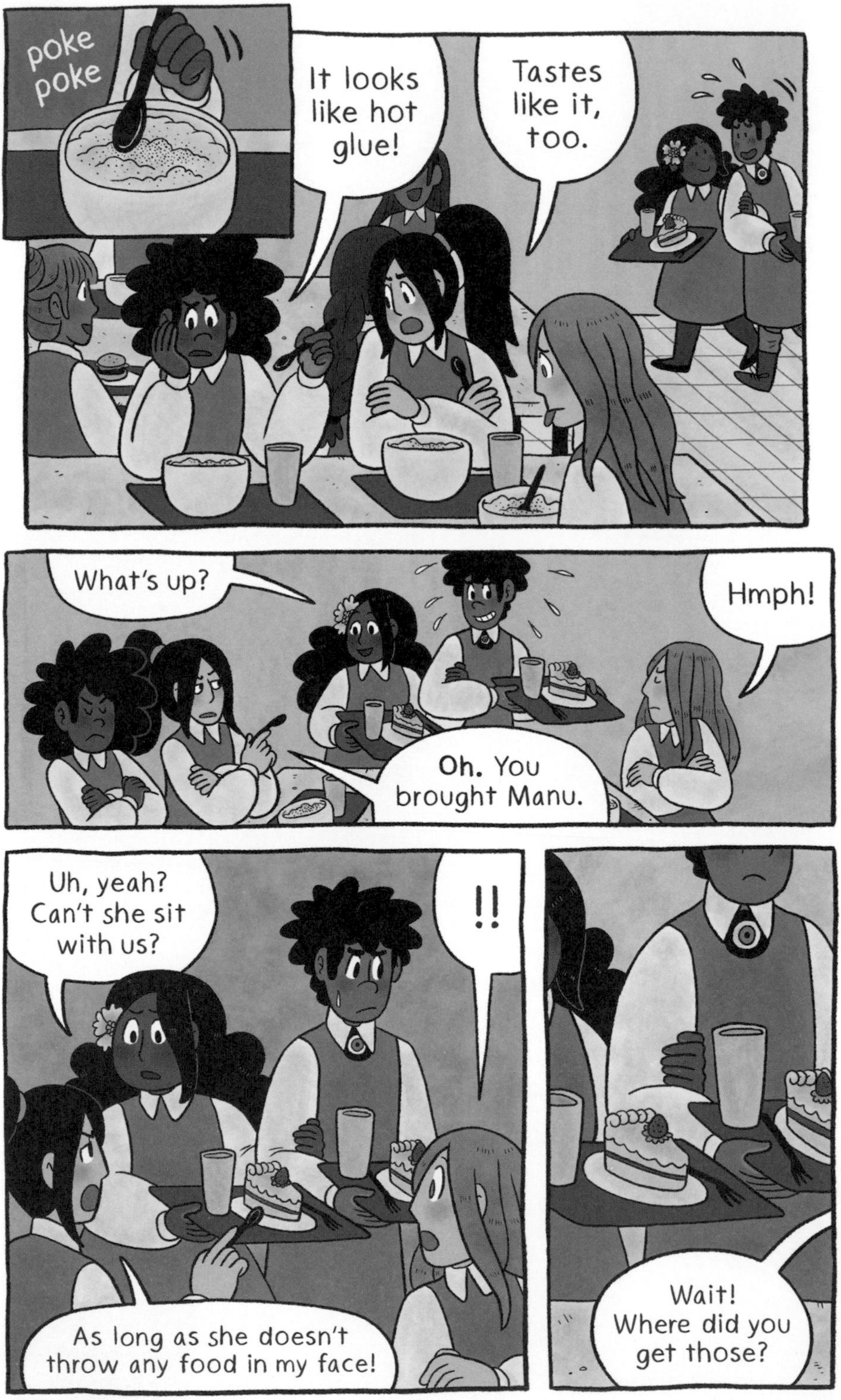
poke poke
It looks like hot glue!
Tastes like it, too.
What's up?
Hmph!
Oh. You brought Manu.
Uh, yeah? Can't she sit with us?
!!
As long as she doesn't throw any food in my face!
Wait! Where did you get those?

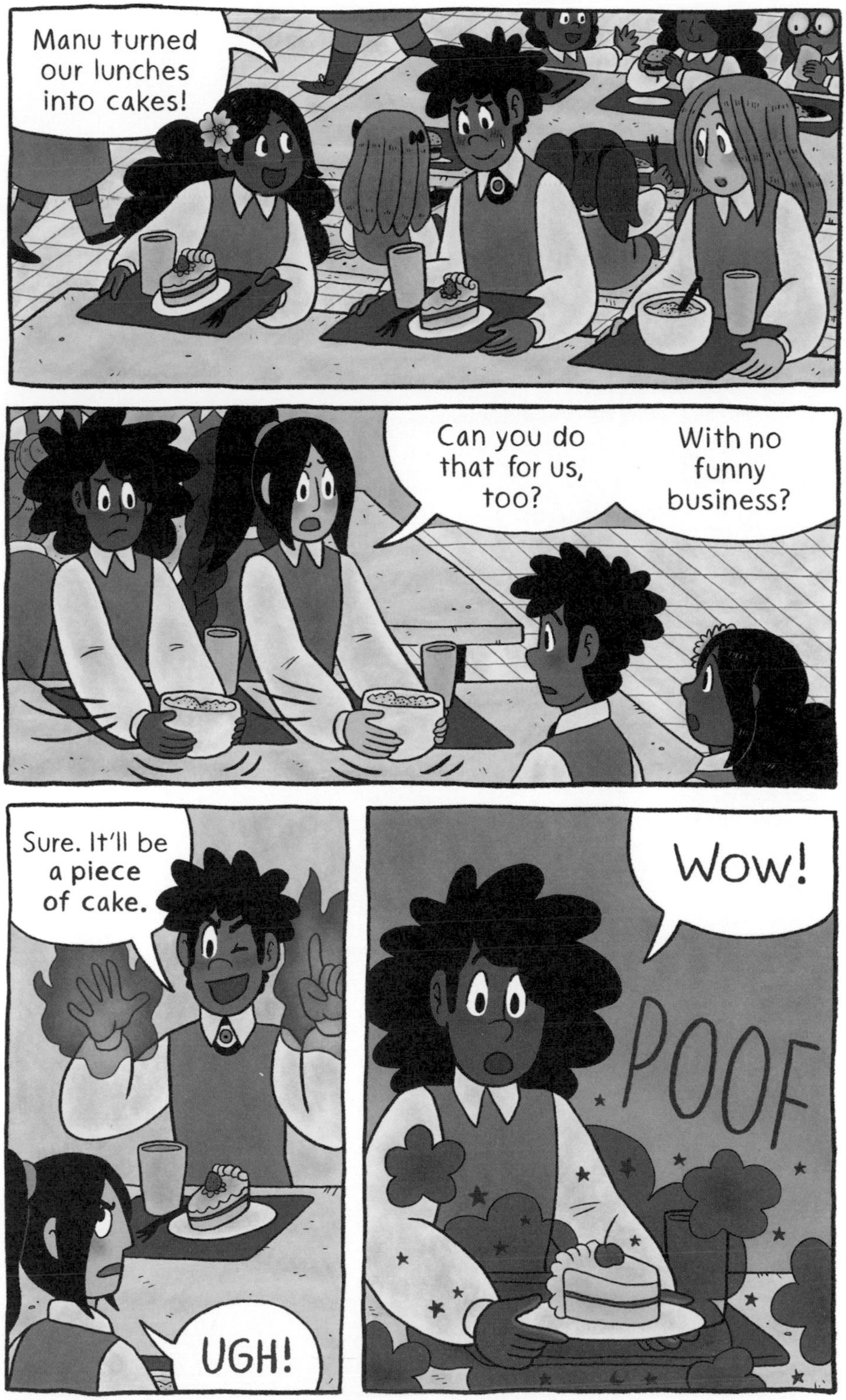
Manu turned our lunches into cakes!
Can you do that for us, too?
With no funny business?
Sure. It'll be a piece of cake.
UGH!
WOW!
POOF

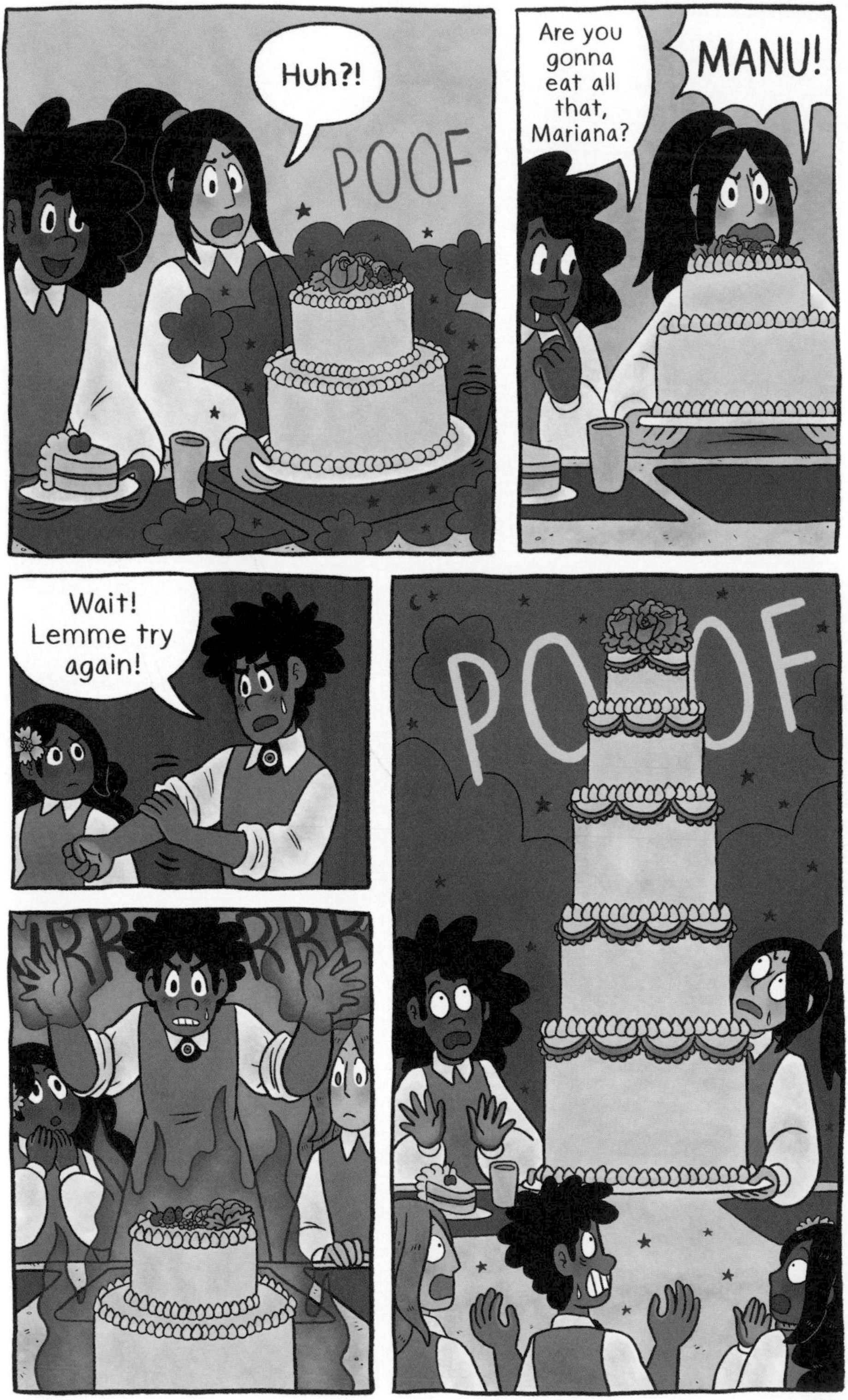
Huh?!
POOF
Are you gonna eat all that, Mariana?
MANU!
Wait! Lemme try again!
POOF

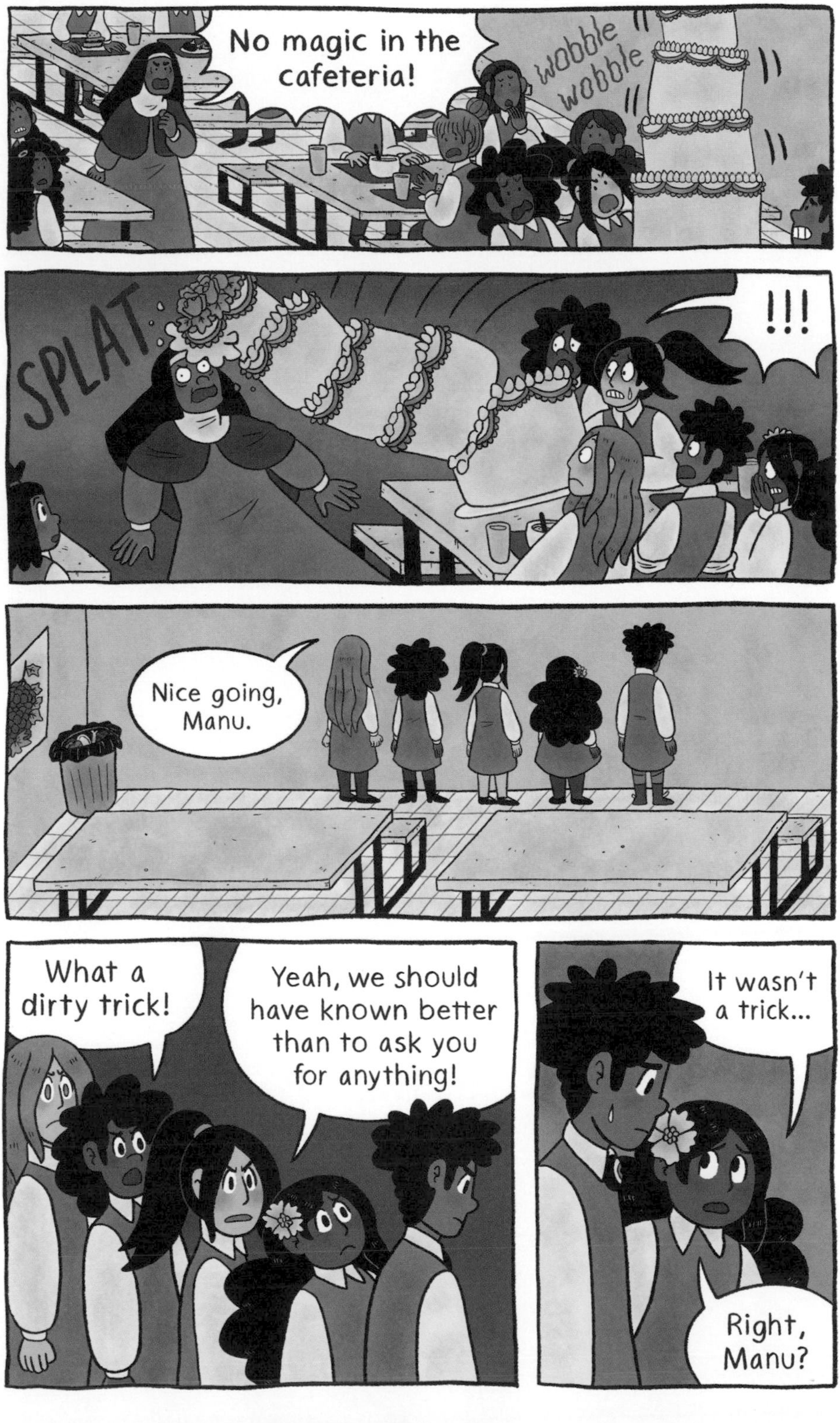
No magic in the cafeteria!
wobble wobble
SPLAT
!!!
Nice going, Manu.
What a dirty trick!
Yeah, we should have known better than to ask you for anything!
It wasn't a trick...
Right, Manu?

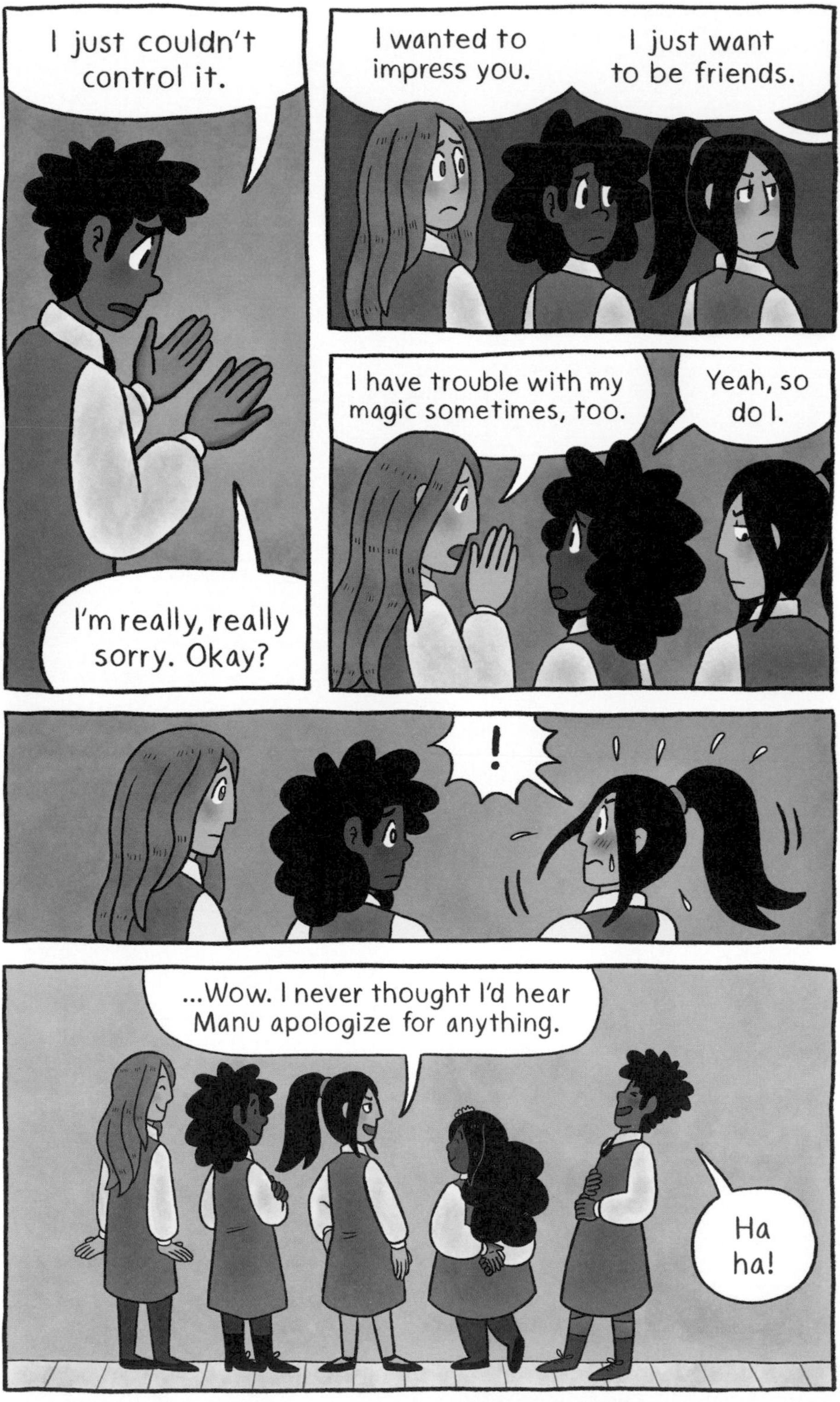
I just couldn't control it.
I'm really, really sorry. Okay?
I wanted to impress you.
I just want to be friends.
I have trouble with my magic sometimes, too.
Yeah, so do I.
!
...Wow. I never thought I'd hear Manu apologize for anything.
Ha ha!

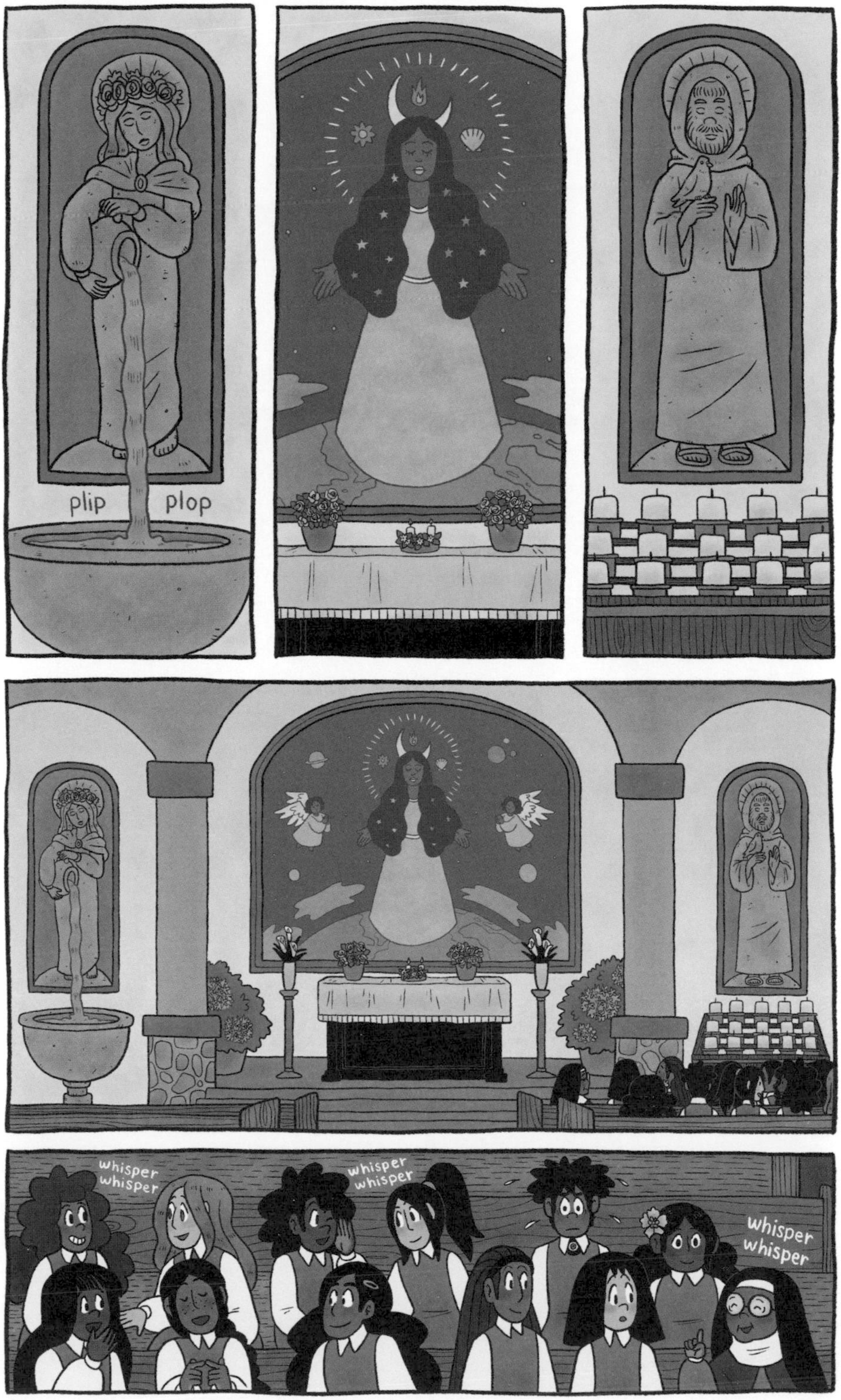
plip
plop
whisper whisper
whisper whisper
whisper whisper

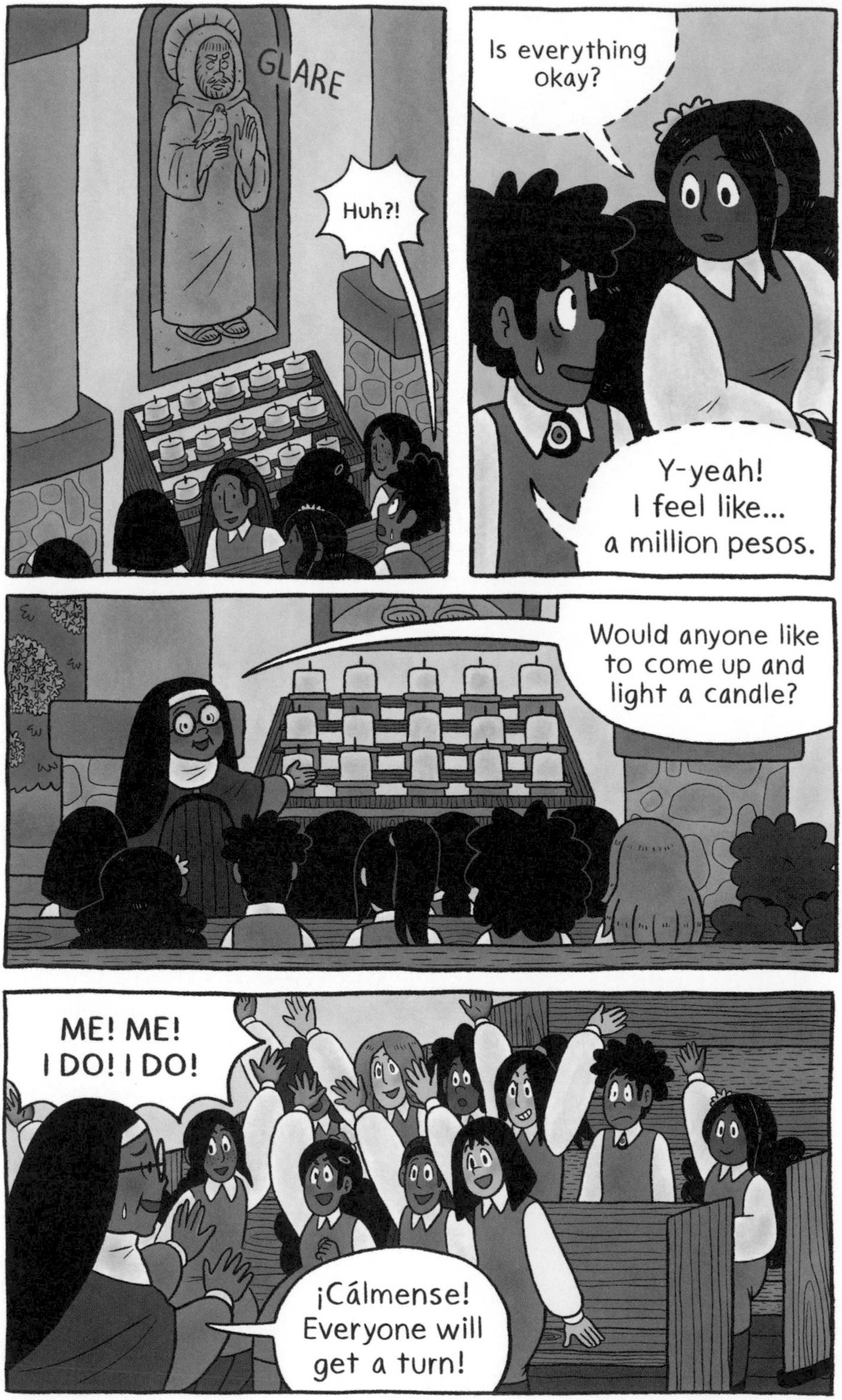
GLARE
Huh?!
Is everything okay?
Y-yeah! I feel like... a million pesos.
Would anyone like to come up and light a candle?
ME! ME! I DO! I DO!
¡Cálmense! Everyone will get a turn!

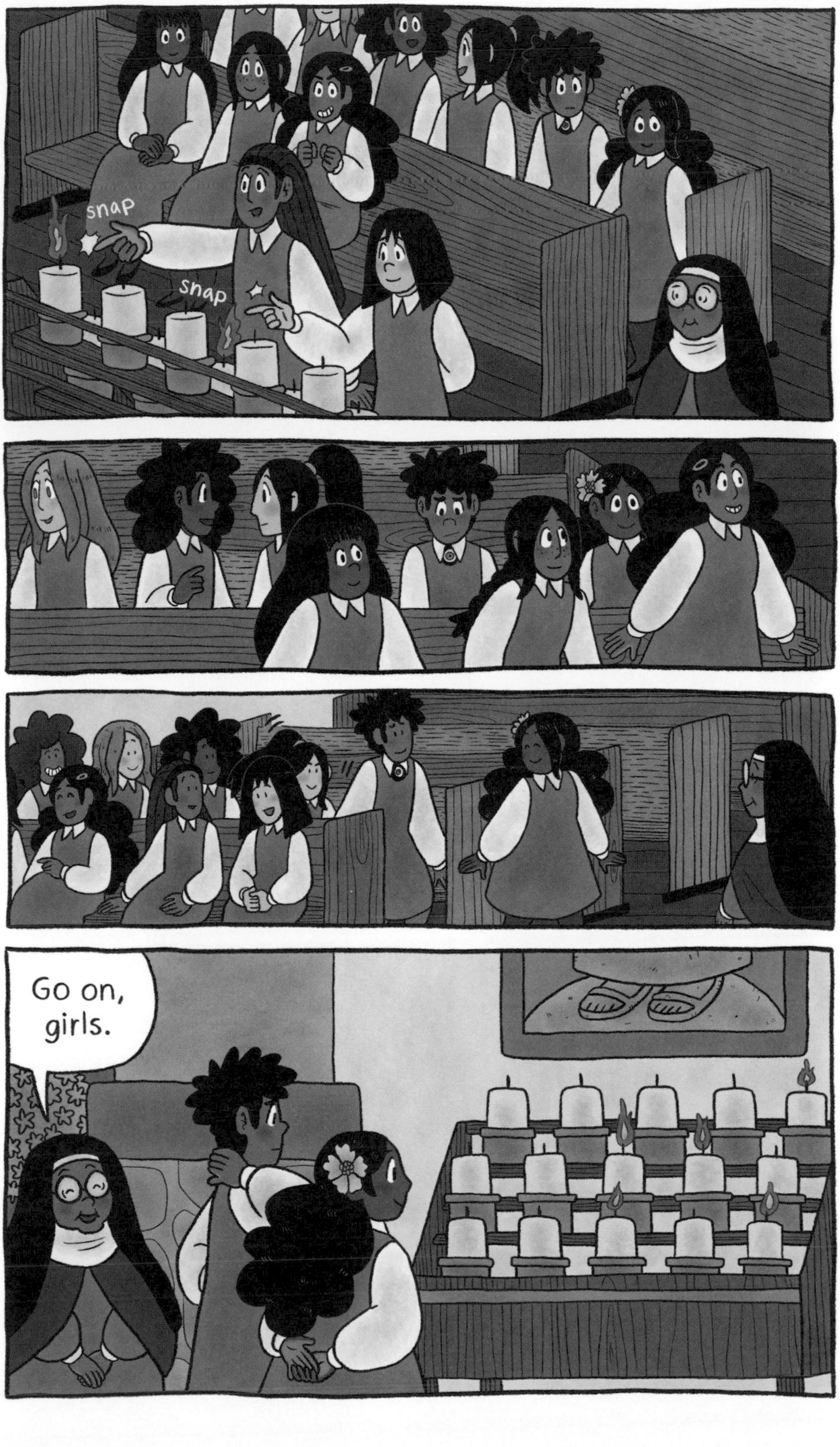
snap
snap
Go on, girls.

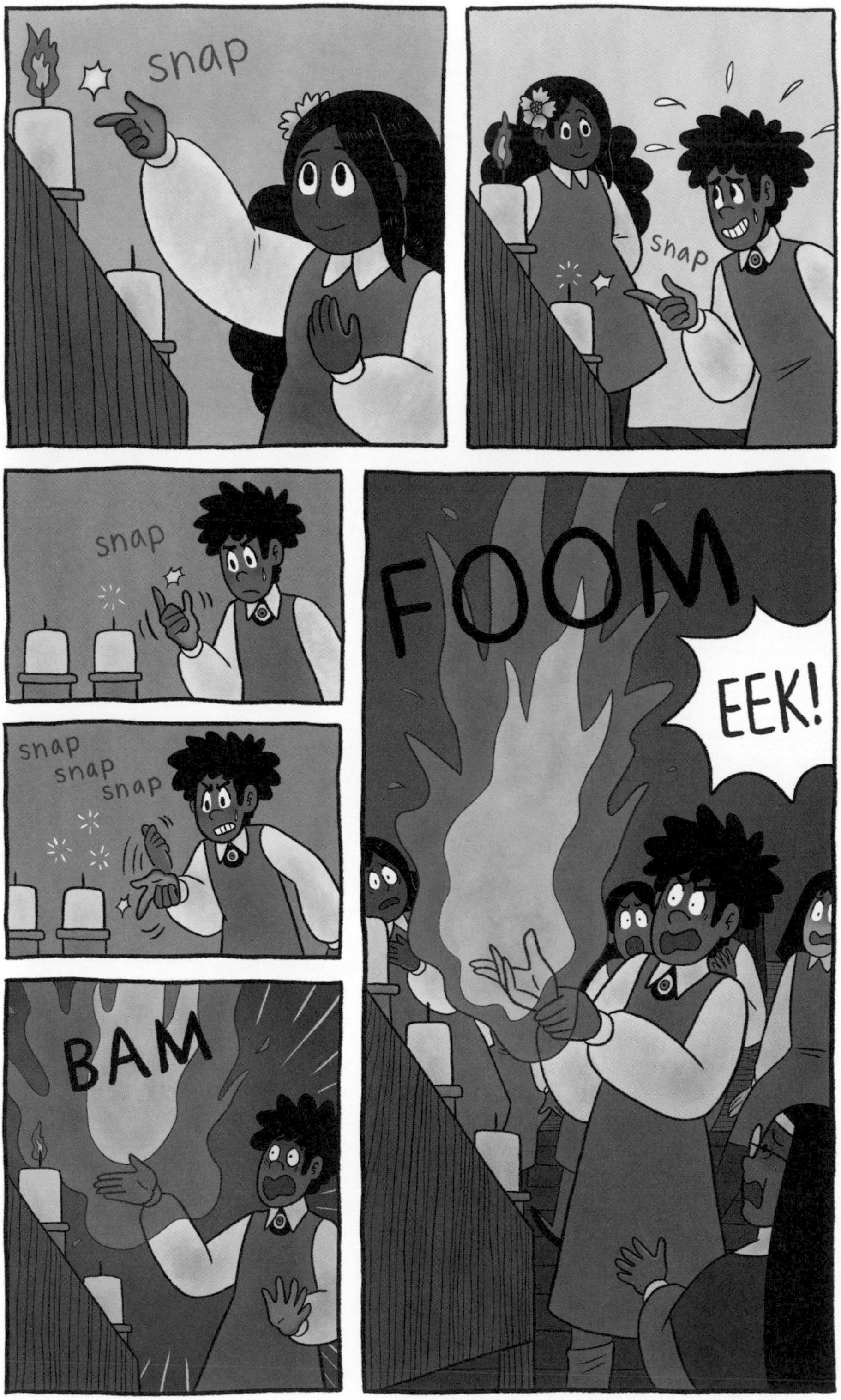
snap
snap
snap
snap
snap
snap
BAM
FOOM
EEK!

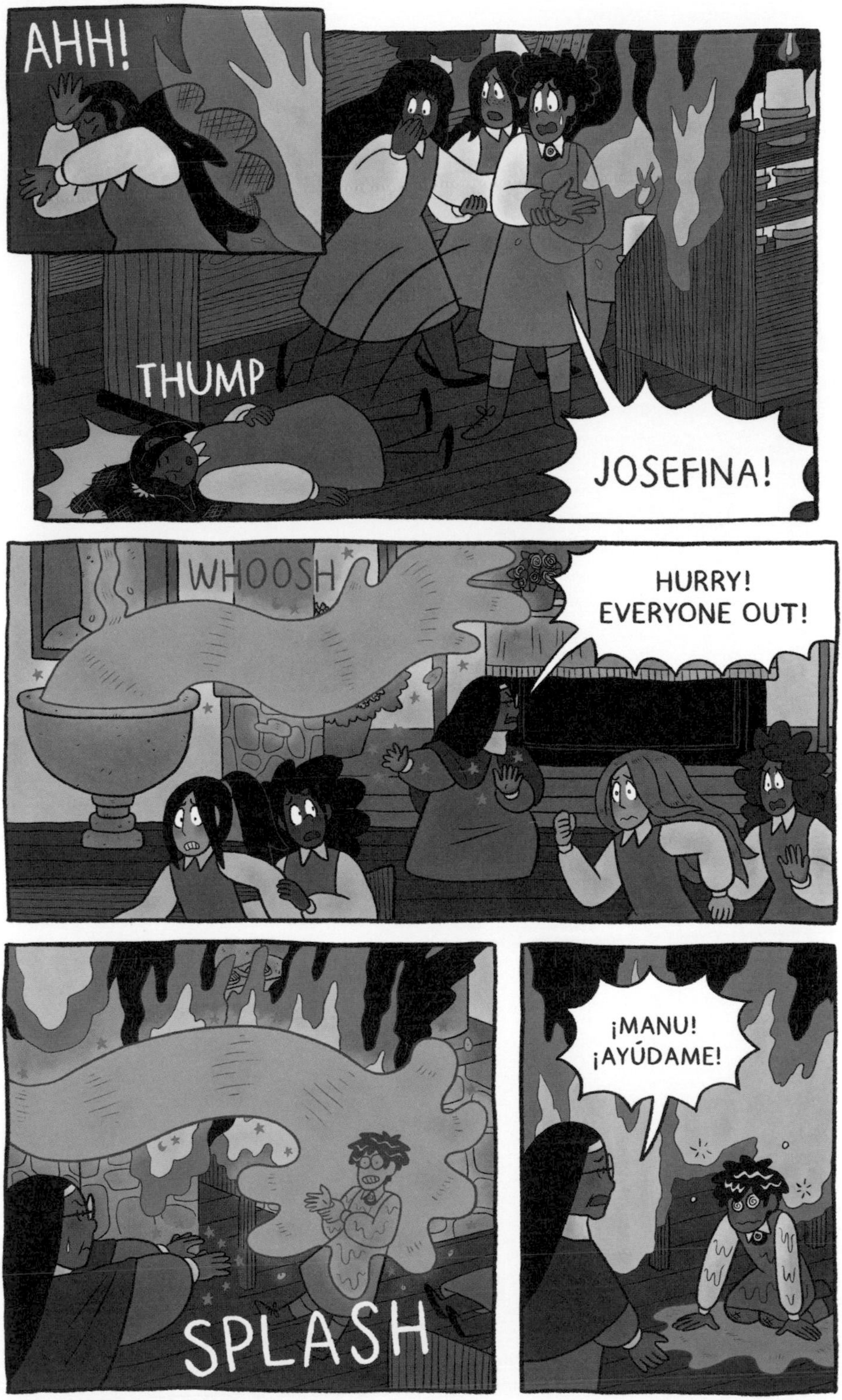
AHH!
THUMP
JOSEFINA!
WHOOSH
HURRY! EVERYONE OUT!
SPLASH
¡MANU! ¡AYÚDAME!

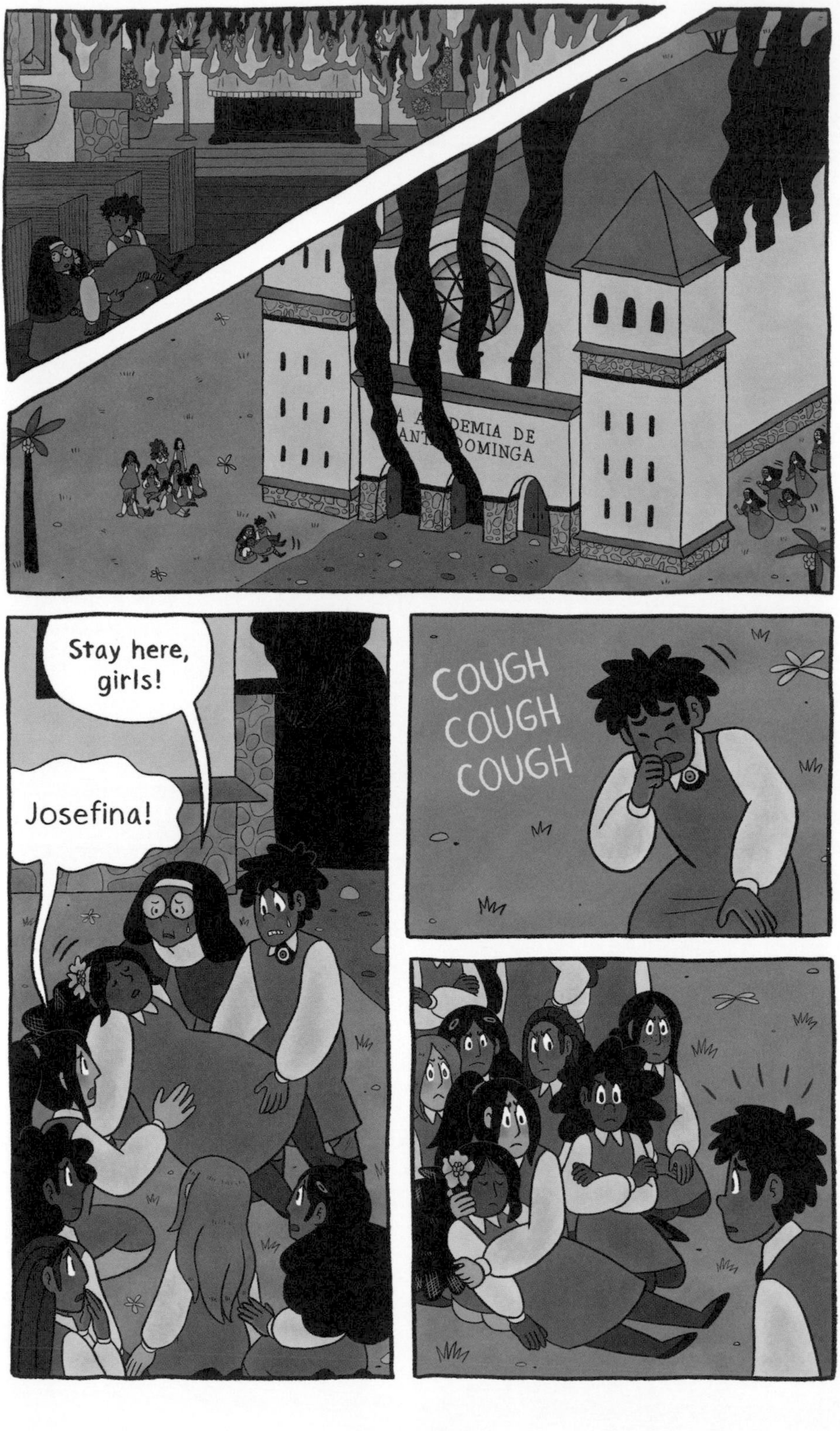
A ACADEMIA DE
SANTA DOMINGA
Stay here, girls!
Josefina!
COUGH
COUGH
COUGH

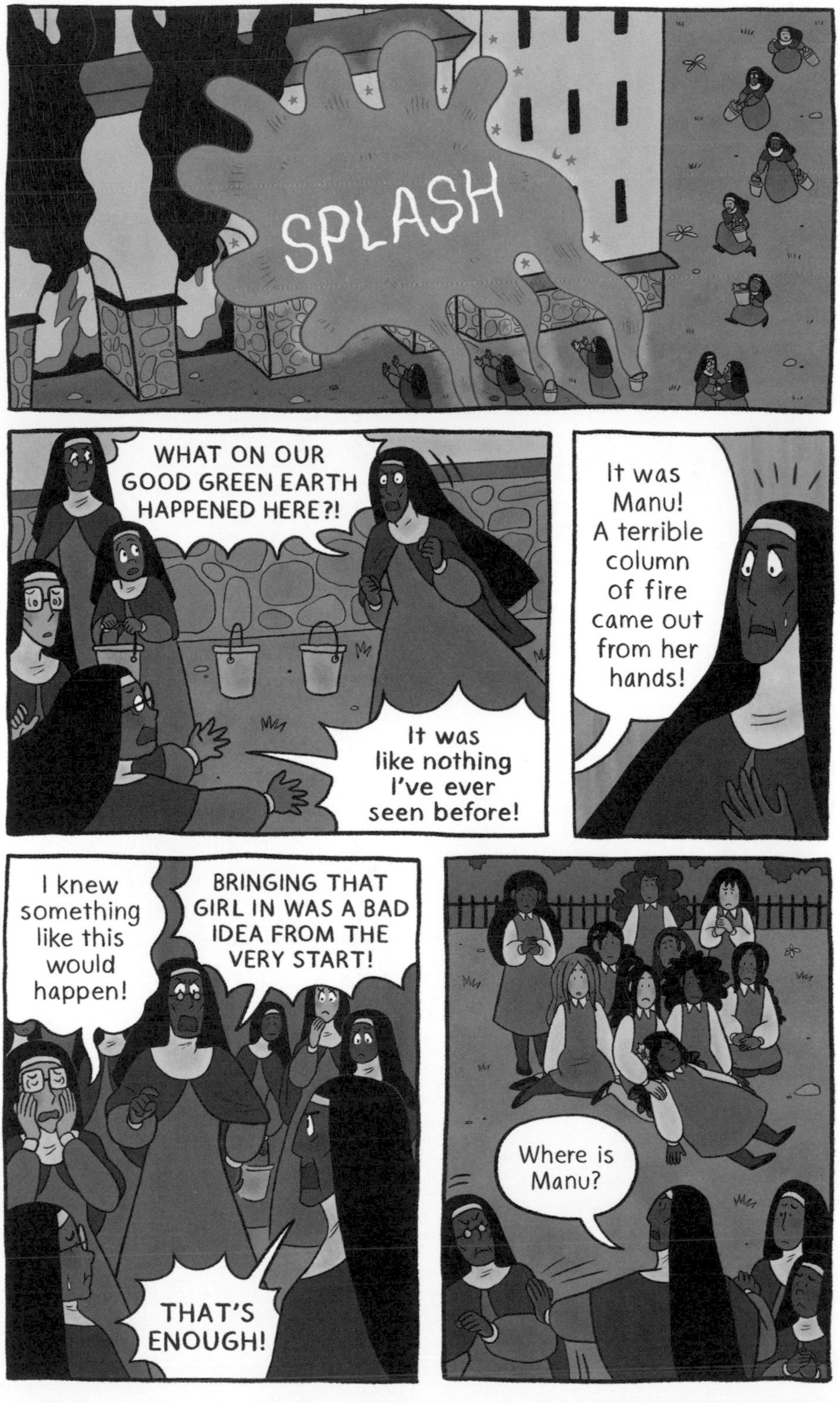
SPLASH
WHAT ON OUR GOOD GREEN EARTH HAPPENED HERE?!
It was like nothing I've ever seen before!
It was Manu! A terrible column of fire came out from her hands!
I knew something like this would happen!
BRINGING THAT GIRL IN WAS A BAD IDEA FROM THE VERY START!
THAT'S ENOUGH!
Where is Manu?

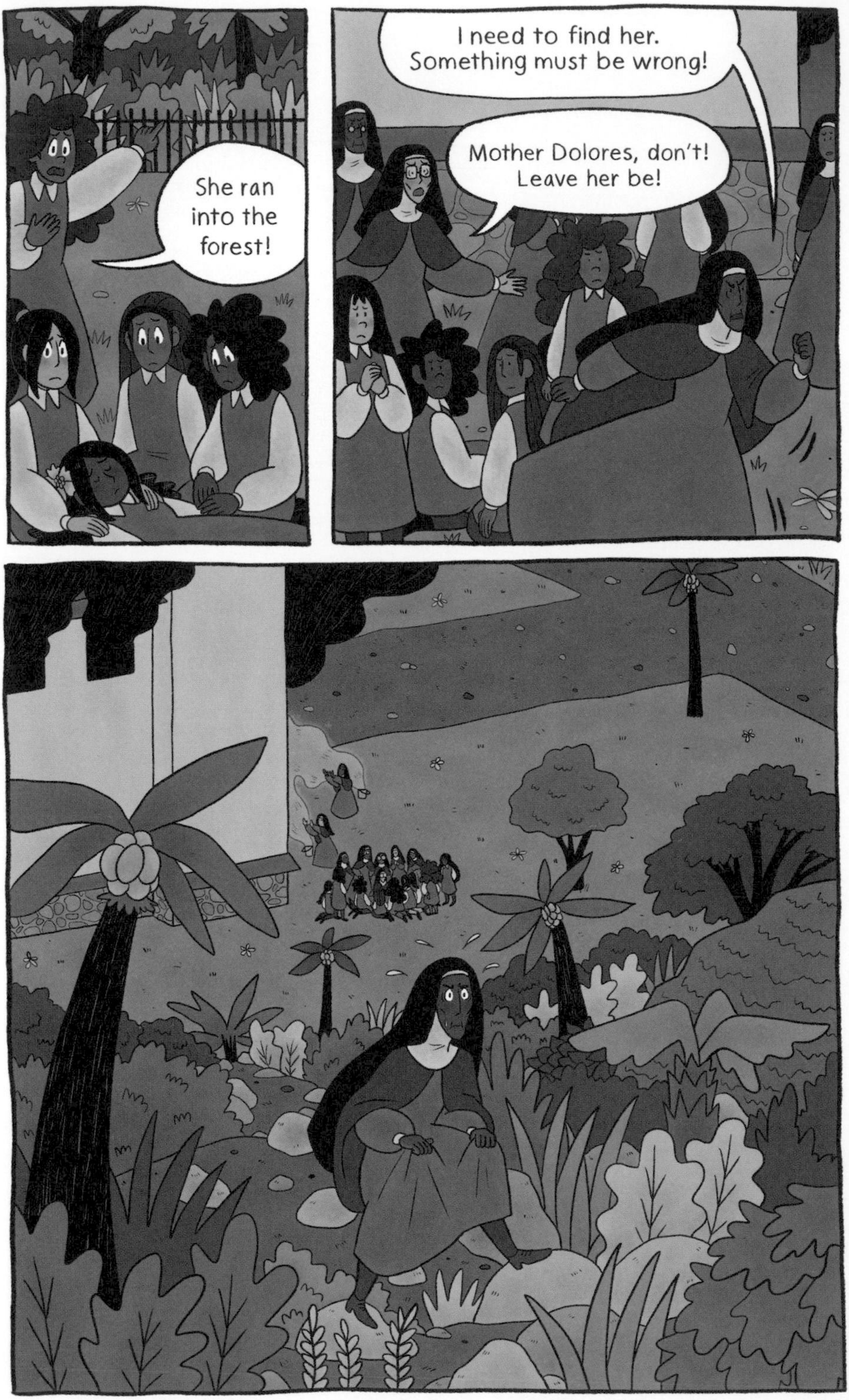
She ran into the forest!
I need to find her. Something must be wrong!
Mother Dolores, don't! Leave her be!

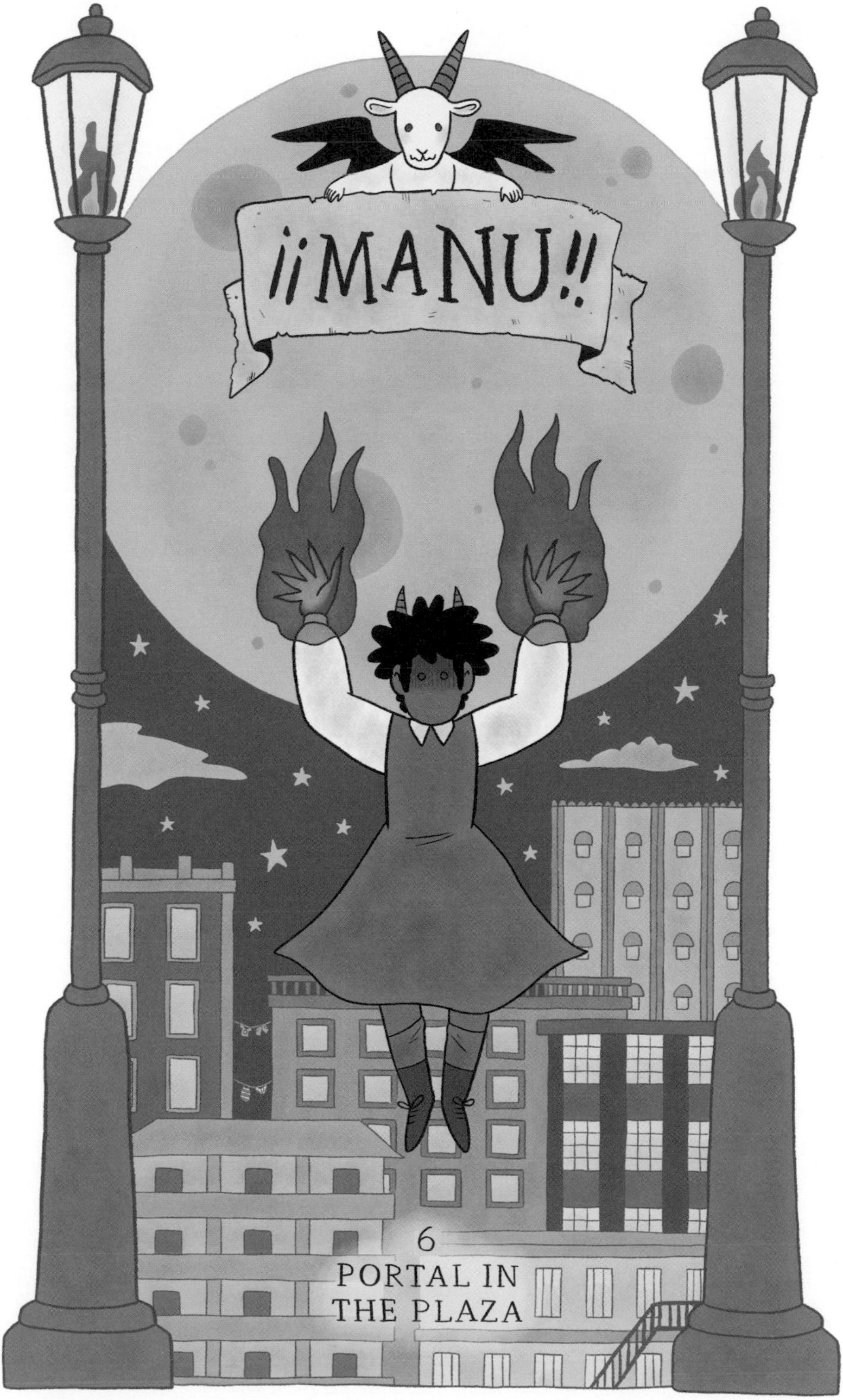
¡¡MANU!!

6
PORTAL IN THE PLAZA

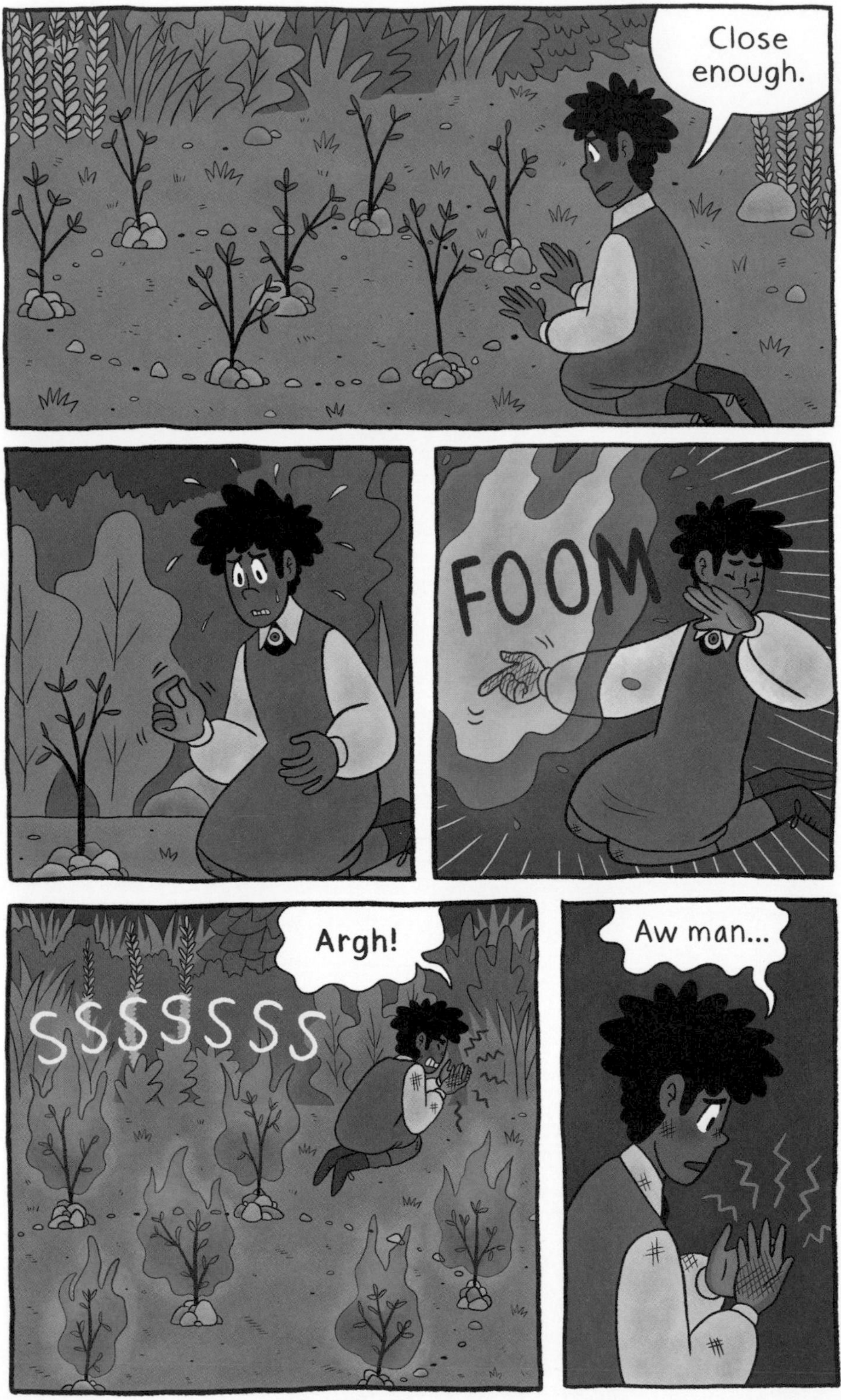
Close enough.
FOOM
Argh!
SSSSSSS
Aw man...

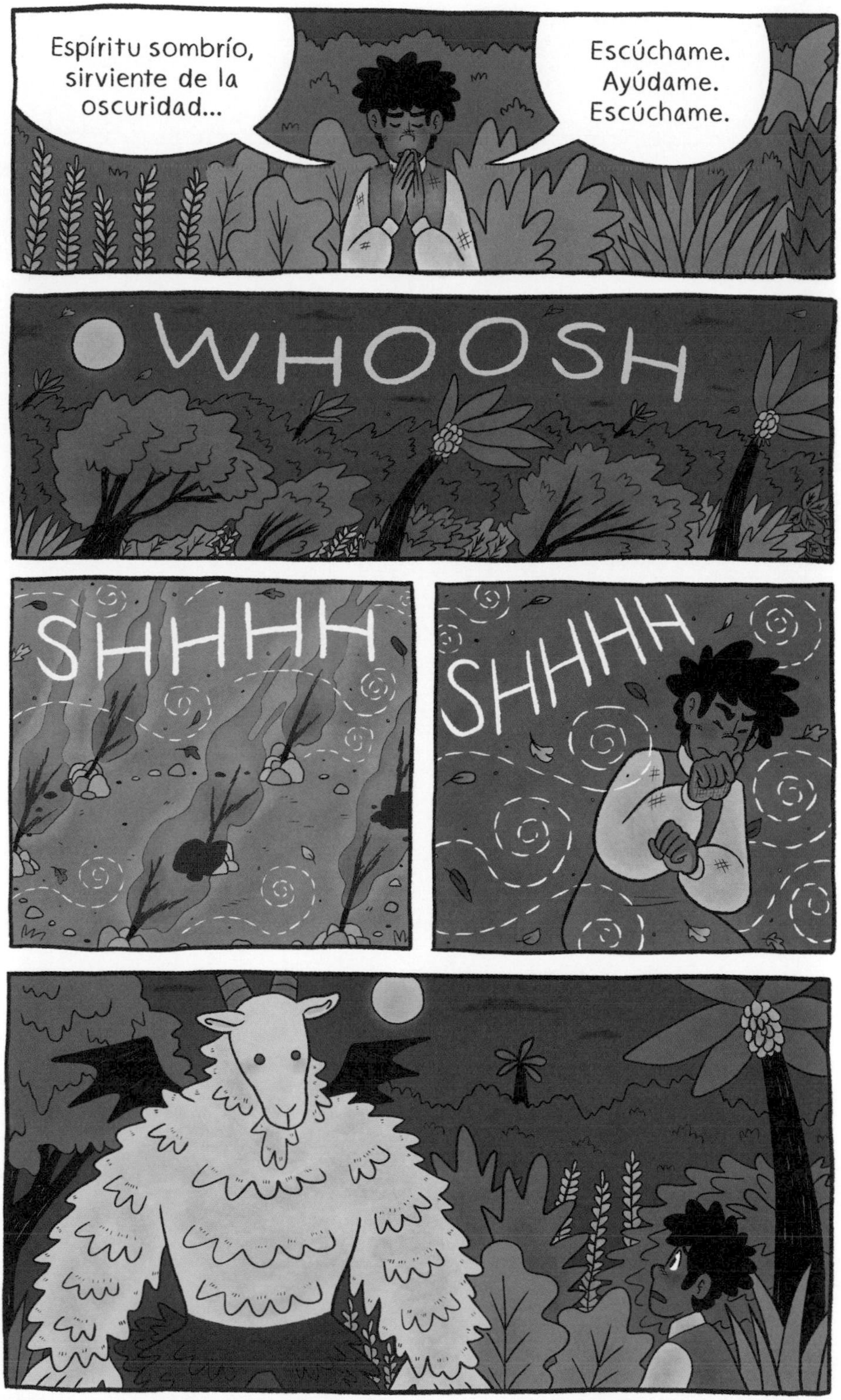
Espíritu sombrío, sirviente de la oscuridad...
Escúchame. Ayúdame. Escúchame.
WHOOSH
SHHHH
SHHHH

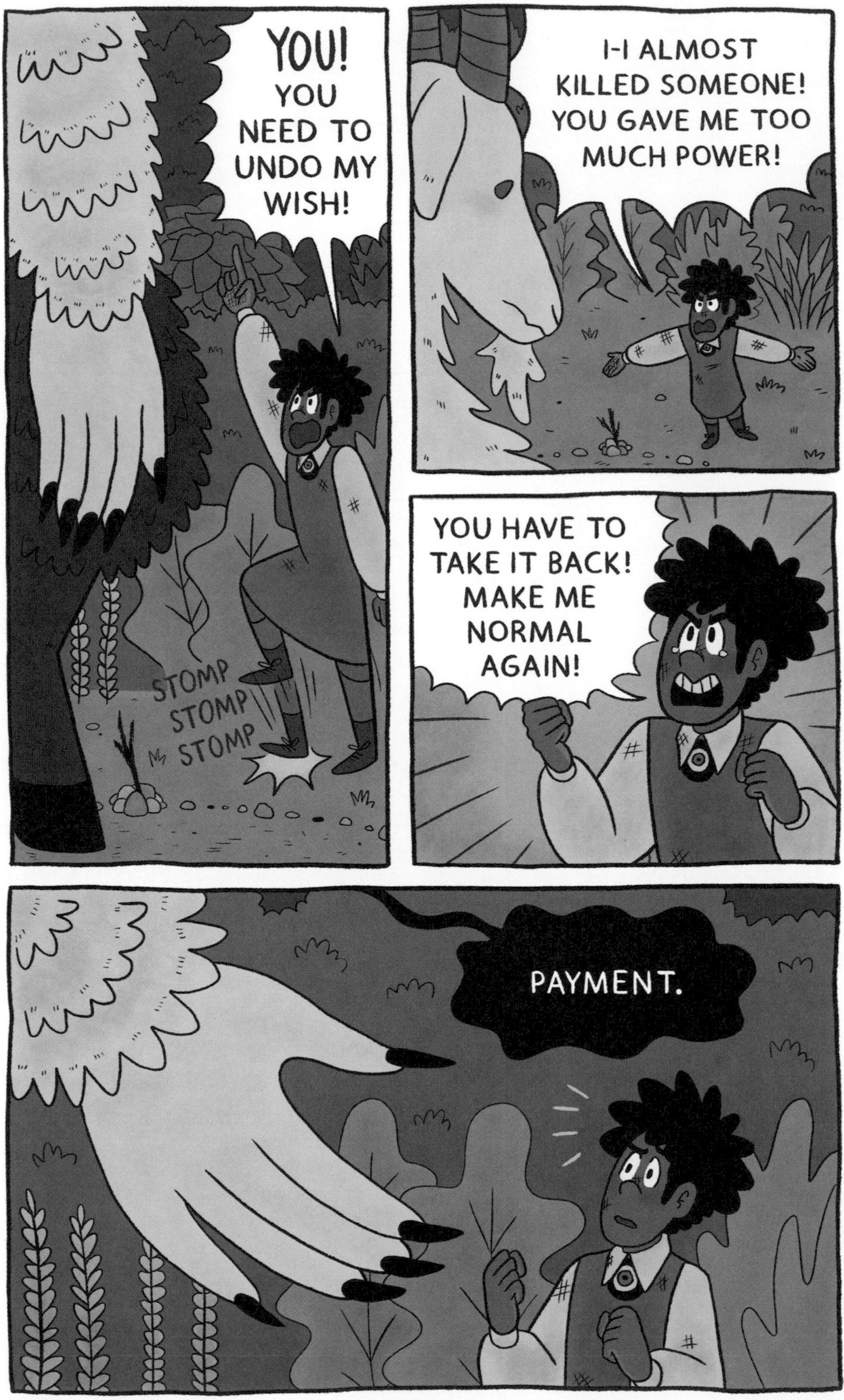
YOU! YOU NEED TO UNDO MY WISH!
STOMP STOMP STOMP
I-I ALMOST KILLED SOMEONE! YOU GAVE ME TOO MUCH POWER!
YOU HAVE TO TAKE IT BACK! MAKE ME NORMAL AGAIN!
PAYMENT.

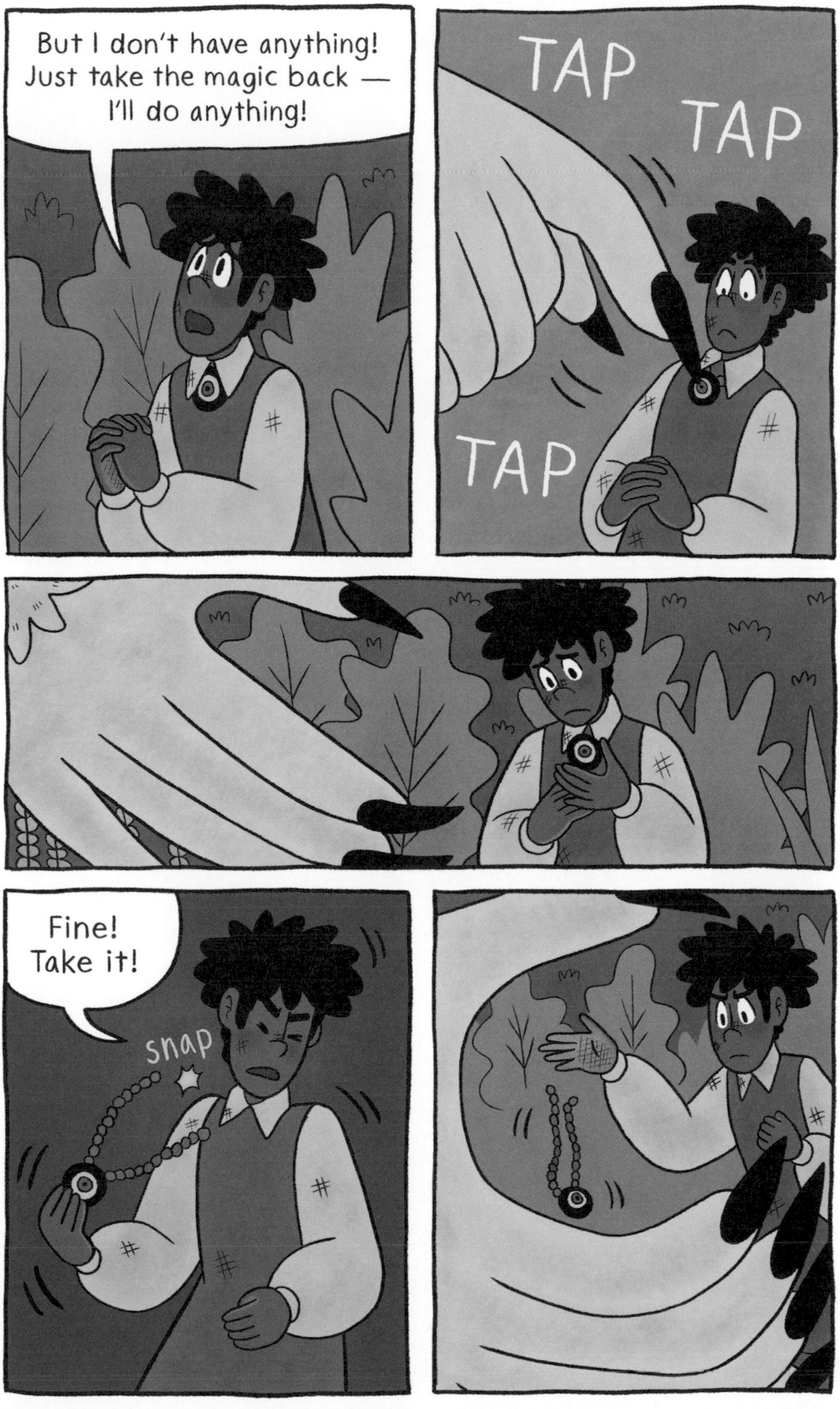

But I don't have anything! Just take the magic back — I'll do anything!
TAP
TAP
TAP
Fine! Take it!
snap

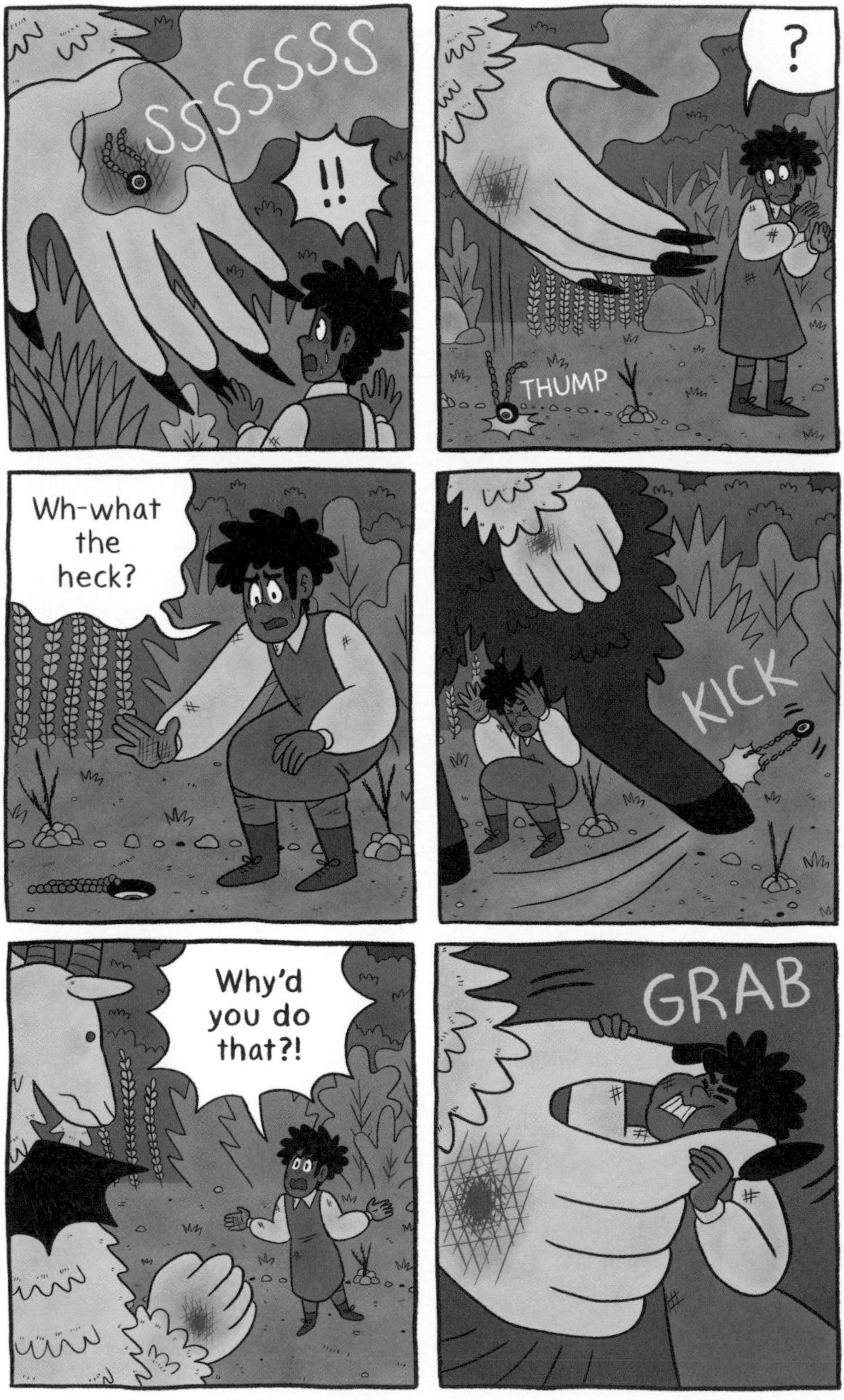
SSSSSSSS
!!
?
THUMP
Wh-what the heck?
KICK
Why'd you do that?!
GRAB

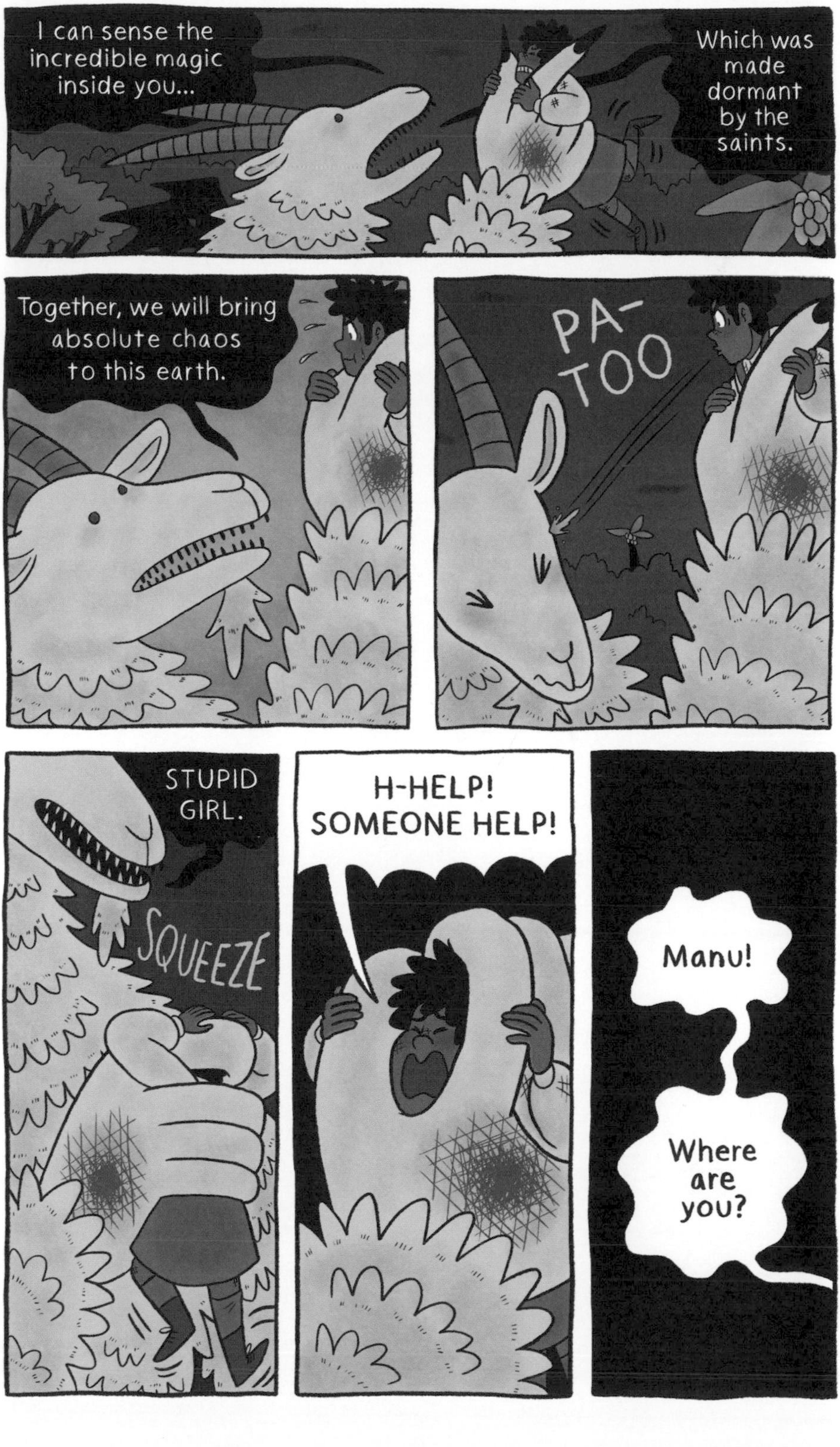
I can sense the incredible magic inside you...
Which was made dormant by the saints.
Together, we will bring absolute chaos to this earth.
PA-TOO
STUPID GIRL.
SQUEEZE
H-HELP! SOMEONE HELP!
Manu!
Where are you?

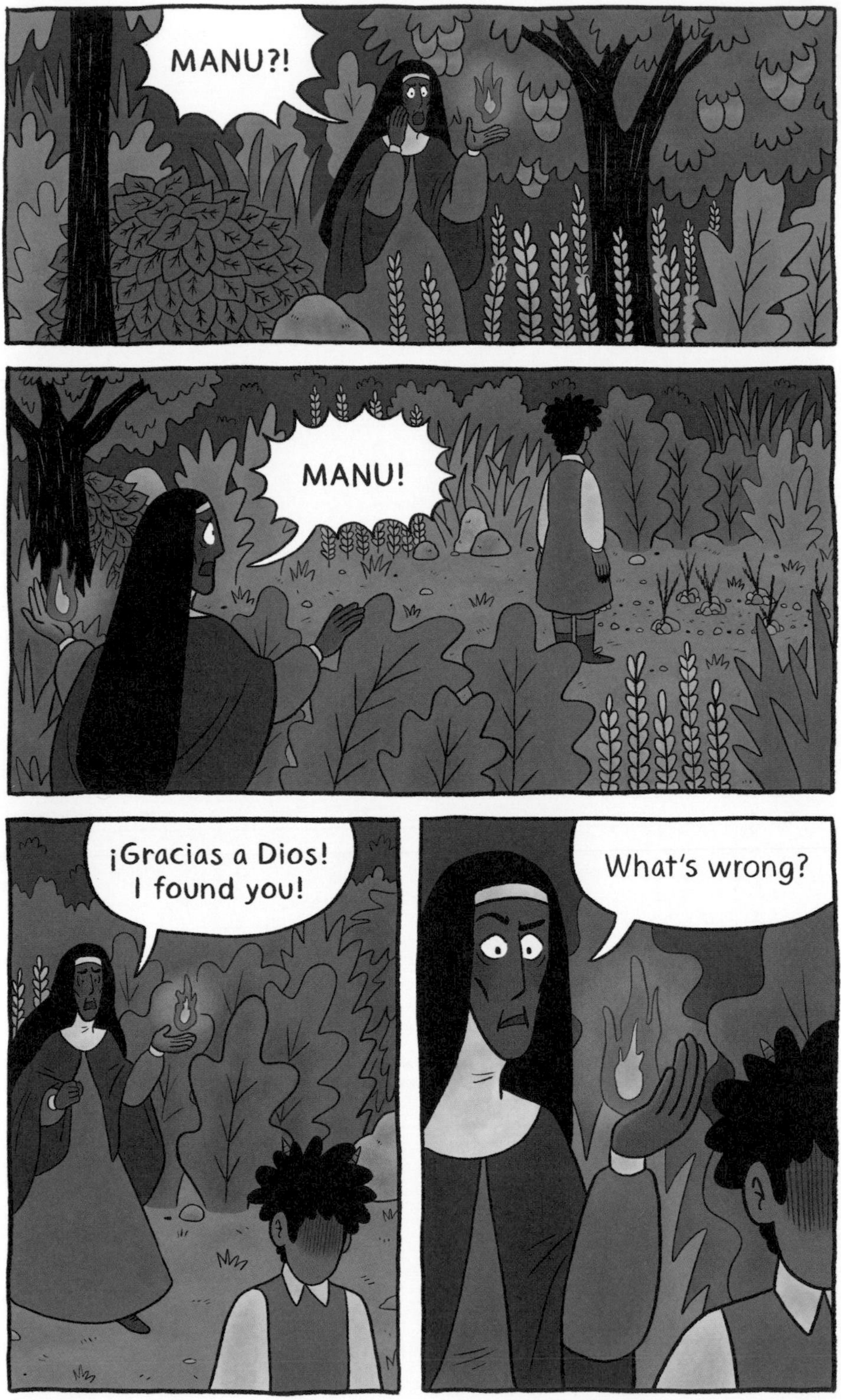
MANU?!
MANU!
¡Gracias a Dios! I found you!
What's wrong?

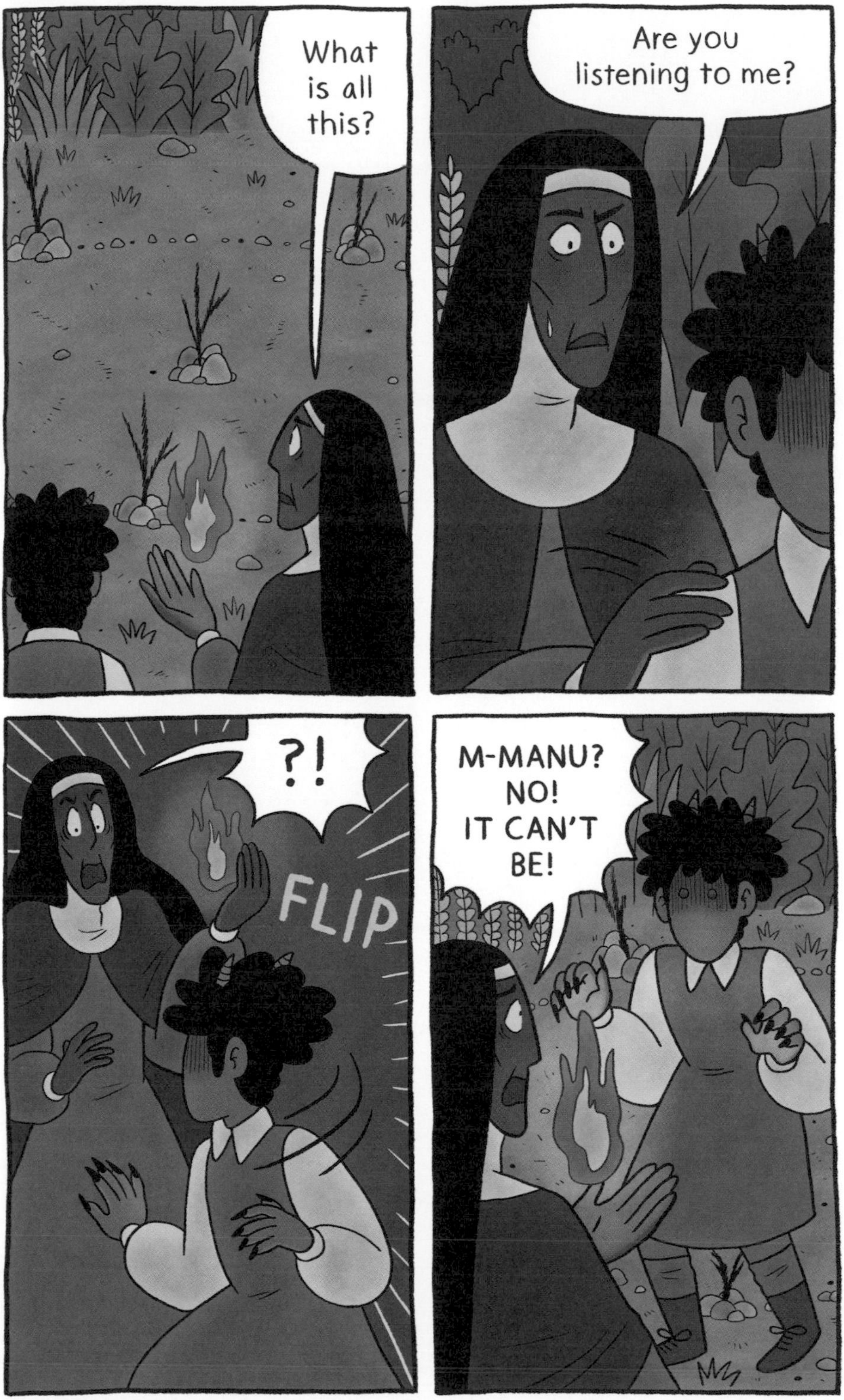
What is all this?
Are you listening to me?
?!
FLIP
M-MANU? NO! IT CAN'T BE!

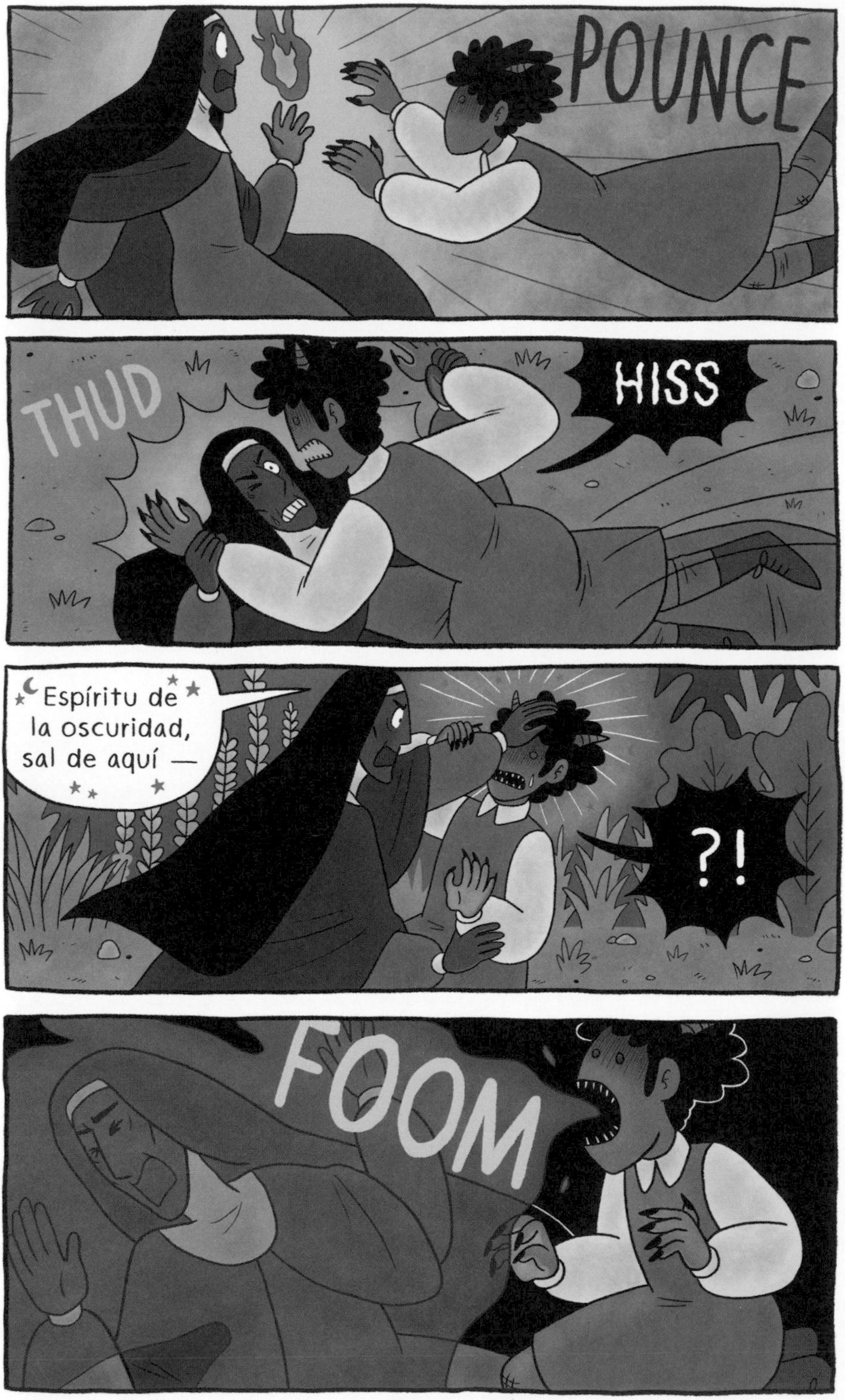
POUNCE
THUD
HISS
Espíritu de la oscuridad, sal de aquí —
?!
FOOM

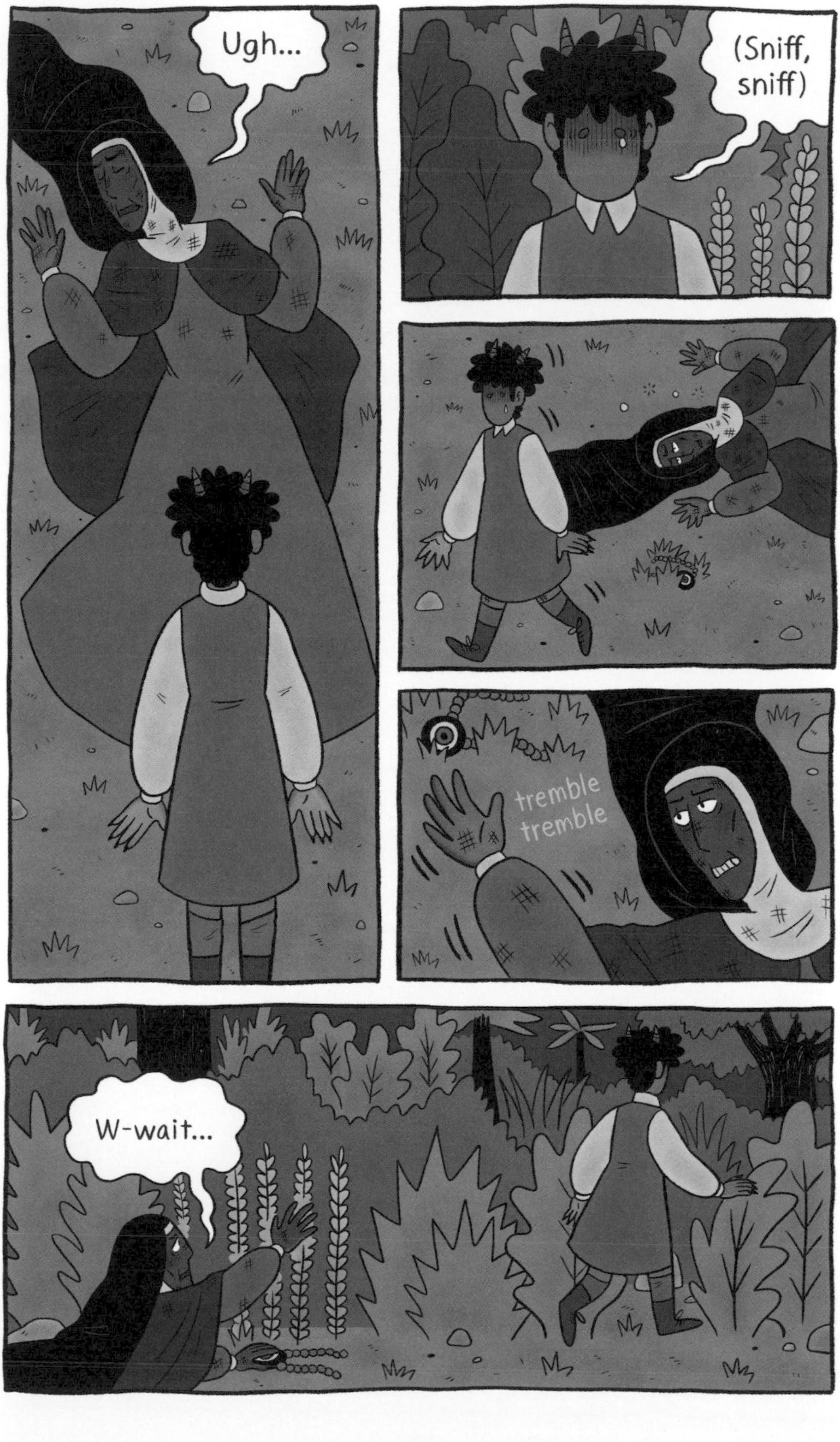
Ugh...
(Sniff, sniff)
tremble tremble
W-wait...

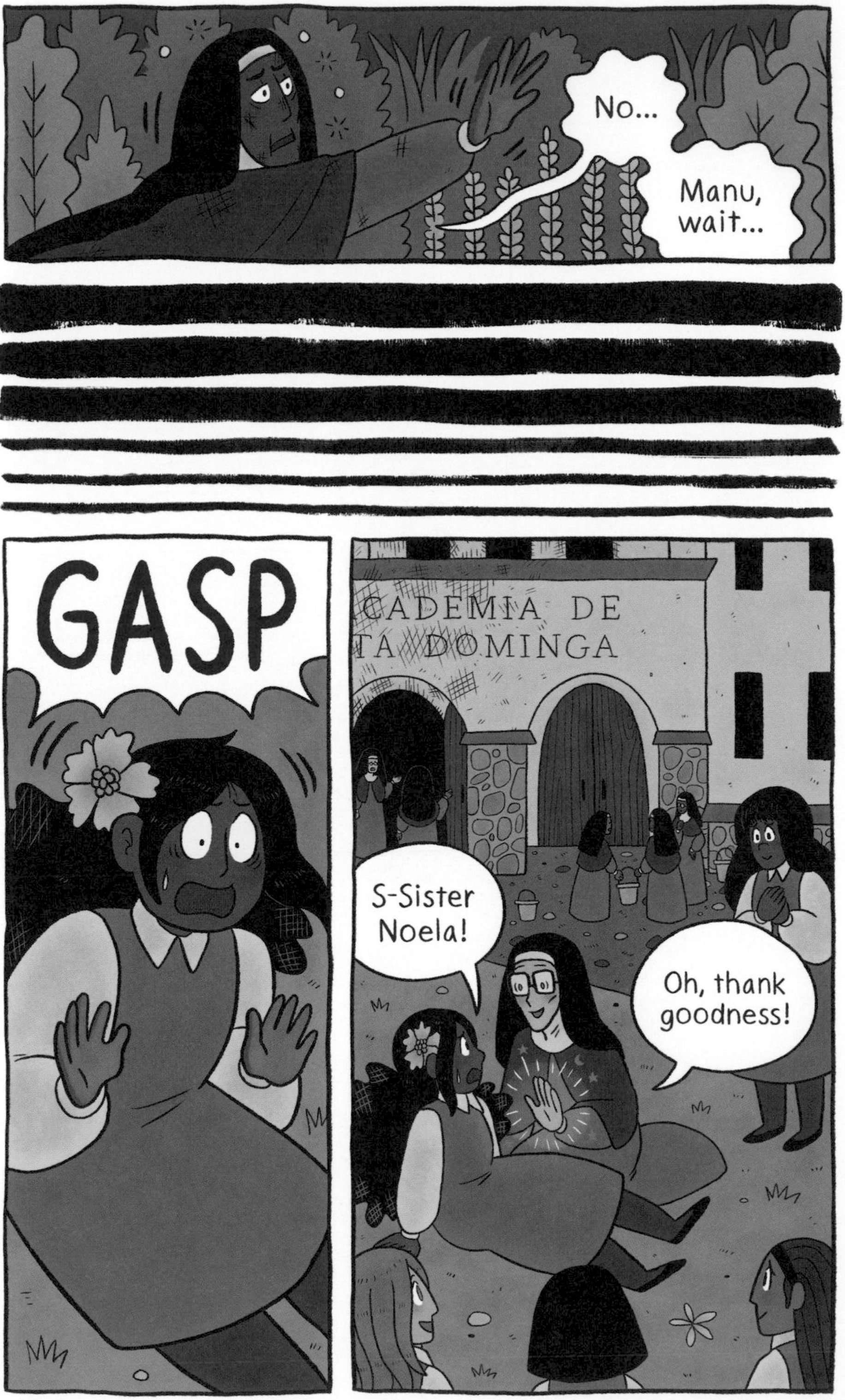
No...
Manu, wait...
GASP
CADEMIA DE
TA DOMINGA
S-Sister Noela!
Oh, thank goodness!

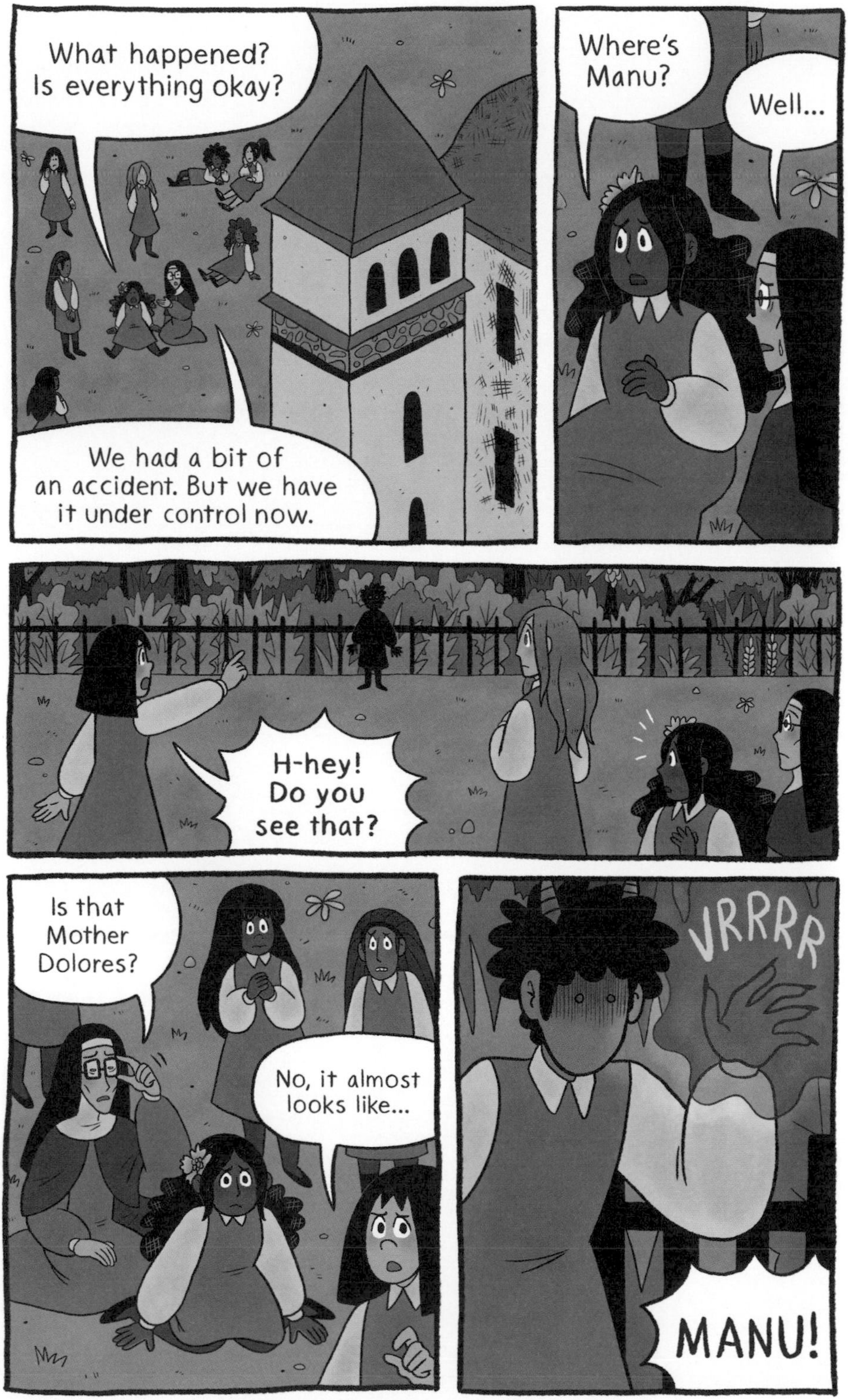
What happened?
Is everything okay?
We had a bit of an accident. But we have it under control now.
Where's Manu?
Well...
H-hey! Do you see that?
Is that Mother Dolores?
No, it almost looks like...
VRRRR
MANU!

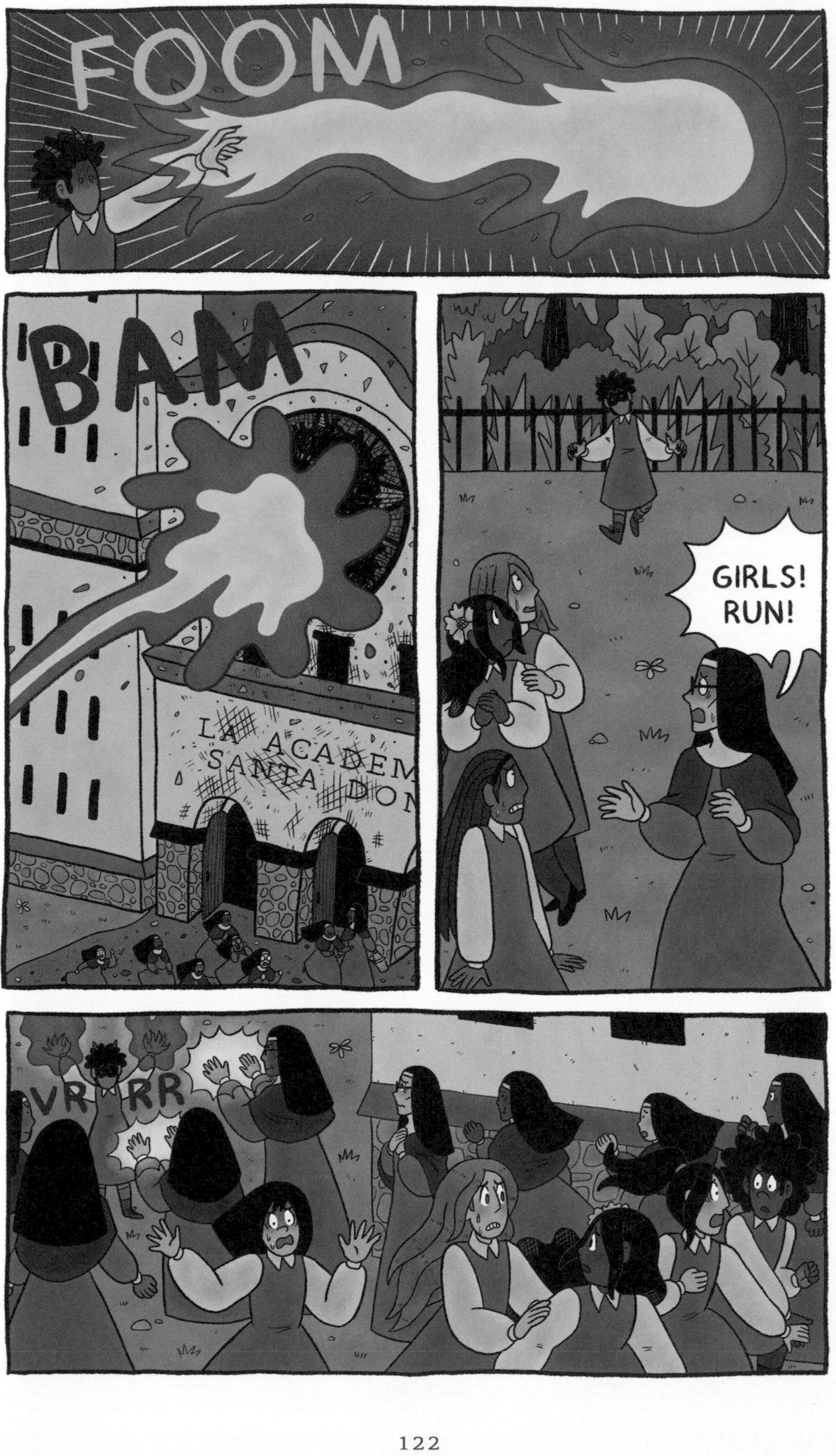
FOOM
BAM
LA ACADEM
SANTA DON
GIRLS! RUN!
VRRR

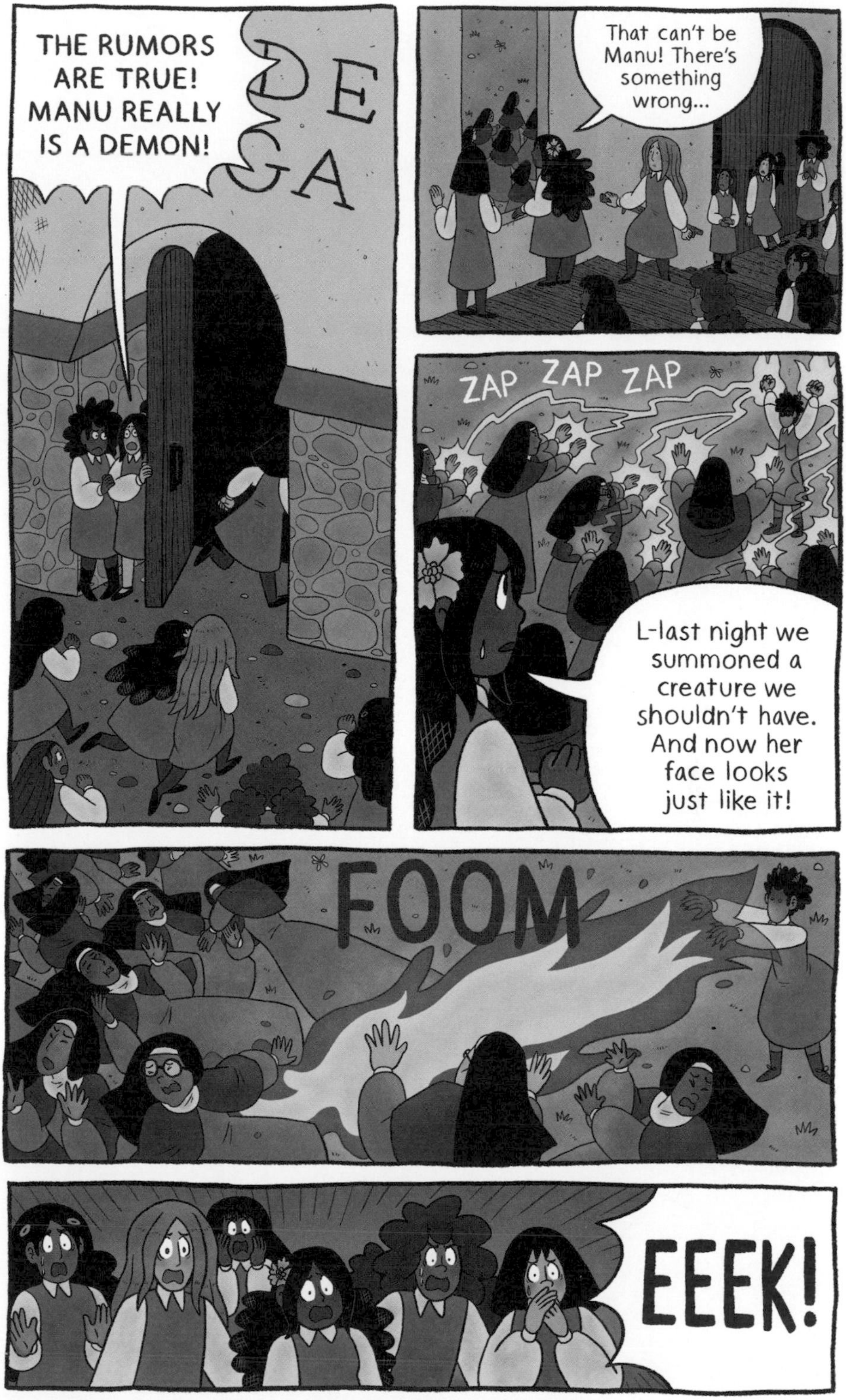
THE RUMORS ARE TRUE! MANU REALLY IS A DEMON!
DE GA
That can't be Manu! There's something wrong...
ZAP ZAP ZAP
L-last night we summoned a creature we shouldn't have. And now her face looks just like it!
FOOM
EEEK!

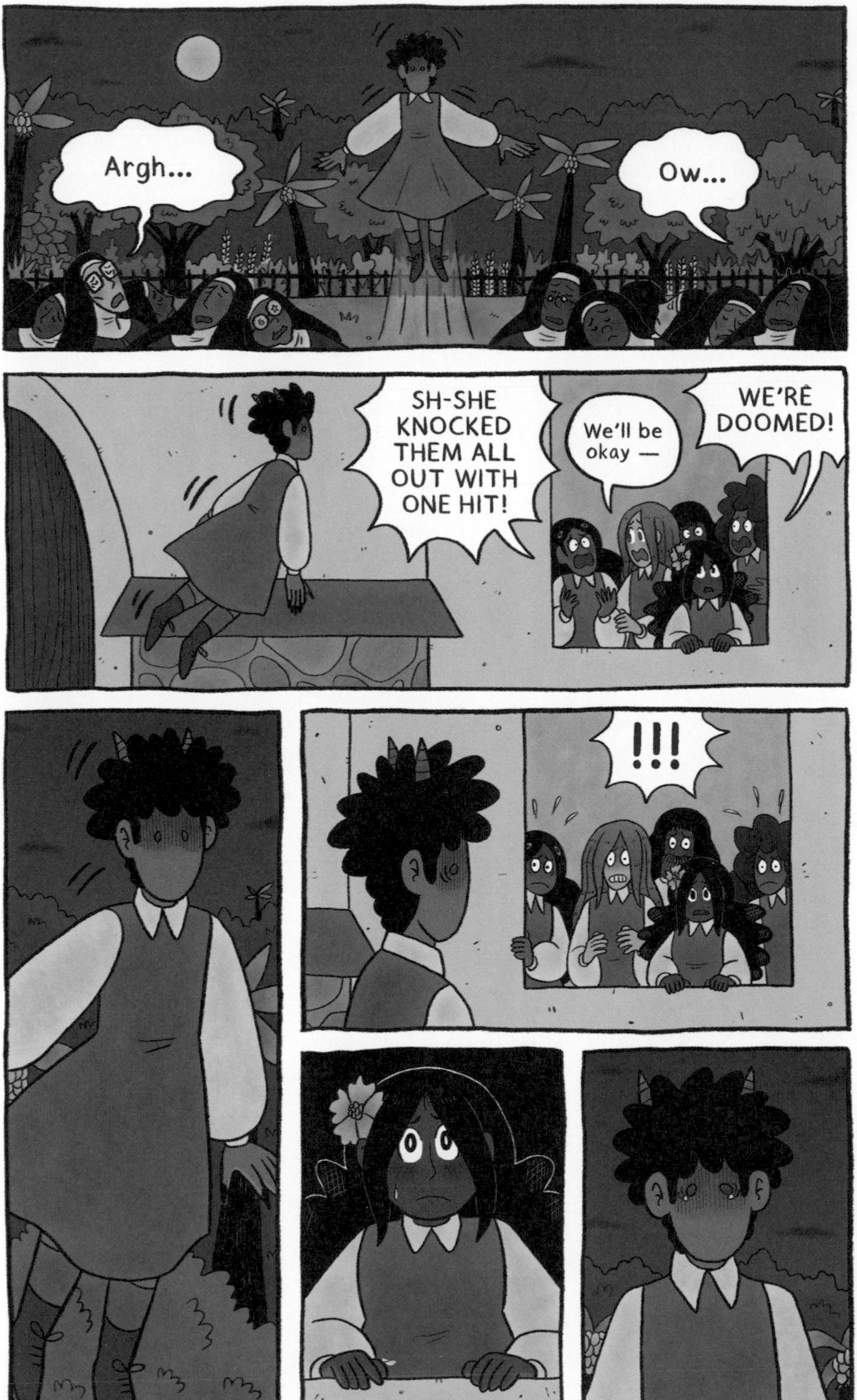
Argh...
Ow...
SH-SHE KNOCKED THEM ALL OUT WITH ONE HIT!
We'll be okay —
WE'RE DOOMED!
!!!

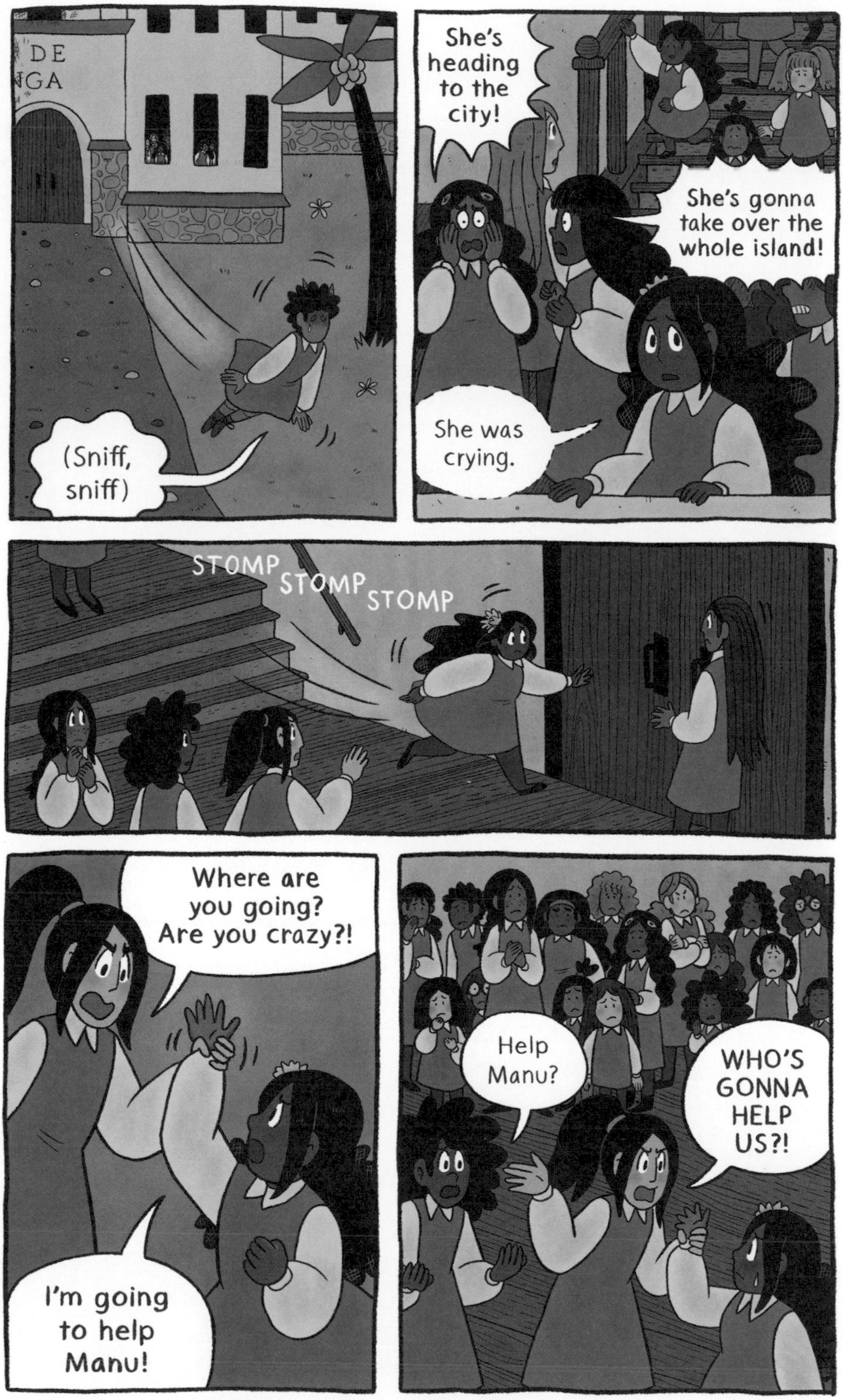
DE
NGA
(Sniff, sniff)
She's heading to the city!
She's gonna take over the whole island!
She was crying.
STOMP STOMP STOMP
Where are you going? Are you crazy?!
I'm going to help Manu!
Help Manu?
WHO'S GONNA HELP US?!

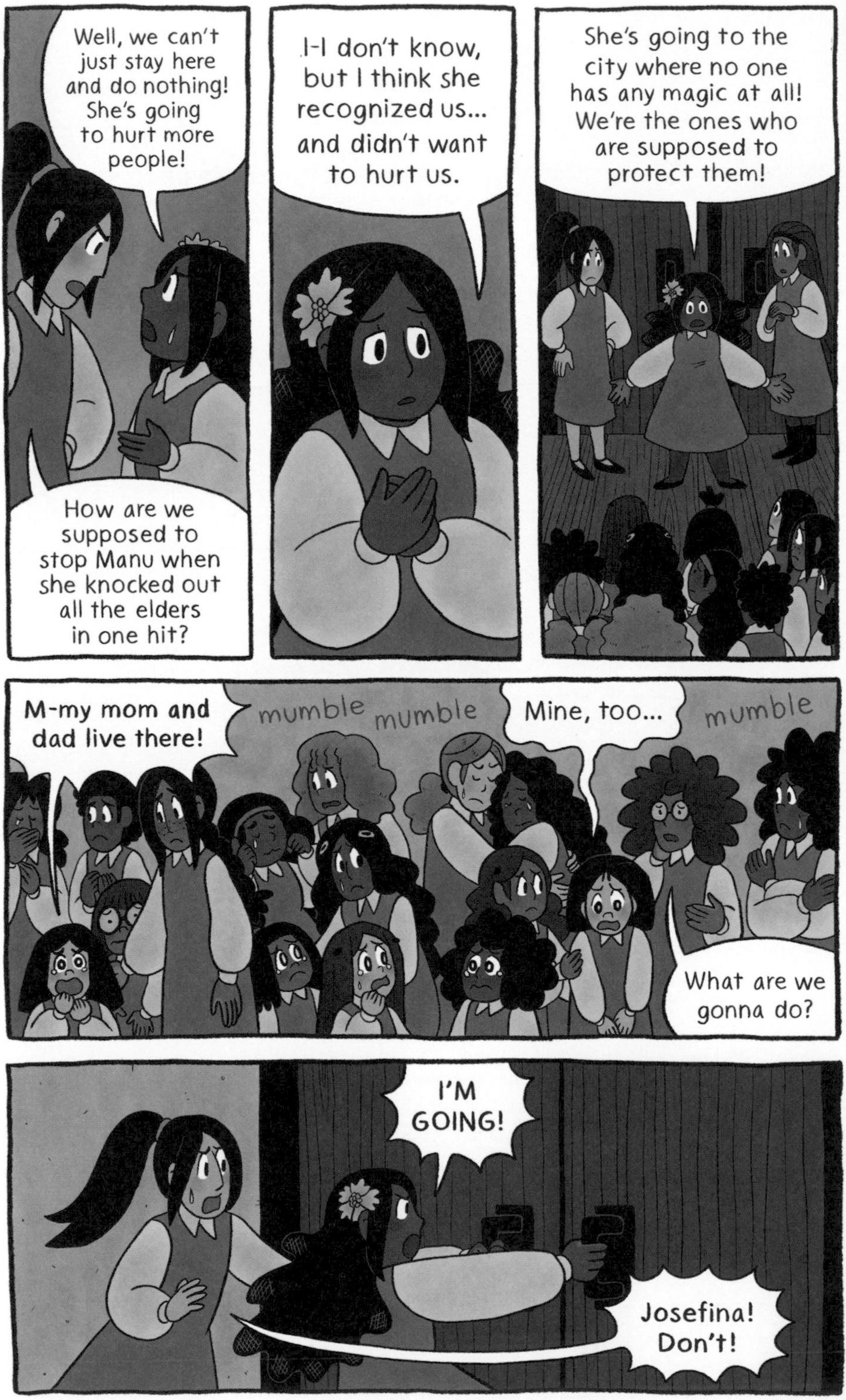
Well, we can't just stay here and do nothing! She's going to hurt more people!
How are we supposed to stop Manu when she knocked out all the elders in one hit?
I-I don't know, but I think she recognized us... and didn't want to hurt us.
She's going to the city where no one has any magic at all! We're the ones who are supposed to protect them!
M-my mom and dad live there!
mumble
mumble
Mine, too...
mumble
What are we gonna do?
I'M GOING!
Josefina! Don't!

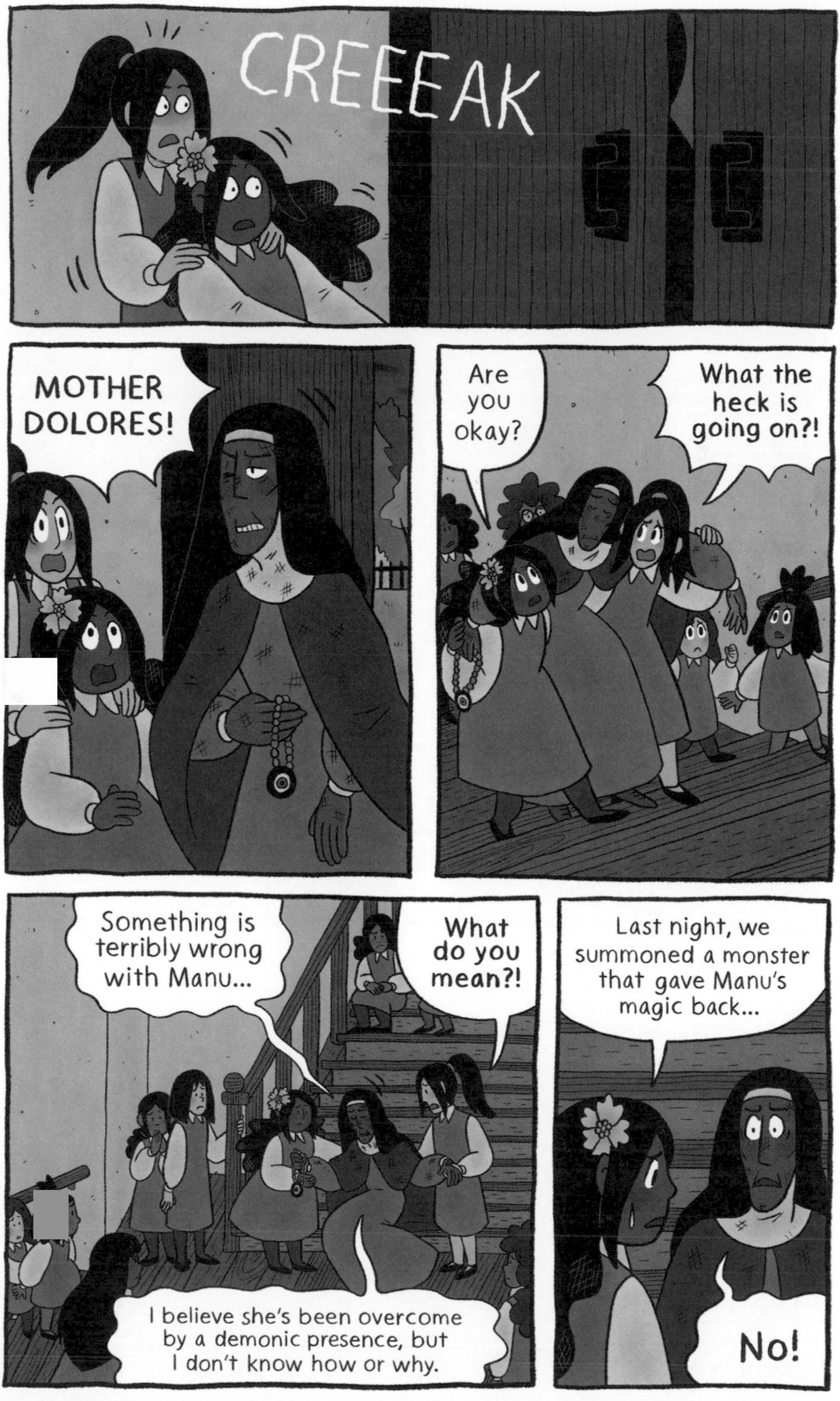
CREEEAK
MOTHER DOLORES!
Are you okay?
What the heck is going on?!
Something is terribly wrong with Manu...
What do you mean?!
I believe she's been overcome by a demonic presence, but I don't know how or why.
Last night, we summoned a monster that gave Manu's magic back...
No!

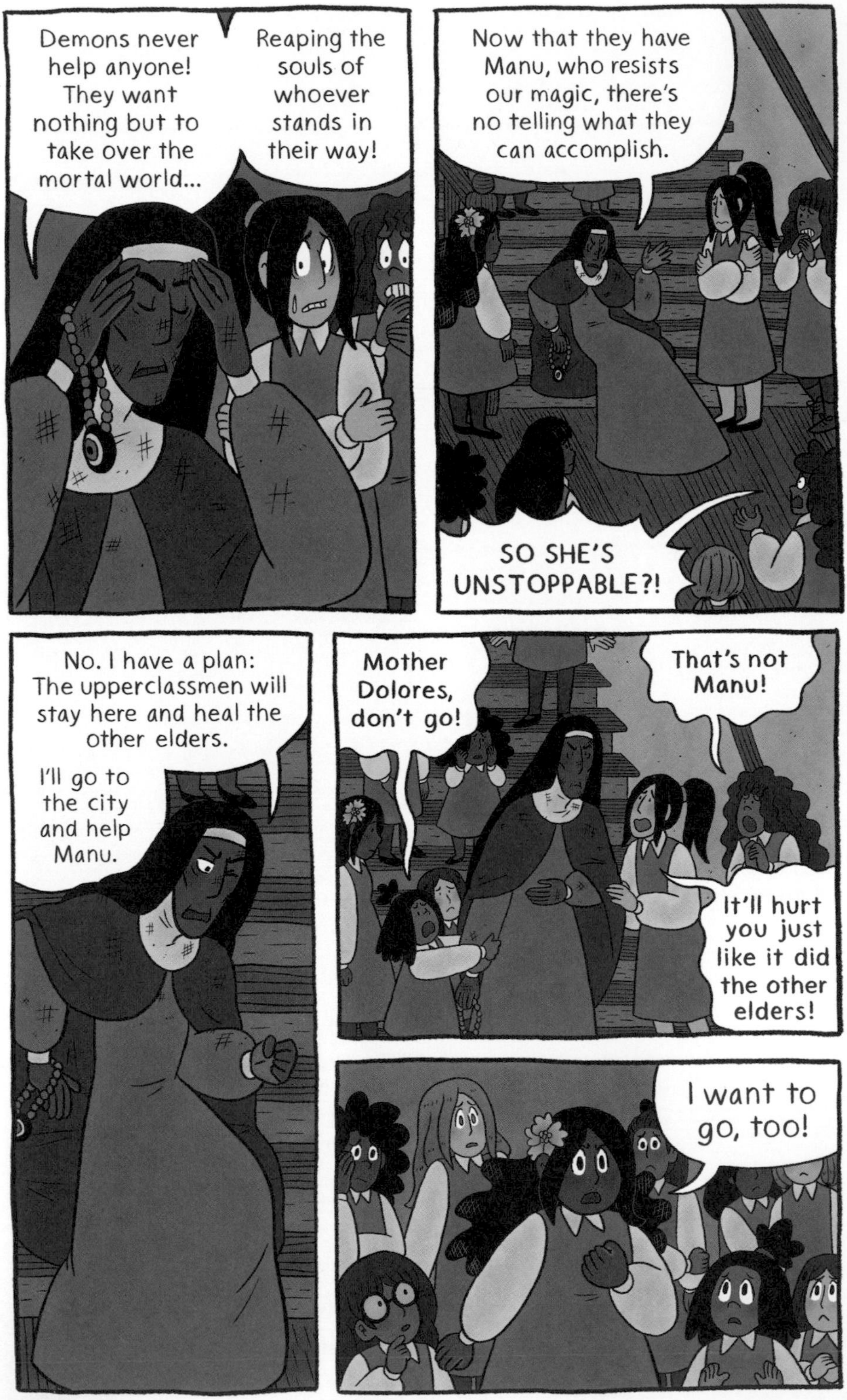
Demons never help anyone! They want nothing but to take over the mortal world...
Reaping the souls of whoever stands in their way!
Now that they have Manu, who resists our magic, there's no telling what they can accomplish.
SO SHE'S UNSTOPPABLE?!
No. I have a plan: The upperclassmen will stay here and heal the other elders.
I'll go to the city and help Manu.
Mother Dolores, don't go!
That's not Manu!
It'll hurt you just like it did the other elders!
I want to go, too!

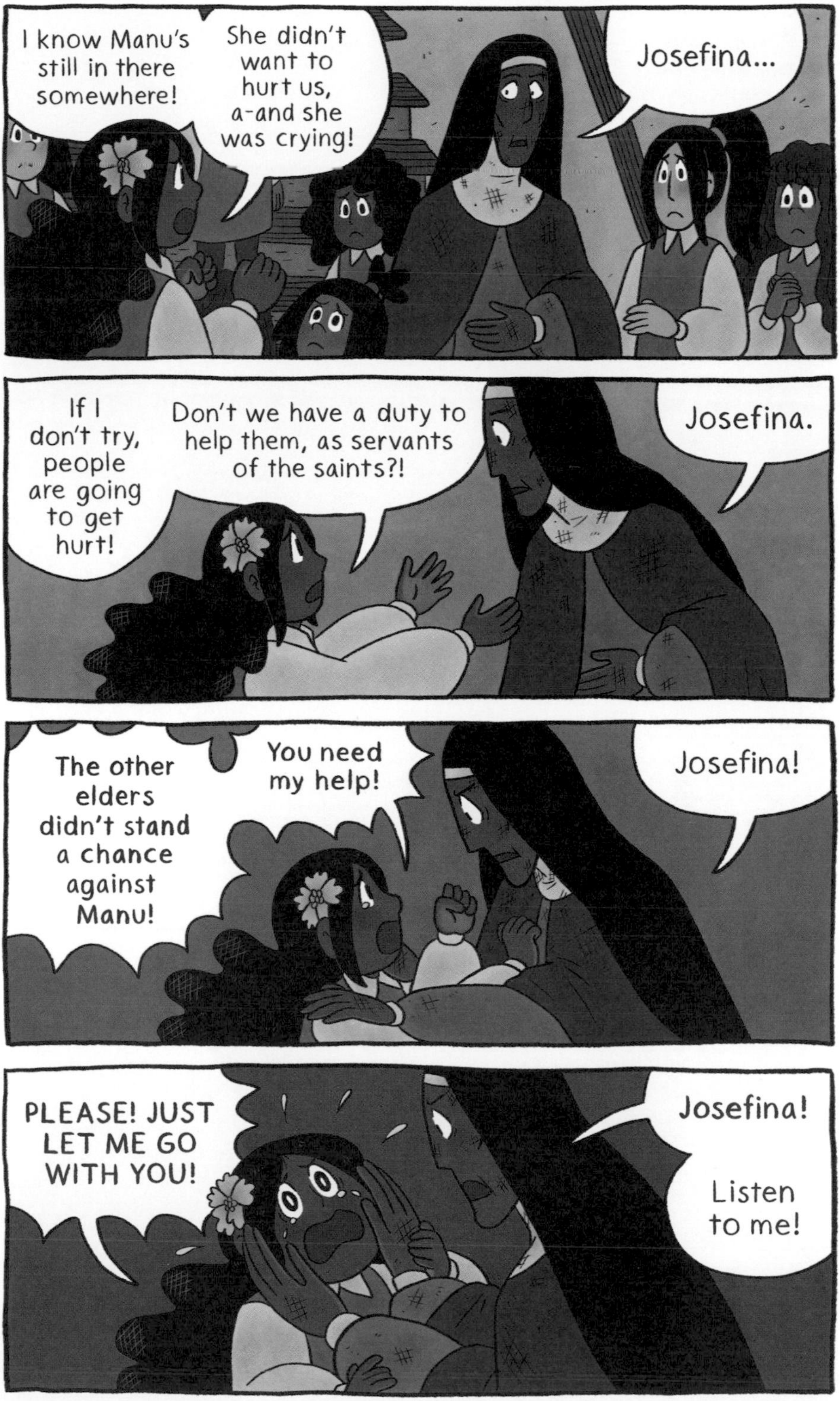
I know Manu's still in there somewhere!
She didn't want to hurt us, a-and she was crying!
Josefina...
If I don't try, people are going to get hurt!
Don't we have a duty to help them, as servants of the saints?!
Josefina.
The other elders didn't stand a chance against Manu!
You need my help!
Josefina!
PLEASE! JUST LET ME GO WITH YOU!
Josefina!
Listen to me!

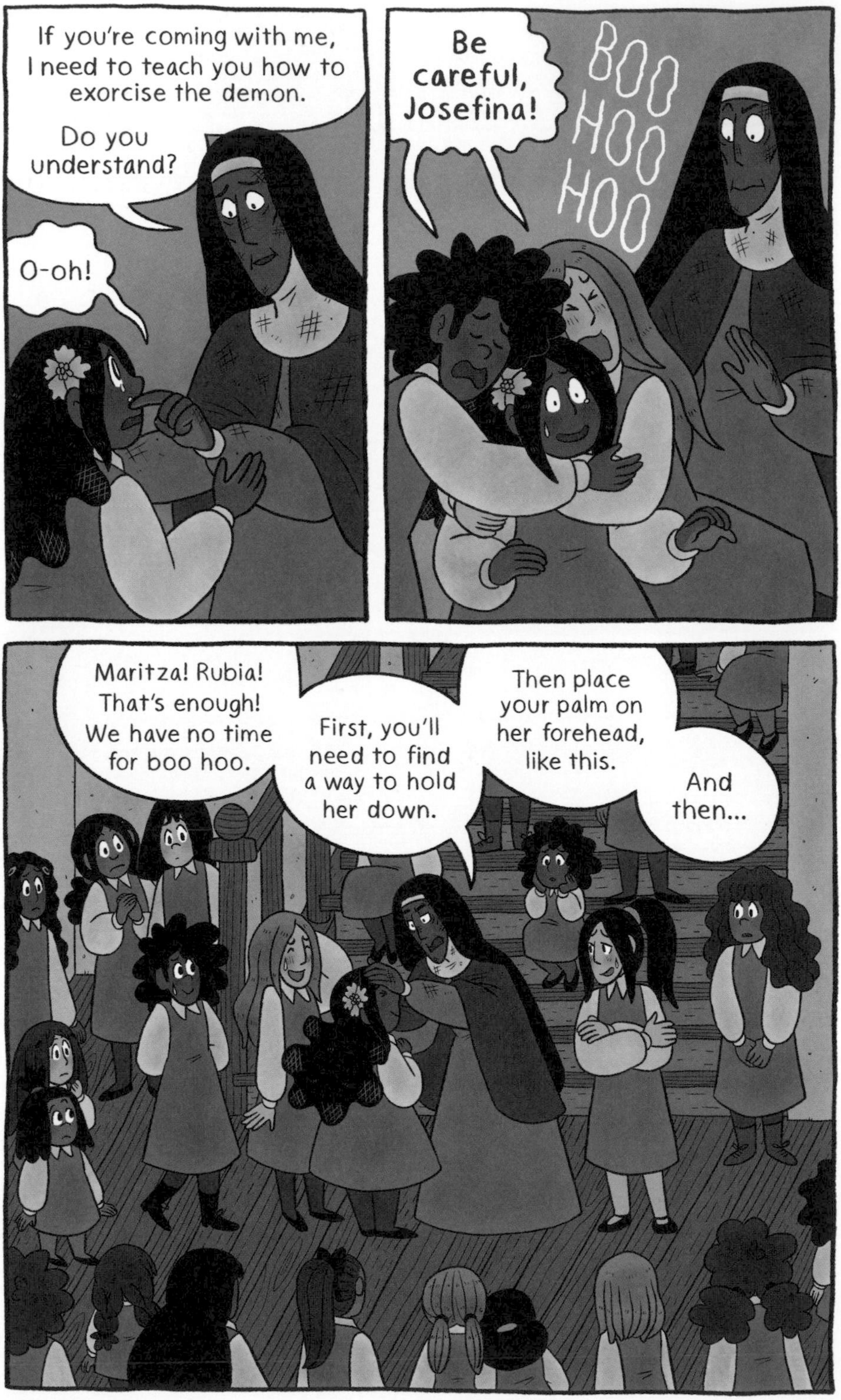
If you're coming with me, I need to teach you how to exorcise the demon.
Do you understand?
O-oh!
Be careful, Josefina!
BOO HOO HOO
Maritza! Rubia! That's enough! We have no time for boo hoo.
First, you'll need to find a way to hold her down.
Then place your palm on her forehead, like this.
And then...

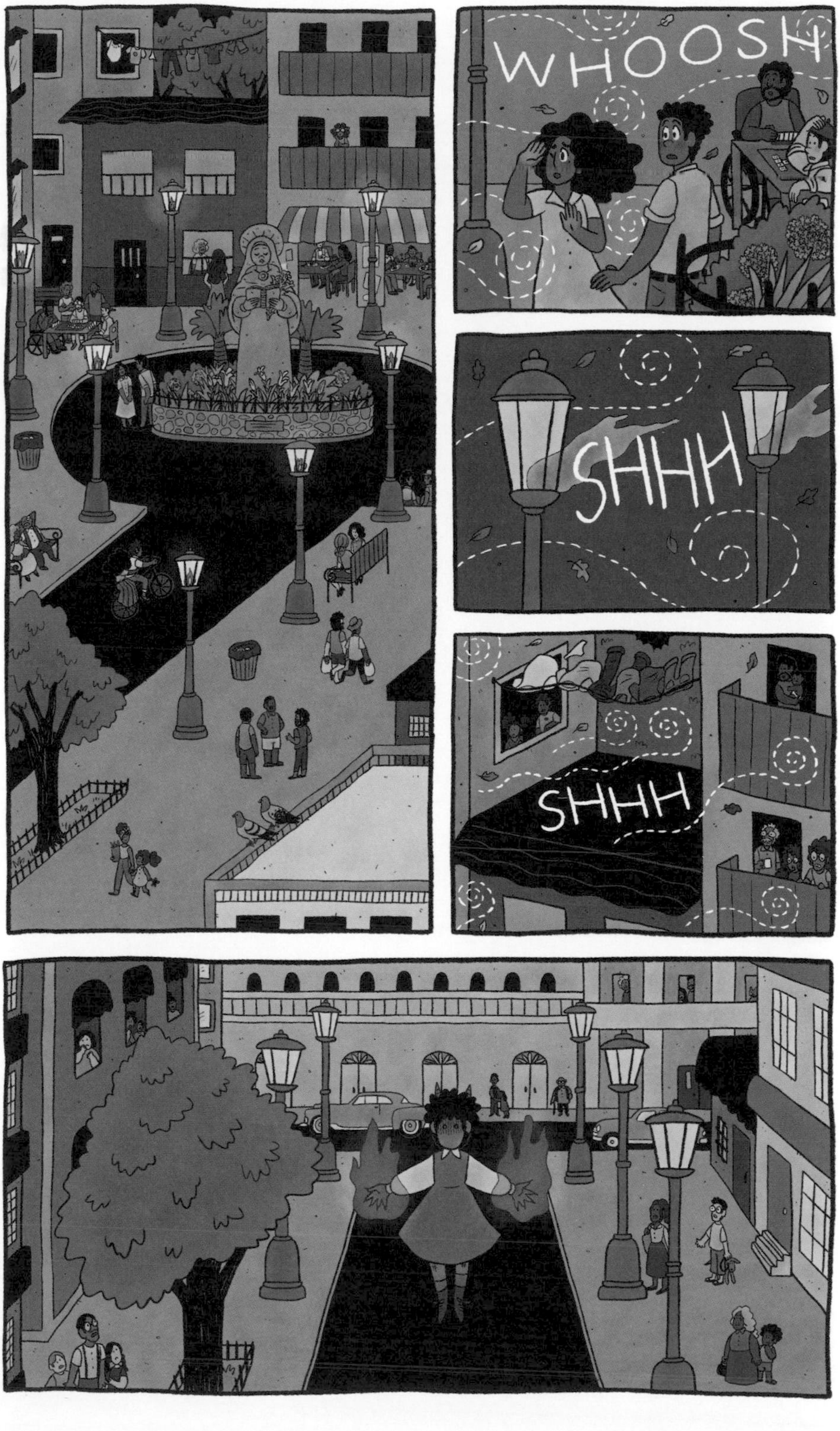
WHOOSH
SHHH
SHHH

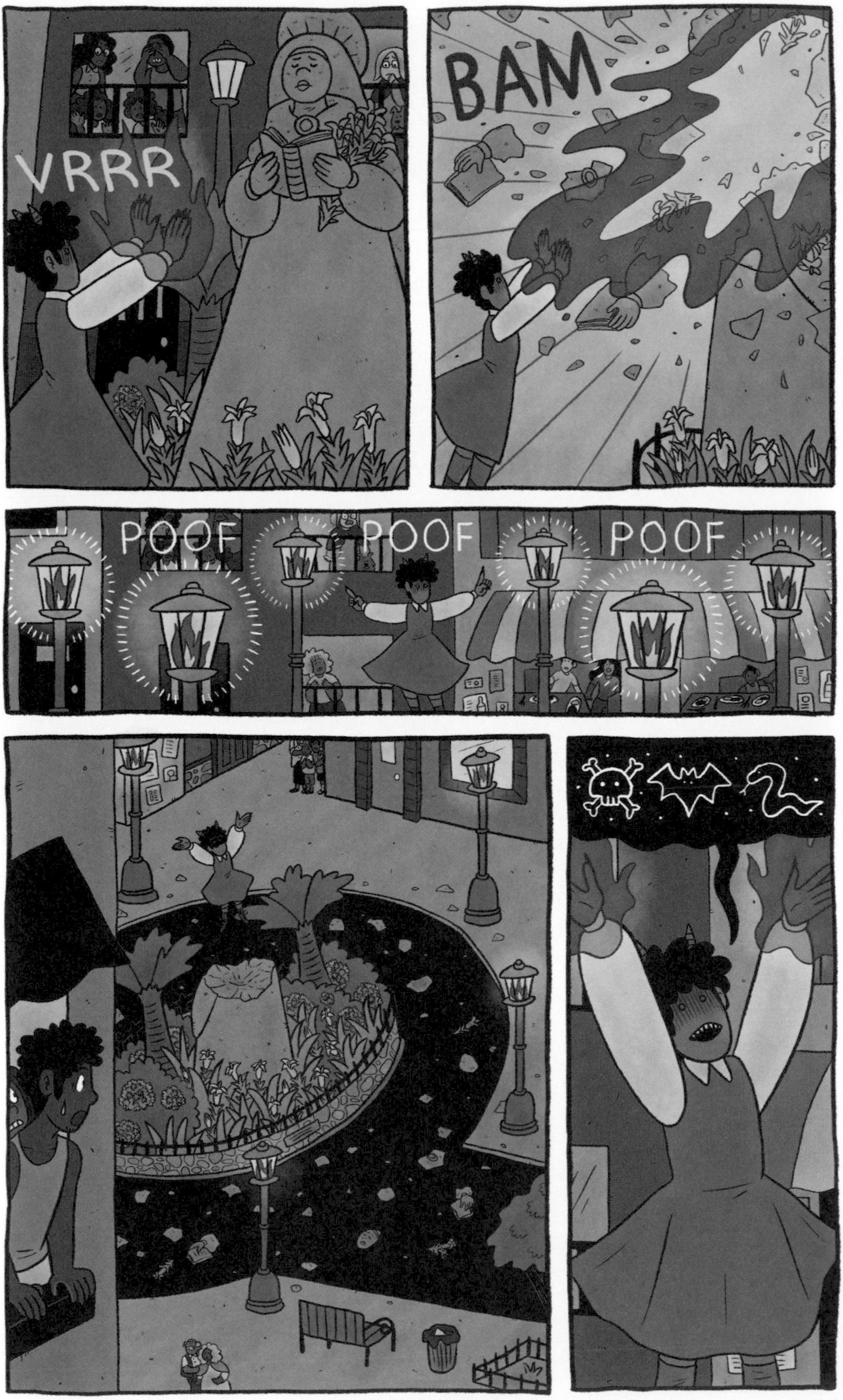
VRRR
BAM
POOF
POOF
POOF

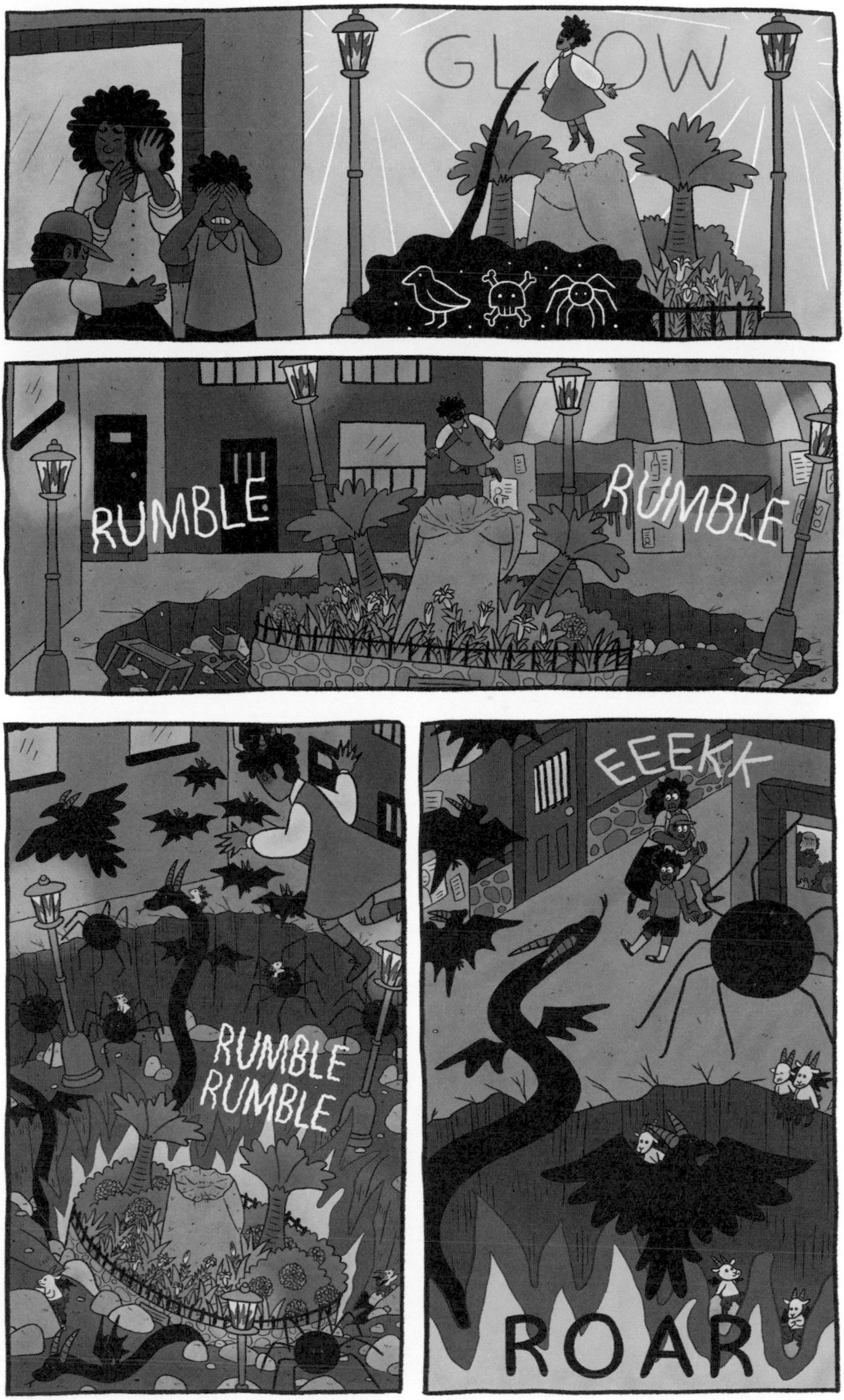
GLOW
RUMBLE
RUMBLE
RUMBLE
RUMBLE
EEEKK
ROAR

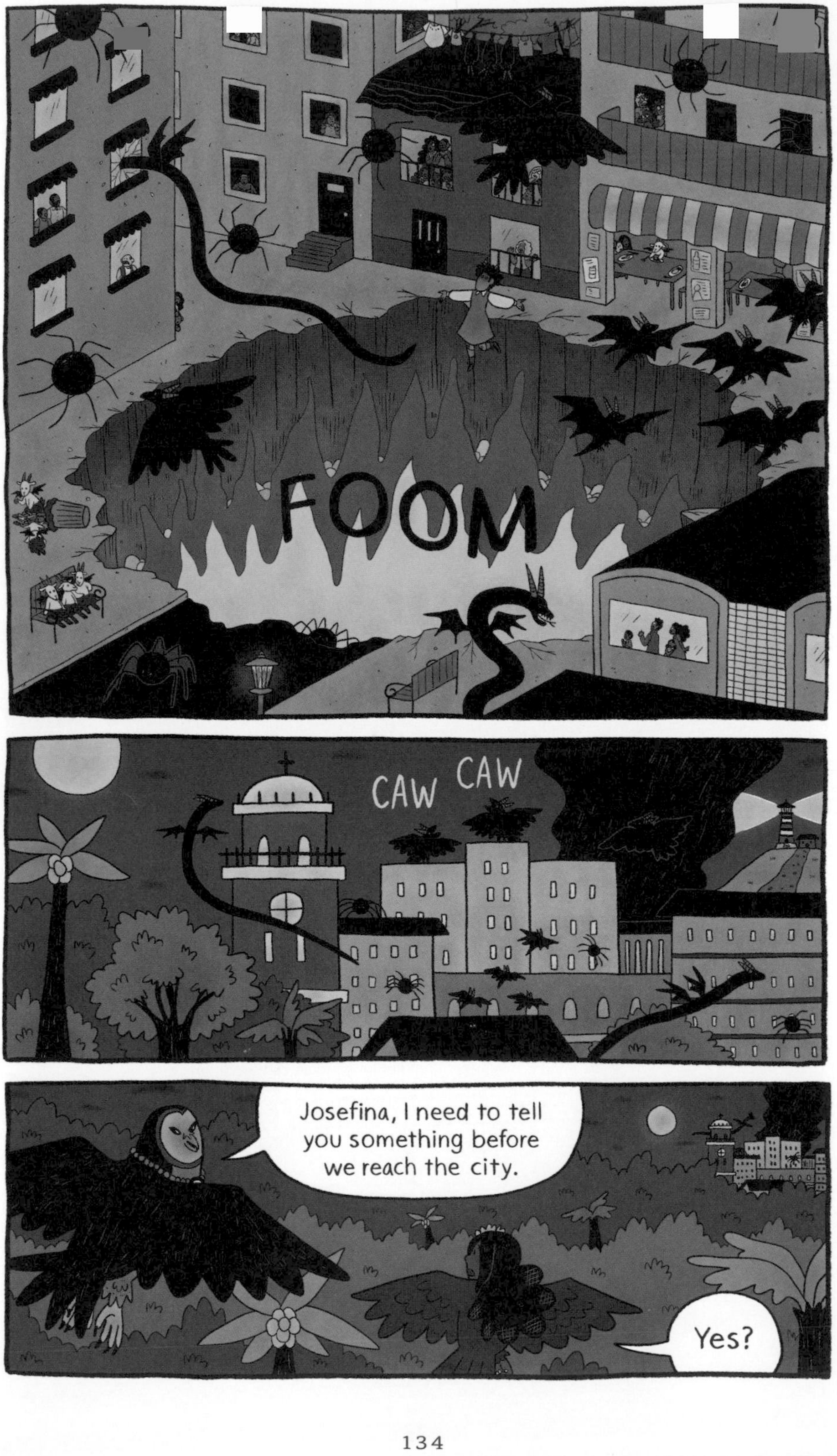
FOOM
CAW CAW
Josefina, I need to tell you something before we reach the city.
Yes?

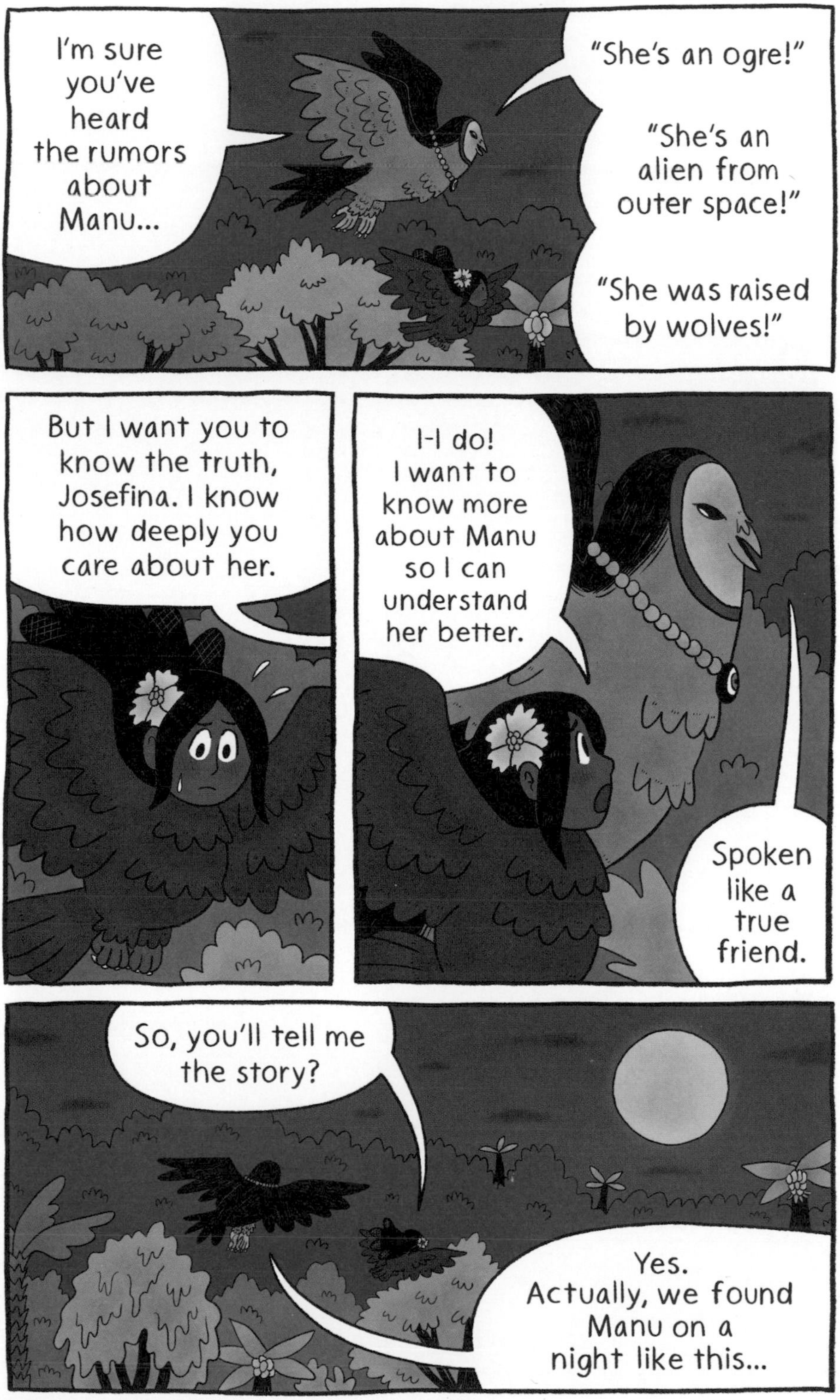
I'm sure you've heard the rumors about Manu...
"She's an ogre!"
"She's an alien from outer space!"
"She was raised by wolves!"
But I want you to know the truth, Josefina. I know how deeply you care about her.
I-I do! I want to know more about Manu so I can understand her better.
Spoken like a true friend.
So, you'll tell me the story?
Yes. Actually, we found Manu on a night like this...

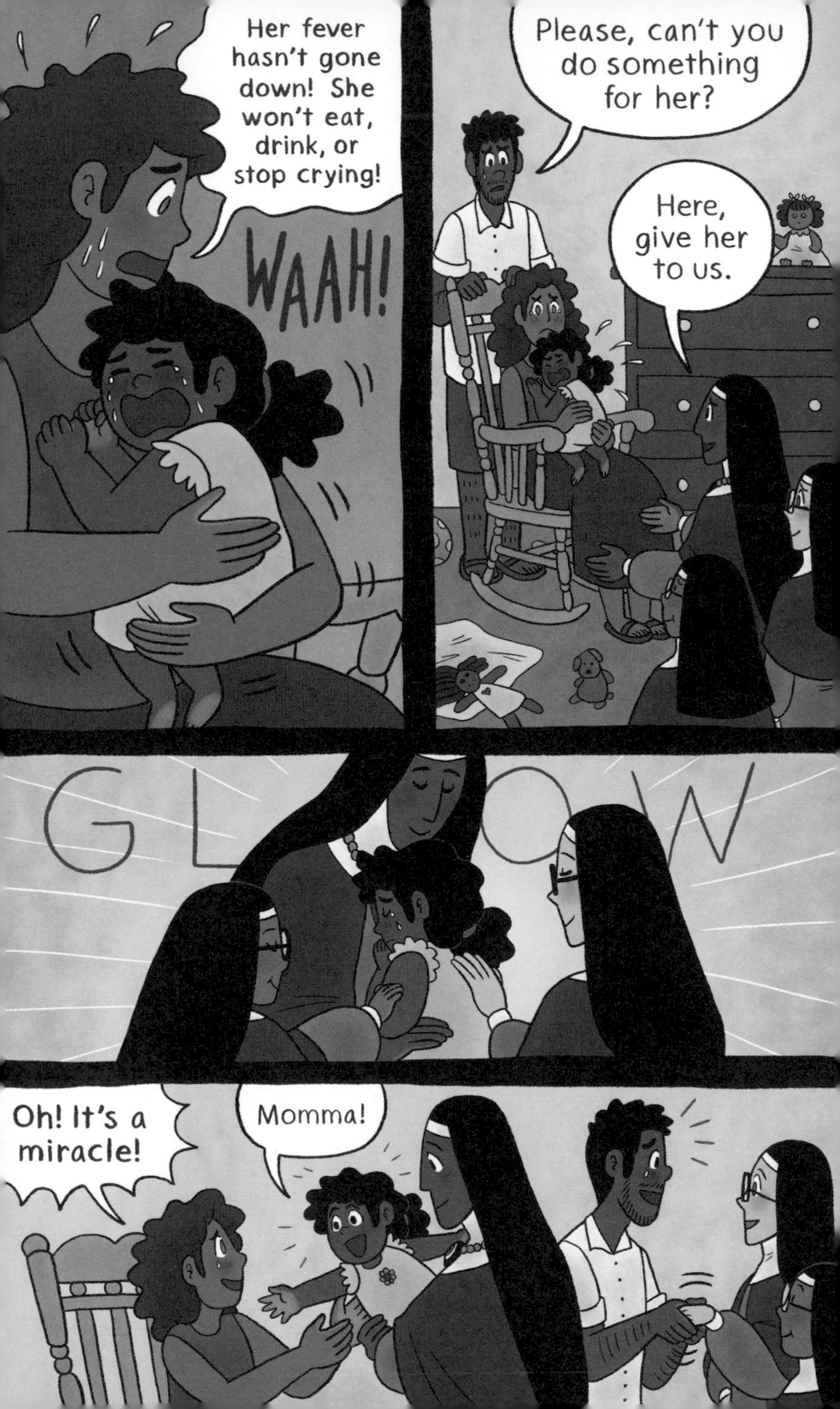
Her fever hasn't gone down! She won't eat, drink, or stop crying!
WAAH!
Please, can't you do something for her?
Here, give her to us.
GLOW
Oh! It's a miracle!
Momma!

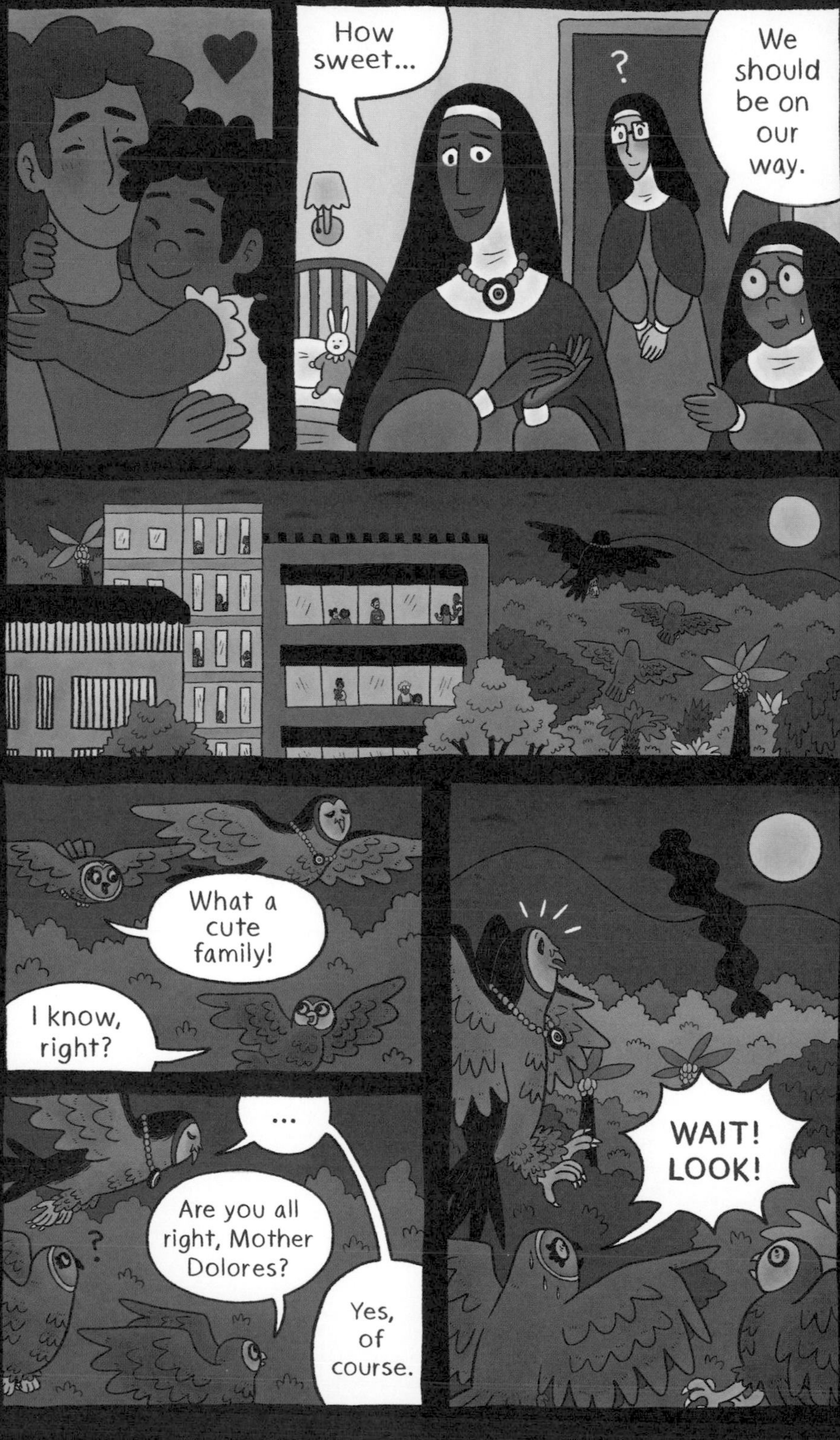
How sweet...
?
We should be on our way.
What a cute family!
I know, right?
...
Are you all right, Mother Dolores?
?
Yes, of course.
WAIT! LOOK!

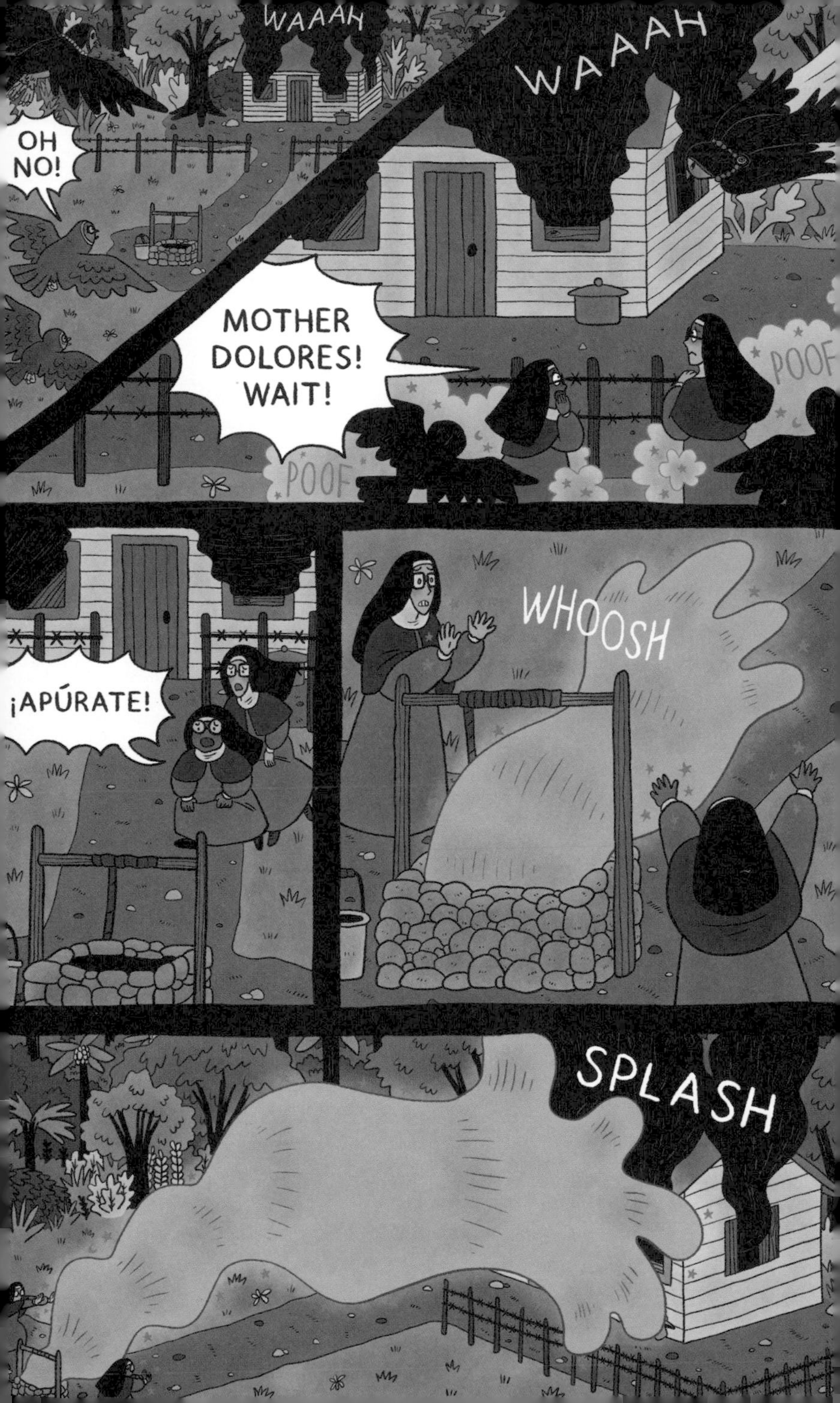
WAAAH
OH NO!
WAAAH
MOTHER DOLORES! WAIT!
POOF
POOF
¡APÚRATE!
WHOOSH
SPLASH

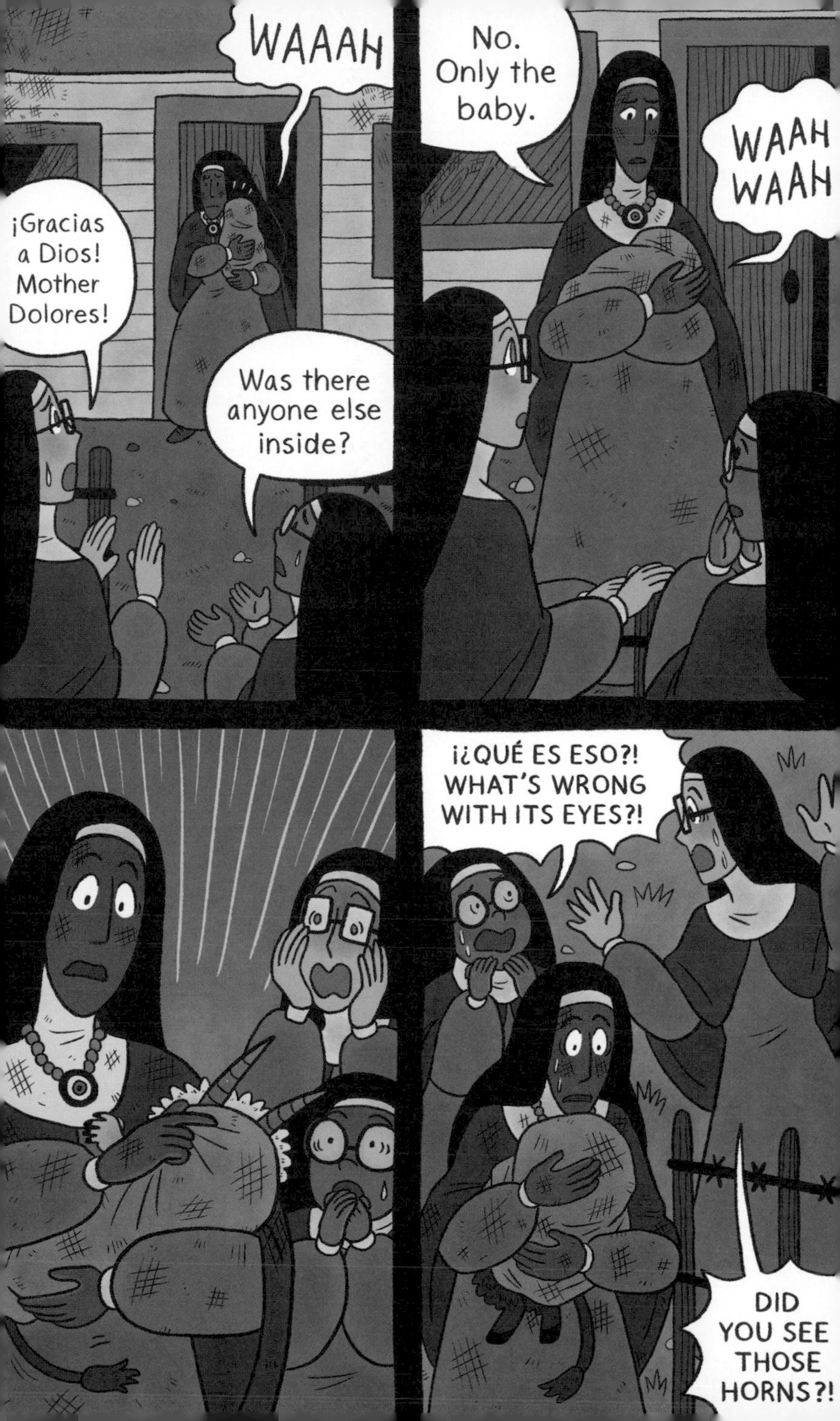
WAAAH
¡Gracias a Dios! Mother Dolores!
Was there anyone else inside?
No. Only the baby.
WAAH WAAH
¡¿QUÉ ES ESO?! WHAT'S WRONG WITH ITS EYES?!
DID YOU SEE THOSE HORNS?!

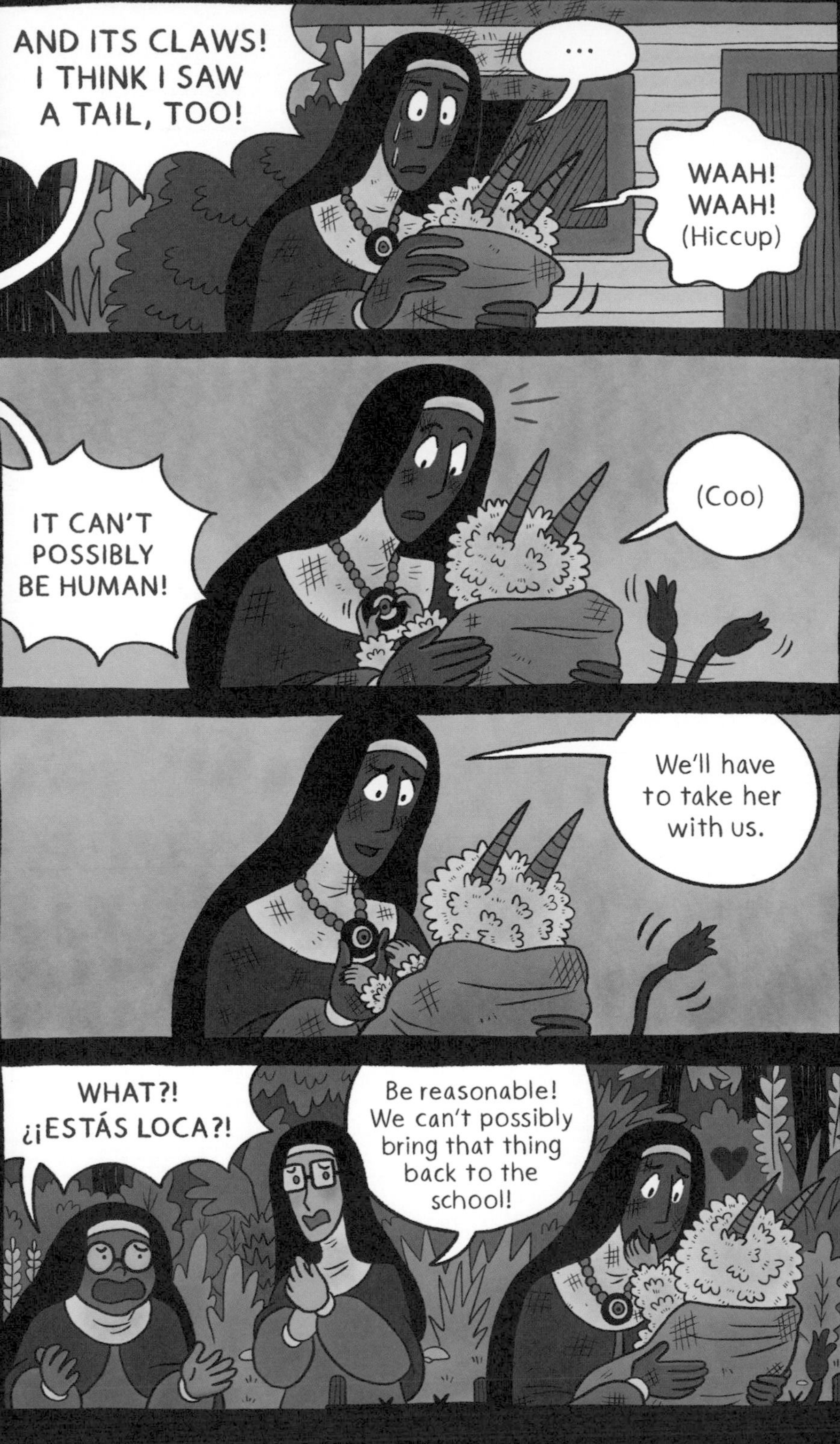
AND ITS CLAWS! I THINK I SAW A TAIL, TOO!
...
WAAH! WAAH! (Hiccup)
IT CAN'T POSSIBLY BE HUMAN!
(Coo)
We'll have to take her with us.
WHAT?! ¿¡ESTÁS LOCA?!
Be reasonable! We can't possibly bring that thing back to the school!

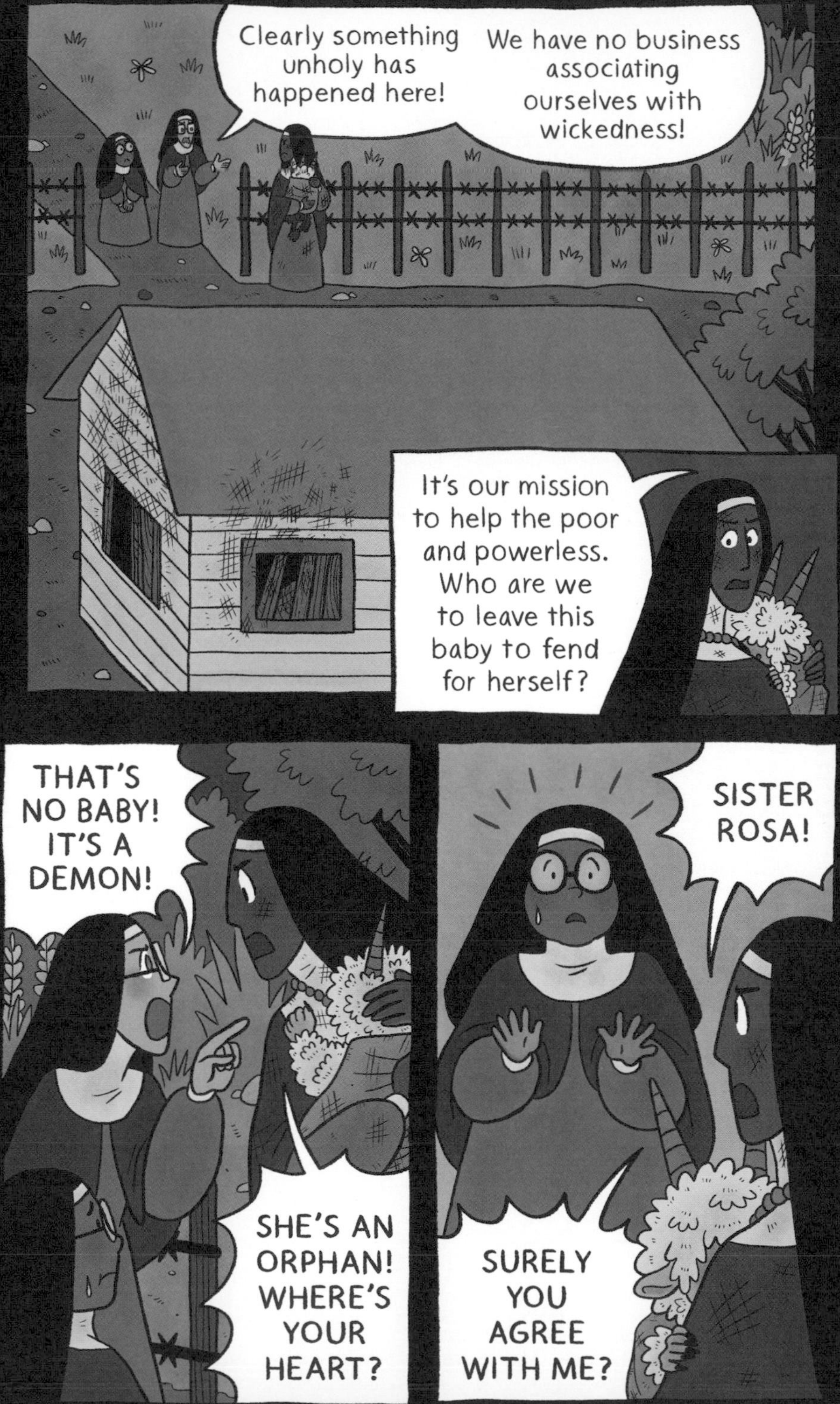
Clearly something unholy has happened here!
We have no business associating ourselves with wickedness!
It's our mission to help the poor and powerless. Who are we to leave this baby to fend for herself?
THAT'S NO BABY! IT'S A DEMON!
SHE'S AN ORPHAN! WHERE'S YOUR HEART?
SISTER ROSA!
SURELY YOU AGREE WITH ME?

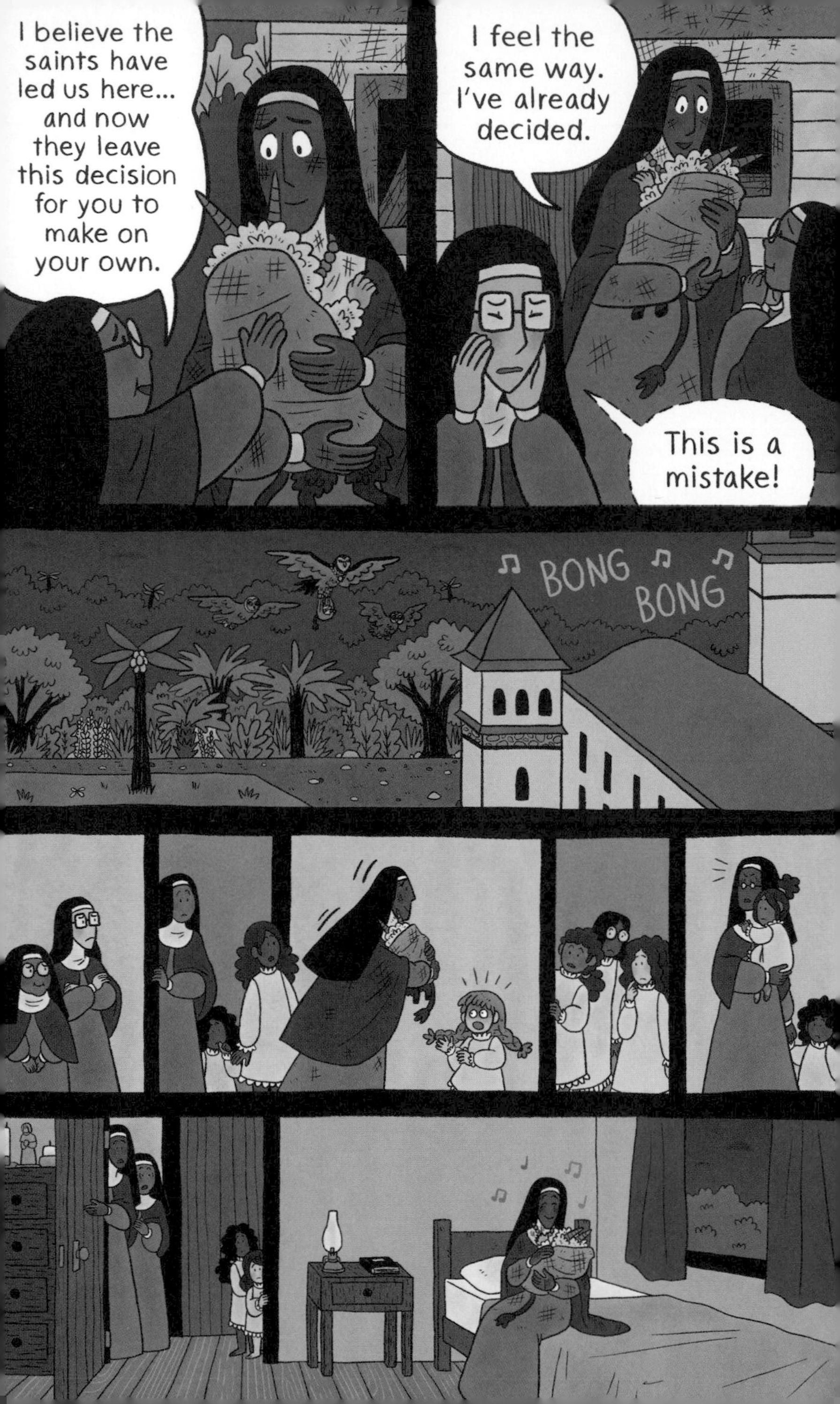

I believe the saints have led us here... and now they leave this decision for you to make on your own.
I feel the same way. I've already decided.
This is a mistake!
BONG
BONG

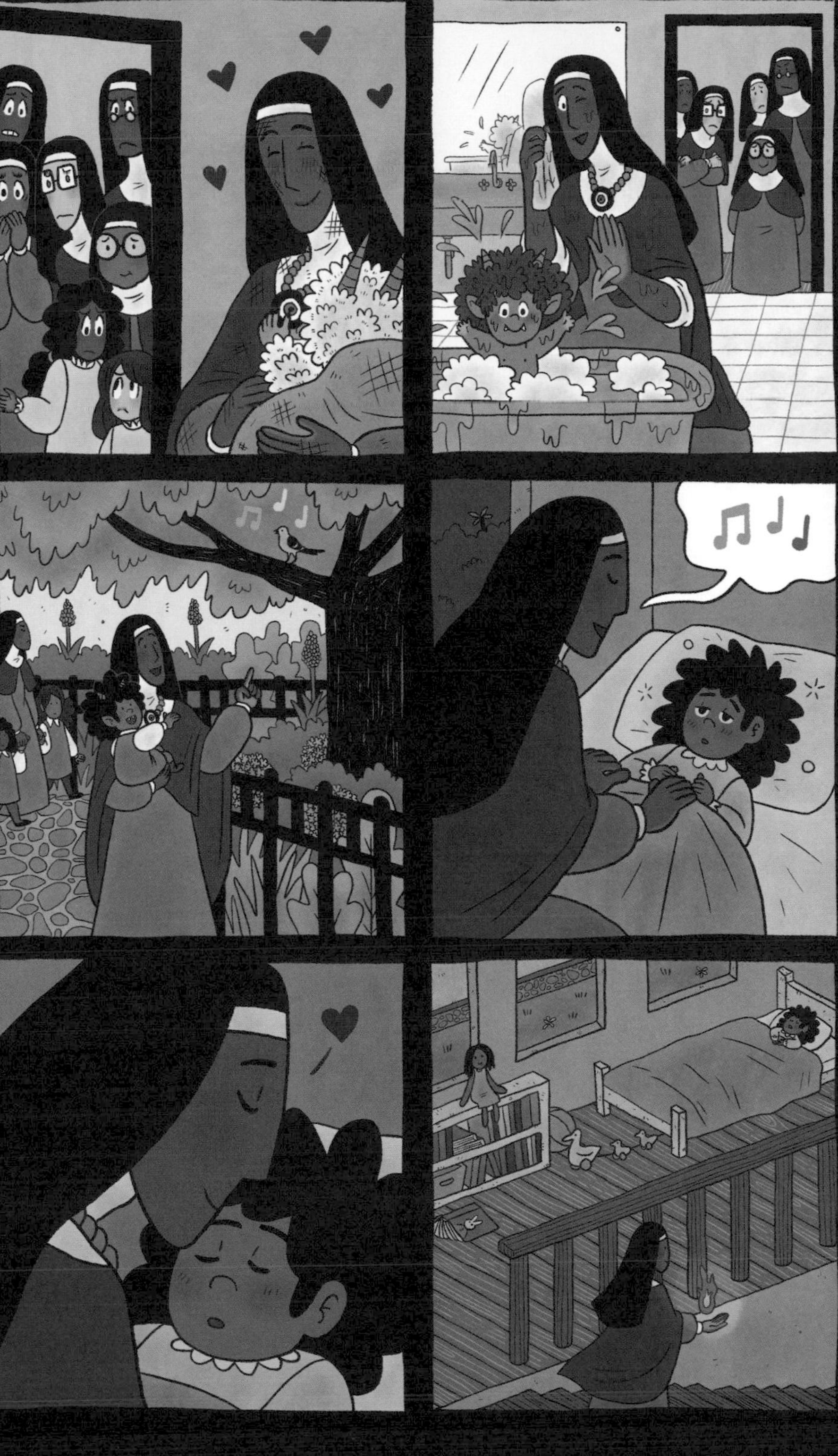

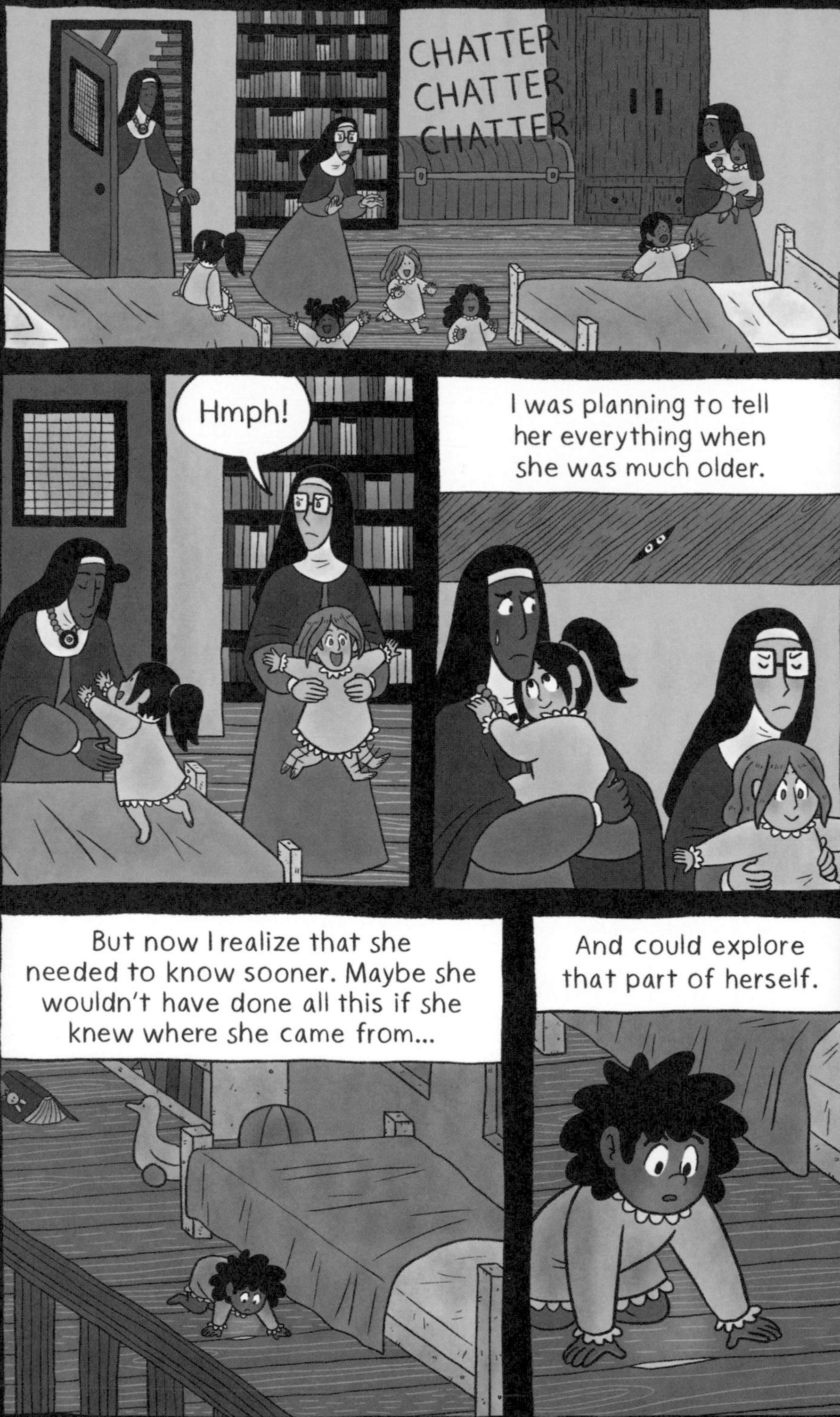
CHATTER
CHATTER
CHATTER
Hmph!
I was planning to tell her everything when she was much older.
But now I realize that she needed to know sooner. Maybe she wouldn't have done all this if she knew where she came from...
And could explore that part of herself.

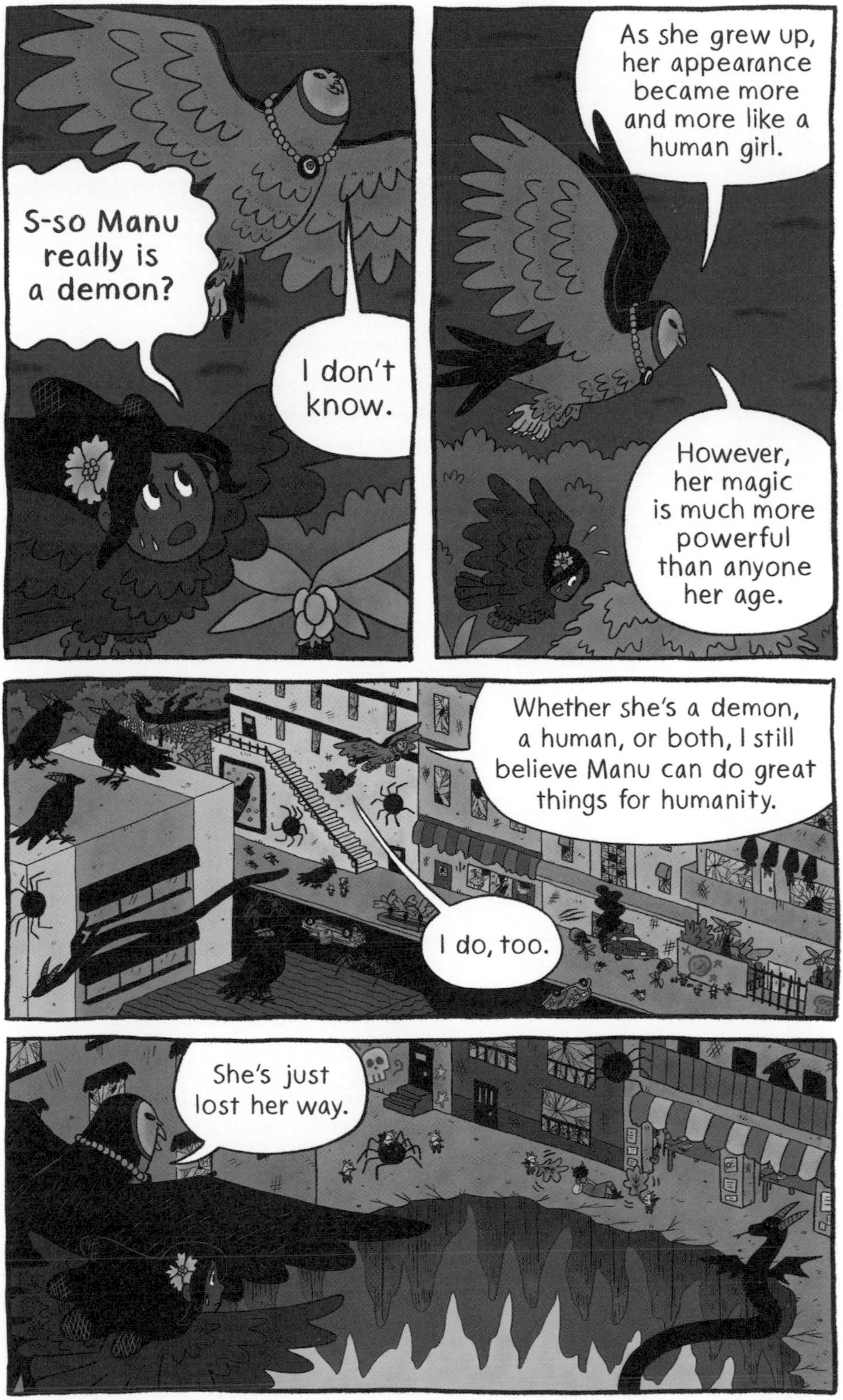
S-so Manu really is a demon?
I don't know.
As she grew up, her appearance became more and more like a human girl.
However, her magic is much more powerful than anyone her age.
Whether she's a demon, a human, or both, I still believe Manu can do great things for humanity.
I do, too.
She's just lost her way.

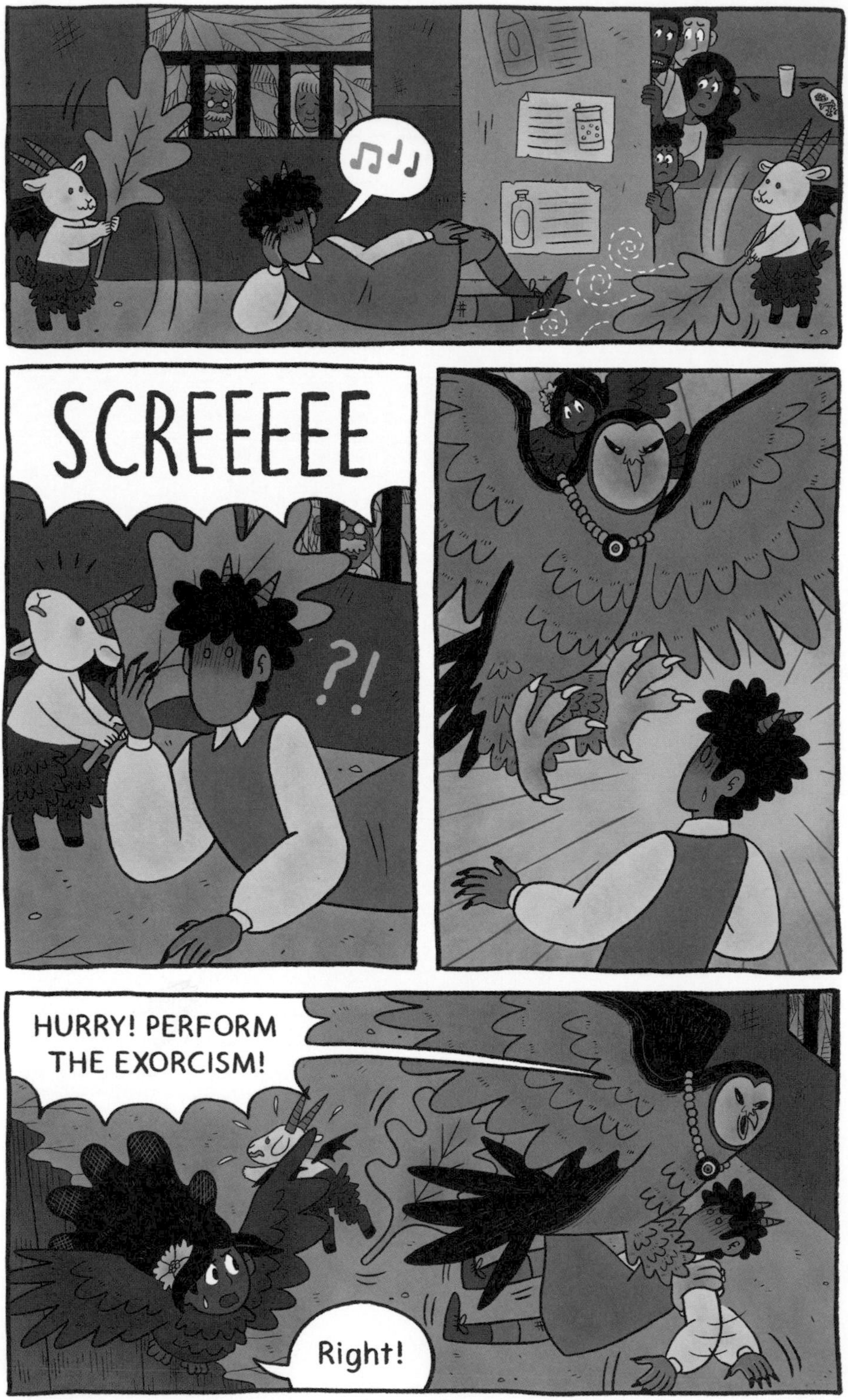
SCREEEEE
?!
HURRY! PERFORM THE EXORCISM!
Right!

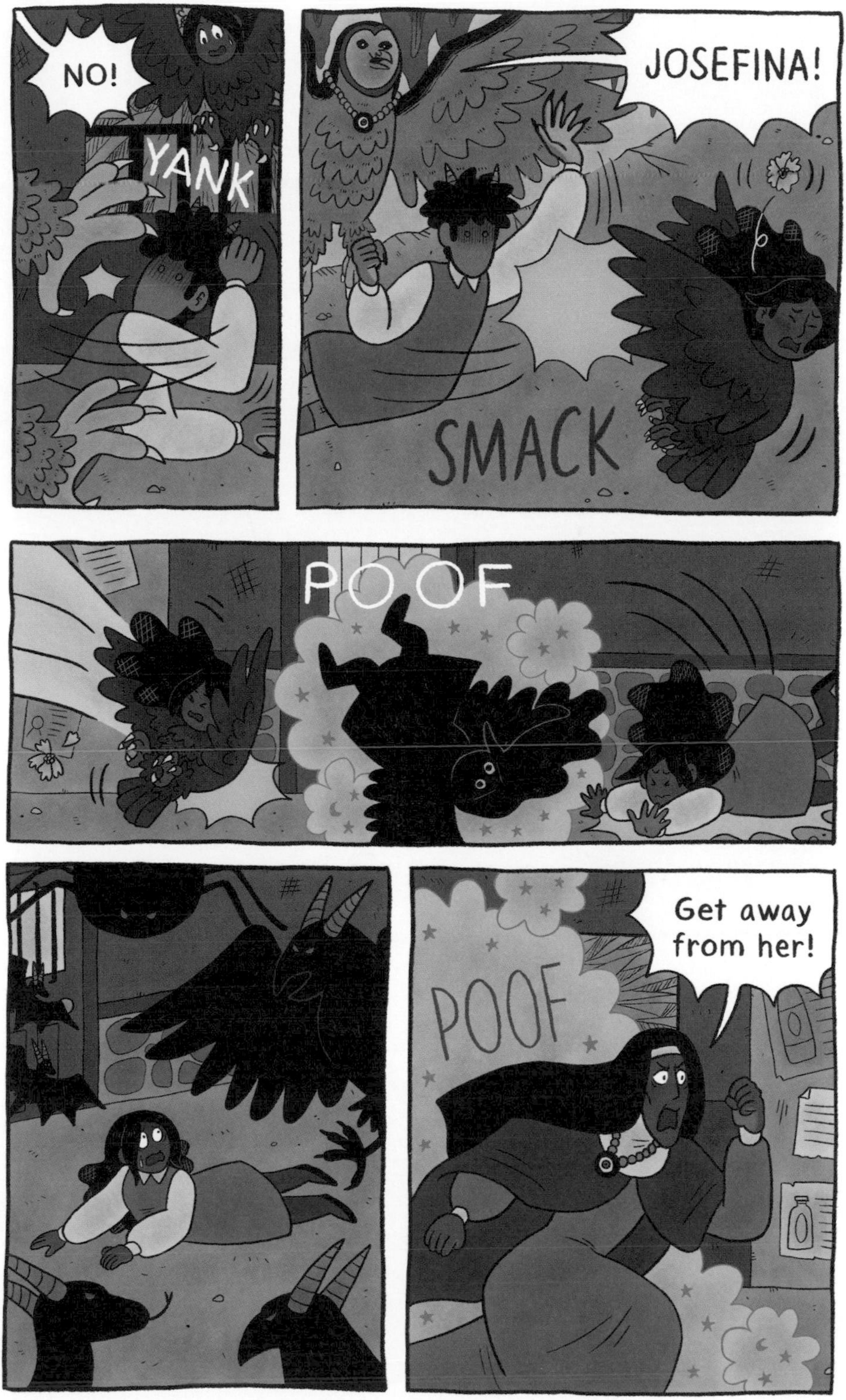
NO!
YANK
JOSEFINA!
SMACK
POOF
POOF
Get away from her!

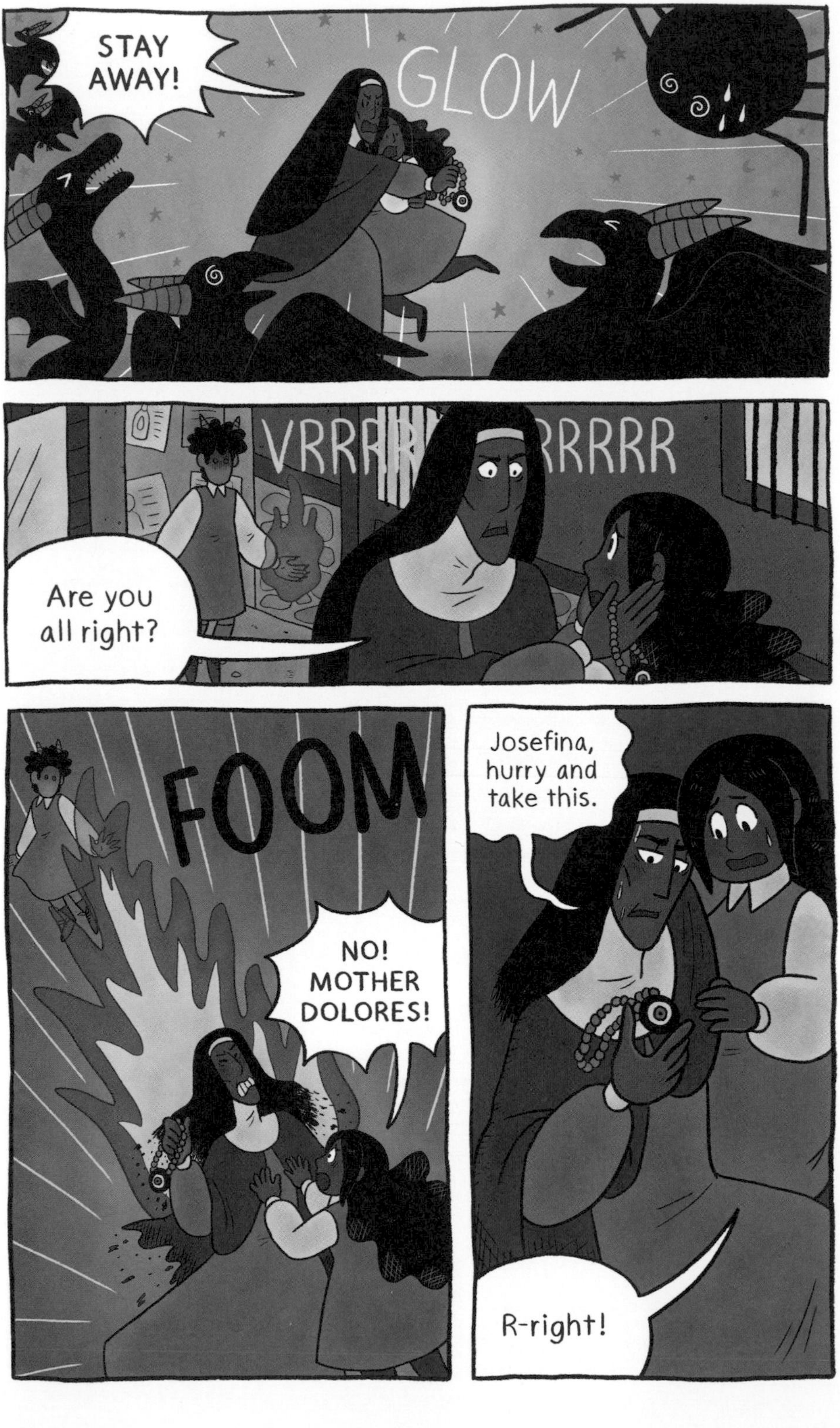
STAY AWAY!
GLOW
VRRRRRRRRRR
Are you all right?
FOOM
NO! MOTHER DOLORES!
Josefina, hurry and take this.
R-right!

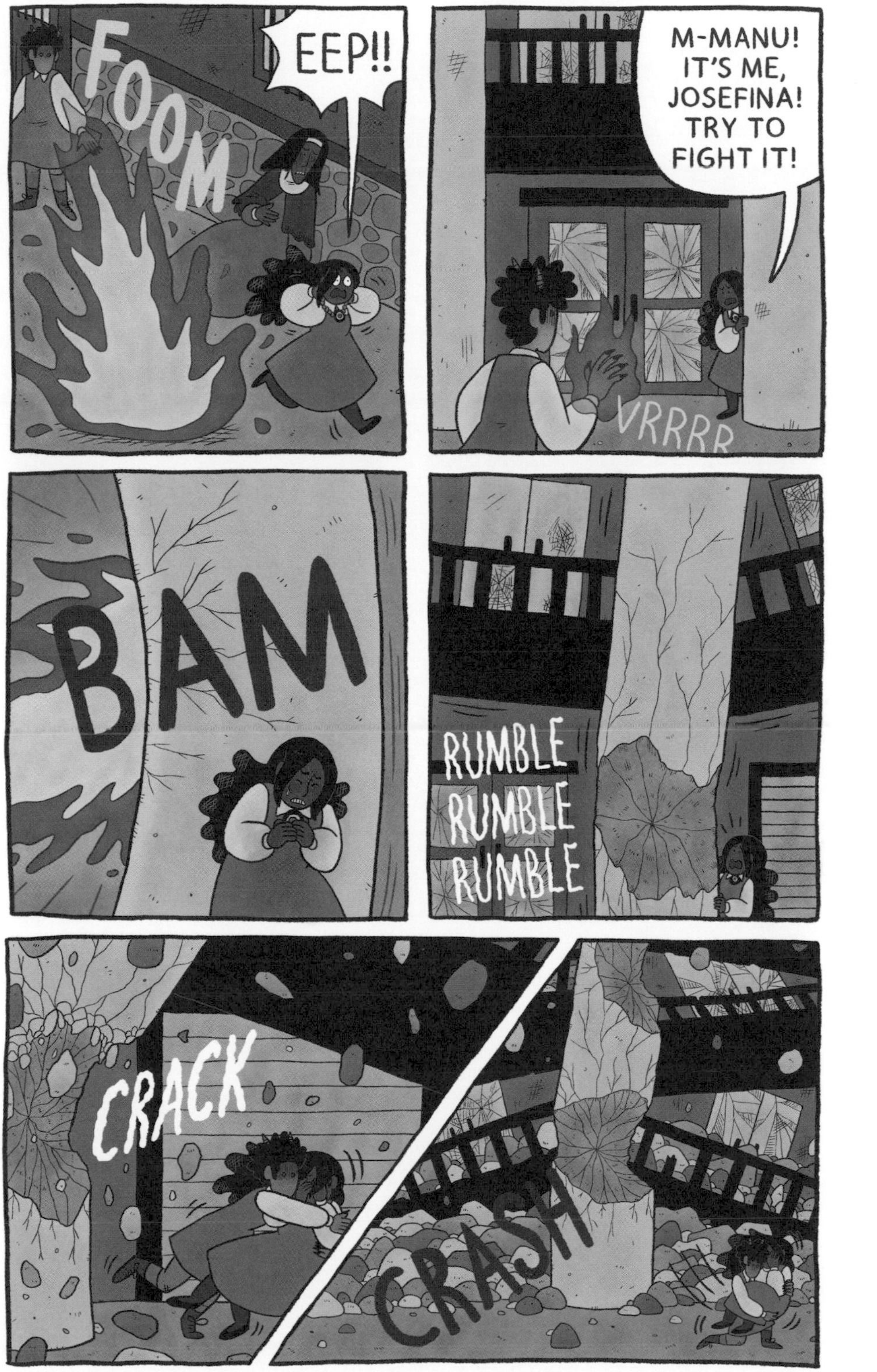
FOOM
EEP!!
M-MANU! IT'S ME, JOSEFINA! TRY TO FIGHT IT!
VRRRR
BAM
RUMBLE
RUMBLE
RUMBLE
CRACK
CRASH

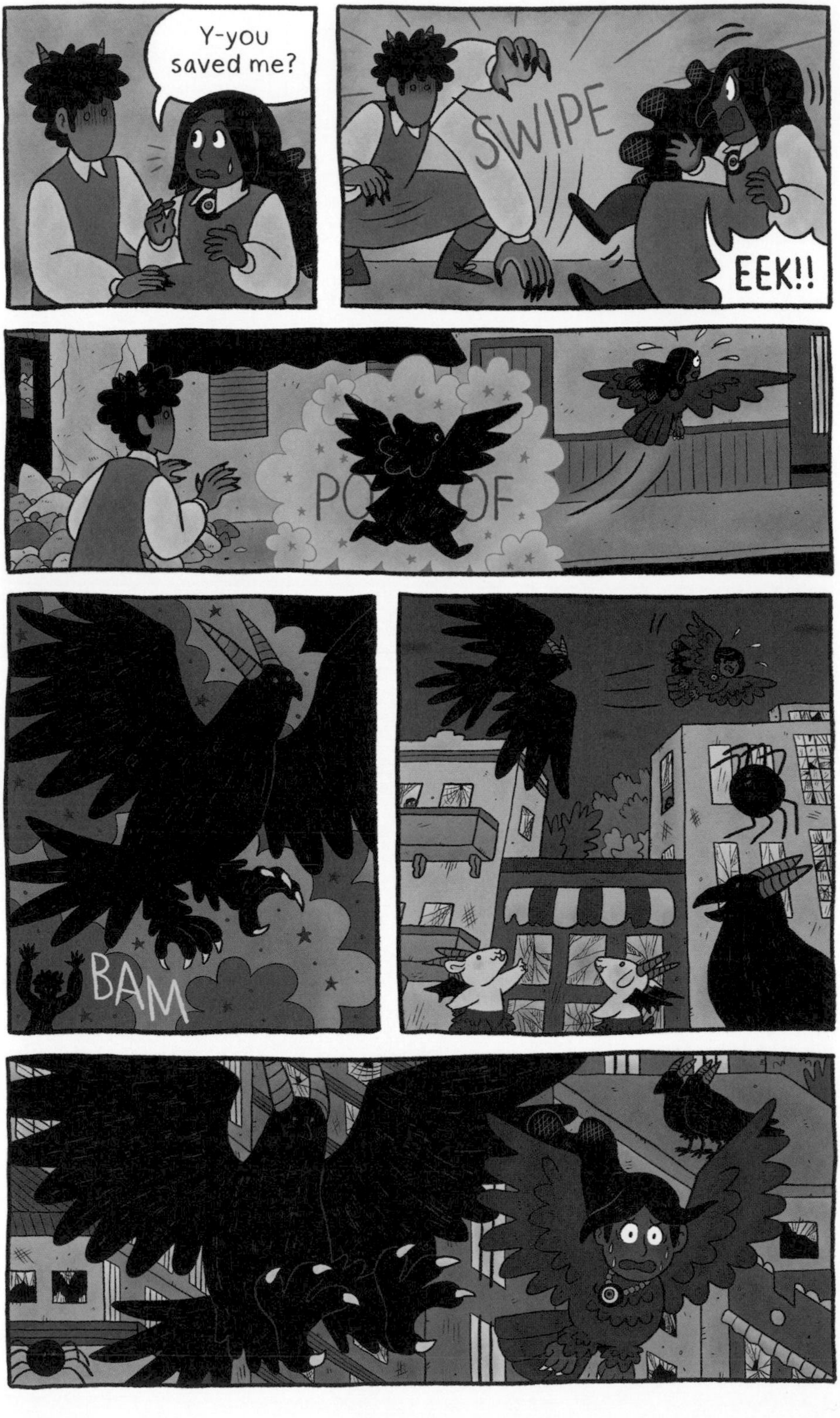
Y-you saved me?
SWIPE
EEK!!
PO OF
BAM

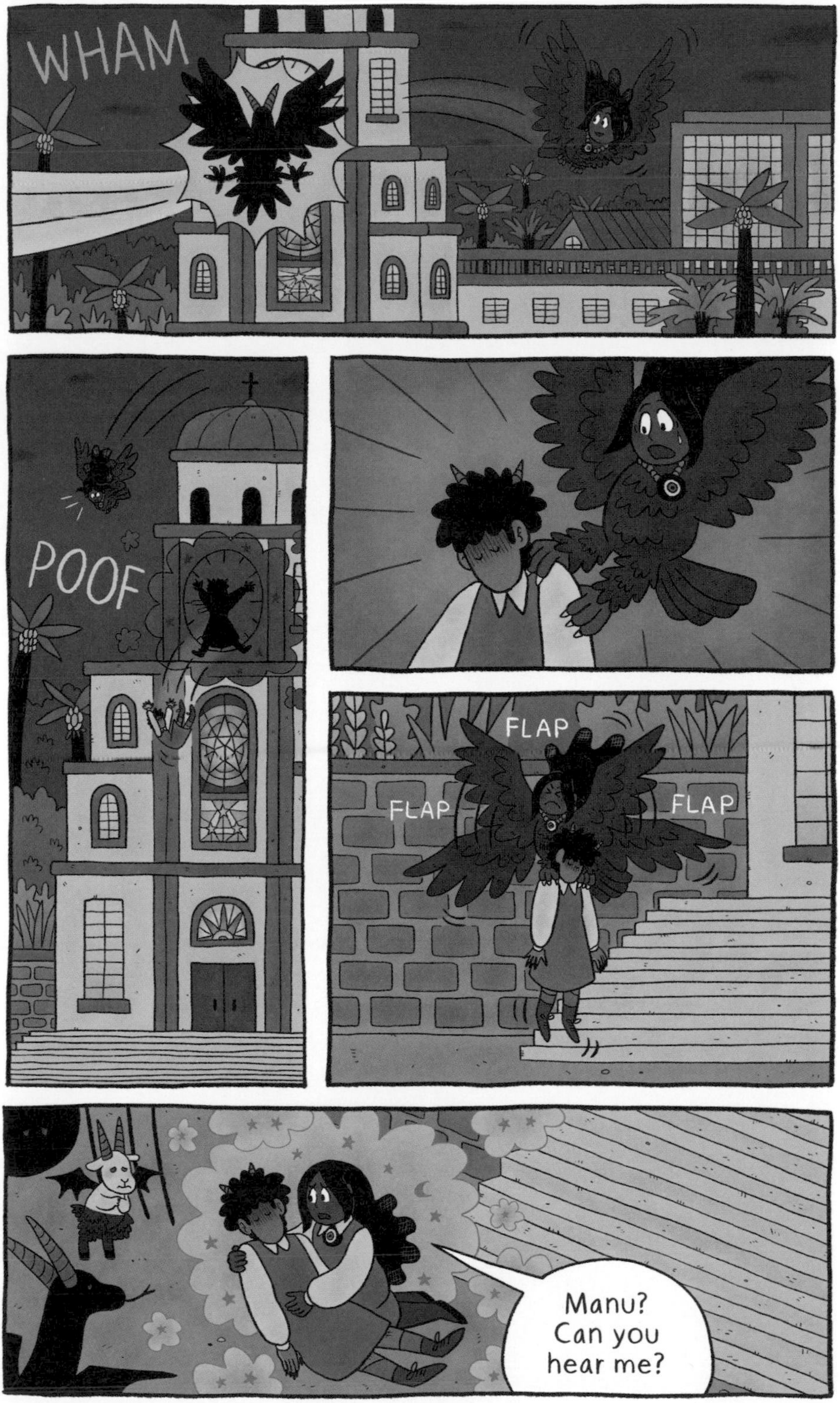
WHAM
POOF
FLAP
FLAP
FLAP
Manu? Can you hear me?

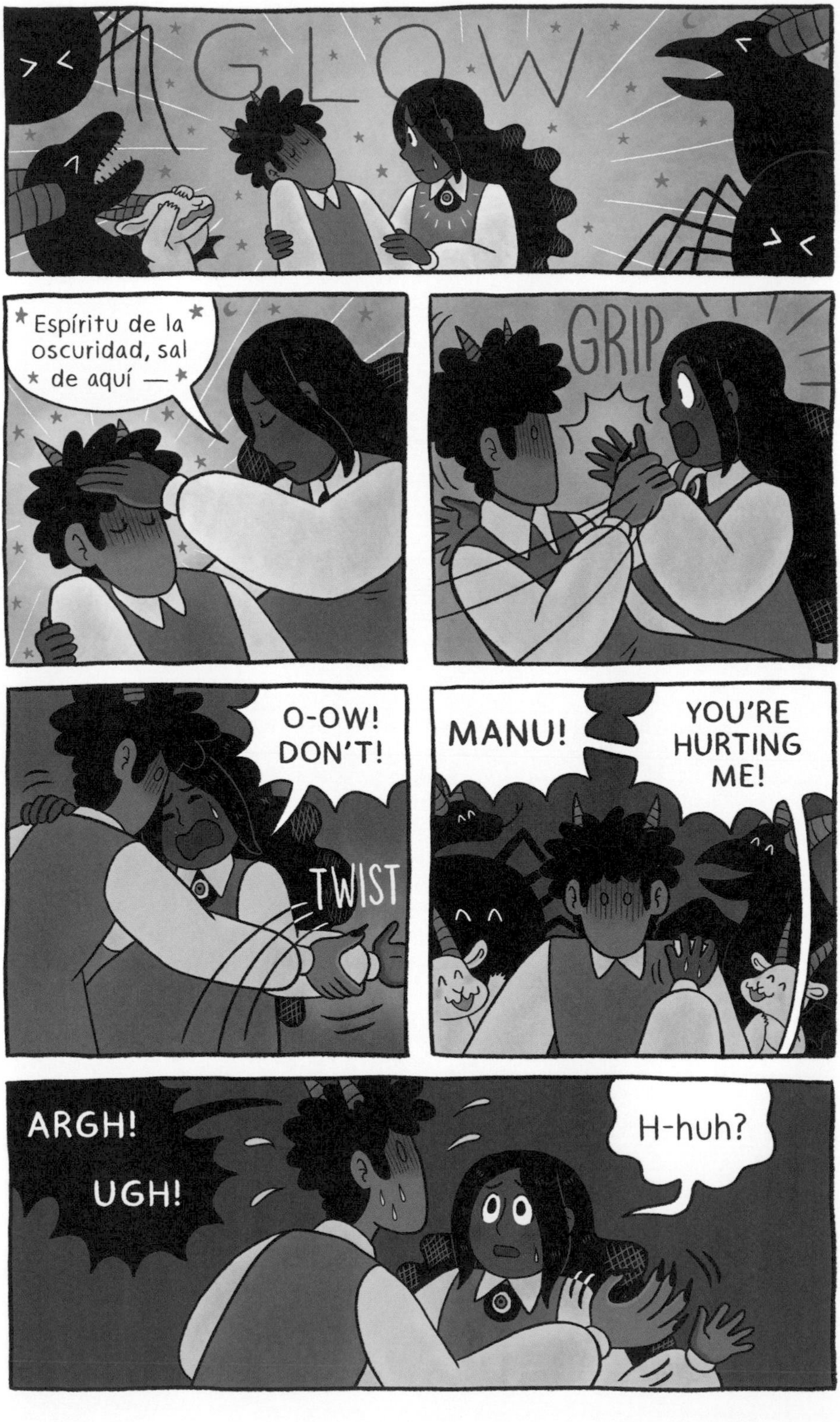
GLOW
Espíritu de la oscuridad, sal de aquí —
GRIP
O-OW! DON'T!
TWIST
MANU!
YOU'RE HURTING ME!
ARGH!
UGH!
H-huh?

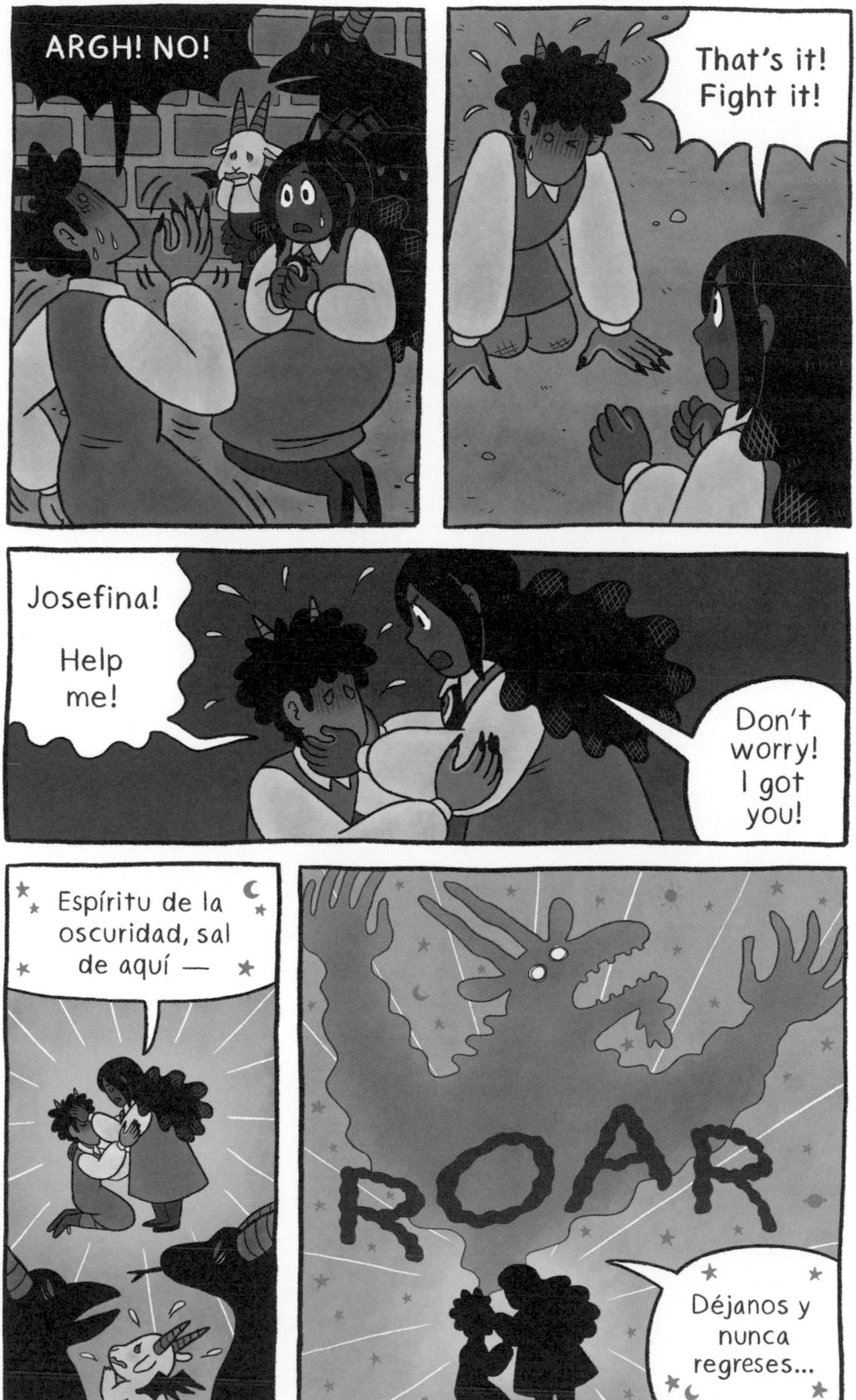
ARGH! NO!
That's it! Fight it!
Josefina!
Help me!
Don't worry! I got you!
Espíritu de la oscuridad, sal de aquí —
ROAR
Déjanos y nunca regreses...

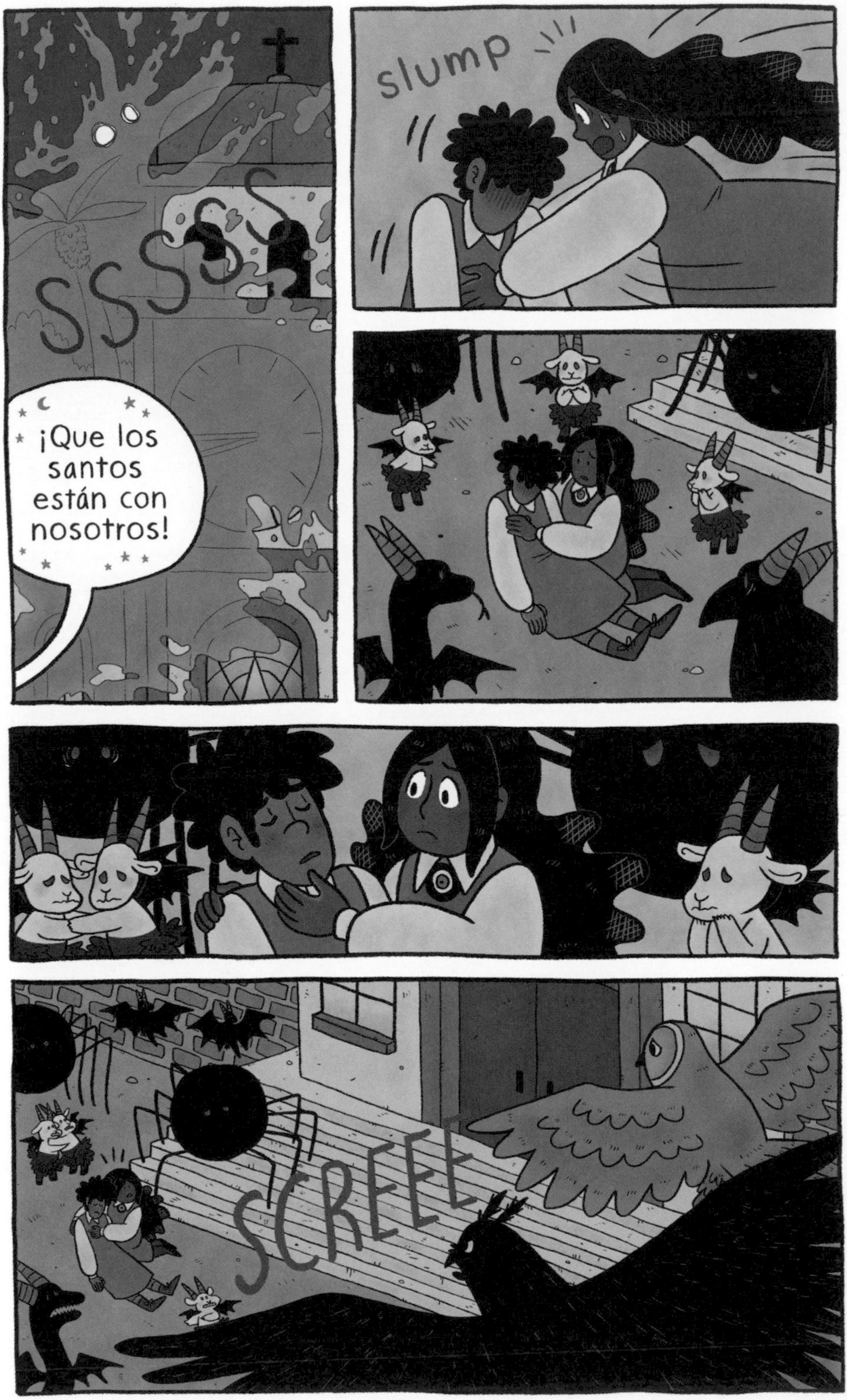
SSSSSS
¡Que los santos están con nosotros!
slump
SCREEE

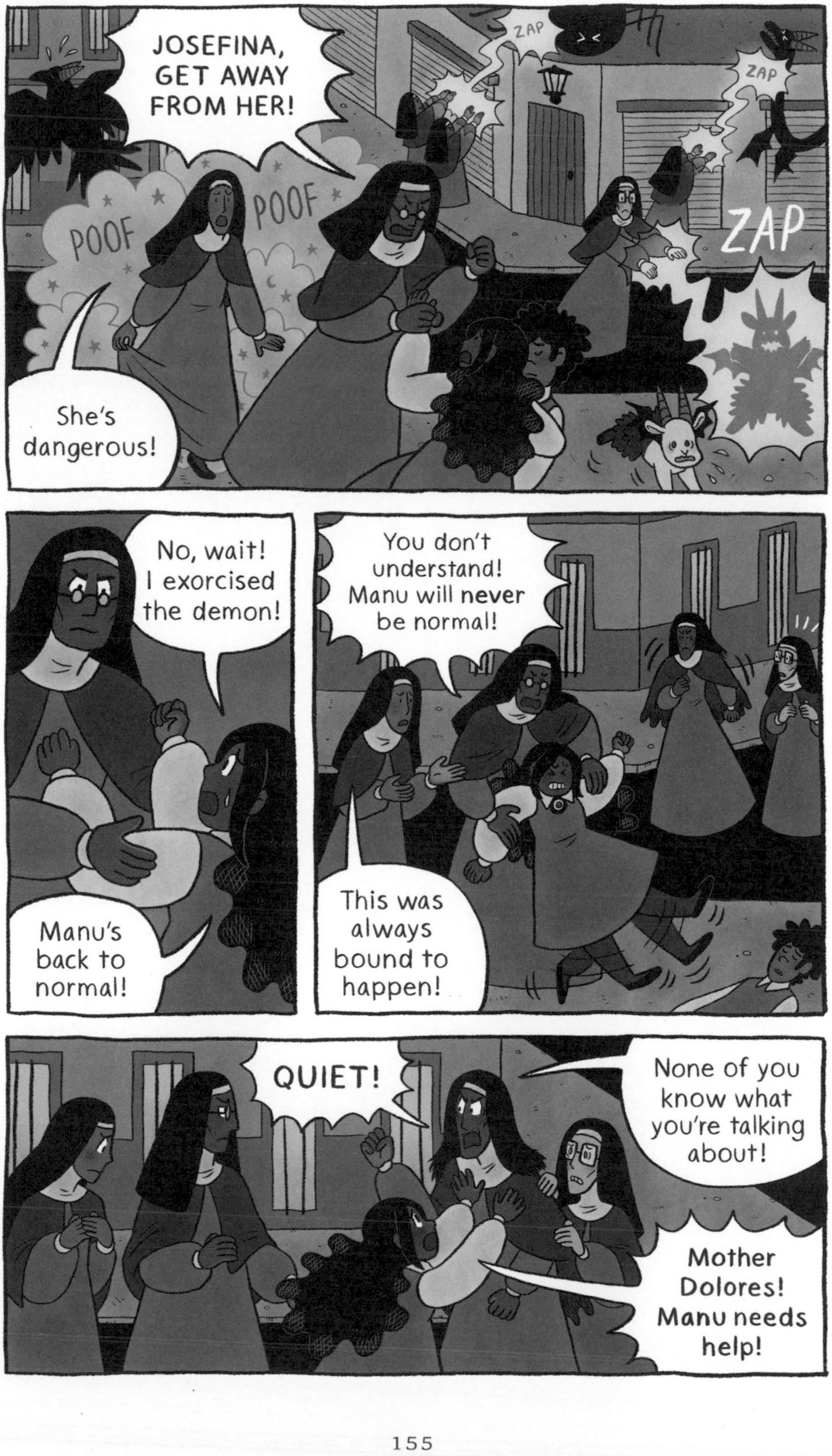
JOSEFINA, GET AWAY FROM HER!
ZAP
ZAP
POOF
POOF
ZAP
She's dangerous!
No, wait! I exorcised the demon!
Manu's back to normal!
You don't understand! Manu will **never** be normal!
This was always bound to happen!
QUIET!
None of you know what you're talking about!
Mother Dolores! Manu needs help!

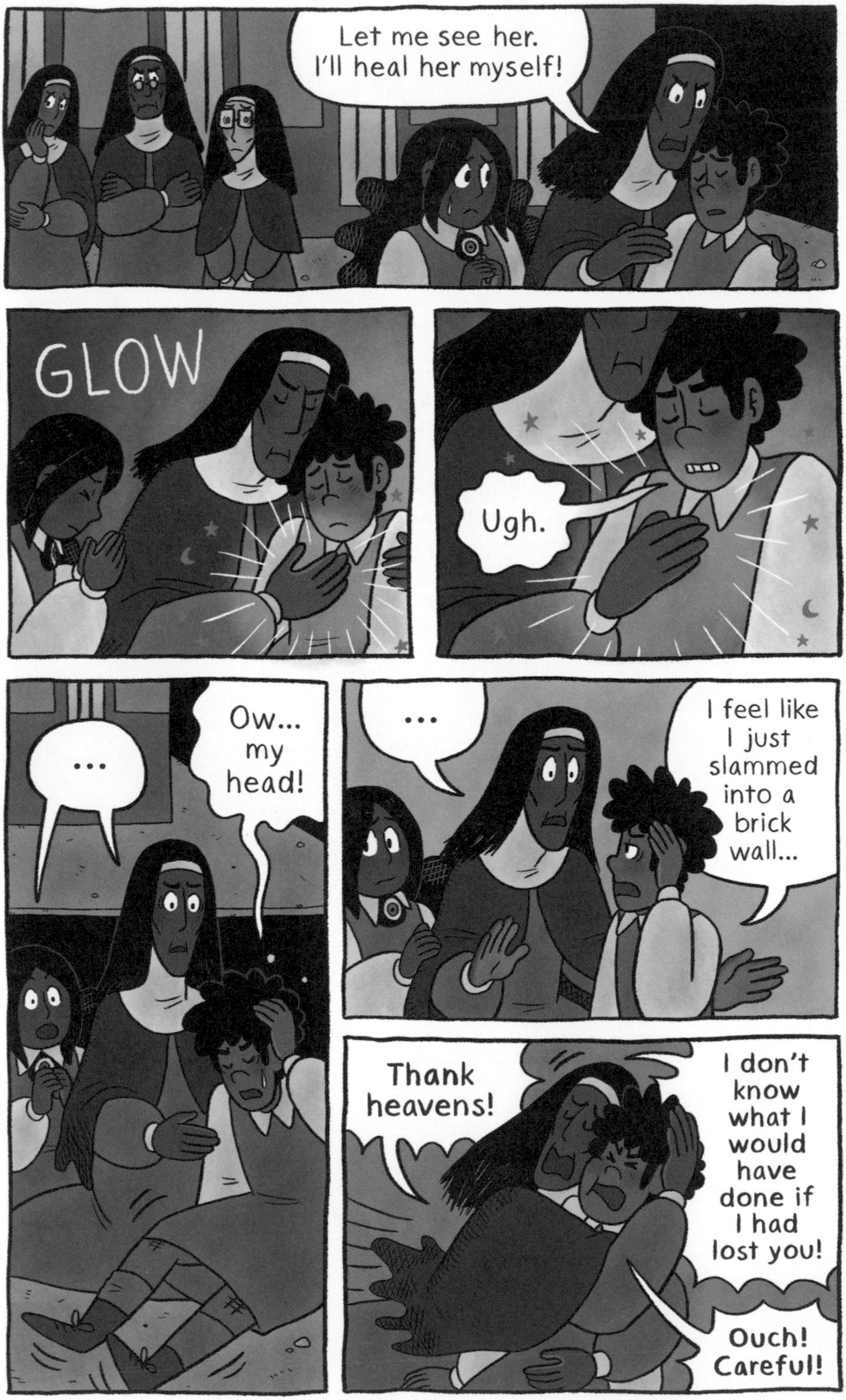

Let me see her. I'll heal her myself!
GLOW
Ugh.
...
Ow... my head!
...
I feel like I just slammed into a brick wall...
Thank heavens!
I don't know what I would have done if I had lost you!
Ouch! Careful!

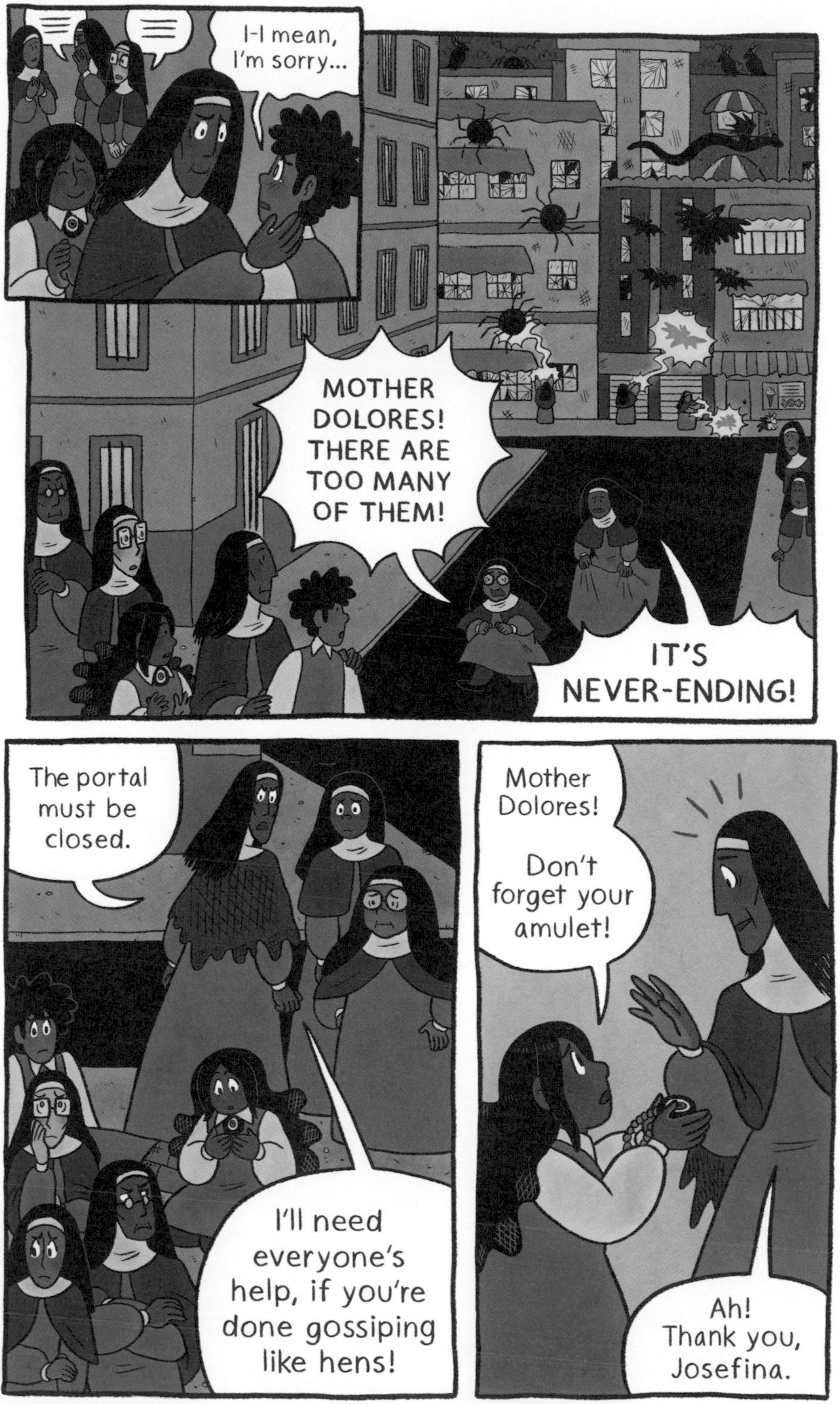
I-I mean, I'm sorry...
MOTHER DOLORES! THERE ARE TOO MANY OF THEM!
IT'S NEVER-ENDING!
The portal must be closed.
I'll need everyone's help, if you're done gossiping like hens!
Mother Dolores!
Don't forget your amulet!
Ah! Thank you, Josefina.

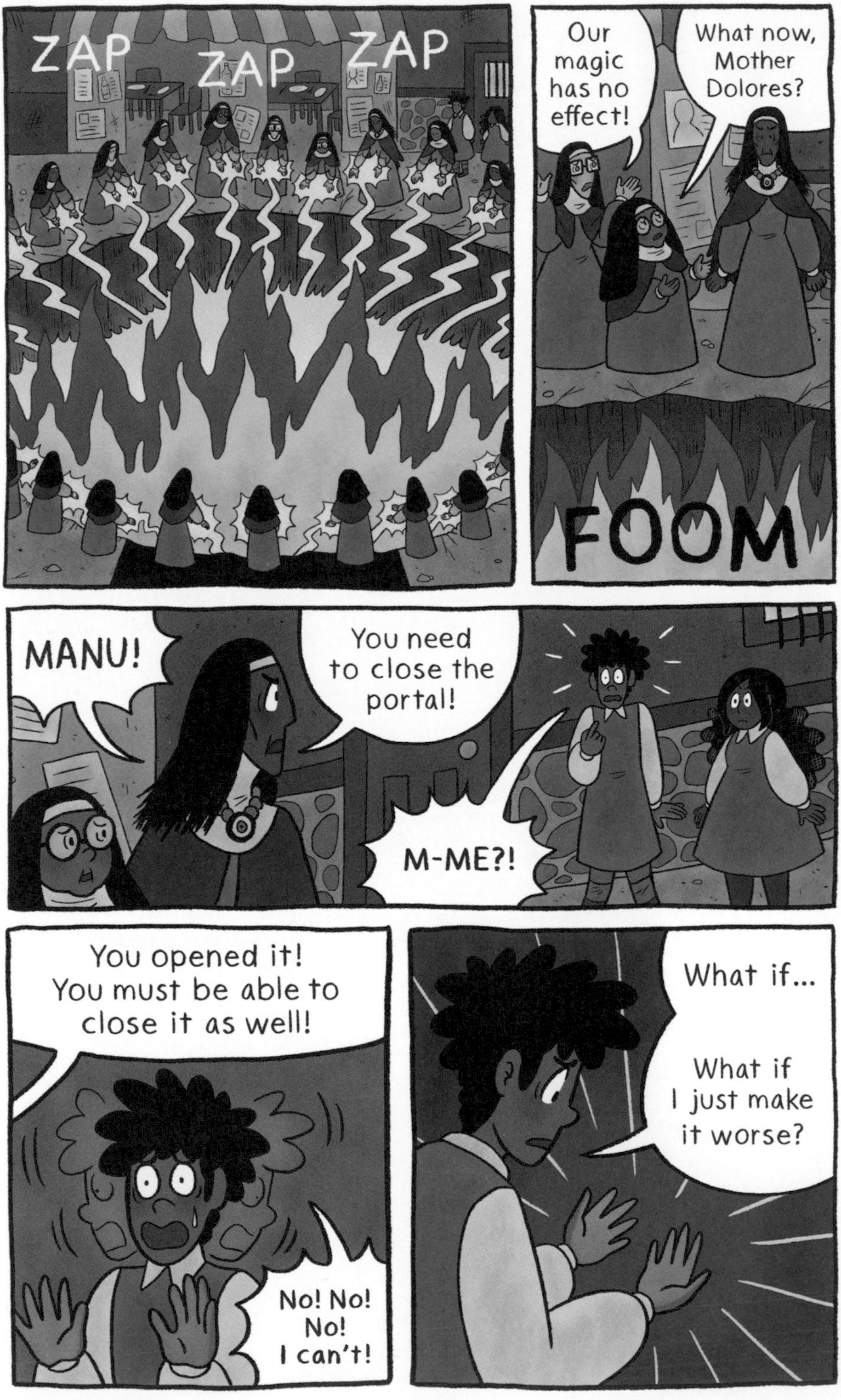
ZAP
ZAP
ZAP
Our magic has no effect!
What now, Mother Dolores?
FOOM
MANU!
You need to close the portal!
M-ME?!
You opened it! You must be able to close it as well!
No! No! No! I can't!
What if...
What if I just make it worse?

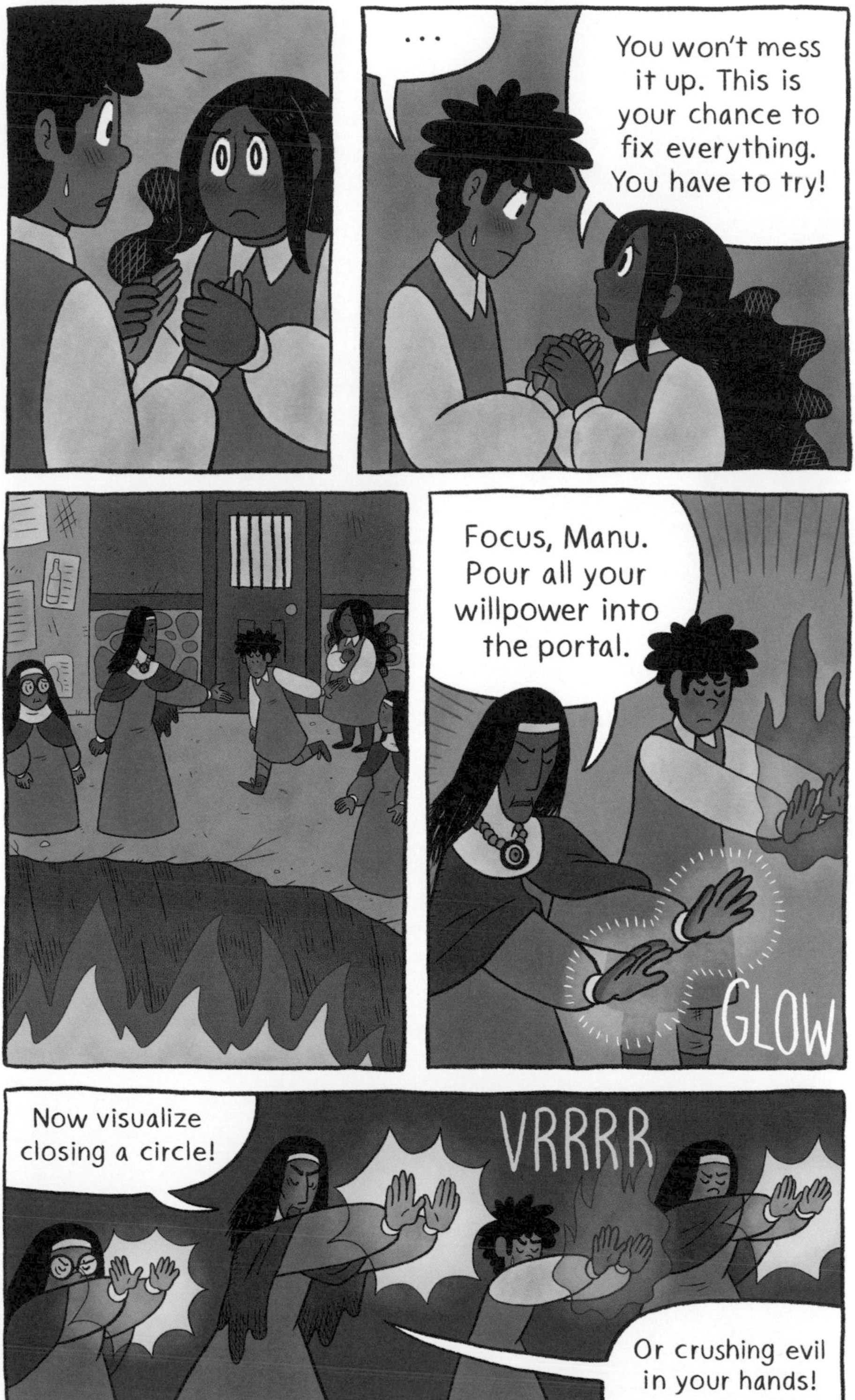
...
You won't mess it up. This is your chance to fix everything. You have to try!
Focus, Manu. Pour all your willpower into the portal.
GLOW
Now visualize closing a circle!
VRRRR
Or crushing evil in your hands!

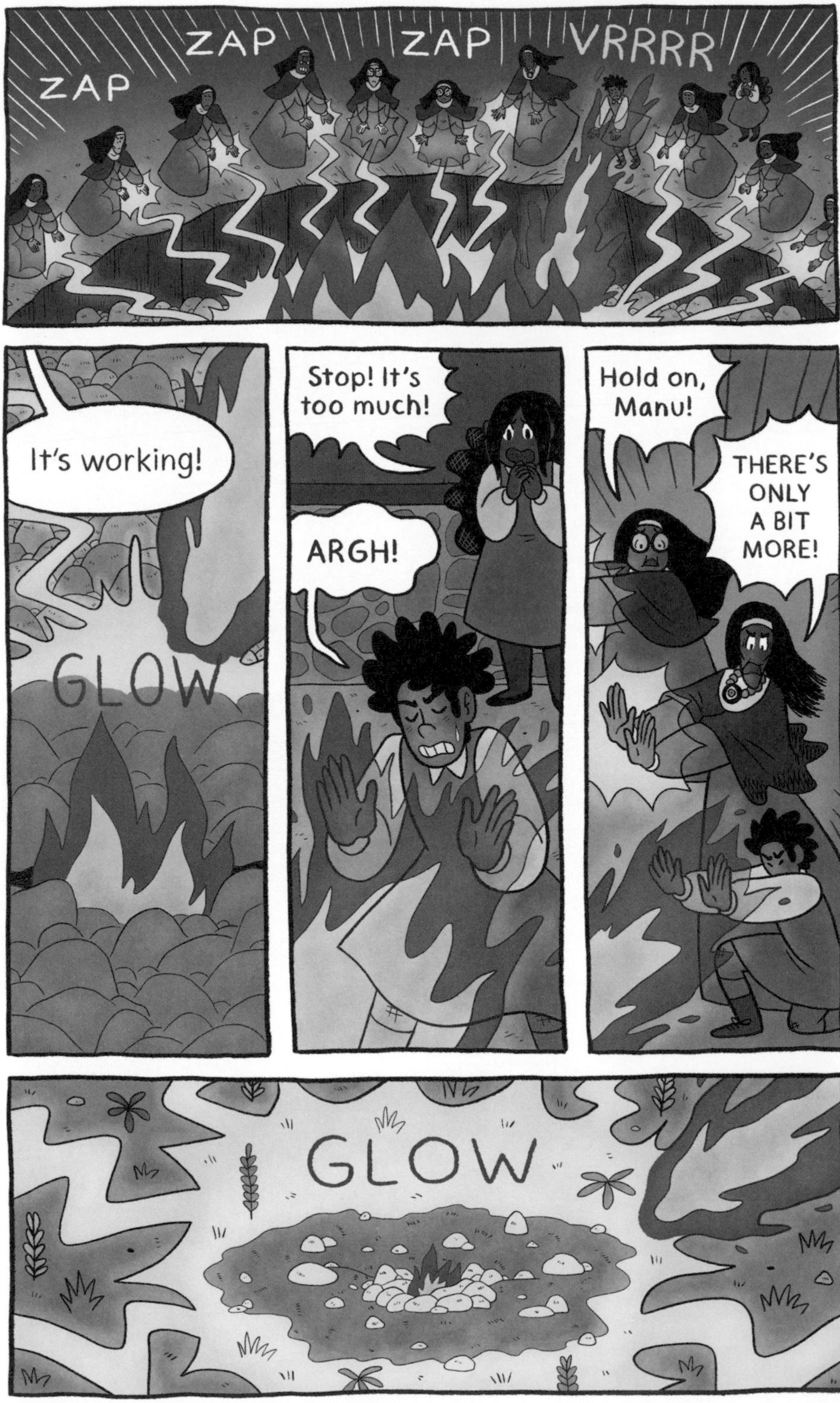
ZAP
ZAP
ZAP
VRRRR
It's working!
GLOW
Stop! It's too much!
ARGH!
Hold on, Manu!
THERE'S ONLY A BIT MORE!
GLOW

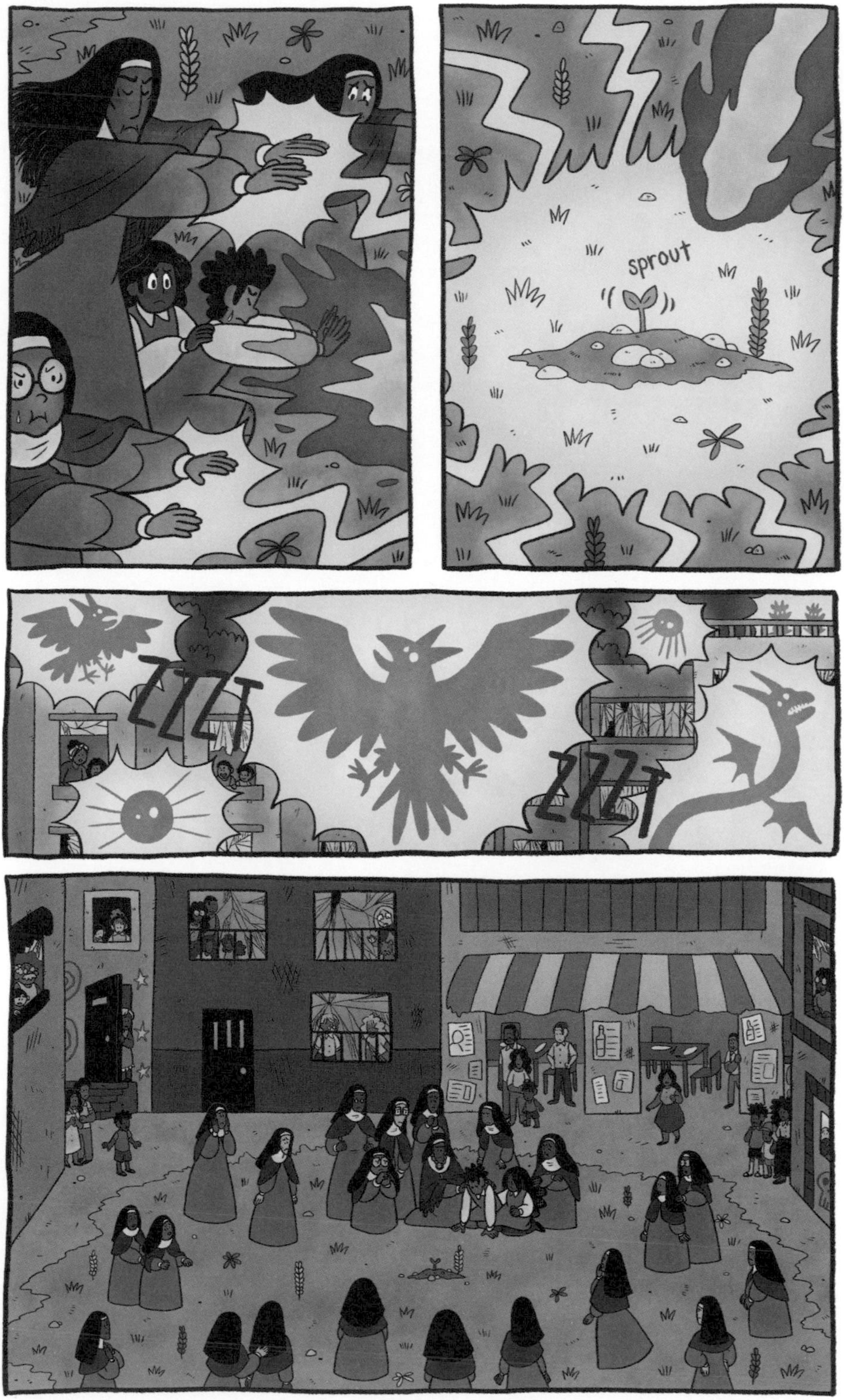
sprout
ZZZT
ZZZT

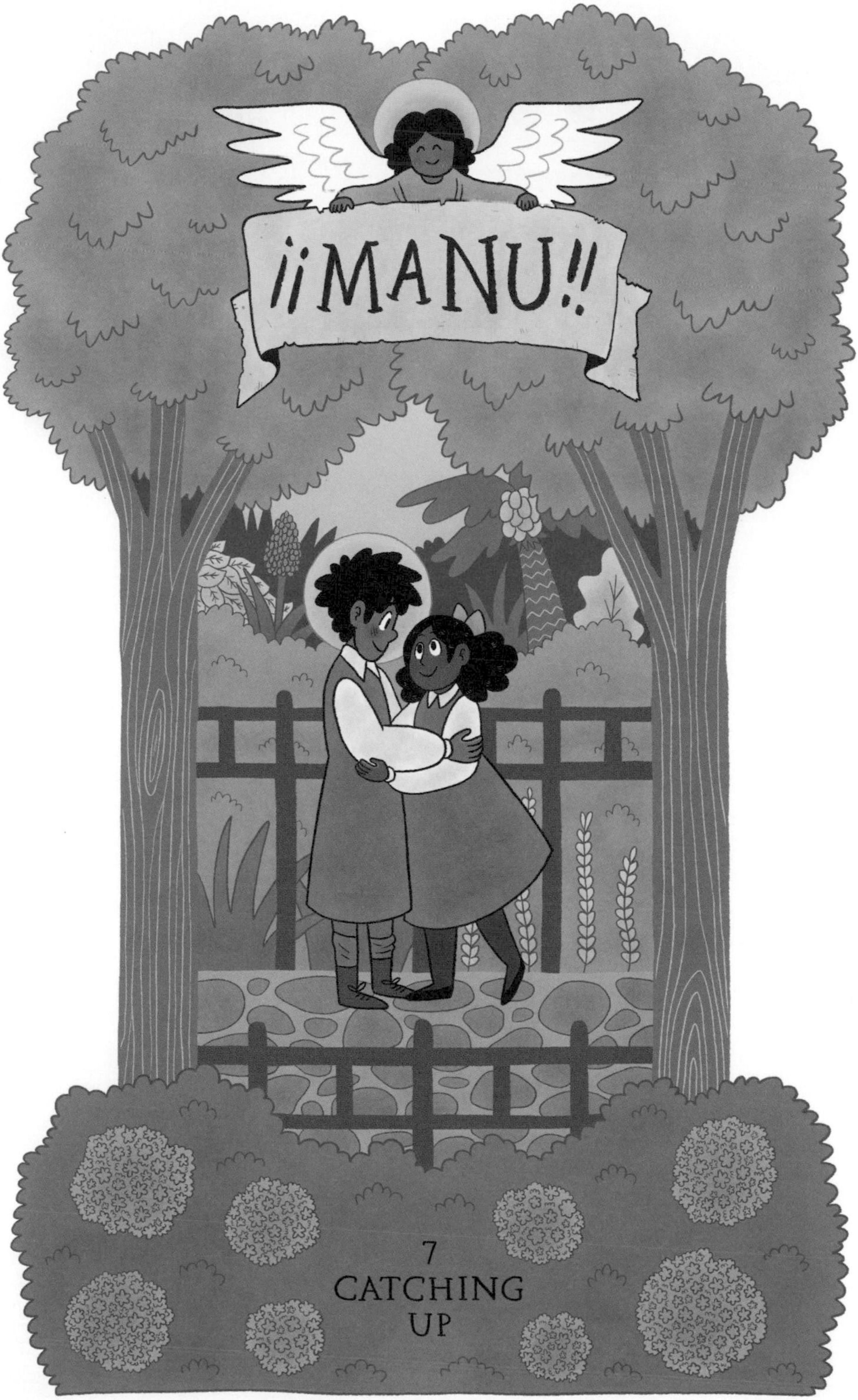
¡¡MANU!!

7
CATCHING UP

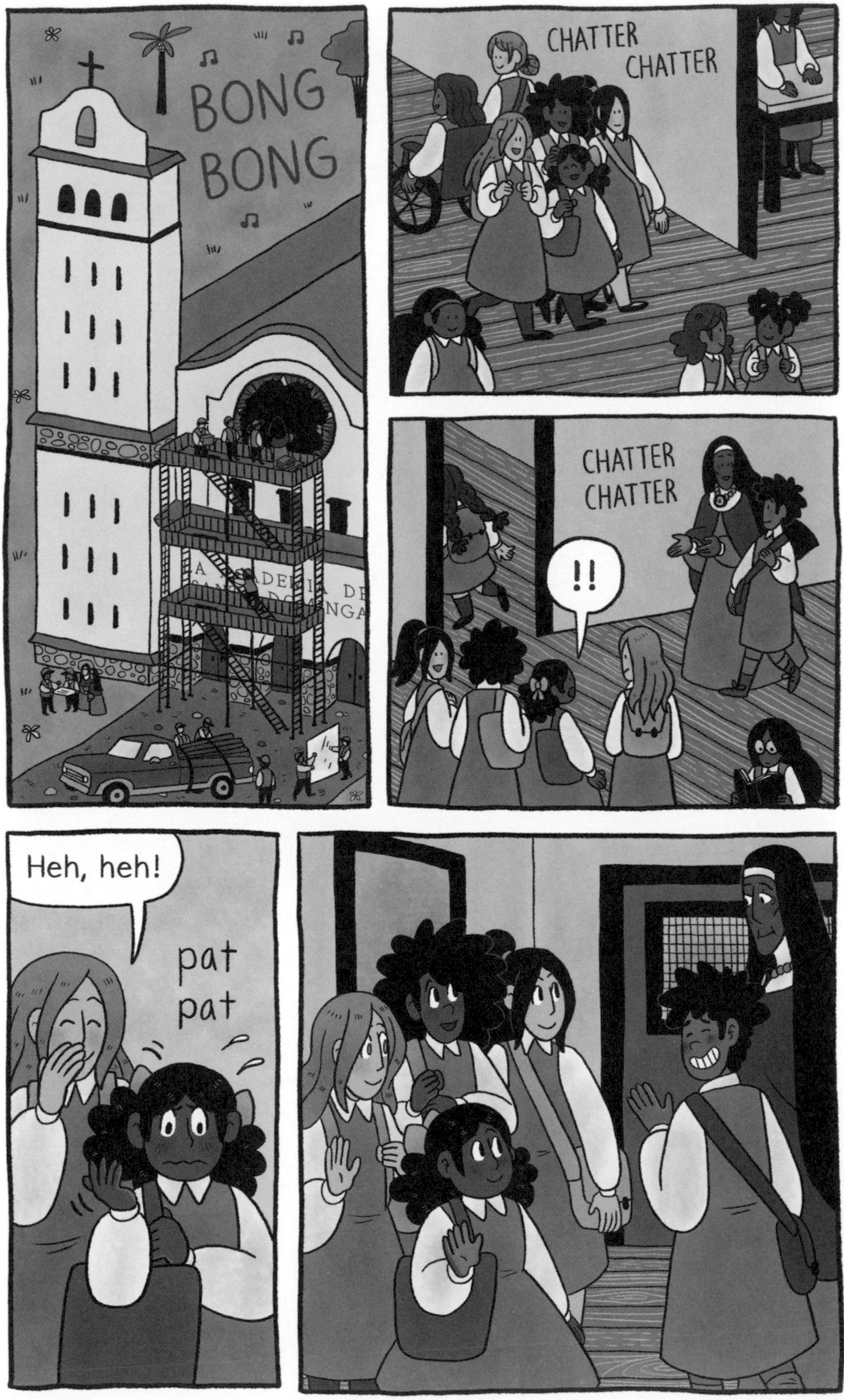
BONG
BONG
CHATTER
CHATTER
CHATTER
CHATTER
!!
Heh, heh!
pat
pat

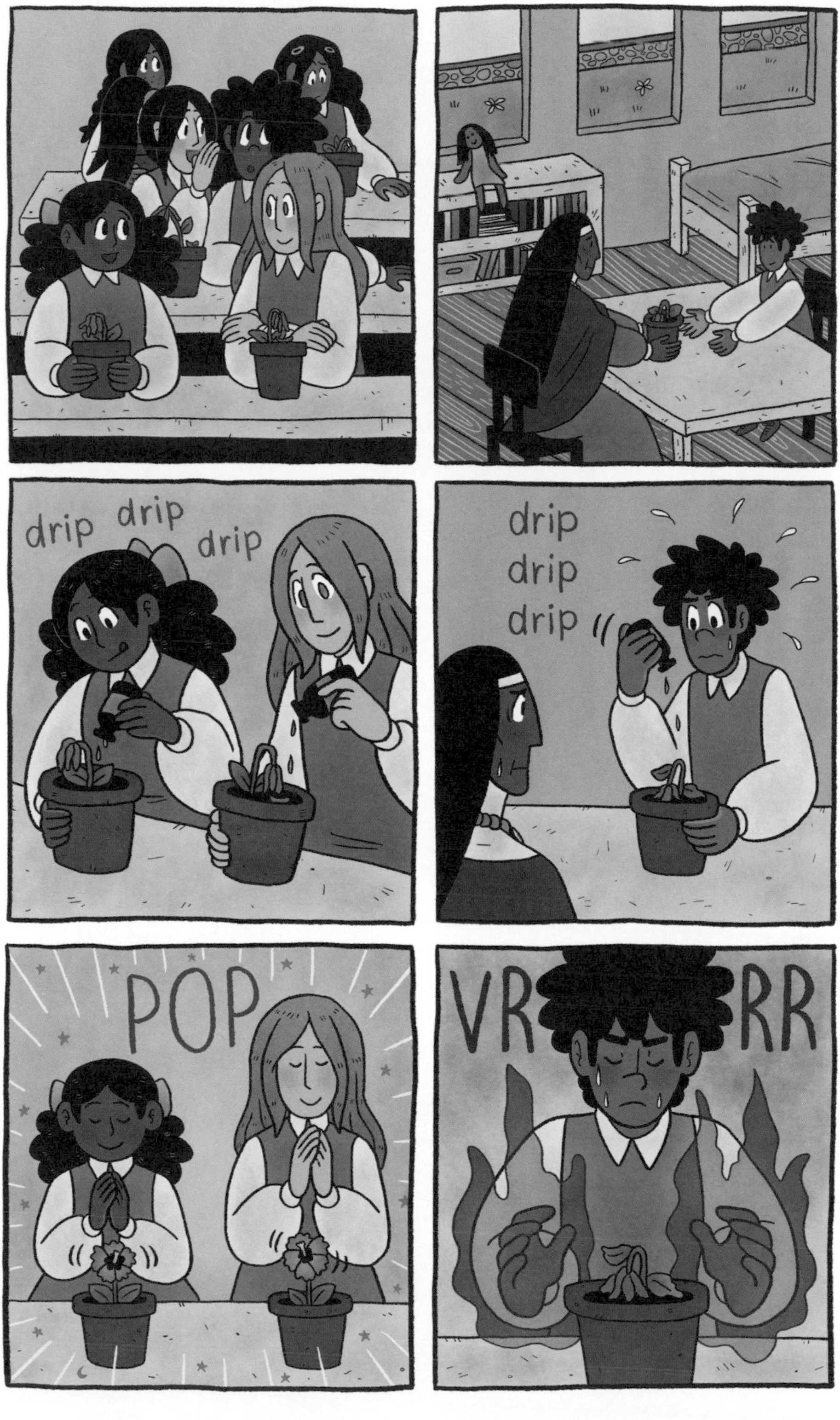
drip drip drip
drip
drip
drip
POP
VR RR

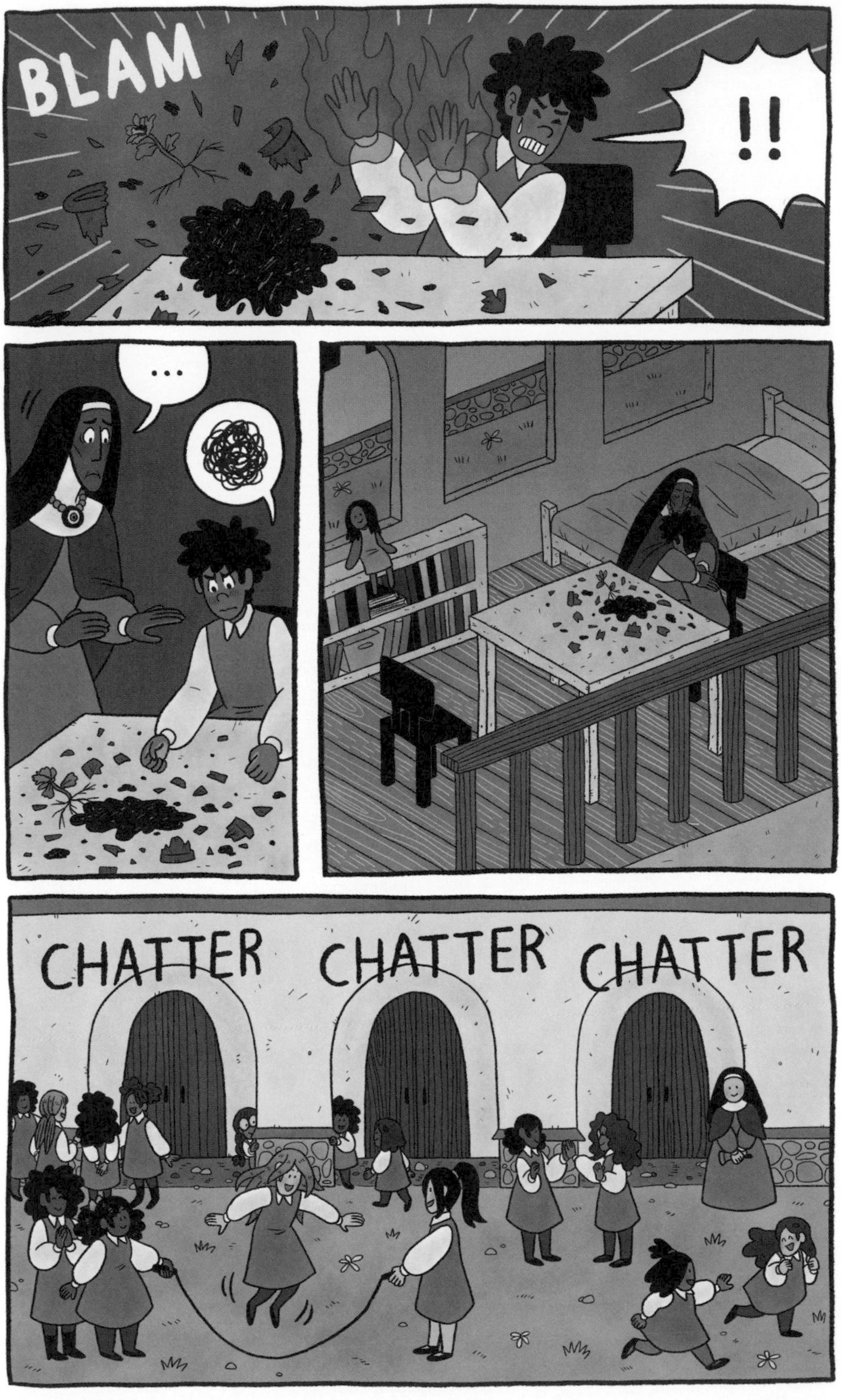
BLAM
!!
...
CHATTER CHATTER CHATTER

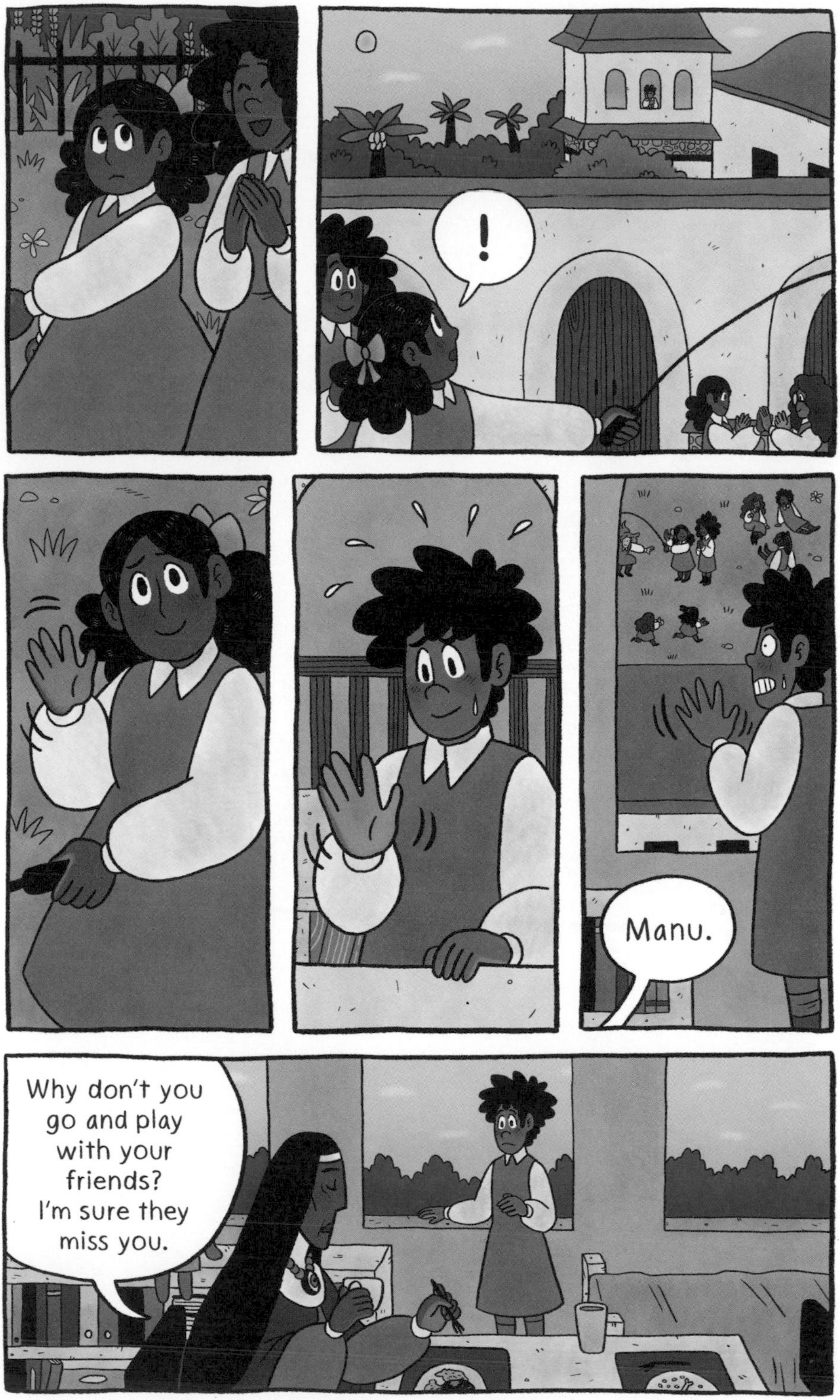
!
Manu.
Why don't you go and play with your friends? I'm sure they miss you.

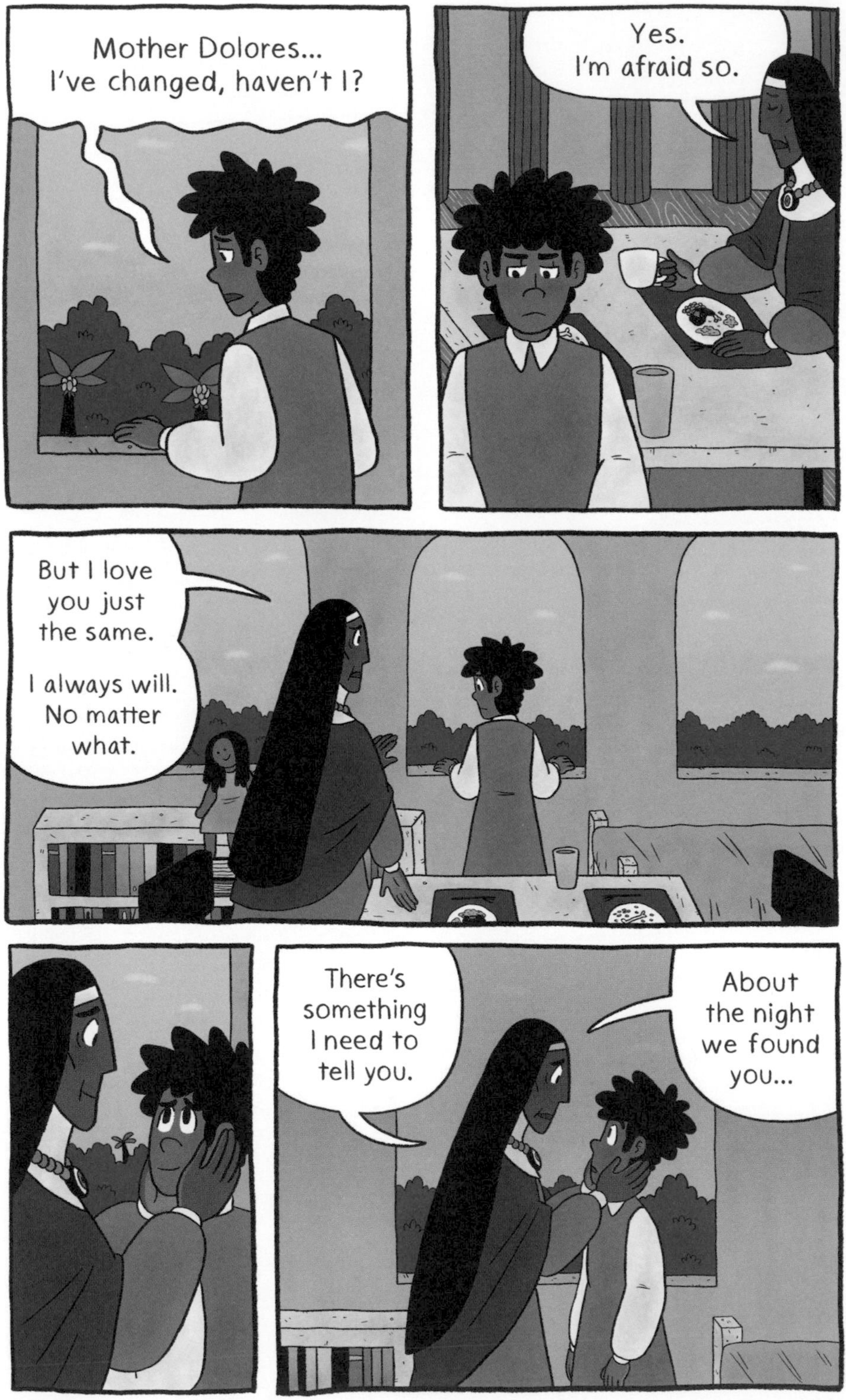
Mother Dolores...
I've changed, haven't I?
Yes.
I'm afraid so.
But I love you just the same.
I always will. No matter what.
There's something I need to tell you.
About the night we found you...

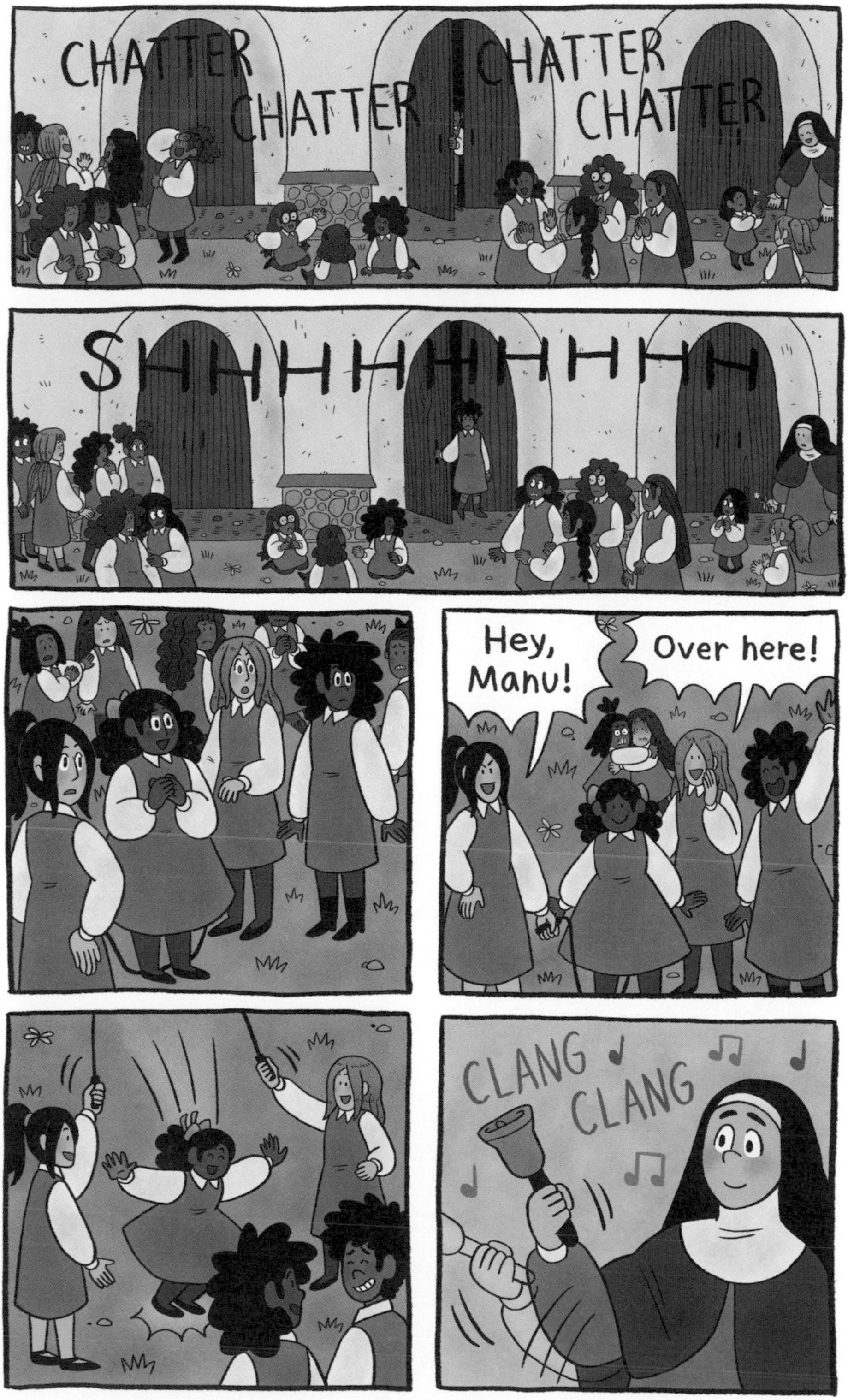
CHATTER
CHATTER
CHATTER
CHATTER
SHHHHHHHHH
Hey, Manu!
Over here!
CLANG
CLANG

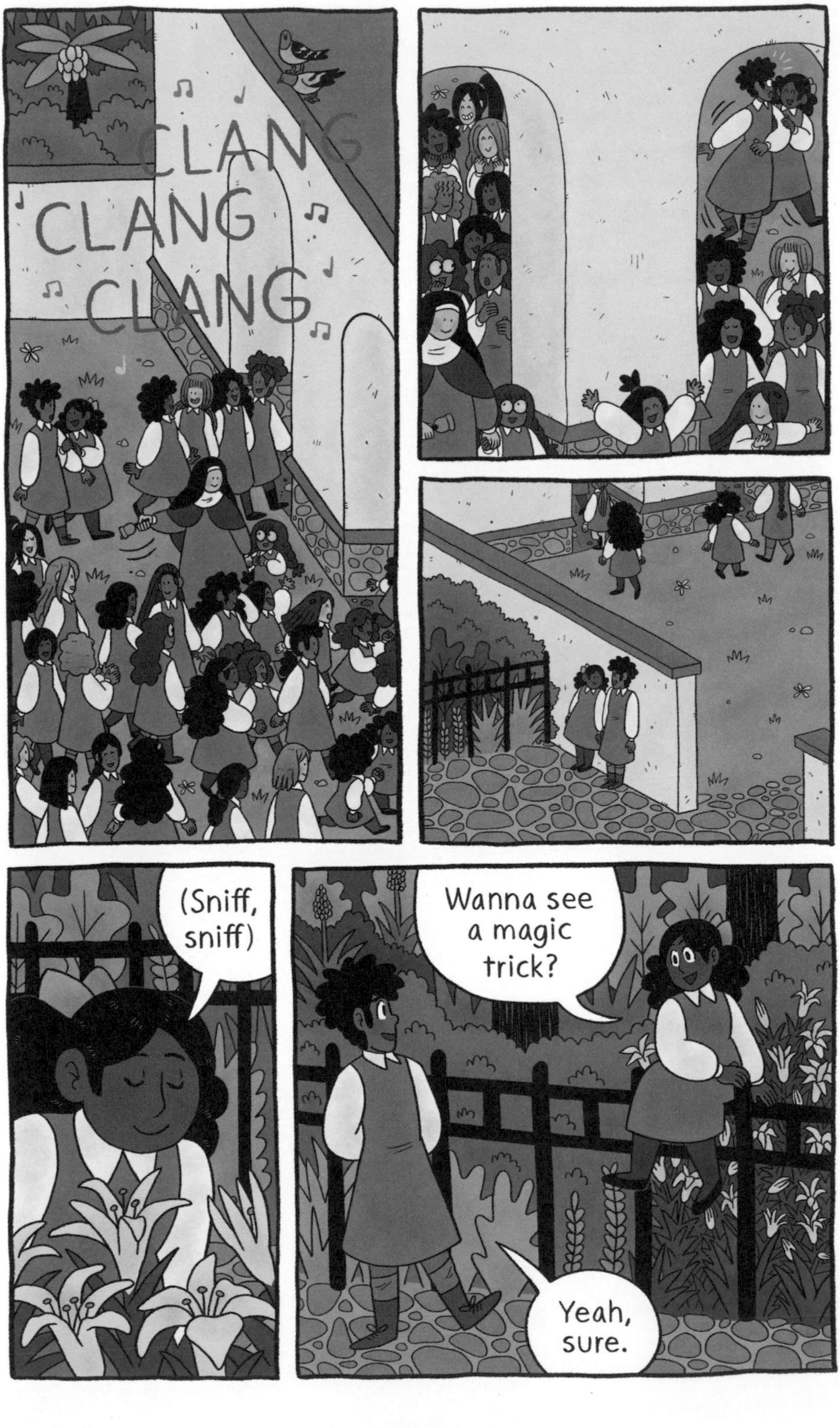
CLANG
CLANG
CLANG
(Sniff, sniff)
Wanna see a magic trick?
Yeah, sure.

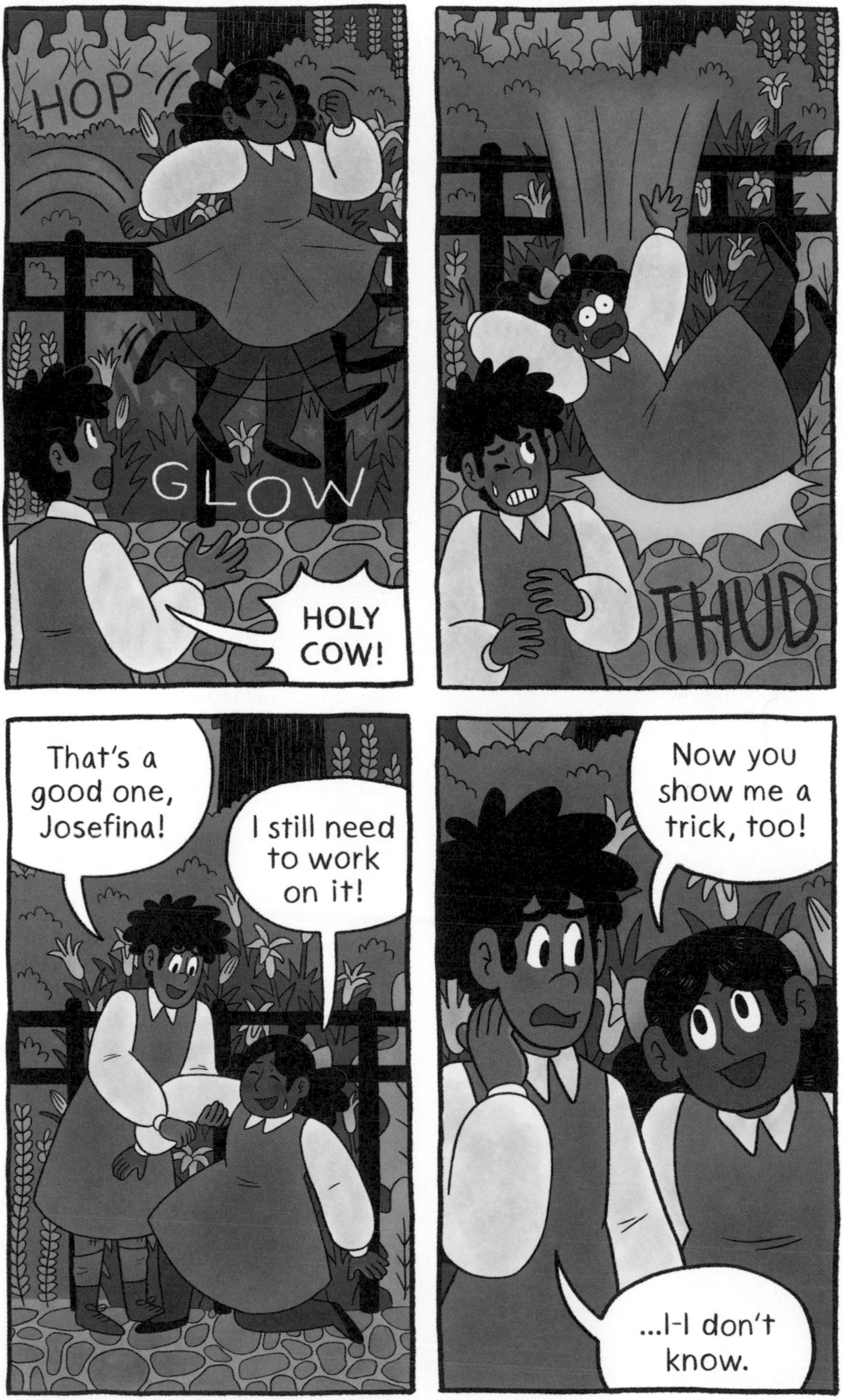
HOP
GLOW
HOLY COW!
THUD
That's a good one, Josefina!
I still need to work on it!
Now you show me a trick, too!
...I-I don't know.

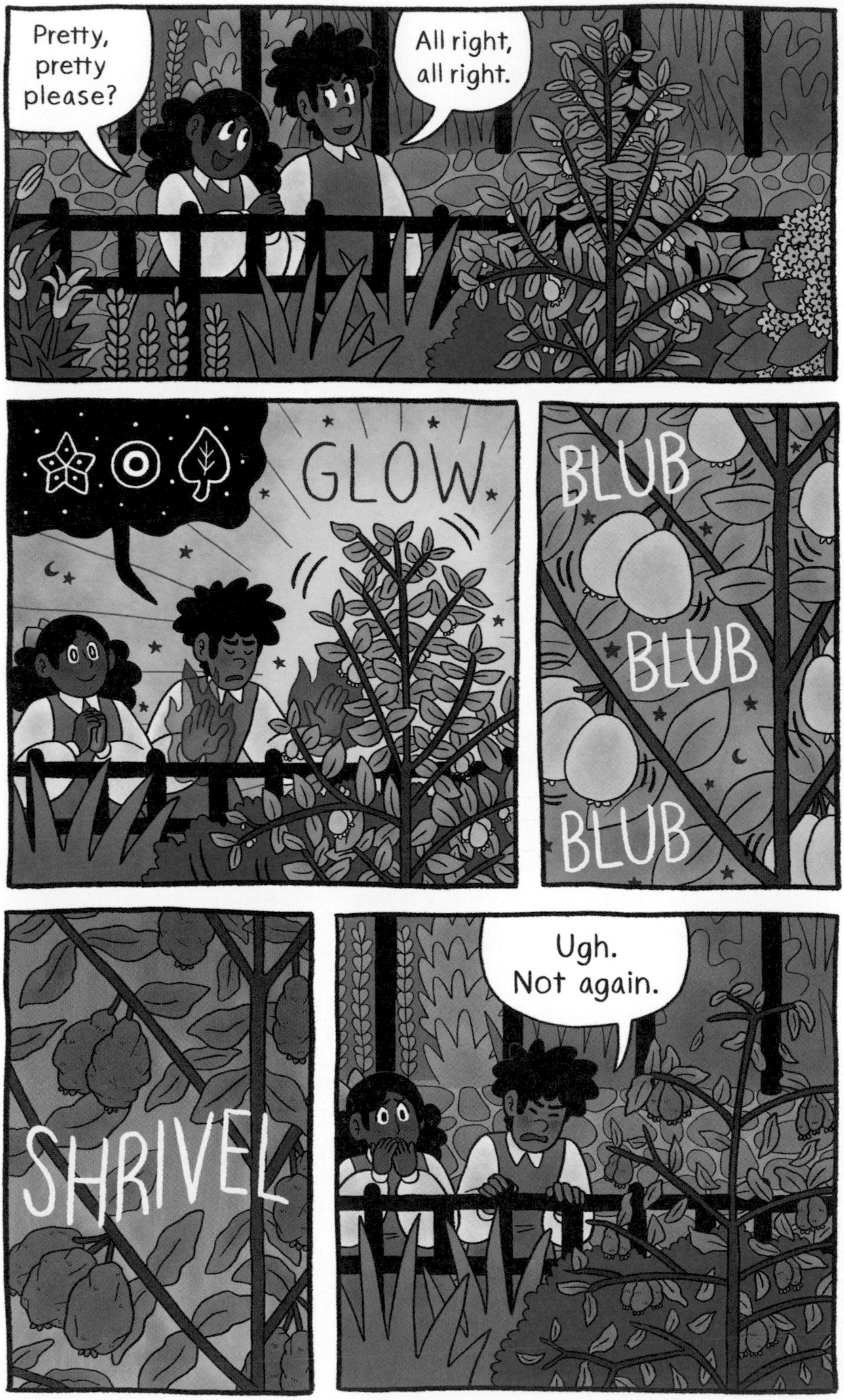
Pretty, pretty please?
All right, all right.
GLOW
BLUB
BLUB
BLUB
SHRIVEL
Ugh. Not again.

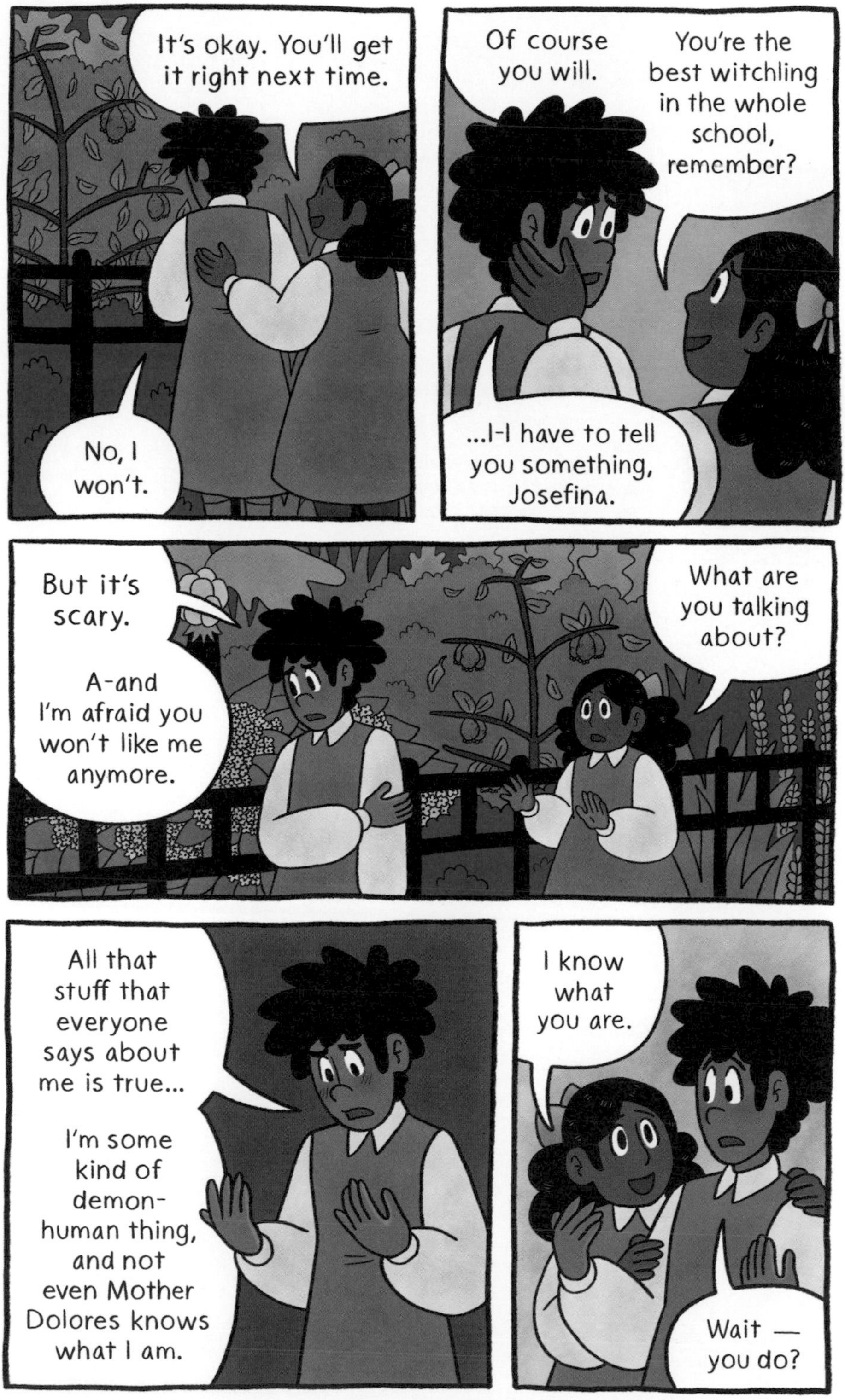
It's okay. You'll get it right next time.
No, I won't.
Of course you will.
You're the best witchling in the whole school, remember?
...I-I have to tell you something, Josefina.
But it's scary.
A-and I'm afraid you won't like me anymore.
What are you talking about?
All that stuff that everyone says about me is true...
I'm some kind of demon-human thing, and not even Mother Dolores knows what I am.
I know what you are.
Wait — you do?

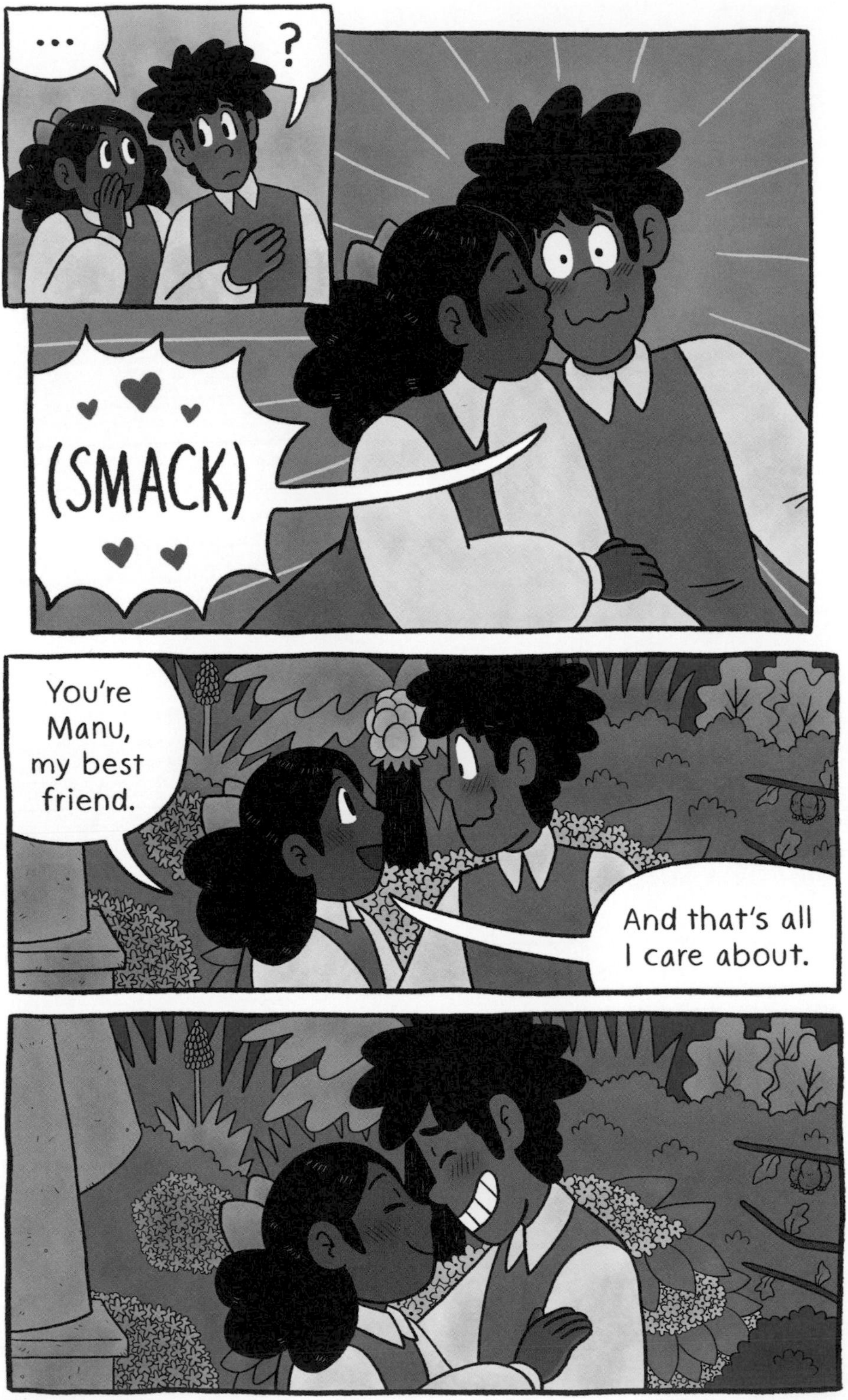
...
?
(SMACK)
You're Manu, my best friend.
And that's all I care about.

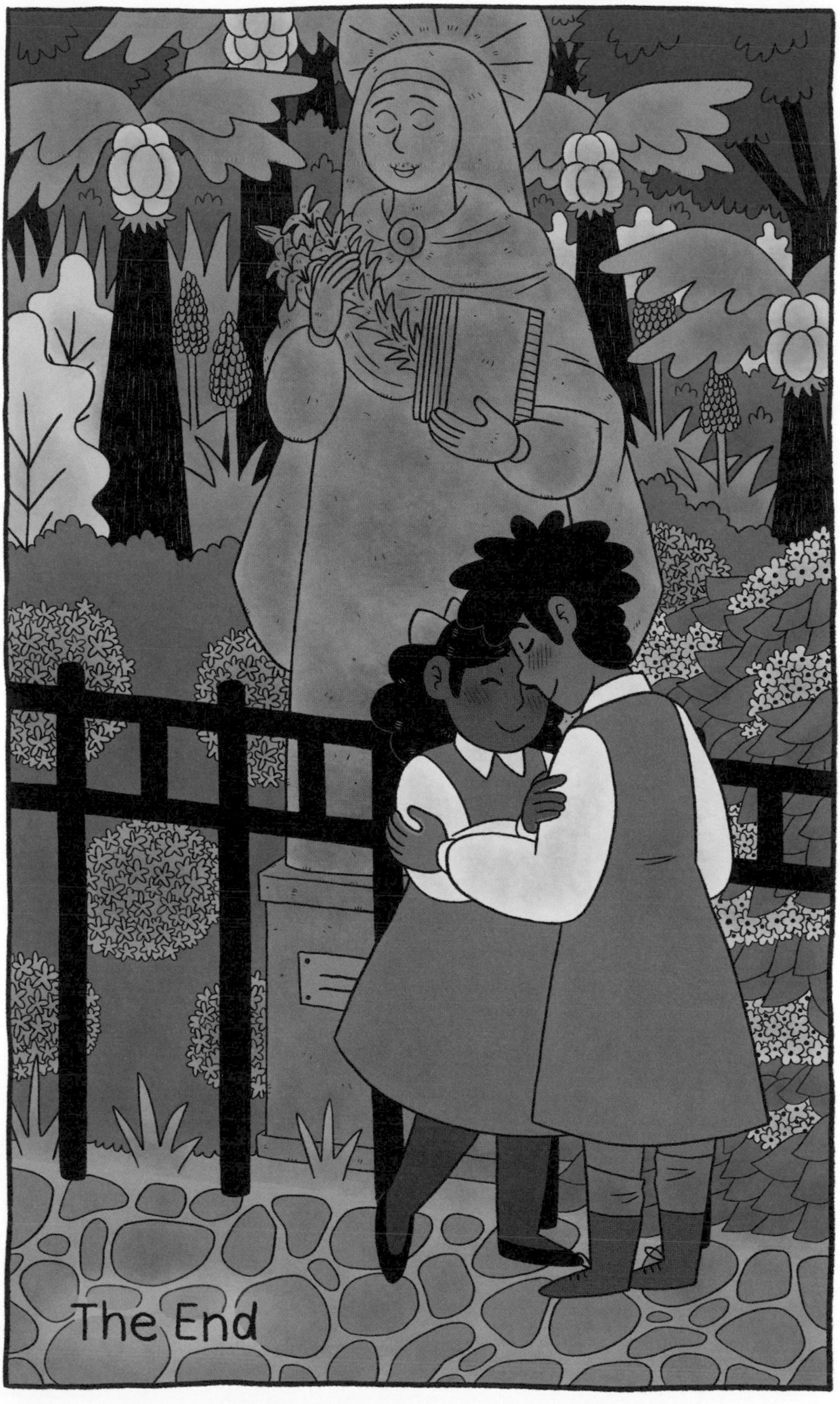
The End

Alumnas de secundaria

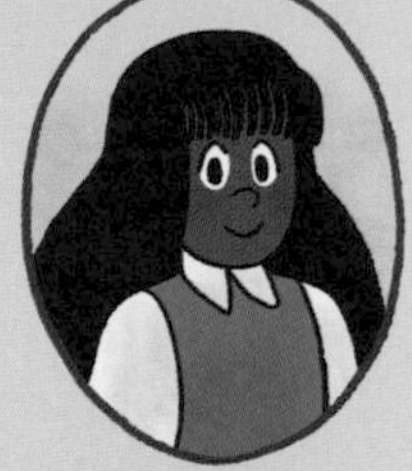

Flor Álvarez

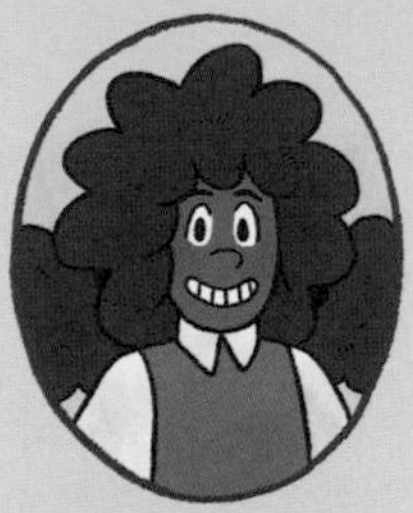

Úrsula Delgado

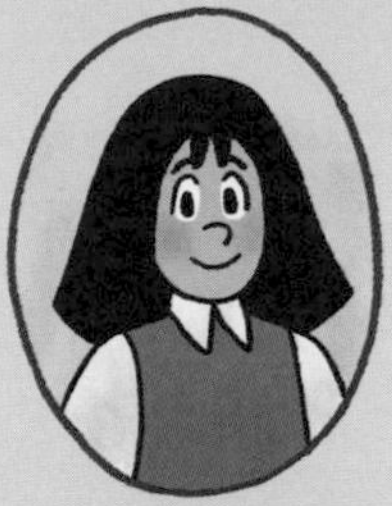

Li Díaz

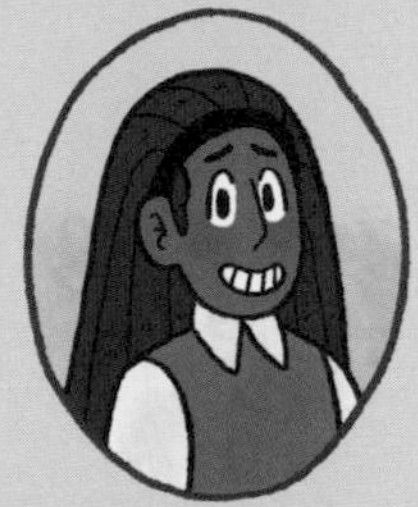

Elisa Fabron

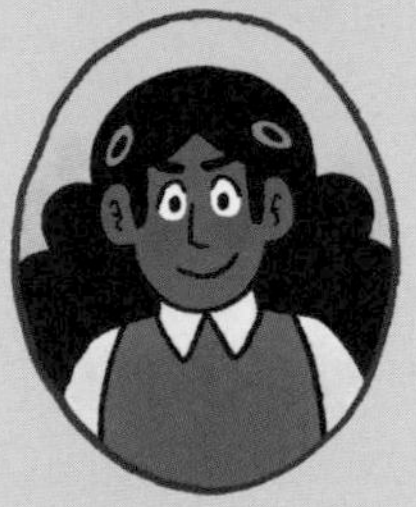

Paola García-Meléndez

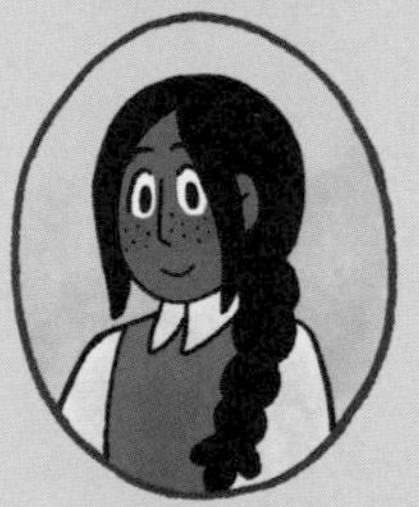

Graciela Mendoza

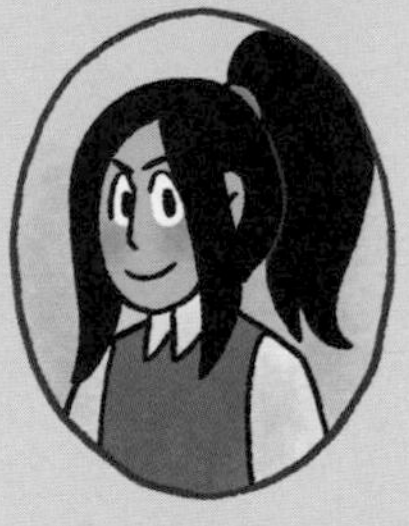

Mariana Morales

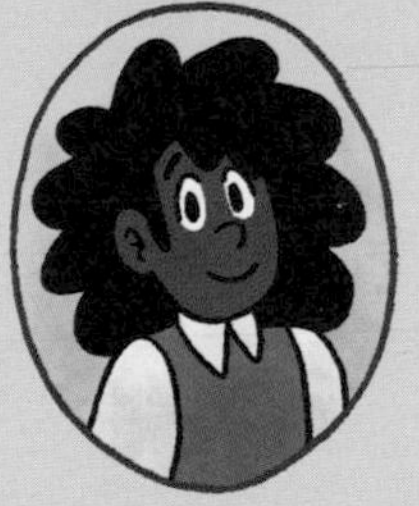

Maritza Núñez

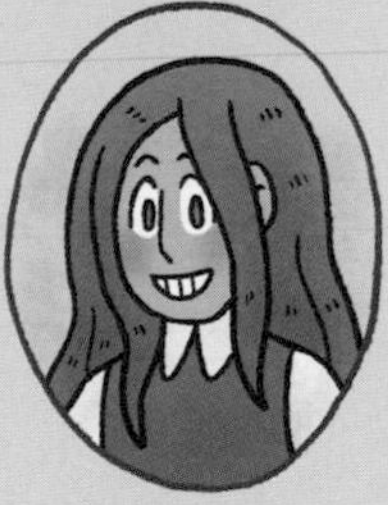

Rubia Pérez

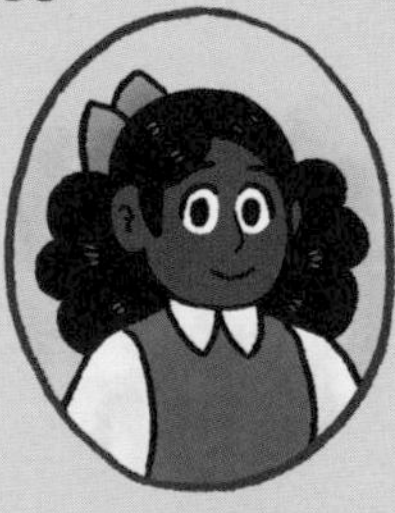

Josefina Teresa Rojas

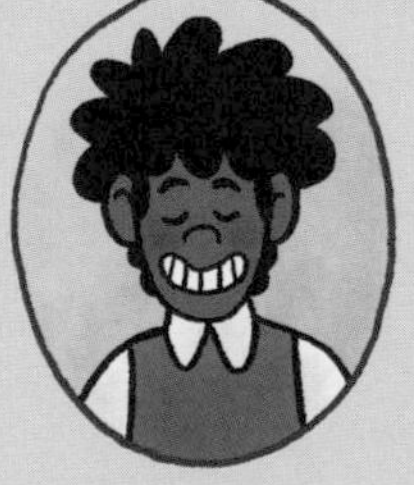

Manuela Santos

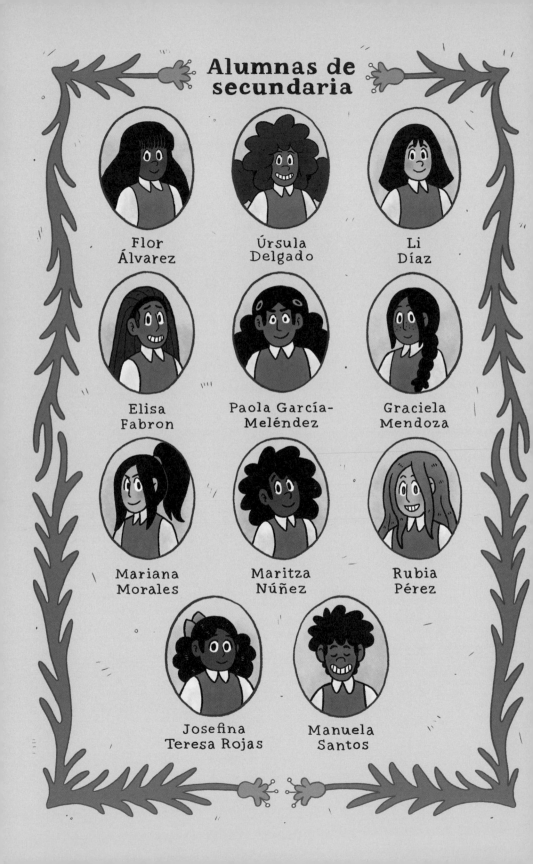

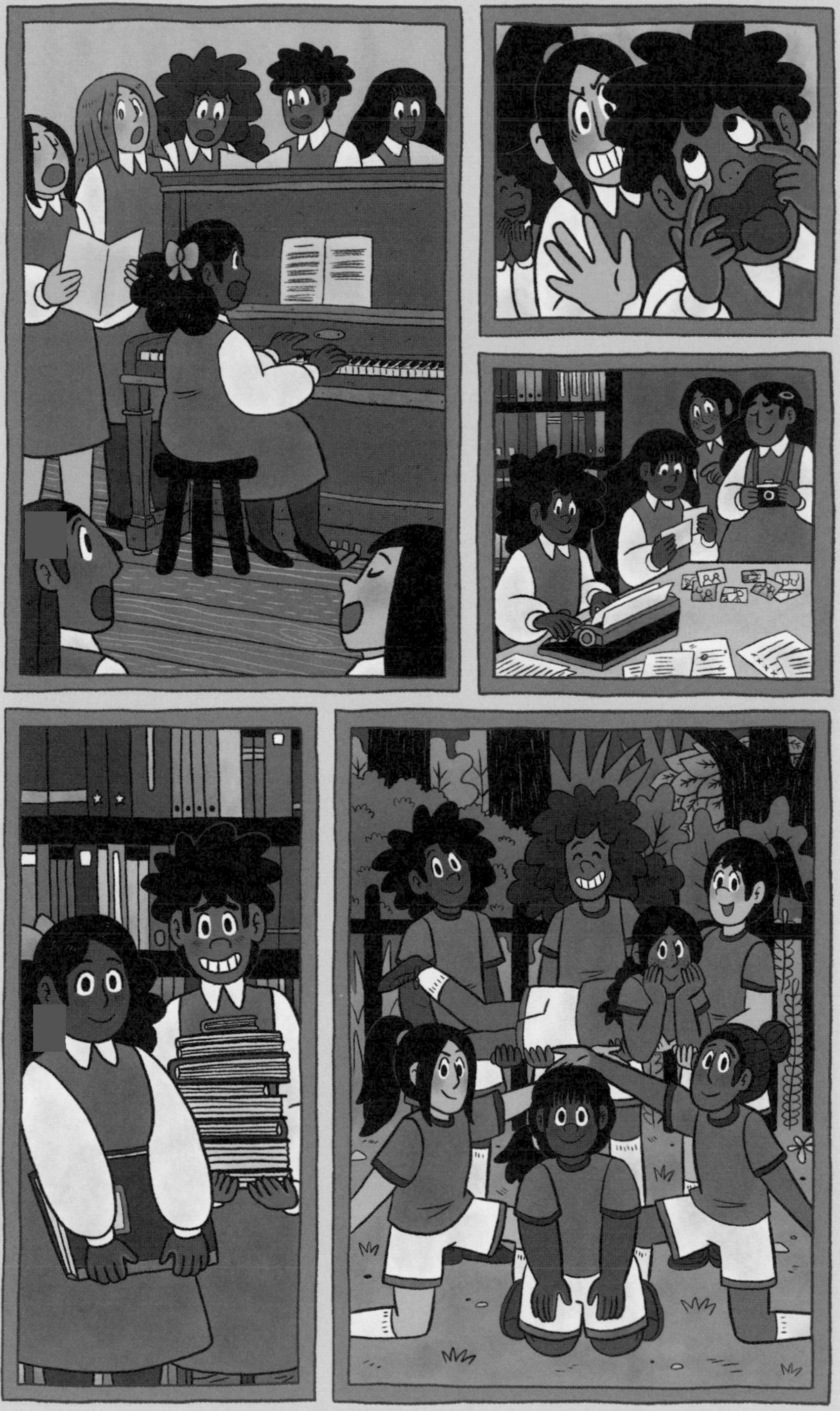

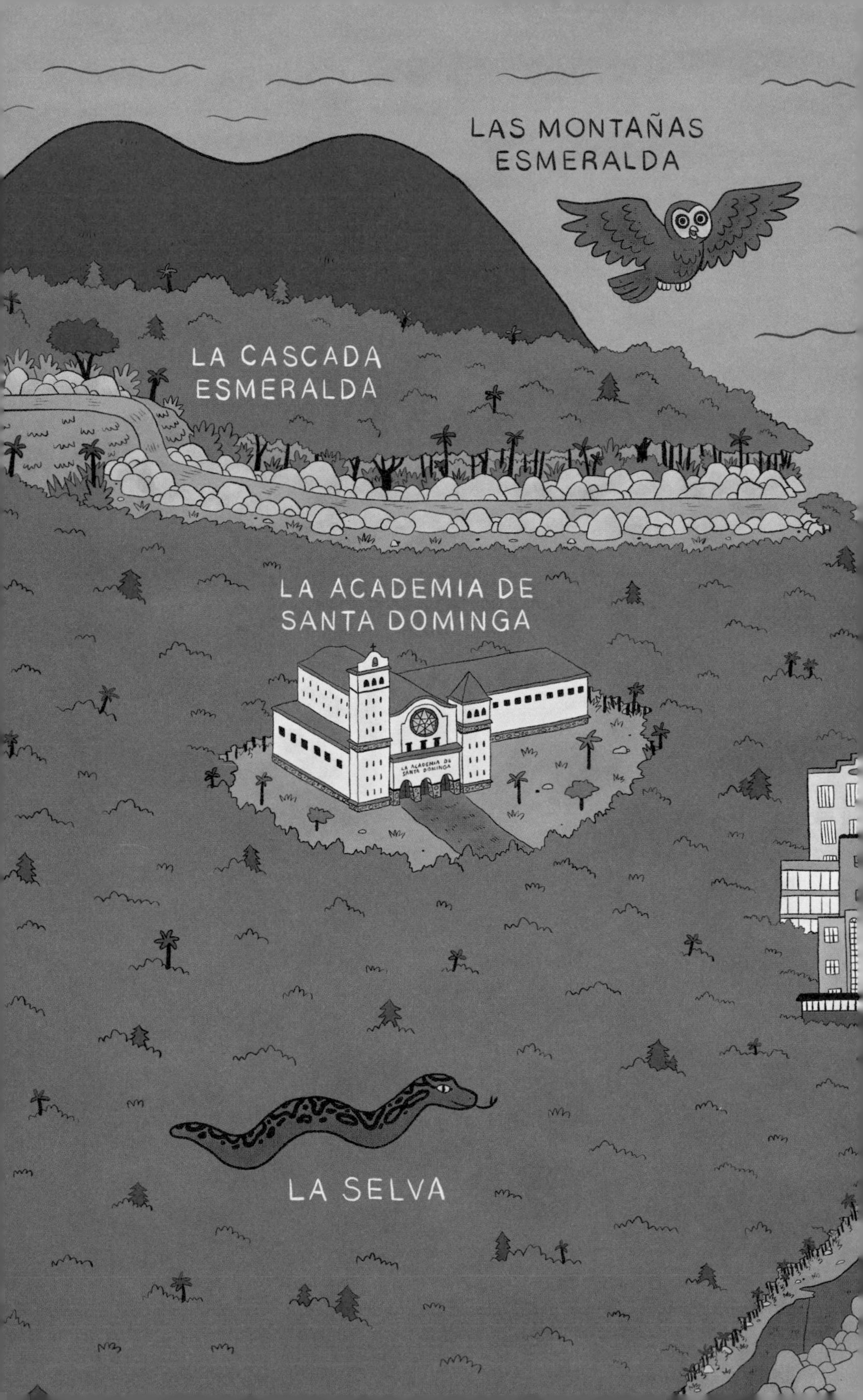
LAS MONTAÑAS ESMERALDA
LA CASCADA ESMERALDA
LA ACADEMIA DE SANTA DOMINGA
LA ACADEMIA DE SANTA DOMINGA
LA SELVA

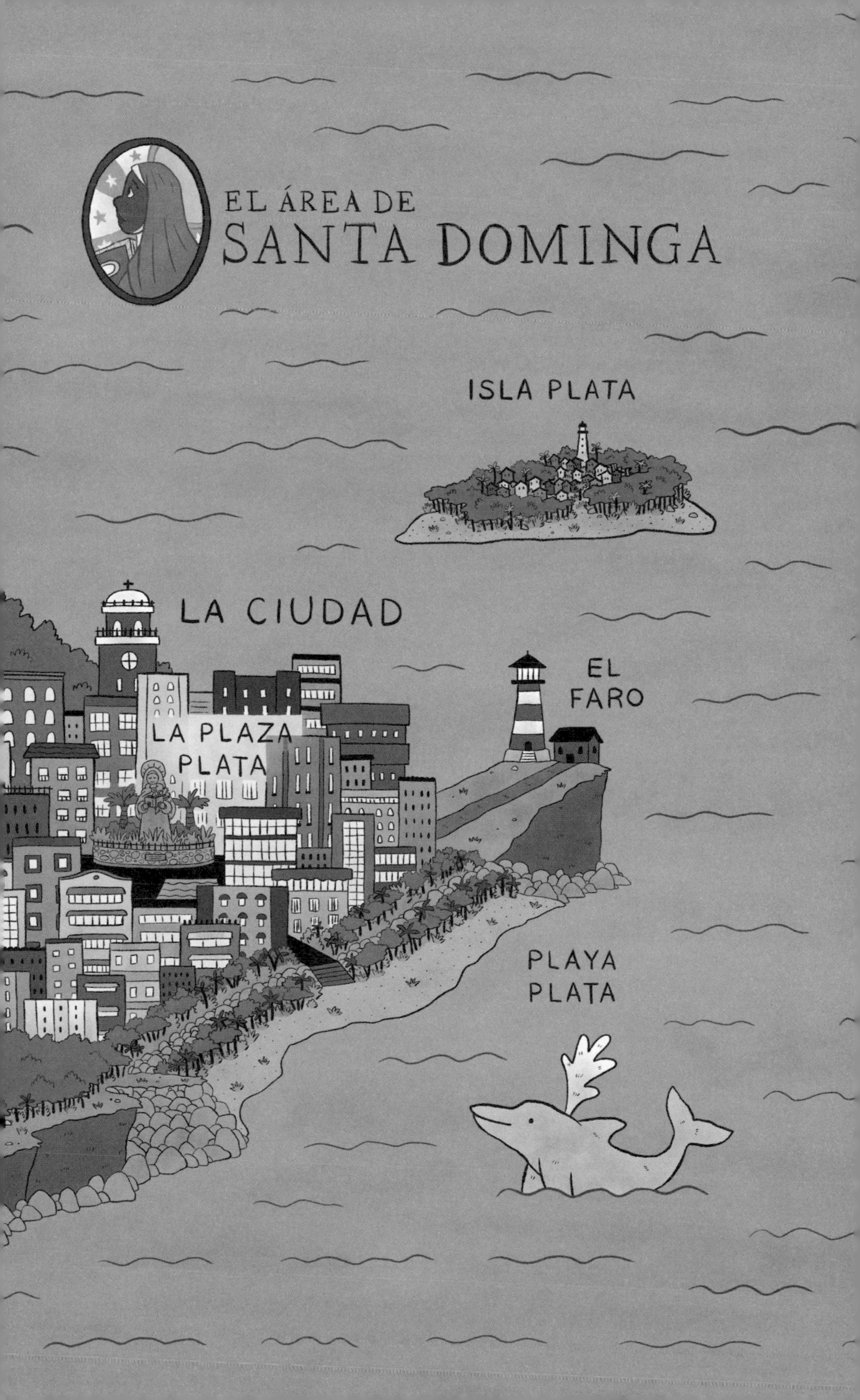
EL ÁREA DE
SANTA DOMINGA
ISLA PLATA
LA CIUDAD
EL FARO
LA PLAZA PLATA
PLAYA PLATA

AUTHOR'S NOTE

While writing this book, I reflected on my childhood and the stories my family would tell about curses, ghosts, monsters, and brujas. It was easy to see how brujería (the Spanish word for witchcraft) was ingrained in our daily lives as Dominicans, including the way we seamlessly wove it into our Roman Catholic traditions. Though we aren't witches ourselves, we heed and respect many of these beliefs and rituals that have taken root in our culture.

From what I've learned through research and speaking to my Latinx friends and colleagues, brujería varies from country to country, culture to culture, and family to family. My personal experiences involved wearing both our mal de ojo bracelets and prayer rosaries as protection from danger and bad intentions, singing the "colita de rana" chant whenever someone hurt themselves, and reciting "Our Father" and "Hail Mary" at bedtime. My newborn cousins never went without spit and thread on their foreheads (for warding off hiccups), and were also baptized in church.

This book is my way of exploring and celebrating the parts of myself that are still mysterious to me. Though both sides of my family immigrated to the United States from the Dominican Republic, there are still things I'm learning about my history, culture, and language every day. I hope *Manu* inspires you not to hide or reject the mysterious parts of yourself, but to embrace and learn more about them.

Kelly

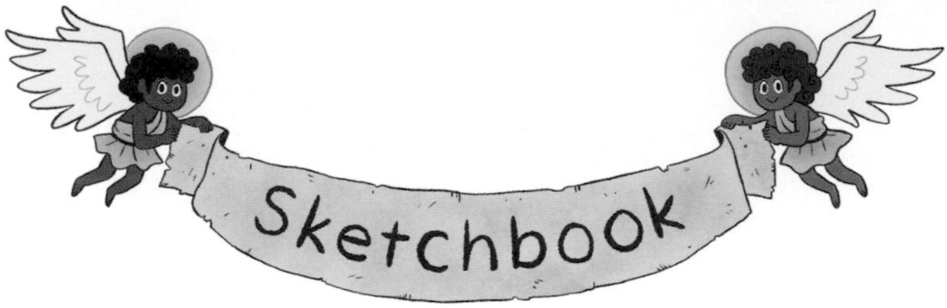
Sketchbook

Here are some drawings and cartoons that I made while developing Manu!

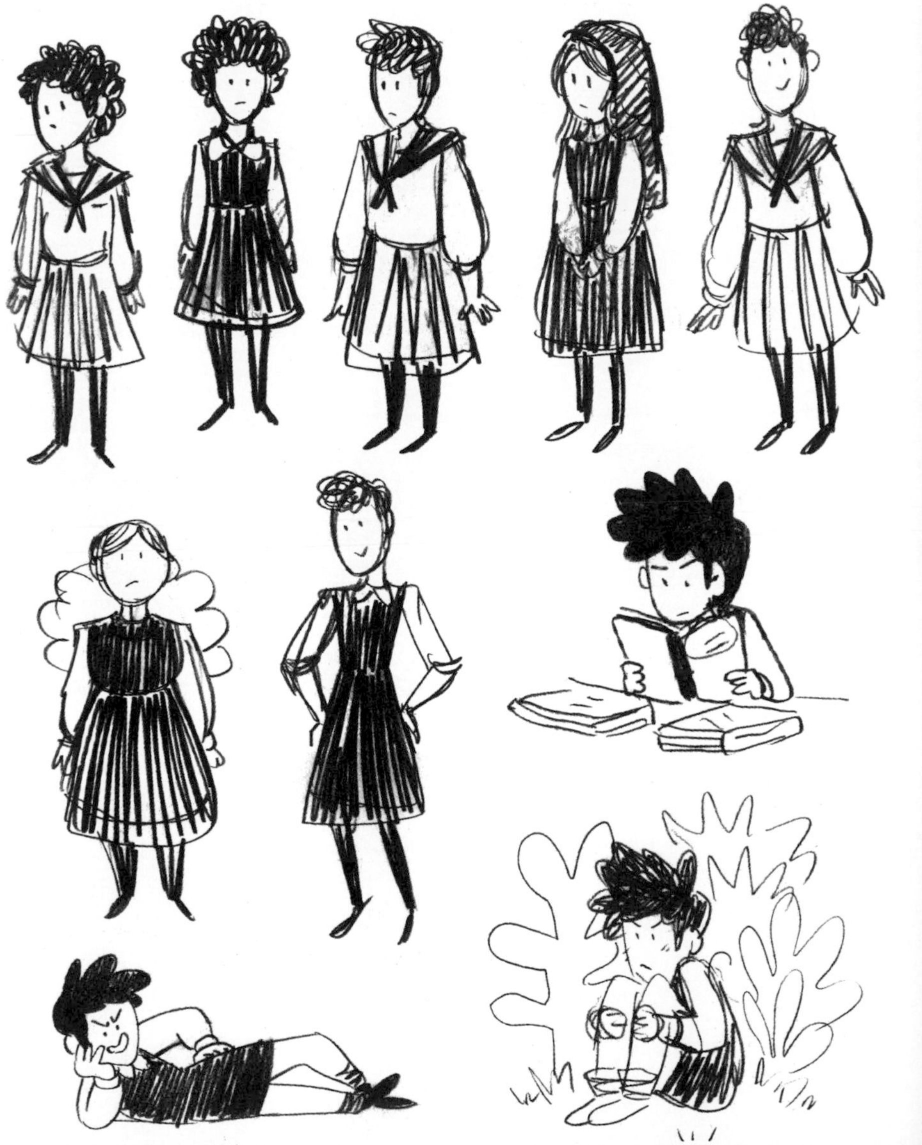

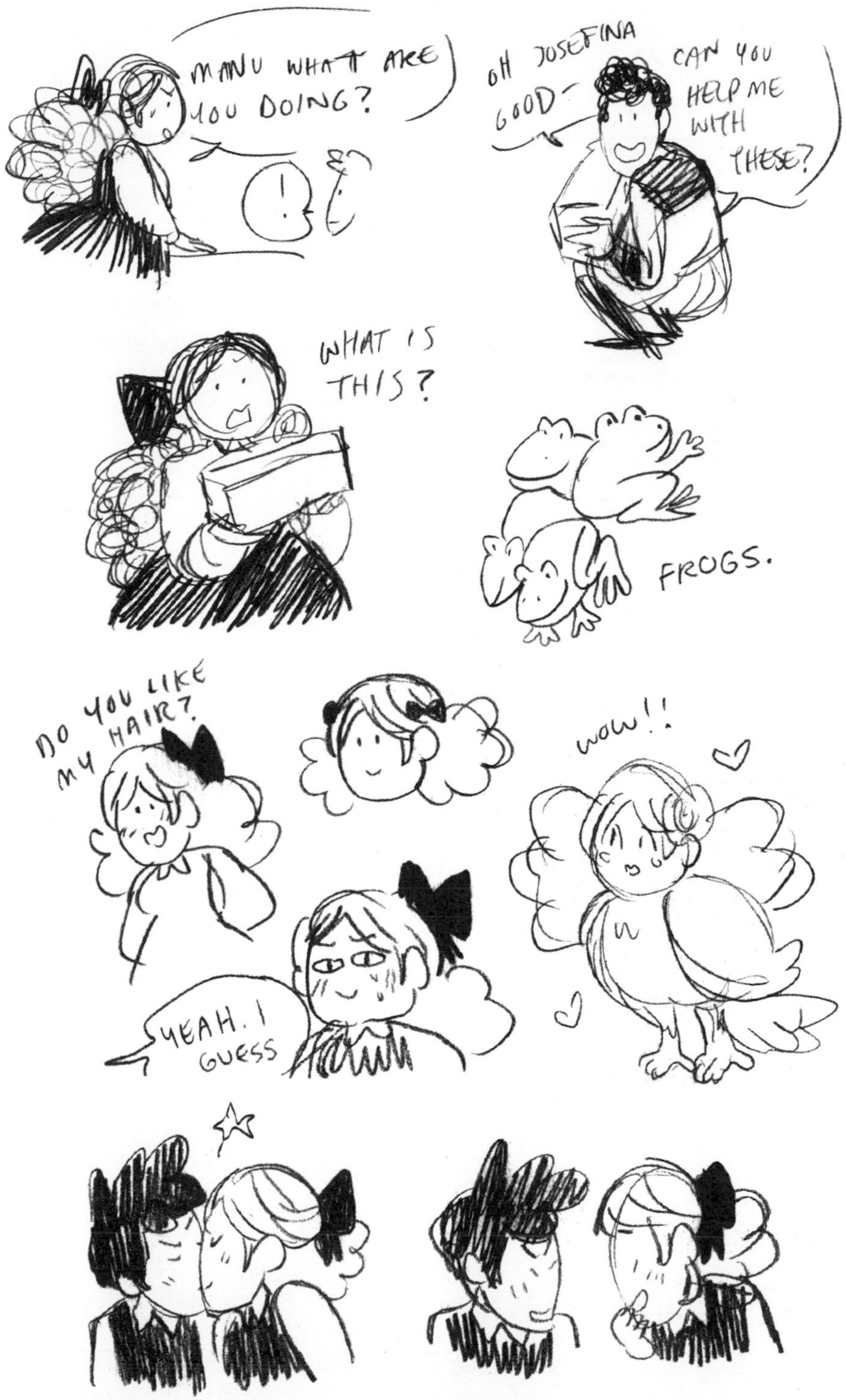
MANU WHAT ARE YOU DOING?
OH JOSEFINA GOOD-
CAN YOU HELP ME WITH THESE?
WHAT IS THIS?
FROGS.
DO YOU LIKE MY HAIR?
WOW!!
YEAH. I GUESS

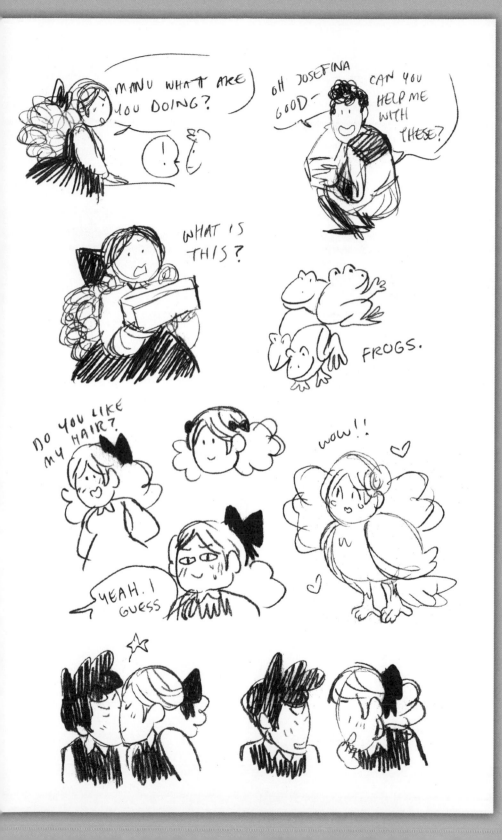

ACKNOWLEDGMENTS

Thank you to my family for being my first fans, editors, and collaborators. To Cassandra, David, María, Phil, Steve, Emily, Holland, and everyone at Scholastic who believed in me and helped make this book a reality — I can never thank you all enough! You've made the dreams I've had since I was ten years old come true.

Thank you to my agent, Tanya, for all your advice, cheerleading, and brainstorming over the phone. To Andrés, Na, Mei Lan, and Pablo, for being the second family I didn't know I needed. To my colleagues at FPPL for all the love you've shown me and for your acceptance. Big hugs and thanks to Kat, Steph, and Lucía for being there when I was at my lowest points. And to everyone who has supported my work online and in person throughout the years. I wouldn't be here without your encouragement!

Last but not least: Thank you, Angelica, for your invaluable assistance, feedback, and love. You're my partner in crime, and I feel incredibly lucky to have you in my life. Whenever you're with me, I feel like a million pesos!

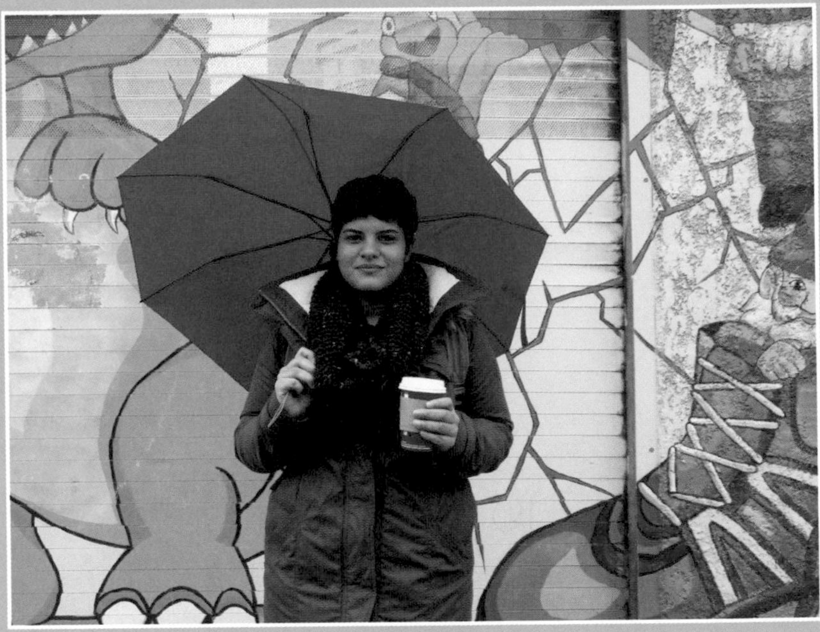

Photo by Angelica Busanet

KELLY FERNÁNDEZ makes comics that are inspired by her daily experiences, Dominican heritage, and American culture. Her work has been featured in comics anthologies, and she won a Chicago Alternative Comics Expo Cupcake Award for her minicomic *Cuidando*. Kelly is a winner of the Get Published by Graphix contest, and *Manu* is her debut graphic novel. She lives in Queens, New York, and you can visit her online at kellyfernandez.net.